From the U.S. electrical grid and all its back-ups, engine control-management systems, early warning systems on U.S. satellites, every motor vehicle, aircraft and ship made after 1985, to even simple memory chips inside children's teddy bears—every electronic fuse, resistor, or connector that was "Made in China" becomes dormant... forever.

At one minute past midnight on January 1st, every modern television broadcast of the U.S. New Year's Eve festivities on the East Coast black-out. Millions of motor vehicles with an engine management system or engine-computerized system suddenly die, causing loss of control and thousands of accidents only seconds into the New Year. Traffic lights, directional beacons, communication stations, and all aircraft landing systems black out a couple of minutes later, as their modern back-ups start failing. Children's Christmas presents, nearly forgotten, stop buzzing, moving, and blinking and go silent. Radios, computers, and all forms of electronic communication devices—even the latest 132 million electronic Christmas presents given only a week earlier (iPhone 5Gs, iPod Nano 4s, iMac Notepads and iPad 3s) go silent, never to blink on again. Ninety seconds after midnight, the entire electrical grid of North America deactivates itself and goes into close-down mode.

The shutdown of the United States of America, and 97% of the entire world, is accomplished by 12:30 am U.S. Eastern time on the first day of the New Year.

It takes only 30 minutes to completely dismantle the whole of modern Western civilization as we know it.

D1737893

INVASION USA IV

THE BATTLE FOR HOUSTON

—

THE AFTERMATH

T. I. WADE

Please visit our website http://www.TIWADE.com to become a friend of the INVASION USA Series and get updates on new releases.

Triple T ProducTions, Inc. books may be purchased for educational, business, or sales promotional use. For information please write: Triple T Productions Inc., 200 Grayson Senters Way, Fuquay Varina, NC 27526.

Library of Congress Catalogue-in-Publication Data
Wade, T I INVASION USA IV / T I Wade.—1st ed.

Editor – Sherry Emanuel, Raleigh, North Carolina
Final Editor – Brad Theado, Stuarts Draft, Virginia

Cover design by Jack Hillman, Hillman Design Group, Sedona, AZ

Print edition layout by eBooks by Barb for booknook.biz

BOOKS BY THE AUTHOR

The Book of Tolan Series (Adult Reading):

Banking, Beer & Robert the Bruce
    Hardcover and eNovel.

Easy Come Easy Go
    Hardcover and eNovel.

It Could Happen
    eNovel.

INVASION Series (General Reading):

INVASION USA I: The End of Modern Civilization
    eNovel – July 2011,
    Trade Paperback Edition – August 2012.

INVASION USA II: The Battle for New York
    eNovel – March 2012,
    Trade Paperback Edition – August 2012.

INVASION USA III: The Battle for Survival
    eNovel – June 2012,
    Trade Paperback Edition – August 2012.

INVASION USA IV: The Battle for Houston …
The Aftermath
    eNovel – August 2012,
    Trade Paperback Edition – August 2012.

INVASION EUROPE: The Battle for Western Europe
    eNovel – April 2013.

INVASION ASIA: The Battle for China
    eNovel – June 2013.

INVASION USA V: The New America
    eNovel – August 2013.
    (Final Novel in this seven novel series)

Dedication

INVASION USA IV – The Battle for Houston
Is dedicated to the Men and Women of the United States
Navy.

Thank you for all you do to protect the United States of
America, its people and many others around the world.

Note from the Author

This novel is only a story—a very long story of fiction,
which could or might come true sometime in the future.

The people in this story are all fictitious, but since the
story takes place in our present day, some of the people
mentioned could be real people.

No names have been given to these people and there were
no thoughts to treat these people as good or bad people.
Just people who are living at the time the story is written.

Are you ready to survive a life-changing moment that
could turn your life upside-down sometime in the near
future?

Read on and find out!

Is your survival knife honed and ready yet?

TABLE OF CONTENTS

THE BATTLE FOR HOUSTON
3

CHAPTER 1
San Antonio Invaded...5

CHAPTER 2
Flight from China – May..19

CHAPTER 3
Houston – May-June...39

CHAPTER 4
We Have Found the Bad Guys, Sir!..49

CHAPTER 5
Seal Team Six..72

CHAPTER 6
The Hurricane with No Name..83

CHAPTER 7
We Need More Men!..113

CHAPTER 8
The Battle of Houston – May-June...127

CHAPTER 9
The End of the Battle for Houston..171

CHAPTER 10
What to Do Next?...177

THE AFTERMATH
183

CHAPTER 1
August 1st..185

CHAPTER 2
Bogotá, Colombia – July..192

CHAPTER 3
The Meeting on Capitol Hill.......................................230

CHAPTER 4
Wedding Days...238

CHAPTER 5
Who Are These guys?...258

CHAPTER 6
Alaska...287

CHAPTER 7
Mike Mallory – The Right Wing Threat....................297

CHAPTER 8
Who is in control of this?...303

CHAPTER 9
We've Found Them!..324

CHAPTER 10
Cold Bay, Alaska...338

CHAPTER 11
The Time for Civilians is Over...................................369

CHAPTER 12
Major Wong and the Seals 373

CHAPTER 13
The Final Cleanup 410

CHAPTER 14
New Government – New Laws 414

EPILOGUE 426

THE BATTLE FOR HOUSTON

CHAPTER 1

San Antonio Invaded

WHILE GENERAL PATTERSON WAS FIGHTING his war on the other side of the world, the local war was about to heat up.

Manuel Calderón allowed his men to rest on May 4th and told everybody they would cross into the United States the next day. May 5th Cinco de Mayo was a good day to attack America. He got his two brothers, Alberto and Pedro, together and invited the leader of the new Cartels to the meeting with the five other family commanders from Venezuela and Brazil. With the combined forces of their first American-Latino family they had 150,000 men all together. The Sanchez family of 30,000 waited just south of Laredo in a community called Rio Brava; here they had found a nearly deserted housing community, murdered the dozen-odd people they found there and moved in to wait for their friends coming from the south.

* * *

The Navistar-P satellite was not picking up these congregations of people massing on both sides of the border. If it had remained over the central U.S., where Carlos left it, the technicians would have seen slightly darker moving shapes of masses of men slowly joining together like mercury. The satellite could have shown a group of 20,000 men in one place, and 100,000 would have blatantly stood out.

Unfortunately, the technicians manning the satellite feed were watching the Chinese coast, Hawaii, and to within 500 miles of the Californian coast. Their viewing range was a great distance from Texas.

Carlos would be told the bad news in a couple of days when he would then give the technicians orders to change the satellite's orbit back to its original position. It would take Carlos and his technicians at least two weeks to get the pictures back over the Texas area and currently he, was just leaving the satellite's viewing field; he was 700 miles away from Elmendorf in Alaska—the U.S. coast—in the AC-130 Gunship *Pave Pronto*.

* * *

Manuel Calderón slowly and carefully entered the Unites States of America on May 5th, his personal army of 2,500 loyal men with him. He entered five miles south of Laredo and about a mile south of Rio Brava.

The Sanchez family had been waiting for him for a week and they had sourced dozens of small boats from the area around Rio Brava to help ferry the men over the Rio Grande. Here the river wasn't very wide and there was a large island in the middle; this meant that it was a hundred yards or so from each side of the island to dry land, and an easy task to transport Manuel Calderón's rested men and their equipment with no one getting wet.

The whole secret operation took no more than twelve hours of darkness to get the 2,500 men across. On the Texas side the Sanchez family provided several old trucks for their pre-planned trip into Laredo to take out the military guard at the only bridge over the Rio Grande in the area, and get the larger army in the U.S. Manuel had selected Laredo due to its being the only U.S.

border city having smaller army bases and its location 180 miles south of the only real Air force Base, Laughlin Air Force Base, 5 miles east of Del Rio. Carlos Sanchez checked out the area days before the arrival.

An hour after Manuel had driven into the base, the border control post and area had been taken using pistols and silencers given to him by Carlos Sanchez. A platoon of thirty U.S. Army soldiers lay in their own pools of blood.

Two army radios were attacked first, their operators quickly dealt with, so that word couldn't get out. Manuel was also handed a working satellite phone found on the lieutenant's bloody tunic. He had never used one of these in his life, but knew that if he used it the people he was ambushing, and who he did not want to know he was there, would have a direct line to him. He crushed it with a rifle butt breaking it into small pieces, and then he urinated on it.

Carlos Sanchez showed him the several small military barracks in the town: a U.S. Army Reserve depot where another thirty men had been shot dead and the National Guard station by the international airport where the army platoon stationed there, had met the same fate. His orders were that no American soldiers would be left alive. Manuel didn't want them to come back and haunt him.

Other than the soldiers, several unknown civilians were seen, mostly carrying guns and, without asking questions, they met the same fate. The city was now empty of people. Manuel suggested to Carlos Sanchez that the military had pulled the population back as a buffer zone in case of attack. Carlos Sanchez laughed at him and said, "What population?" Most of them were dead, shot by his men.

Sanchez also told Manuel that the army had come through here in large numbers a month earlier and had ordered any civilians to pack up and head north.

"One week there were people shooting at us, the next week it was a ghost town. We heard the army was coming, thousands of men and small civilian aircraft, and they rounded up the people and left. We had to cross the border to escape being noticed. Even the stinking dead bodies were counted and burned in huge piles of thousands," he told Manuel. "The city was cleaned of dead and the area left to the three army stations to control."

"How far north have they gone, the people, I mean?" asked Manuel.

"I sent out some guys to head up I-35 and Highway 59, north and east and they got as far as San Antonio before seeing anybody. Even then soldiers were still moving people north-wards. It will be hurricane season soon and I think they have moved people out of the coastal cities like Houston as well. The men I sent in that direction, to Houston, will be back in a few days," stated Sanchez.

"What about the air force base to the north?" Manuel asked over a meal of fruit freshly shipped over from Mexico. He watched thousands of his men stream over the bridge spanning the Rio Grande. The deserted city of Laredo was filling up again with his men.

The loud roar of weapons being fired around the three small military installations had attracted men, mostly Latinos, hiding in the countryside around the area. Any men other than Latinos were shot on sight.

By the time they rested and had a good night's sleep in real beds, 300 Latino men had arrived at the guard posts, armed and ready to join the army. The commanders slept in a heavily guarded motel, a ransacked, but still usable Days Inn on the outskirts of Laredo.

It was at midday May 6th, when they again got together at the Days Inn; Sanchez's men still hadn't returned as they sat down to a good meal to discuss a battle plan. It was the first time Manuel Calderón and his brothers had ever visited the country;

he had sent over billions of dollars of drugs, but had never set foot in the United States.

This city, Laredo, looked like most of the cities he had passed on his journey northwards. Panama City was a massive city; their police force tried to find out who the traveling men were, and after several hours of fighting, retreated, leaving hundreds dead on the often dirty and low-income suburban and shanty-town battlefields where they had collided.

The same had happened in Honduras and other countries they passed through. The partially destroyed communication systems prevented the country's leaders from knowing what was going on, and the armed forces fighting against the Calderóns didn't have backup or the stomach to take on the large well-armed groups more than once. In the U.S., it was the first time the brothers had seen empty towns and cities.

Something was different here. Manuel could see by the large numbers of local banditos arriving to join his invading army that the men had already helped themselves to local military or civilian weapons.

"Why are they making this large piece of country empty of people, Alberto? Pedro? Carlos?" Manuel asked the group the next day over a lunch of good American steaks. A large bull had been found totally mad and wandering around the outer city area a few days before their arrival and Carlos Sanchez had it shot and butchered. After hanging the meat for a couple of days, it was soft enough to eat.

"The men think that there were so many dead bodies," stated Carlos Sanchez, "and so many civilians being shot, that the American government decided that they cannot control the whole country. I think they have moved all the remaining civilians into smaller areas to protect them. These American banditos told me that they have all killed many people for anything they had: food, money, old trucks, farmhouses, beautiful women, even for a new cell phone which they know doesn't work. Some of these people are pretty crazy people, Manuel."

"Get me some of the new arrivals who have travelled the furthest to get here, let us find out what they know," ordered Manuel to several of the group commanders and they headed out to search. "We will meet with them tomorrow over lunch."

The next day, over a large bottle of bourbon provided by Carlos Sanchez, a group of three men arrived to tell their stories.

"Name!" ordered Manuel to the first man. He was a mean-looking ox of a man, six feet tall and had one tooth sticking out of his smiling mouth. He was filthy, the smell from him worse than their dirty bodies, but he was a killer, a real killer and a real asset to his army.

"Antonio Pedro Muñoz Izquierdeas, Señor Calderón. I used to sell cargo from you in Dallas and Fort Worth."

"Where have you come from, Antonio, and how did you know I was here?"

"A man who I used to deal with from Señor Sanchez's family told me that an army was coming, Señor, your army, and that if I wanted to shoot soldiers, it would be better to fight with your army. I met the man at our old connection point outside Austin and came south with him last week."

"Tell me what you have seen north of here," demanded Manuel.

"Lots of dead Americans, Señor! Lots of dead people, mostly shot by other Americans, and helped by other friends I know. There were no American police after February. We shot anybody who had a uniform and a gun, sometimes three or four a day. In Fort Worth where I live, I had to kill several men who even attacked my own house. Lucky, I had several machine pistols and shotguns and I killed those men. There were others who killed my neighbors and I shot them and then ate the food they had stolen. At one time, at the end of January, there were bands of police trying to keep law and order, but snipers killed them one by one until they didn't come around anymore. Then the National Guard arrived and more army soldiers and the fighting got very bad. These soldiers were better equipped than the stupid policemen and many of the banditos left town. So did I, and me and my family crossed the border into Mexico to stay with my wife's family south of here. I returned, Señor, and got as far as Austin, before coming up to roadblocks and small aircraft flying around looking for us."

"Why did you come back?" Manuel asked.

"Hey, Señor! There's lots of stuff to steal here. Even though there was little food, many people were protecting their houses full of things to steal. In one house alone in San Antonio, Señor, I found $100,000 stashed away in the farmer's mattress. $100,000, Señor, is a lot of money and American dollars still buy things in Mexico, Senor Calderón; a lot of Tequila and nice things for pretty girls.

"How much money did you find, Antonio?" was Manuel's next question.

"A lot, Señor... millions! I worked with this team of five men during March and April, until I heard about you. We killed about a hundred gringos and black people, and often their whole families. We even killed scared Latino families; some of their women were very pretty and would do anything we asked once their husbands and sons were dead. One even cleaned my clothes," he laughed, the men around him grinning at the joke. "We always killed everybody and burned their houses, Señor. Now that the army is patrolling San Antonio, and they have moved all the people to the north, many of the men we knew were shot and so I left the city. There were only a few thousand soldiers, Senor Calderón, but for us, there were too many."

"So you are a rich man, Antonio. I don't need to pay you, just give you houses to clean out once we win the fight," suggested Manuel.

"None of the men need your money, Señor, just a nice piece

of land or a nice big American house to live in and people to work the lands for food. Just like in the old days in Mexico—people to work while I drink Tequila, Señor Calderón; people to be servants, nothing more!" Antonio smiled.

From all three people, it was the same story; the army had moved the remaining people north to areas of safety. It didn't sound like very many were still alive from the stories the three men told. That meant that he could easily take over a good piece of Texas without a big fight.

Manuel knew that he would someday come up against the might of the U.S. military, but it didn't seem that there were very many. Surely they were still stuck in Iraq and other places in the world. Also during his entire operation in Mexico he hadn't been attacked by one American aircraft. Maybe they didn't have any more than the Mexican military and he still had 30-odd ground-to-air missiles to surprise them.

He felt pretty confident about taking over Texas and declaring it his own country. His uncle had told him that it used to be one of the twenty biggest economies in the world, and that alone could make the Calderón family nearly invincible.

"OK, guys, we take over everything between here and San Antonio," declared Manuel that evening. "Me and my brothers and our main army leave at dawn tomorrow morning and we will travel fast on I-35 directly into San Antonio. Carlos Sanchez, you attack Corpus Christie and then go southwards to Brownsville and McAllen with your men. Kill all military you see and then attack and ransack any military barracks for weapons and equipment. There should be lots of ammo around for you to arm your men. Leave any civilians alone and let any Latino men join you who want to. Grow, Carlos Sanchez; grow as big as you can. Force any man who speaks Spanish to join your army. No gringos or black men, we can't trust them. Don't kill the farmers, we will need food in our new country of Texas, amigo. Once you have the area controlled by your men, leave two thousand men in each of the three cities, heavily armed under disciplined leaders. I will wait for you for one week after I attack San Antonio and then I will attack Houston. I want to make Houston our new capital. It's big and a good place to fight the Americans when they come. Carlos, you must find every vehicle that works and get your men to look for food as you move, or your army will grow hungry. Comprehend?"

Carlos Sanchez nodded his head and gave orders to his men to get ready to move out. He wanted to be moving down the dual carriage highway towards Corpus Christie by dawn.

"Remember, Carlos Sanchez, your men will need food. You are not going to find any food in the cities, the best place to find food is in army barracks or places that are defended. There is no law and order in this country, no such crime as murder just the crime of survival. Alberto will give you three of the radios I captured from the Mexican army. I will keep a radio team at the edge of my army and always on a hill. That means you can talk to me once you are within one hundred miles of me and my men."

There wasn't much sleep that night. It took a lot of work and organization to move an army of men. All the leaders and commanders got trucks packed, munitions counted, fuel dispensed and by dawn the next day the two highways out of Laredo were full of men and trucks heading away from Laredo.

Carlos Sanchez, with most of his men already stationed further out of the city of Laredo, left first on a different highway due east to the Calderón armies.

The weather was blustery and overcast, the winds from the south, and rain squalls hit from behind as Manuel led his mobile army of 25,000 men north on I-35. His 3,000 vehicles, mostly jeeps and civilian cars, and Mexican military troop carriers pulling the fuel tankers, covered both sides of the highway northwards for twenty miles, and they managed a good speed of ten miles an hour. His vehicles included three old Mack U.S.

army trucks pulling fuel tankers, captured from the U.S. National Guard base in Laredo.

Alberto's army of 25,000 men was crammed into 2,000 mostly slower military and civilian trucks of all sizes. He had found several dozen old trucks with flatbed trailers, and the hundreds of vehicles started the journey an hour after Manuel's group disappeared over the horizon.

Pedro's much larger army was next and was due to leave immediately after Alberto's last vehicles left. He only had 40 percent of his 60,000 men in vehicles and most of his men had to walk.

All three armies had several hundred men on horseback who rode out a couple of miles on each side of the highway in case of surprise flanking attacks. They were also there to ransack farms, ordered to leave any civilians or farmers alive, but take any food, fuel, vehicles or horses they could find.

The last army of 25,000 was to leave the next day on foot under the command of Pedro's second-in-command, leaving the last 15,000 men to guard Laredo and search every inch of the town for food and any vehicles with fuel. Manuel had decided to leave a relay radio station every fifty miles along the road, on a hilltop. They had several extra radios, ransacked from the Mexican army, and would need communications if and when attacked by American soldiers.

For three hours Manuel and his army surged forward covering 20 miles an hour. The highway was clear with many crashed or non-working vehicles neatly moved and placed on the sides of the two stretches of asphalt. They saw no one and it was as if they were the only people on earth.

Manuel thought that they certainly weren't expected yet and they could get into San Antonio in a surprise attack. He had a list of military installations he needed to engage and could not understand the American logic; one military base covered nearly the whole city. There were two Air Force bases and an Army base, Fort Houston.

He wasn't worried, he had a big army and it seemed he wasn't expected. He decided just to take one at a time.

It was impossible to hide so many men from prying eyes but there was no need to stop and regroup. His three armies were moving and within six hours his group reached the outskirts of San Antonio. Manuel wanted to attack the first base at dawn to get a foothold in the city. He found two small municipal airports on his map and he decided to aim for Castroville Municipal Airport; Alberto would overnight at the Devine Municipal Airport several miles further out of the city and directly on I-35.

To get to the Castroville airport, Manuel's men needed to leave the Interstate, and he picked a couple of side roads to get his large number of vehicles through. This took time and he arrived just before dark.

If the people who had lived down these small roads were still there, they would have seen hundreds upon hundreds of vehicles, much like rush hour traffic, moving on the narrow roads in front of their rural houses.

There were no people to be seen. Manuel thought he saw a person watching them here and there, and he had seen several men drive or ride up to their group of men on horseback and get in line to help the cause.

Now that they had reached the limits of rural living, he could see what the men who had travelled overland to join his army had told him back in Laredo.

There were no houses without damage. Most were broken down blackened ruins where once families lived. There were wild-looking and barking dogs everywhere; and his men wanted to shoot them from the vehicles, but orders had been given for silent travel. Every shopping center or strip mall he passed was nothing but broken bricks and blackened ruins. The only thing that he saw which looked undamaged was one McDonalds sign on the corner of a strip mall. He saw the famous sign, but he couldn't see where the McDonalds had stood. The whole strip mall was nothing more than blackened rubble.

The airfield was small, but at least there was enough room to park many of his trucks on the asphalt runway and taxiway in long lines. There was one empty hangar which still had its structure undamaged, and he turned it into his overnight headquarters.

Manuel radioed Alberto and was told that he too had reached his airfield and would set up camp. He would be the backup army for Manuel, who didn't want to show anybody watching, the size of his forces just yet.

Pedro's army was still twenty-odd miles behind and was to camp in a town called Pearsall. There they found several men, who were waiting to join their army. They had accumulated around a thousand cans of food from several unoccupied houses; the food would only feed a small part of the army, but they and their rations were welcomed. Pedro set up camp in the whole town, his men taking ruined houses for their overnight accommodations.

Here they were far enough away from listening ears to solve the growing dog-barking problem and many animals met with quick deaths before the rest decided to retreat and head out of the danger area.

Carlos Sanchez had told him that he thought San Antonio had no more than three thousand American soldiers guarding the town, but he didn't know where they were based. He anticipated a thousand in each of the three bases.

Early the next morning, May 10th, Manuel's army cut hundreds of openings into the perimeter wire around Lackland Air Force Base while Alberto's army continued up I-35 into the center of the city and towards Fort Houston, the second base on his list. His men were to divide into two groups, one half attacking Fort Houston while the other half headed to Randolph Air Force Base a couple of miles further east.

It was impossible to take the whole city by surprise, but Manuel's armies needed to take over the bases and make sure that the food supplies and anything else they could scrounge out of the bases wasn't destroyed by the Americans.

At exactly 06:30 Manuel's army attacked the installations at Lackland. In hordes his men spread out, shooting anybody who fired back at them. There were good defenses, but not good enough to repel an army of 25,000 men and slowly the firing ceased as American soldiers who weren't immediately shot surrendered their stations. It wasn't worth fighting when you saw thousands of enemy advancing at you.

By 07:30 hours Fort Houston was attacked and much the same happened there. At 08:15, Randolph Air Force Base was attacked and, with only a couple of hundred men defending this base, the battle was over within 30 minutes with many of the still sleeping soldiers either shot in their beds or taken prisoner.

At all three bases, the radio areas were hit first. Unfortunately for the attacking armies, at Randolph the commander had a satellite phone connection and called the president telling him of the attack by thousands of civilians. One of Alberto's men saw the man on the phone, quickly put a couple of bullets through his head, and then crushed the satellite phone with the butt of his AK-47.

At the other end of the phone, the President of the United States heard the gunshots, heard the Air Force Commander grunt sharply and then fall. The last thing he heard was somebody shouting orders in Spanish and then the phone went dead, and his face went white.

"Where the hell is Randolph Air Force Base?" he thought to himself and immediately got on the phone to Carlos to find out if

he knew, tell him what he had heard, and find out where the video satellite was focused because he wanted it to focus on the area where the base was situated.

Carlos also didn't know where Randolph was so the president immediately phoned General Patterson in China. He got the answer that it was Joint Command in San Antonio, Texas, and a now pissed-off General Patterson would be back as soon as possible.

CHAPTER 2

Flight From China – May

COLONEL PATTERSON HEADED DOWNWARDS to the underground level, stepping over three bodies his grenade must have taken out. There were lights, and he carefully stepped into an empty corridor which smelled badly of explosives. He backed into the stairwell and watched a line of guys looking at him from the stairs above.

He didn't want to leave the surface, but he knew that the Marines would follow his orders and fight until there was no more opposition. What worried him down here was not only meeting the enemy but coming face to face with American soldiers who shot first and asked questions later.

There was nothing else to do, but bite the bullet and go forward. He grabbed his third grenade and slung his M16 over his shoulder and took his pistol out of its holster.

He looked back into the empty corridor and decided that to the right was the correct way to proceed and it should take him towards the rear of the base. He silently headed to the next left hand corner and peeked around it. Again the short corridor was empty and it turned right again twenty feet ahead. Also there were two doors on either side of the corridor.

The general reached the next corner and peeked around. It

opened into a large cavern, but he couldn't see anything past the entrance. He nodded to the Marines to open the side doors and they loudly crashed the doors open.

"Who's there?" shouted an American voice from the cavern around the corner. "Show yourselves or we send in grenades, we have dozens of guys, so make my day!"

"U.S. soldiers, Air Force and Marines checking out these doors," shouted out General Patterson and he peeked around the corner to see three Chinese-American Marines dressed in red army uniforms ready to blow his head off. "OK, men, it's me, General Patterson. We are checking these doors."

"Um, sorry, Sir!" stated one Marine as the general showed himself and the three men saluted. "You shouldn't be doing this special work; it's far too dangerous down here. We are making sure no enemy pass this point. We have several other squads guarding other entry points so you'd better let us guide you. Those doors were locked and we didn't bother to open them, it would have made too much noise.

"Two store rooms with cleaning equipment," added the Marine captain coming around the corner. Again the three men saluted.

"We heard you guys blasting the hell out of the enemy up there," continued the Chinese-American Marine sergeant taking off his Red Army outerwear to show his U.S. camouflage. "I suppose we can get rid of this borrowed gear," and he and his two men discarded the enemy clothing. "Unfortunately we have had only a little fishing down here, caught only three fish since you guys arrived. Come see."

The general followed him and found three Chinese soldiers tied up and gagged. One had the rank of major and the other two looked like sergeants. General Patterson asked the Marine to take off the major's gag and he ordered Major Wong to ask the man if the man knew where Colonel Zhing was.

"He was blown up and killed on the wall, sir," Major Wong

translated, getting a quick answer out of the man. "This man is his second in command."

"Ask him why he was coming underground," commanded the general.

"There are systems to activate if they were ever attacked and with the colonel dead it was his duty to make sure that the underground sections were closed and made secure. Unfortunately, it seems that he was too late and he can't understand where these soldiers came from."

"Ask him if he would like to guide us to the main area. If not we can find it ourselves and then we won't need him and I will shoot him," stated General Patterson raising his pistol towards the man.

The major immediately agreed to show them around, and the Marine sergeant stated that he would go on ahead and make sure the other men wouldn't shoot first. They still had their issued dog whistles which would warn the others of their approach.

They were still only twenty feet underground, and they could hear that the battle above them was dying down.

Two men pulled the major up on his feet and tied a rope around his arms. He had been well frisked and only had his tunic, shirt and trousers on. His shoes and the rest of his equipment were in a pile with the other men's clothing and weapons several feet away.

With the sergeant leading, they slowly moved forward, the Chinese major several feet behind him and the general behind the major with his pistol in his back. The underground room, with unpainted cement on all four sides, was empty of people. In the middle were several 50-gallon drums of what looked like gasoline and several large wooden boxes on pallets.

The room looked much like the armory at the airfield and again there was the same green button Preston had found on the opposite wall in the airfield's armory. Actually there were three of them across the rear wall, not just one in the middle.

General Patterson wanted one of the boxes inspected and two soldiers got to work opening the closest one of five. Inside was what looked like spare parts for the helicopters. Looking around carefully he noticed an elevator door, painted grey, on the side of the room. He wanted to use it to go up and check what was happening above but thought it was a little premature and he might get his head blown off by both his men and the enemy, so he postponed his rise to the surface.

"Have your men gone through this section yet?" the general asked the sergeant.

"No, Sir. We have been using that other door over there only," he stated pointing to a second open door on the front wall and to their left. "It leads to some offices and sleeping areas. We didn't realize that those buttons would open doors; we thought they were for the elevator or something."

General Patterson asked the sergeant and Major Wong to push the buttons to the outside doors first. This time thick wooden hallway doors opened, nothing happened and the general told the major to push the middle door.

The major pushed the button and waited. A larger ten-foot by ten-foot concrete door opened in the wall and showed a cavern behind, which was in darkness.

"Sergeant, go find some of your men, we'll wait here. I want these two smaller doors guarded while we inspect the cavern behind the large door," ordered the general. They waited and a few minutes later several more Marines arrived. "I want one of you with a whistle to come with me. I can't hear it, but you guys can. Major Wong, ask our captive what is behind that large door." The conversation was quite long.

"It's the entrance to the nuclear missile chambers and there are five silos. He also said that three silos are empty and two still have missiles in them," replied Major Wong.

General Patterson's face went white with shock.

The captured man went first and when he hit the light switch the general's mouth opened and his face drained of blood.

He was at upper missile height and only a steel chain stopped him from falling into an empty silo a hundred feet or more deep. The walls were blackened and it still stunk from the blast when the missiles had left the silo. They were in the middle of the silo room. The next two silos on either side of the ones he was standing next to were fifty feet away and behind armored glass to the roof. Both were empty.

General Patterson believed that one of these had killed General Allen and most of Beijing.

This was what he had come for, but he counted only three; and he had been told five silos. He looked at the Chinese major and the major pointed to two more green buttons behind protective glass on the other side of the cavern they were standing in. A narrow corridor between the glass dividers led to the other side.

General Patterson asked the captured major to go first and he headed over and pushed one of the two buttons. Again a large door opened and this time, once the light was turned on, the general's mouth opened and shut like a fish. He was in silo number five and it was much bigger and deeper, and had a large rocket still in it. Major Wong opened the other door and walked into a separate room.

"Bloody hell!" stated General Patterson in total shock. The tip of a Russian R-36M multi-head Intercontinental Ballistic Missile stood in front of him, above him, and a hundred feet below him in its massive silo. He looked around and the mouths of all the men were open.

"What is this Russian 1970s missile ready for?" the shocked general asked Wong to ask the major.

"If the invasion failed, Colonel Zhing had orders to fire this missile. You can see on its side the writing of the Supreme

Commander. This Russian-purchased R-36 has 10 warheads, and the Supreme Commander wrote on its side where he wanted each warhead to go. I was coming down to begin the firing sequence manually from a control station over there," he added quite calmly pointing to a command room in the corner of the silos where one of the smaller doors was; the center looked like six inches of armored glass protected it from blasts.

"Who has the codes to fire this weapon?" asked the general looking at the scribble written in English on the side of the missile less than a foot away from him.

"Just the colonel and I," replied the major, still calm.

"Is there another Russian missile next door?" the general asked Wong. The answer wasn't what he expected.

"The second silo blasted our three Zedong satellites into space in 2009 on one of these same Russian missiles, stated the major. "Our Chairman then placed this Russian missile in here, in case something might go wrong in America. The three smaller missiles arrived a few months later from Pakistan, also in 2010, and were for our own Chinese cities if the Chinese government tried to stop our plan. They were given suggestions from the Chairman that he had these missiles in a secret location here. The Russian missile in the silo next door is the same as this one, General, but it still has three of the latest Chinese communications satellites as its payload, not an atomic warhead, and was to be used as a backup if the first three satellites didn't make orbit. The Chairman wanted to purchase a second R-36M multi-headed intercontinental ballistic missile from the Russians, but they didn't want him to have more than one. He was made to sign an agreement in Vladivostok to state that he would send this missile to America if he ever needed it, or if the Russians wanted him to use it."

General Patterson was still in shock and awe of how this Chairman had planned the destruction of the world while listening to Major Wong's long interpretation. For the second time he read the names of the cities written on the missiles surface.

"Major, you are now my captive. Is this missile in safe-mode, and how do we destroy it?" the general asked.

The major suddenly refused to say anything, gave his name, number and rank as he was supposed to do under the rules of The Geneva Convention, and the general ordered the Marines to take him away and keep him alive. He still needed the codes if they wanted to send the three satellites into space.

General Patterson ordered the Marine captain to find a hundred men, arm them to the teeth, and get ready to sleep in the empty room with the helicopter parts. The captured major had already shown them that this was the only entrance to these silos. He closed the doors as they exited the different areas and posted men at each door while they waited for the captain to return. He needed time to think, and there was still a battle to win.

By the time General Patterson had climbed the stairs back up to the surface the fight was over. A company of Marines were guarding a large group of prisoners, and the rest of Colonel Zhing's men were strewn around the base.

"Casualties!" shouted General Patterson, looking up and finding two gunships circling overhead.

A Marine major came over, the man who had been in command of the parachutists, and saluted.

"We have lost 29 Marines sir, 13 men shot while they were under their chutes and another 16 men in ground skirmishes. We have 31 men wounded; three pretty critical... They won't make it. I don't have the other section's casualties report, Sir."

"Medics should have arrived at the airfield by now. We have no large choppers to ferry the wounded, so get the dead and wounded onto the trucks and back to the airfield ASAP, Major," ordered General Patterson. "Also, Major, check with your men underground and make sure you don't leave any of our dead or wounded behind. You'd better have your dog whistle with you."

"We are doing that, Sir, and should have our wounded out of there in a few minutes," the Marine replied, saluting.

An Air Force Chinese-American Medical Captain came up and saluted. He had blood all over him.

"I was in one of the trucks behind you, Sir, when we entered the base. We have nine men dead and 11 wounded. We lost that one helicopter with Air Force personnel aboard so my latest count is 11 dead. The dead and the wounded are being loaded into the trucks, and one has already left for the airfield."

"Thank you, Captain. Go back to the wounded; get the major's dead and wounded aboard the same aircraft. Load all the bodies and every wounded man on one 747 only, and get the crew to fly you into Misawa. They have a full and operational medical hospital there. Many of their personnel will already be at our airfield, and they are here to help the wounded. And tell the pilot not to save gas on the way, I want him there yesterday!"

The numbers weren't bad for such a vicious battle, and he was thankful that he had had the idea to send the Marines in early to get down into the underground bunkers. Otherwise, they would not have stopped the Chinese major from destroying the entire East Coast.

Suddenly the general lurched, and Major Wong immediately grabbed him to help him stand.

"General Patterson, you haven't slept for over 36 hours, you need some rest," stated Major Wong and whistled for the jeep to drive over to them.

"I'm fine, I'm fine, Major. There is more work to do still," he replied, his face white, but he didn't resist as he was helped into the passenger side of the jeep. Major Wong gave orders to get the general to bed in Colonel Rhu's old quarters for the rest of the day with guards and a "Do Not Disturb" sign on the door.

Major Wong didn't feel too good either; he had snatched only a couple of hours sleep in the same period and he would need help pretty soon.

The major got on the radio to tell the two circling gunships to land and rest. The helicopter crews were already at the airfield, and he told them to stand down. The Marines who had been awake all night in the enemy base were relieved and told to head back and get some sleep. They would be back in action the next day. He found the Marine captain, the one who was detailing the guard, and told him to pick another 200 fresh men; he would be in command of this base with 300 soldiers for the next 24 hours.

A few minutes later he found another Marine major and two captains checking the enemy dead.

"We have counted 397 dead, 21 slightly wounded and 63 non-wounded enemy combatants, above ground, "stated the Marine major. "We also found the remains of the enemy colonel, and we are still searching the dozens of corridors underground for their dead. It will take another hour. My men placed 13 of their badly wounded soldiers with our wounded and they will be on that 747 to Misawa; we have a lieutenant and his platoon of 30 flying with them. What do you want me to do with the dead?"

"Do we have any machinery here to dig a hole?" asked Major Wong.

"Yes, there is a Chinese type of Caterpillar back-end loader with a digging attachment in the motor pool at the rear with several other vehicles. It's next to the helicopter repair hangar. We could use that to dig a massive hole to bury the enemy. Do you want us to keep their uniforms?" Major Wong said no. Zedong Electronics no longer existed and they still had enough Red Army uniforms for soldiers if they needed them again.

Within an hour Major Wong saw the single 747 taking off from the airfield with the dead and wounded bound for the base in Japan. He shouted for any men who hadn't slept in 24 hours to get on the trucks, and he climbed into one and headed back for some sleep. The rest of the world could wait.

Forty-eight hours later the battle briefing took place. Twenty of the C-130s had already left for Misawa with 1,600 Marines heading back the long route with the tankers to the states, via Elmendorf in Alaska. Another 100 Marines had headed out on each of the other three fully loaded 747s which took off an hour after Major Wong got to sleep. He had taken care of those issues.

General Patterson then ordered a second load of 100 Marines to head back to the U.S. with the first four 747s which returned after loading them again with electronics and took off as Major Wong surfaced from a needed twenty-six hours of sleep.

Carlos and Lee Wang left with the second load of Marines and flew in the comfort of the several passenger seats in the 747 Transporter. Carlos wanted to get back and reposition the satellite over the central United States. It would take him a week and, unbeknown to him, he was already too late.

The general had told Carlos about the three unused satellites aboard the missile, and he said that he would be back in a week. He wanted to get them into space.

"A battle with honors, gentlemen," shouted General Patterson through a megaphone to the 800 remaining Marines, 100 Air Force personnel and 150 engineers and technicians standing in formations in front of him; they were on the apron where the 747s were being loaded. Another 100 Marines and 50 Air Force personnel were still on guard duty at the other base and a radio mike had been placed in front of him to allow them to hear his briefing. "Yes, we lost many fine men and yes, our enemy lost over ten times more men than we did. Any battle commander would be proud of his men with those numbers. I'm here today to tell you that my worst nightmares did come true in the underground area of the last military base controlled by our enemy. We found a fully operational R-36M Russian Intercontinental Ballistic Missile aimed directly for Washington, DC. As many of you already know, this missile is capable of sending 10 separate warheads over to the United States, or anywhere else in the world for that matter. On the side of the missile, and in the enemy leader's own handwriting, were ten cities he wanted wiped off the map.

"If his mission to invade and take over our country had failed, he wanted the base commander to fire that missile. The major was on his way to do just that when we attacked yesterday morning; he was captured alive by our Marines who had infiltrated their underground sections the night before and prevented him from achieving that mission. I don't know how many people still live in those cities, and I'm sure many of you might have grown up in those cities; but yesterday we saved those Americans who are still there. Those cities are Washington D.C., New York, Trenton, Boston, Indianapolis, Chicago, Pittsburgh, Columbus, Ohio; and Richmond, Virginia. Any areas within 200 miles of those cities would have been death zones."

Preston, upon hearing the news for the first time, was shocked. His farm and airfield were within the Richmond range.

"Again, we have won the right to survive and again we will do so," continued the general. "The last military base of Zedong Electronics is ours, but many of us will stay to clean up the spoils of war for our country which desperately needs them. Once we are done, all enemy soldiers below the rank of captain will be released and allowed to go home. By the time the thousands of Chinese soldiers we sent on leave return, I don't want one item of value to be at either of these bases. We will not destroy any living quarters, and we will leave a small amount of food for the returning soldiers, but that is all. Another 600 of you Marines will head back to the United States tomorrow with the remaining C-130s. We will keep a Marine commander and 300 men here in case we come up against hostiles. All our Air Force personnel will stay, except the C-130 crews flying our Marines home with three of our Gunships. The rest of us will pack up and load everything we can and get it home to start our country's machines again. We will fly all of the captured officers to Japan.

When we leave here they will be returned and freed. Thank you gentlemen for a job well done!" and the general applauded his troops.

"That means all our guys back at my airfield would be toast by now," stated Preston having a drink in the Officer's Mess of the enemy base with General Patterson, Mo Wang, and Major Wong. Everyone nodded agreeing with him.

"I knew the Chairman was up to something bad," added Mo. "He was so secret about this base and especially about that second one. Even I was never allowed to visit that top-secret base. All I was allowed to do here was to track stores in and out, train men, and visit the arms company in Harbin from time to time."

"Is that the company that produced the helicopters?" asked General Patterson.

"They completed the final assembly of several of Zedong's military weapons," he replied.

"A large company?" Major Wong asked.

"Yes, it has a hangar at the city airfield where you first landed your aircraft in Harbin," Mo Wang replied, "and a large factory about a mile north of the airport. It is a big company and the factory grounds are about half the size of this airfield."

"I think a visit is in order," suggested the general. "I will schedule it for late tomorrow afternoon. In the morning I want to check all the underground corridors for any areas we have missed, and then get those twelve remaining helicopters over here and have the men dismantle their rotors for shipping. I also want to find every missile around here, air-to-ground and ground-to-air.

They had a sort of celebration that night. There wasn't much good alcohol around Mo showed them how to drink the local Harbin rice wine, heated. To Preston even a simple cold Yuengling tasted better than this stuff.

After an early 04:00 breakfast the next morning, the twelve

troop carriers and the general in his Chinese jeep headed over to the other base. Six American and six guarded Chinese pilots were to fly the Z-10 helicopters back to the airfield. Preston and Mo Wang went along to look at this secret missile. Mo did not believe that his ex-Chairman had such destructive weapons.

The dead had been removed and buried in a freshly-dug, nine-foot deep trench a hundred yards long. The Marines had completed the grizzly task within 24 hours, and nothing more than a long, wide pile of dirt showed where the remains of the defending base soldiers rested.

A temporary base camp had been set up on the green parade square, and the general was saluted from all angles as he drove in. He checked the walls and found squads of men on guard around the base.

The first visit was to the Marine officer who he had ordered to protect the missile silos at all costs. Preston and Mo went with him. In the rooms around the entrance to the silos, the guard detachment of the 100 men was steadfastly guarding the area.

"Anybody gone through here since I left?" he asked the man.

"No, Sir. We have had two men at the door 24/7 and a machine gun over there with six men around it pointing at the entrance to this room," he added pointing to the machine gun placement behind sandbags. "We bedded down in the several rooms around here. Nobody could have gotten through this room."

"Found any secret doors?" General Patterson asked.

"How did you know, Sir?" the captain asked.

"Well, we haven't found an armory or magazine. Every base has one somewhere, so may I assume you found it, Captain?"

"Yes, Sir! It was in the extra wide corridor as you go left out of here, and on the wall several yards away was one of the same little green buttons in the middle of a blank wall. A ten-by-ten foot stone door opened, and it led us into an ammunitions magazine. It has taken us a whole day with 50 men to record what is in there."

"How many helicopter missiles?" asked the general, now looking straight at the captain who pulled out a long piece of what looked like legal paper and scanned it for a few seconds.

"Missiles in total: 600 cases, 3 missiles to a case," he replied.

"Air-to-air and air-to-ground I assume," suggested the general.

"Exactly 200 cases of three types sir; air-to-air, air-to-ground and also ground-to-air," replied the captain. We also found a couple of those stored ground-to-air missile-launcher units on wheels, the ones they kept pulling out of the ground yesterday."

"And I would assume a secret elevator with a grass top to take everything to the surface, Captain?"

"Correct, Sir," replied the captain, "except that it was a concrete top, part of the actual area the helicopters were stationed on. It's going to take the 747 Transporter filled to the brim to get the whole armory out of here."

"We are going to exhaust those 747s before we are finished here," added the general "We still have a whole factory to check yet."

The general's transportation problems were growing. The president wanted all the men returned from Europe ASAP while General Patterson now wanted all this valuable modern military weaponry flown back ASAP.

He would have to use the fleet of C-130s until the troop return was completed. He began to realize that it was going to take weeks to get out of here, and he didn't want to hang around that long. The general remembered that the first flight of C-130s should still be in Japan and he headed for the surface where he could satellite phone Misawa.

The C-130s at Misawa were about to head off to Elmendorf when he reached the commander of the base. It was still early; dawn was rearing its head over the eastern horizon.

General Patterson told the colonel to load up the 1,600 Marines tightly into the C-130s; they should take 110 men with only basic equipment and squashed into each aircraft. That should free up five of the aircraft. The general told the commander to return the extra aircraft to Harbin. He also gave orders for the flight crews of the C-130s going into Elmendorf to offload the Marines at Edwards Air Force Base temporarily, and then return to Harbin via Elmendorf. General Patterson needed to return the tankers to Harbin once they had air-refueled the outgoing aircraft on their long flight into Elmendorf. Instead of going into Elmendorf, the tankers were to return to Misawa, refuel themselves and then head back here to Harbin.

General Patterson wanted these valuable attack helicopters transferred, and one helicopter with dismantled rotor blades could just fit into the cargo hold of a C-130. With the 16 C-130s still on the apron and the five returning aircraft, he could load all of the remaining choppers; 17 in one flight stateside, and the four extra aircraft loaded with their valuable air-to-ground missiles. That would leave the transporter for the electronic supplies.

He, Preston, and Mo Wang then checked the silos again and made sure everything was safe. He didn't like guarding a missile with so much destructive power; and he ordered a couple Air Force nuclear engineers who had worked on the American versions of this type of missile to make sure that if it was launched, it would never deliver an active warhead. General Patterson anticipated that he might come across this problem and had brought the two specialists with him. He already knew that there was a fourth Pakistani missile which needed to be terminated, forever.

They left the base with the eleven still-operational troop carriers behind the jeep and, under Mo's guidance, headed to the city of Harbin. There were few people around, and those who did see the convoy must have been shocked to see U.S. soldiers driving around in local Chinese military trucks.

They drove for 30 minutes and found the airfield. It was as the Marines had left it, stated Lieutenant Colonel Clarke who had returned with the general. He had been stationed here for two days waiting for the attack.

The large warehouse was off to one side and was surrounded by a type of high fence normally found around a prison. The gate was not guarded, and the two large entrance gates had large padlocks and several signs saying that anybody entering would likely end up dead.

It didn't take long to open the gates, and they drove up to the large aircraft hangar doors. Preston noted that a C-130 or several of them could be stored in this one large hangar. He was wrong; it was totally empty, except for three more Z-10 Helicopters parked there, totally alone, and looking rather small in the large space. He radioed Major Wong who was in the air with the first transfer that he needed to collect another three helicopters here and the group then left for the factory.

It was another 20 minute drive to the factory through more densely populated areas, and through the built-up areas the convoy really got interesting stares.

This time the factory gates did have two armed guards—security guards, not soldiers—guarding them. The general drove up and waited for them to open the gate. It was a weird scene; two security guards standing there, one phoning into the main office that there just happened to be a convoy of 12 Chinese military vehicles full of American soldiers.

It seemed that nobody believed him; a third guard, their superior, walked over to check out the story.

"Mo, tell him who you are and to allow us in, or we will just drive through the closed gates and declare war on this establishment," stated General Patterson sitting in the front seat of the jeep. Mo did and, shaking his head, the third soldier got onto the phone to relay the latest demands.

A few seconds later a man in command gave orders to the two security men who opened the gates to allow the convoy to drive through. Once through and in front of the main office, the Marines erupted out of the trucks to make a perimeter defense for the general still in the jeep. There was still no opposition.

Again the general just sat there with Mo and Preston waiting for something to happen. A single, older man in a smart civilian suit exited the main swing doors to what looked like the front office building in front of a much larger factory complex. He walked up to the jeep and bowed deeply.

"What can I do for you?" he asked simply in Chinese.

"I am Mo Wang. I was on the Politburo of Zedong Electronics under Chairman Chunqiao. The Chairman is dead, and so are Zedong Electronics and its Politburo. These men would like to see the working of your factory, and what it makes."

"I'm sorry to hear about the death of our beloved CEO and president," the Chinese man replied bowing again. "Since it now seems that I am in charge, or maybe it is you, Comrade Wang, who is in charge. I would be honored if you completed a tour of our facility. We are the only operational complex and factory left in Harbin with electricity and the only operational factory left in China I believe."

Once General Patterson was told what the man had said, he climbed out of the jeep, the man bowing to him as well.

"Honorable General, I also speak perfect English. I received my doctoral degree in Mechanical Engineering at MIT in Boston twenty years ago."

That shocked General Patterson who quickly regained his composure. "So you know U.S. military uniforms, then?" he asked.

"Yes, I spent a month stationed at your McGuire Air Force

base on the East Coast studying the principals of military helicopter flight and engineering."

"Well, I'm very impressed with your Zhi-10; I haven't had the pleasure to fly one yet, but they seem a pretty neat machine," replied the general.

"They should be, General," the man replied. "They are a well upgraded copy of your first American Apache designs with more modern Russian production ideas."

The general realized that he had just hit the lottery; a fully working engineering factory that he would have the pleasure to take piece-by-piece back to California.

"Would you like the opportunity to return to my country?" the general asked simply.

"That would be an honor," the man replied. "I never liked my superiors in Nanjing and regretted being forced to hand over the 50-year old company my father started, for nothing. As long as I can take my family and my workers and their families, if they want to join me, I would enjoy working with others in your country."

"How many people do you have working for you?" General Patterson asked.

"In total, 4,500 men and women, from design engineers to assembly technicians; we even forge many of our own metals and alloys here at our factory."

"How many people in total would you need to transport?"

"General, I will need to check with my personnel, but if everybody wanted to go with their families, I would say around 25,000 people," answered the man.

"If you can show me why I would want to move that many people I will get on the phone right here and begin the airlift of your entire factory, its machines and its people over to Silicon Valley in California."

Within 30 minutes of arriving, General Patterson was on the satellite phone to the U.S. president asking him permission to hold all troop flights for a week and get every flying machine in here to begin transporting equipment into California. The president wasn't happy until he was told of the R-36M Russian missile pointing at his very office and he then relented. Although over ninety percent of the troops had already returned, he had so far not kept his word to the American people about troop numbers and withdrawals during the current year; one more reschedule wouldn't really make any difference.

General Patterson had seen what he had wanted to see. This company made things, electronics, from scratch. There were over a dozen modern, big and heavy machines making things so small he needed a microscope to see the parts. There were two completed Z-10 helicopters close to completion and another two in the building stage. There were also two of the mobile ground-missile launchers on the building blocks, and they also made the entire missile itself, including its electronic control parts and guidance systems in-house.

For Michael Roebels, and the other engineers and technicians in California, it would save them years in designing and in making these parts; they could be redesigned to do a hundred different tasks, not run a helicopter or a missile launcher, but maybe liven up the electrical grid or an operating theater in a hospital, and many other important systems the USA needed right now.

General Patterson, Preston, and even Mo Wang were stunned by the treasure trove they had just stumbled upon.

Within an hour the general had phoned Andrews and told all the base commanders, until further notice, to halt the 747s still bringing troops home, leave only one aircraft to airlift any needed supplies to the men, and, fly them all into one location: Ramstein in Germany. He also instructed them to protect the U.S. base there and bring its allotted 600 troops home on its return flight.

He then gave orders for the entire fleet of 747s to refuel and fly the Arctic route to Harbin. One was to stop at Travis and pick up three hundred engineers and technicians to help the Chinese in Harbin dismantle and pick up every piece of equipment on the two bases and the factory. The troop transporters could truck everything to the airfield immediately. He phoned Michael Roebels, who was spending the day at Silicon Valley, and ordered him to get 300 men ready for pickup.

It was a whirlwind of activity for that hour. Preston was swept away by how fast the general worked and directed the Air Force personnel to organize themselves to get to China to collect needed electronic equipment. He was still touring the plant a few minutes after the call to Andrews when the general's phone rang.

General Patterson listened for a few seconds and his face went white with anger. He put the phone down and looked at the ground for a second before telling the several people around him what the conversation was about; the President of the United States had just told him there had been an attack from the southern border and San Antonio, Texas had been taken by an enemy army of what they believed to be a large number of armed civilians.

"Shit!" he stated to nobody. "Mo Wang, Lieutenant Colonel Clarke," he stated to Mo and the Marine officer, "I need to get back ASAP. It looks like we are in trouble, and I'm needed back there. Preston, Lieutenant Colonel Clarke, you are coming with me. We will take *Blue Moon* and *Easy Girl* back to Misawa and I will have to figure out this new problem in the air. Now I know how General Allen felt trying to keep up with all this dammed new stuff happening all at once. Major, leave your second-in-command here and Mo Wang, you will be our person in charge to pack up and get all this stuff stateside."

Mo nodded, glad to be part of the system of trust.

CHAPTER 3

Houston – May-June

GENERAL PATTERSON WAS TOLD BY the president that there were perhaps as many as 50,000 men in the civilian army that had attacked San Antonio. The base commander had estimated far more, hundreds of thousands, and by the time word got to General Patterson in China the suggestions had increased to 300,000.

The number wasn't that far from accurate. Once the several bases had been overrun in San Antonio, and Manuel had no opposition to fight on the fourth day, word got out that there was a foreign army taking over Texas; and the numbers of armed men had already increased by 20,000 to 170,000. Manuel had lost several hundred men at the three bases. The Americans had fought hard; and once they understood the magnitude of the attack, they fought like madmen.

It was not possible for 3,000 men to fight 50,000 and, within several hours, the fighting had ended at the bases called Joint Command San Antonio. Then they cleared the smaller National Guard base and several other bases and storage facilities around the city. Manuel was lucky that at the time he had attacked, there wasn't one military aircraft in the whole of Texas that could fly. He didn't know that all the Texas-based aircraft were further north on food duty, or over in Japan and China.

Manuel's next problem was what to do with the 900 captured Americans. Killing the enemy whilst in battle was part of war, but to murder nearly 1,000 captured men and women by firing squads was far above the nastiness of even the Calderón Cartel. His men had done well losing only several hundred to over 2,000 American dead.

He couldn't stop his men playing with the female soldiers, that was part of the spoils of war; but it took a day, his fifth day in America, to decide what to do with the prisoners once he had given the order for the men to leave the women alone.

"Alberto, we must let them go. We can send them out in their underwear and boots and tell them they have 24 hours to get going. They should scamper north like cattle, and hopefully we never see them again."

"I think we should just shoot them all, or they will head to other bases and join forces," replied Alberto.

"Less than a thousand soldiers, already beaten in battle, will not be our problem in the future, Alberto," added Manuel. "We have grown by thousands just in the last few days, and if we keep growing at this rate, we could have more men than the whole American army soon. That, my brother is not impossible! Where are their aircraft? Their fancy fighting Marines and Special Forces? Where are their parachutists? Everywhere in the world except where they need them: here. We saw more aircraft in Mexico, and shot all of them down! Alberto, just in case, we, the Calderón Cartel should not be accused of mass murder."

Slowly Alberto agreed. The prisoners had already been collected from the several bases where they had waved their white flags and were encamped at Lackland Air Force Base.

Later that day and just before dusk, they stripped the soldiers of their uniforms and burned the lot. The prisoners, 848 men and the 69 women, who had suffered the brutality of the men, were driven out of the base like cattle, dressed in underwear, hats and boots, and told they would be hunted down, starting in 24 hours. The soldiers knew what that meant and, helping limping and injured soldiers, they hobbled off and scattered like leaves in the wind, much to the men's laughter and merriment. He gave his men the rest of the day off and the next day to rest

The next morning, May 14th, Manuel left San Antonio and headed towards Houston leaving 10,000 men with enough captured American MRE rations and food at Lackland to keep the base intact. The men had orders to empty the other bases of vital equipment and raze the bases to the ground. They had found a couple of dozen old military troop carriers, a dozen jeeps, and several artillery pieces which they took with them.

Manuel also left his army with far more than they needed to defend themselves. He also had his men destroy the quantities of U.S. Air Force modern fighter jets, bombers, and dozens of useless modern attack helicopters on the airfields. Manuel's men found a couple of 707 tankers at Randolph and blew them up. Fort Houston experienced the same treatment, except the weapons of destruction were furniture and gallons of aviation gasoline which was no good for Manuel's transport, but excellent for setting the base on fire.

Massive black clouds of smoke began erupting out of San Antonio, a couple of hours after they left the base. It would give notice to anybody who could see them that the invading army was not afraid of the Americans knowing that they were there.

Radio communications between the Sanchez Cartel in Corpus Christi and Manuel was constantly relayed, and Manuel heard that they also had captured Corpus Christi. Carlos Sanchez had killed every one of the 300 American soldiers found there, loaded important food and gas supplies, and departed with part of the city burning.

The Sanchez Cartel was to travel northeast and meet Manuel on I-10, halfway to Houston.

* * *

By this time General Patterson was landing at Edwards in California. It had taken him only six hours to get airborne out of Harbin, and over the aircraft's radio he gave instructions to his men remaining in China. He had waited for the five C-130s to return; the 16 others were already loaded with the first rotor-less helicopters. The five C-130s from Misawa took less than two hours to load the last helicopter and 200 of the 600 cases of missiles in the other four aircraft.

He refueled in Misawa, organized and checked on weather from Carlos's satellite for the long and heavy flight into Elmendorf, and took off in a heavy rain storm from the south, knowing that the 18 C-130s, two Gunships and seven tankers would have tailwinds for at least the first couple of hours to help them get the range into Alaska. It was touch and go with the heavy choppers aboard.

On board, General Patterson acted much like General Allen had done before him. He contemplated every fact, and then phoned people to get their input and give orders.

No, nobody knew what was happening in San Antonio. No, there were absolutely no flyable aircraft in the whole of Texas. Even the Laughlin Air Force Base commander said that he had nothing flyable. Everything was north feeding people. The commander had 3,000 men on the base and had heard over his satellite phone about the attacks 200 miles to his east in San Antonio. No, he would not go and see what was going on. He had 3,000 men versus hundreds of thousands. He was going to stand and defend his base and wanted backup.

It was same at Dyess, Goodfellow and Shepherd Air Force Bases in the rest of Texas. There were less than 12,000 men at these three bases, no flyable aircraft and nobody knew who the attacking army was.

General Patterson's brain was working as fast as it could

while the pilots flew northwards enjoying a 50-knot tailwind for the first three hours. They would make it.

Refueling was completed six hours later, halfway to Elmendorf in Alaska. General Patterson phoned Carlos in California, who was now able to send orders to the satellite via the observatory from "The Cube" near San Francisco.

"How long before you get our observation satellite back over Texas?" he asked Carlos.

"It took two weeks to redirect it from Kansas to directly over Hawaii. I think we will have visuals back over western Texas in about ten days," Carlos replied.

"Do you need to be there? Can Lee do your satellite commands for you, Carlos? I need you in Texas," replied the general.

"Give me another day and I'll be ready to leave."

"Good, you still have the AC-130 Gunship *Pave Pronto* with you don't you, Carlos?" the general asked. Carlos acknowledged that he did. "Get her refueled and head for McConnell Air Force Base in Wichita, Kansas once you are done. I want you to phone Preston's farm and order the Super Tweets airborne and get them over to Kansas within 24 hours. I'm scrambling the F-4s and F-5s and they will be heading into McConnell today. We are at war, it's going to take us 24 hours to mobilize our aircraft and base ourselves in that area for our next battle. Get there fast, I have 18 of the attack helicopters aboard and will fly them into Edwards; get the choppers out of our holds and to our technicians to get them operational again, and then fill our 130s up with Marines. It will take 48 hours from now for me to get out of Edwards, and then we should be able to see what we are up against. I'm sending a couple of Cessna 210s south as spotters, and we should have eyes by tomorrow. Call me when you get to McConnell. Fly safe!"

Next the general called other bases and scrambled all the jet aircraft at the bases. It wouldn't take them long to get to Kansas and he would brief them once somebody knew what the hell was going on. He couldn't fight a war blindfolded.

Fifteen hours later he landed in Edwards and hundreds of extra technicians at Edwards, flown in by small civilian aircraft from the surrounding bases, began taking the Chinese helicopters out of the thirsty C-130s which were immediately refueled. The first flight of 18 C-130s and three of the six gunships, which had brought in the Marines from China 48 hours earlier, were ready to go with a few of their bellies full of soldiers.

Another 2,200 Marines from the 1st Marine Division were picked up at Camp Pendleton, They had only returned from Europe a week earlier and were still getting used to Pacific Time. The total number of Marines from this division now numbered 4,000 and the C-130s, like a swarm of birds now with five gunships also full of soldiers, headed for McConnell in Kansas. Nobody could tell where the enemy was, and McConnell was far enough away to regroup and prepare for whatever was to come.

* * *

Manuel looked at the sky. He was worried. It was a beautiful day with no wind and not a cloud in the sky. It was very hot and more humid than usual. The weather was too perfect and he thought a storm was brewing as he closed in on the intersection where he was to meet Carlos Sanchez.

Both armies were growing rapidly, sweeping up any Hispanics and Latinos who had a gripe against the United States, or were just bad guys at heart. For many of them this was a dream come true. Manuel's soldiers were ordered to shoot any gringos or black men who wanted to join his army, and dozens of warm dead bodies littered the Interstate behind them. Many of these unfortunate people arrived on horseback; the horses were taken for the army, leaving the dead riders to rot in the sun.

The Sanchez Cartel radioed in and told them that they were two hours from reaching the intersection; their highway was only a two-lane road and they couldn't travel as fast.

By nightfall Manuel saw the southern army coming over the dunes to meet them.

* * *

By nightfall of the same day, May 14th, the eight F-4s and three F-5s had already been waiting a day for the swarm of C-130s to arrive from the west. There wasn't much they could do and they weren't built to be slow spotter planes.

A spotter plane, a Cessna 210, had been sent southwards and flying high at 25,000 feet over San Antonio saw the smoke from the burning barracks. That was all it had time for before returning at dusk to Dyess to report as the small aircraft's 800 mile range couldn't get the two pilots back into McConnell.

The Super Tweets, coming in from Preston's airfield in North Carolina, were eight hours ahead of the C-130s the next day and landed right behind Buck coming in from Andrews in the Colombian DC-3. Carlos arrived an hour behind the Super Tweets, flying in from California, and excited to see Sally for the first time in weeks. He knew Preston wasn't far behind and was surprised to see his Colombian gunship standing there with Buck walking up to say hi.

The slower C-130s finally arrived in a line ten miles long and began turning into finals for McConnell's two major runways from the north east. There was a brisk constant wind coming in from the south.

Martie ran into Preston's outstretched arms as he exited *Blue Moon*. He had been away forever and she had much to tell him about her new flying abilities. It was time for the two couples to have a little time together and General Patterson, who rested a little during his long flight, called for a briefing in an hour.

The first spotter plane had gone out again early that morning and was followed by a second one an hour later and a third, an hour after the second one.

"OK guys, get settled, we have another bloody war to fight. When are we going to end these battles?" he asked aloud from the podium as everybody took their seats. "What do we know other than what has been explained already?" he asked. The report from the pilot of the spotter plane told the briefing room that he had seen two major columns of smoke exactly where Fort Houston and Randolph were situated. He had to return due to the lateness of the day and had seen no more.

General Patterson got on a radio on the desk next to the podium and called in the first spotter plane.

The aircraft's pilot replied that he had again seen the same fires over San Antonio, and he was currently 50 miles west of San Antonio over Interstate 10 at 10,000 feet and heading west towards El Paso. So far he had seen no movement.

The second pilot reported that he was west of Dallas directly over Dyess Air Force Base, southwest of Abilene, and he was to fly southeast to San Antonio to see if any enemy were using the major secondary roads in that direction, and if they were planning on attacking the next Air Force Base, Dyess. The pilot's instructions were then to fly east over Interstate 10 towards Houston.

The third spotter pilot stated that he was 100 miles north of Dallas and was to head down Instate 35 over Waco and then to circle over Austin to see if he could see any movement anywhere. So far none of the aircraft had seen any movement.

* * *

Manuel Calderón had spoken with Carlos Sanchez the previous night and was happy to learn that a new cartel out of North Texas, the Santana Cartel of 15,000 men, had been found by Carlos just outside Corpus Christi and had happily joined the army. The Santana Cartel knew of and had radio contact with another Mexican Cartel which was heading south from Lubbock, Texas and were currently 50 miles north of Houston traveling south on I-45. They had another 5,000 men.

Carlos Sanchez also had good news which explained why he had taken longer to get to the intersection. He found a large storage warehouse on the Naval Air Station in Corpus Christi he had attacked. There had been only 200 men at this base.

His men had destroyed all the aircraft they found there, dozens of useless pieces of metal. In one of the warehouses was a mountain of army rations. This base looked like it had not been visited for a couple of months by any outsiders as the American soldiers were unshaven and dirty. The only thing they had apart from a couple of operational vehicles and a jeep was this mountain of food. He had stacked the two troop transporters full, and he suggested that they send a dozen trucks back immediately to fill them with MRE rations.

The Cartel members couldn't keep count of all the men and now with so many men, they would be like locusts on the ground; they would need to find food supplies in large quantities. Hopefully Houston had some sort of food supplies and only military installations seemed to have ample food stocks.

Manuel agreed with Carlos Sanchez and looked at his map. There were smaller roads direct from Houston to Corpus Christi and if he had a problem, he could send out trucks at night which could return the next night.

Manuel estimated that now he had well over 190,000 men with still more joining every day. He had ordered his commanders to check on food stocks throughout the night and several hours later he was given vague amounts that he and his men had enough for less than a week.

He ordered hundreds of men out of dozens of troop transporters and told them to walk. They were only 30 miles from the outskirts of the massive city of Houston and once he was in there, he knew that he would have better cover from future air attacks, if any came.

He asked Carlos Sanchez for one of his commanders and told him and the thirty drivers of the now empty trucks to immediately head south on the smaller roads, fill the trucks with food and return to Houston. The trucks headed southwards with a fuel tanker, two of the valuable missile launchers and fifty heavily armed men to help load the food.

An hour later he was still discussing his "Invasion USA" plan with Carlos Sanchez when they heard the drone of a small aircraft high in the sky coming from the west, behind them. The enemy aircraft would have seen the rear armies by now, and it was also the first time that he had seen or heard a small aircraft in the U.S. This one was certainly not a fighter aircraft, and his three armies began to move eastwards again as he knew that they would now be monitored by the U.S. Air Force. He hoped the pilot didn't see his trucks traveling south, now at least forty miles away heading towards the food.

CHAPTER 4

We Have Found The Bad Guys, Sir!

"GENERAL PATTERSON, SIR! WE HAVE communication from the second spotter plane," stated a radio operator entering the briefing room an hour later, and all eyes turned to the woman. "The pilot has spotted a large number of people heading eastwards along Interstate 10 towards Houston. They are around 40 miles from the outskirts of the city."

A second operator arrived seconds later as the general was about to bark out orders. This time the operator was a male.

"Excuse me, Sir, the same pilot has just reported a second and third group of men; he estimates there are about two hundred thousand in total, and traveling at approximately 15 miles an hour, all in the direction of Houston. The vanguard group is about twenty miles west of the outer rim of Houston, and the second group is about five miles behind the tail-end of the first group, and about fifteen miles behind the lead vehicles of the vanguard group. It seems the three groups have a five-mile space between them, and the third is the largest group by far."

"Thank you, please get coordinates from the pilot and tell him to refuel at his closest base and to stay overhead as long as he can; we will have attack aircraft incoming within an hour," replied General Patterson thinking fast. Maybe we can halt their progress into Houston. "F-4 and F-5 crews scramble and get out of here towards Houston at high cruise. It's a long flight for your fuel reserves so fly steady at medium to high cruise until I give you further orders. I will brief you while you are in the air."

Several crews in the briefing room already in flight suits collected their notes and readied to run to their aircraft waiting on the apron. All the eight F-4s had been refueled with two extra wing fuel tanks fitted per aircraft and armed for ground attack with six veteran 1970s Maverick air-ground missiles and one 250 pound older 1960s-era Walleye bomb under the belly. The other two wing connectors had the fuel drop tanks for further range. The F-5s, being only single-seat fighters, were much smaller and a faster high-cruise aircraft. They carried six Mavericks, three under each wing, and their two under-wing fuel tanks.

General Patterson immediately realized that he was too far away from where the enemy was situated, and he needed to get closer.

"Dyess Air Force Base in Abilene, west of Dallas will be the next base of operations, ladies and gentlemen; pilots head back to Dyess on your return flights. Now get airborne." He had ordered the preparation of the jets for as long a range as possible, thinking that any enemy would head straight for Austin and then Dallas. He had been wrong.

All the jets had under-wing fuel tanks, which gave them at least a 900 mile range at high cruise with a light weapons load, but it also increased the time the aircraft would take them to reach Houston, a little over 500 air miles south. Also none of them had fuel reserves to make it back to McConnell after their attack; hence the immediate change to Dyess, 150 air miles closer.

"All six AC-130 Gunships and Tankers," began the general rapidly giving orders, "I want you out of here within thirty minutes. Carlos and Buck, you guys fly your AC-47. It will take you just under two hours to get there, so hurry and I want you out of here in five minutes; go now and I'll get some men to collect your personnel belongings. You are returning to base at Dyess tonight as well. Go! You six Super Tweets, I want you ready for takeoff in 45 minutes. I will lead you in Carlos's aircraft, *Hector*. Get your stuff packed and outside your doors; Air Force personnel will load it aboard a C-130 bound for Dyess. Get going flight crews!" and the room emptied of pilots.

The general now turned to the men on the ground. "Lieutenant Colonel Clarke, I want you to start hounding the rear of this enemy army. We are not going to be able to stop their entering the suburbs or even the inner city of Houston with only 3,000 men, it would be a suicide mission, but we can certainly try and wag the tail of the dog. I want as many parachutists as you can muster with two days of food, armed to the max, and in by midnight. I will get mortars and a couple of jeeps packed up for a second drop by dawn tomorrow morning." The last person left the room.

The room was now empty apart from the two radio operators and General Patterson asked them if they had radio contact with Dyess. They didn't.

"Colonel Marks, Patterson here," stated the general talking to the commander of Dyess after looking through his satellite-phone book for the phone numbers for the two nearest bases to the enemy—Dyess in Texas and Barksdale Air Force Base in Louisiana. "Commander, I'm setting up my base of operations later today at Dyess, what are your fuel and food reserves?"

Between the two soldiers they agreed that there was enough fuel and food at Dyess for two weeks. Colonel Marks was told to get his base in readiness for operations immediately.

General Patterson then phoned Colonel Montgomery at Barksdale. After several minutes General Patterson realized that Barksdale had much more fuel and food than Dyess; he might need to set up mission headquarters there in a week. He ordered the base to be ready for anything, and then he ran out to get into flight overalls.

McConnell's base commander, about to enter the briefing room, ran along beside him. "Colonel, we are moving out to Dyess, I will leave you three C-130s. I want all your usable missiles, rockets, bombs and 20mm ammo transferred to Dyess ASAP!" the base commander of McConnell stopped, acknowledged, and headed off in another direction.

Three quarters of an hour later the last of the attack aircraft, the seven Super Tweets took to the air with General Patterson in the lead aircraft. Even though it was a two-seat aircraft, he could fly it solo from its left seat and control what he needed in the way of aiming and firing its weapons.

He had ordered the seven Tweets to be equipped with 14 MK40 air-to-ground rockets, each in two launch pods of seven, fitted a few weeks earlier. These aircraft had used them successfully in Vietnam and the MK40 rockets were light, High Explosive missiles, good for use on enemy troops. He had been told about the missiles by the McConnell base commander who, upon checking for supplies, found the stash of a couple of hundred of these antiquated rockets in an old underground storage armory; it had taken the technicians only a couple of minutes to refit the aircraft for their use.

With the two fuel tanks beneath their wings they had extra range and like the rest of the aircraft had 20-mm cannons in the form of Miniguns for backup. Carlos's aircraft, *Hector* was different than the other six. It hadn't arrived in time and General Patterson had only four weapons of high explosive under his aircraft, namely four large 500-pound bombs. He would have preferred the missiles but whatever they could throw at the enemy was better than nothing.

Once the attack aircraft were away, a single C-130 took off with the crews' belongings for Dyess and, thirty-two of the C-130s were being filled with 100 parachutists per aircraft under the command of Lieutenant Colonel Clarke. The three remaining C-130 aircraft, the only aircraft left on the apron, were busy being loaded with enough explosives to blow the enemy into tiny fragments.

The F-4s and F-5s were five minutes north of Interstate 10 when General Patterson rose through 5,000 feet and ordered the Super Tweets, with a larger range than the faster F-4s and 5s, to head south at maximum speed, 500 miles an hour.

Unfortunately the spotter aircraft, all short of fuel were already returning to Dyess.

"Foxtrot Fours, I want you to go in first from the west," stated the general giving orders as soon as he got into radio contact. "The sun should be well down and you should be able to come right out of it from the west. You have enough fuel for one run only, so come in at no less than a thousand feet—and fast—and use all you have and then head back to Dyess. First, I want you to circle for 15 minutes away from the convoy; that will allow us to catch up and be 30 minutes behind your attack, and the C-130s 30 minutes behind ours. Foxtrot Fives, I want you to go in a minute behind the Fours at 500 feet. Mind the F-4 bomb explosions and complete one run, empty everything you have at them before you, too, head back to Dyess. Start your attacks from the west as well, thirty miles out, and keep ten seconds between you; they might have ground-to-air missiles. Good luck and keep your radios open."

The six AC-130s at 300 miles an hour were still 45 minutes out and Carlos and Buck at maximum speed of 250 miles an hour were already about to be overtaken by the gunships and the seven Super Tweets high above at 15,000 feet.

"Foxtrot 4 leader going in; watch for ground-to-airs!" everybody heard 15 minutes later as the next battle for U.S. survival began on May 16th.

* * *

The outskirts of Houston were just coming into view when Manuel heard Pedro shout over the radio that he thought he heard jet aircraft somewhere around them. He wasn't sure but several of the men had said that they had heard something.

"How many of those missiles do you have?" Manuel asked his brother.

"Six with three shoulder launchers," Pedro replied.

"Get them ready Pedro, but don't stop moving. We need to get all our men into the built-up areas before dark. Alberto, how many missiles do you have?"

"Six, and two of the missile launchers, Manuel. I gave two of mine to the trucks heading south," he replied.

"If they are American jets, they will be fast; you and Pedro order your men to fire as soon as you see anything up there. My men will do the same," and he gave orders for his four men to also prepare. He had twelve missiles and his men were ready to fire the first salvo. He couldn't hear anything until he heard Pedro order his men to fire towards the sun and then Manuel thought he could hear something towards the west.

Pedro's men hadn't seen or heard the first two jets sweep in from the sun, but when the F-4s swept over, traveling just under the speed of sound, the ground a few miles behind him literally began exploding in all directions. His army stretched out for ten miles and the air was still silent as he gave the order to fire missiles. Suddenly the ground around him erupted everywhere, and his jeep leapt into the air and threw him out as it turned over in the air and somersaulted forward; the truck a dozen feet behind him disappeared into a fireball.

Alberto had more time. He was ten miles in front of Pedro and saw the first shape coming towards his location; he shouted for his men to fire at will and a missile streaked up towards the lead aircraft. He watched in wonder as the missile missed the aircraft coming in from the rear by feet and kept going. Then his area of the road began jumping up and down as cannon fire opened up a path of destruction behind him. He jumped out and dived for cover. He looked back and saw one of his men in an open Toyota truck 50 yards behind his jeep about to fire a missile. As he released the missile, the man erupted into fragments and then his missile blew up and all of the ground bounced under Alberto's body; the force of the blast blew him into a ditch.

"Incoming missiles hot," stated one of the F-4 pilots calmly as he missed one by several feet and he continued forward throwing everything he had at the road below him. It was like herding cattle there were so many men down there.

"More incoming missiles from the front of the convoy... go low!" shouted the lead F-4 as he reached the end of his cannon rounds and sped over the front of the vanguard group two minutes after he had started. The most forward men were just about to enter the outskirts of Houston. He pulled up and on afterburner went vertical to get rid of any missiles following him.

The same happened to the second F-4 and he went vertical several seconds later, but the third one wasn't so lucky; a missile hit him head-on right down the centerline of the road and his aircraft blew up over thousands of enemy shooting at him. His aircraft, now in millions of hot tiny fragments went straight into the mass below him. The fourth and fifth F-4s were lucky and also got out alive but the sixth F-4 was also hit and it too went in hard over Manuel's scrambling men, clearing a swath of asphalt nearly a mile long.

The seventh and eight got a couple of their rockets off before they had to get out of harm's way as several missiles locked onto them. As they turned hard towards the sun, they warned the rest of the incoming pack.

There was a break in the action as the last two F-4s fought to evade the missiles and a minute later they swooped down vertically towards the road, five of the seven missiles turning to follow them. The experienced pilots leveled out just over the flames and continuous explosions and began a second attack. The missiles, sensing the loss of the jet exhausts and the higher heat of the flames, followed the F-4s but didn't level out and all five missiles went into Pedro's troops in close proximity to each other. The tightly knit explosions disintegrated a large area of soldiers and trucks, and starting a chain of explosions that followed behind the F-4s as they released what they had left on the road and directly over Alberto lying in the ditch facing upwards, then broke off to the south and away from the explosions.

In all, only three minutes had elapsed since the beginning of the attack and the five remaining jets, low on fuel, headed towards Dyess.

"Foxtrot Fives, change tactics, go in from the east, I say go in from the east," ordered General Patterson still a hundred miles away and twelve minutes from the action. "Go in close and fast. Do what you can to the vanguard area and then get out of there. All other aircraft go low, they have missiles; Super Tweets will go in next. Foxtrot Four Leader your aircraft report, please."

"Two aircraft down, low on fuel and heading to our new base," he replied.

The general heard the Foxtrot Five commander give the order to go in. The F-5s were over the city as they swept down fast, above the empty buildings of the city of Houston.

* * *

Manuel got away scot-free on the first round. He and his men were watching the skies and the devastation behind him. He could hardly see anything as he shouted on the radio for Pedro or Alberto. The F-5s came in fast and silent and only one man saw them. The ground around Manuel erupted as he heard and saw someone shout and point to the front. Manuel immediately fell into the rear bed of the empty jeep and pieces of stone and metal began hitting the low sides of the jeep from every angle. It felt like he was in the middle of a tornado, the wind around him trying to suck him out of the jeep.

Seconds earlier he had ordered his driver to drive twenty feet off the road and he let out his man carrying the missile launcher. His jeep had just climbed a low slope by the side of the road and he stood up so that he could see what was happening. He felt his jeep going over as if it was blown by the wind and it landed on top of him, the rear gun holding the vehicle off his body.

His eyes and nose filled with dirt and dust, and he closed his eyes and stayed in a fetal position under his protective roof in shock, not knowing what was going on.

The man with the launcher was able to get his missile off and he watched it go straight into the air intake of the second F-5 a hundred yards in front of him; the aircraft blew up and, as he watched, the debris came straight down towards him and he dissolved into a billion pieces; so did thousands of men around him as millions of pieces of metal traveling at nearly the speed of sound scythed through anything in their way. Trucks and other vehicles blew up as the angry shrapnel passed through killing them all and igniting their fuel tanks. Again a long stretch of road nearly a mile long disintegrated under the heavy force of the exploding aircraft.

The two remaining F-5s finished their runs and peeled away heading for Dyess.

"Foxtrot Five Leader, my number two took a direct missile hit," reported an F-5 pilot. *"Two aircraft are OK and there are no*

missiles airborne on my radar. We are right behind the Foxtrot Fours for Dyess. Fuel levels good."

"Well done, men," replied the general, saddened that he had just lost a few good men and very valuable aircraft. "There should be ground crew ready for you when you arrive. There are C-130 tankers airborne if you need air refueling, but you should make it. Don't take any chances and, Foxtrot Leaders, I want you refueled, armed and ready ASAP. We might be able to get a night raid in. Did you see much down there?"

"We hit them good, exploding damage for twenty, thirty miles. There isn't a part of their convoy which isn't a mile within smoke and or fire. The rear section got hit real bad from the Fours, and we did a smaller number on the vanguard group. They have missile launchers everywhere, so watch out for incoming."

"OK, Super Tweets, we are next and ten minutes out. The sun will be setting by the time we get there, and I think since we are slower we will split up. Powers, Roebels and Smart, you are with me, we are going in straight from the east for the vanguard group. You other three Tweets form up under Watkins; come in from the south turn eastwards and get the sun behind you. Go into the rear group and complete one pass. Look out for us we are coming in from the east and we will break south before we get into the second groups area. We are slower and the missiles will have more time to lock onto us, so we are going in at nosebleed level above the ground and we will stay there; don't climb if there are hot missiles. Second group, attack in sections of about a mile; get off several of your rockets like you did in training and then turn away to the south and come around and get back into what's left of the sun. If you see or hear missiles stay as close to the ground as you can for three to four minutes. I believe the missiles are heat-seeking and there is a lot of heat on the ground. Then, go in for a second and a third attack.

"Watkins, aim your second attack on the second group and then hit the rear group again.

"My group will concentrate on the vanguard group from the east. Gunships, the sun will have set by the time you get there. I want all of you to come in south of the road and from the west once the Tweets are out of there. Pick the largest black areas on your heat sights. Use your infra-red to fire, stay as far out as you can and stay low, we can't afford to lose more aircraft. We have *"Puff"* twenty minutes behind us to pick up any downed pilots, so find roads if you need to land.

"Carlos, AC-47, you are last and tie in with any emergency commands. Everyone, stay low and strafe the ditches and holes where soldiers could be hiding. They should run out of stuff to throw at us sometime so every missile they launch means one less they have."

As planned it was getting dark when the two groups of Super Tweets went in together twenty minutes later, the first time many of the girls were seeing real action. They had trained for this for six weeks now, including how to dodge ground-to-air missiles, but were still green behind the ears and each one scared, but the time was now and they needed to concentrate.

Manuel crawled out from the remains of his jeep. His ears hurt like hell, and he looked around for the radioman he had with him. He found part of his body and a useless smashed radio.

He couldn't hear the remainder of the jets heading out, and he looked at the trail of chaos left behind. The one jeep and three transporters behind where he had left the road were nothing more than a burning mass of twisted metal. It was hot and the smoke burned his lungs but he ran ungainly down the road until he reached one of his commanders shouting orders for the men to get into town. Manuel had passed twelve burning vehicles before he found his man in an untouched jeep.

Here there were hundreds of men getting out of the ditches in the middle of the Interstate and into twenty undamaged trucks, two of which had fuel tankers behind them. Then his eyes fell on the next swath of burning debris where the F-5 had gone down; even he was shocked at the destruction. It was as if a stretch of the Interstate had been cleared of everything that was on it. There was broken metal and fire everywhere on both sides of the asphalt for as far as he could see. It was pure devastation.

"Manuel, do you want to use my radio?" asked his commander. "Manuel, Manuel, can you hear me?" Manuel raised his arm which hurt to show that he did and staggered towards the jeep.

"Alberto, Alberto, report! Pedro, Pedro, report in! Are you OK?" There was silence as nobody responded. Manuel tried again and again and the fourth time Pedro replied. He was OK but his men had taken a beating. Alberto also came over the air and he said the same thing.

"I don't know if there are more, but leave your dead and get into town. The buildings will help protect us from the air. He reiterated his orders several times telling the men to fan out and get into town as fast and in any way they could. Do you have any missiles left? Did we shoot down any aircraft?"

"I saw one go down. It came out from the sun, a missile blew it up," stated an unknown man.

"I saw a second one right behind it. It also blew up a mile in front of me, and the explosion killed hundreds of my men," stated Carlos Sanchez. *"It took out a whole mile of people and trucks."*

The commander next to him stated that he saw one from the east go down right behind his jeep.

"We got three aircraft. How many missiles and launchers do we have?" One man said he had one and suddenly the world around Pedro tossed him around, his body blew backwards toward the way he had come, and this time he hit his head against the side of his commander's still unscathed jeep and he blacked out.

* * *

Martie Roebels, going in behind the general, fired her first two rockets at the first group of trucks Manuel was looking at behind the jeep and he bore the brunt of the edge of the explosions as the trucks and men he was facing flipped in the air in front of him. He didn't even know what was happening.

General Patterson was a hundred yards in front of her, and he ordered the girls behind him to peel off; a 500-pound bomb was not something to fly over. He saw where he wanted to deposit his first bomb, at the next group of undamaged vehicles on the north side; and he pulled the stick back to gain altitude so that he would also be out of harm's way.

The small twin-engine jet screamed upwards and rose 3,000 feet before he forced the stick forward. It felt like he was on the fastest roller coaster in the world as his belts stopped his head from being flattened against the canopy above his head and he shouted "Bomb gone!" as he released the 500 pounds of pure destruction.

He had seen a large group of trucks and men, Carlos Sanchez's group, and he released the bomb for that precise area. As the bomb dropped he hauled the joystick to the left, pushed both throttles to maximum and dipped south as fast as he could.

Several seconds later the blast caught up to him and rattled the thirty-year-old aircraft around him. He was pushed here and there, and then it was over.

* * *

Carlos Sanchez was trying to get his machine gunner to aim at the aircraft, and his man fired off his first rounds as General

Patterson pulled the stick back, climbing steeply, and the man's tracers headed out behind the little jet. The machine gunner didn't have time to catch up with the aircraft as it quickly rose several hundred yards ahead of him and his commander, and the next thing he saw was a shape drop from underneath the aircraft as it dived away and headed southwards.

He froze as he saw the shape slowly descend towards him and he forgot all about trying to shoot the aircraft as his body was vaporized by the explosion.

Carlos Sanchez had also seen the shape leave the aircraft, and he was about to tell his men to scatter when it hit the ground several feet from where he and hundreds of his men had just congregated for orders.

* * *

The sun had half sunk behind the horizon as one man in Alberto's group saw more aircraft coming in, turning in from the south and trying to hide with the dying sun. He shouted the alarm; one man turned fast enough and got a missile off. It passed harmlessly between the first and second aircraft and then all hell broke loose as the incoming rockets blew that immediate area of his convoy to pieces.

Six rockets from the three aircraft hit in a pattern on the north side of the highway, the first one hitting a full fuel tanker. The blast was so big that the jets veered off passing the mush-rooming firestorm on each side and were hit hard by the blast.

On the ground nobody cared about the aircraft as several vehicles around the tanker blew up and connected the explo-sions from the five other rockets.

Alberto's troops, a hundred yards away and on the north side of the highway, could only watch as the line of explosions travel-ed down the southern highway at the speed of sound. A truck on the north side and directly opposite the mushroom fireball exploded, spewing men all over the place. Seconds later there was a mass of bodies heading for cover anywhere they could find.

* * *

Martie's aircraft began to act weird as she veered away from the road; a machine gunner got in several shots into her underbelly and hit her hard.

"I'm hit, I'm hit!" shouted Martie into her radio as the cockpit filled with smoke. Preston in *Blue Moon,* still twenty miles away, felt his stomach tighten. Up to now it had been exciting, but suddenly the scene turned personal. This was something he hadn't expected. He heard Sally Powers tell Martie that she had her visual and ordered Martie to turn the aircraft to the right.

"Try your gear, Martie, try your landing gear, get it down, does it work?" Sally ordered sternly.

"Super Tweets break off, congregate south of the convoy!" ordered General Patterson. Everybody stay off the air until we solve this problem. I'm going in to get rid of my heavies. *Puff...* Carlos, location please?"

"Twenty miles out from estimated problem point and turning towards it. Sally, I think we have you visual on radar."

"Martie, I see your wheels going down. Do you have green lights?" continued Sally. *"Martie, Carlos, we are about three miles south of the middle convoy. Martie, I see a tarred road about a mile in front of you. Do you have it visual?"*

"I have green lights, I think so, it's dark in here and the smoke is bad," Martie responded, coughing badly and grunting to control the aircraft.

"Martie, zero wind, take her in to the south and I'll help you in."

"I'm losing thrust, airspeed just over stall," stated Martie.

"Hey girl, remember that Cessna flies like a Cessna. You

know what to do. Martie, she has a glide pattern, use it and kiss the asphalt gently for me. Turn south slowly now! You should see the black tarmac below you," stated Sally calmly.

Preston held his breath and prayed; this was where every ounce of her thousands of flying hours would be the most important thing in her life. He saw three large fireballs erupt into the air ten miles in front of his aircraft. General Patterson was still nailing the enemy.

"Is it the black stripe below me? No power. She's going down fast," responded Martie.

"Let her go, Martie. Point her nose down a bit more and then flare out when I tell you, your height is about 300 feet. That's right, let her go, keep her speed up, concentrate on the air speed and I'll get you in."

"I can see a white line, Sally," replied Martie a second later.

"Flare now, Martie, just like we taught you in training school. You have fifty feet to go, forty, thirty..."

"She's stalling!" shouted Martie.

"Let her, Martie, twenty feet, Martie, ten..." and Martie's Super Tweet hit the asphalt hard as it fell the last few feet out of the sky and she began to apply brakes.

"You have flames behind you, Martie! Blow the engine extinguishers! Martie, use the brakes and open the canopy. Martie, get out! Martie, get out now, girl!" shouted Sally.

Martie pulled her release and stood up; now, adrenalin taking over, she jumped onto the left wing as her cockpit was engulfed in flames and she jumped down to the side of the asphalt, rolling as she hit.

"Run, Martie, run!" shouted Sally in her radio knowing that Martie couldn't hear her anymore; she was detached from the aircraft.

Sally circled as slow as the aircraft could as Martie, now a dark shape on the ground, rose to her feet and began to sprint. Sally knew she was fast and she watched as the distance widened between her friend and the aircraft which was going to explode at any second, and still had armaments aboard.

She then noticed a Super Tweet landing a mile further south of the burning aircraft. It had its full landing lights on and was dropping fast.

"*Puff!* Come in on my landing lights south of the fire," ordered General Patterson

Then the area lit up as Martie's aircraft fire-balled and blew a sprinting Martie over hard as the blast hit her yards from the aircraft.

"*She's fifty yards east of the aircraft. I think she had enough time to get clear!*" shouted Sally.

Her aircraft turned and she banked over the stopped aircraft. It was her old one, the twin-seat General Patterson was flying, and she saw a dark shape run towards where Martie had fallen.

There was silence on the airways, and Sally with tears welling in her eyes waited with the rest for word from the ground. She looked over to the north and saw the mess they had made of the convoy. There was a line of fires from horizon to horizon and the ground was flat.

"I got her, I got her," stated General Patterson into his radio back at the aircraft, a few minutes later as "*Puff*" could be seen with full lights going into land half a mile behind the general's aircraft. "She's unconscious but breathing. Carlos, I need help. Get over here with a medical bag; she needs two of us to get her into your aircraft. AC-130s, commence your attacks at will, stay low and blast anything you see. Commander of *Blue Moon*, take over air command until further notice. Out."

Preston, co-pilot of *Blue Moon,* got a slap of encouragement on the back from the engineer behind as his commander began giving orders. They were five miles away to the north at the end of the convoy and still thirty miles from the downed aircraft. Carlos must have pushed his throttles to the limit and he had watched "*Puff*" on his radar scope go straight over the convoy.

The captain shouted orders into the radio system to turn on all instruments to control their altitude above ground and all aircraft not to go below 300 feet. There were few hills or rises that high in the area. He then ordered all weapons to test as they turned eastwards and headed towards the end of the area where there were fires.

"Gunships, we are going in a mile south of the highway, in a line; stagger your distance between a mile and two miles. Gun controllers, if anybody sees a missile launch I want that area hit with the 105-mm. Shout missile launch, and pilots dip fifty to a hundred feet. Engineers, shout out height above ground continuously. Let's do one full run, and then break to the right on my command."

They went in low and fast, the Gunships' machine guns and howitzers began shooting into and between the flames on both highways a mile to their north. With such heavy weaponry, a mile distance was nothing.

"There is more damage on the southern highway; gunners aim more towards the northern asphalt strip," stated *Blue Moon's* commander.

At 250 miles an hour, it took twelve minutes to reach the front of the three convoys. By this time all guns were hot and needed a break. Over a ton of explosives had exited the six gunships with not one missile coming up to meet them.

"Shit!" stated *Blue Moon's* pilot as his aircraft suddenly lurched. "That must have been a gust of wind or something. It nearly took the stick right out of my hands. Radar, what do we have in the way of weather? Extend your view to maximum, also, damage report in case that wasn't a breath of fresh air."

"Dangnatious!" replied his radar operator excitedly. *"It looks like something coming in from the south. There are rain squalls coming in lines, I can see three thick green lines of rain on the screen thirty miles to our south."*

"No damage to report, guns are cooling and we are down to

about 40 percent of our ammo," stated his weapon systems operator over the aircraft's radio.

"I heard that," stated General Patterson coming back on air. "There was no wind a few minutes ago when I landed, and now it's like gale-force winds coming in from the south. *Puff* is taking off and I'm a few minutes from being airborne. Gunships complete one more attack, *Blue Moon* and *Easy Girl* concentrate on the vanguard area and level any buildings where you believe the vanguard position may be; the other four head westwards and use up everything you've got. Then head back to Dyess."

"Mike Task Force to command, we are twenty miles out and north of the western end of the fires. Over," stated the lead C-130 bringing in the Marines.

"Mike Task Force, the road is pretty straight east to west, but you should be feeling a headwind. I recommend a thousand foot altitude drop half a mile to the south of the highway and a mile west of the first fires. That should drift the men towards the road. Over," replied the general pulling his aircraft off the gusty road. "We have a bad storm coming in, and I will get you resupplied by morning with extended rations. Mike Task Force, I first want to know who these guys are, and where they've come from. Don't take prisoners; I'm sure they didn't take any of ours. Report in when you have your cloth stacked and packed, and we'll send in someone to collect them. Command pilots, find a north/south intersection before you let the dogs out, so that somebody can come in and retrieve. The wind is too strong for side-wind landings. Out."

Puff rose steeply out of harm's way south of the convoy; Buck was flying as Carlos and two of his crewmen tended to Martie. She was still unconscious; the blast had hurt her and must have thrown her to the ground hard. He checked for broken bones and didn't find any. She had several cuts on her face from flying debris and a large gash on her left upper arm which was bleeding badly.

He cut off her flight suit at the shoulder, bandaged, and tightly bound the wound. It certainly needed stitches. Her face was a mass of tiny scratches, so he cleaned her beautiful face with cold antiseptic gauze which brought her around slowly.

"Gee, Carlos, did you sock me or something? Boy! Does my head hurt," she stated, her blue eyes looking directly into his, blinking. "Did I make it, or are you an angel looking after me?" she continued. She was slowly coming around.

"Move your arms and legs, Martie, show me that you can move them," ordered Carlos and he was relieved to see her four limbs move slowly. "Martie, move your neck, can you lift your head up?" Martie complied and she grimaced with pain as she moved her head.

"Am I in one piece, lover boy?" she asked.

"It seems so, Blondie, your spine isn't injured and your head and mouth work, so your neck and one brain cell are fine!" he replied smiling at her. "You are going to need stitches in your left arm and I'm sure your head hurts badly, so the medic is giving you something to take away any pain and make you sleep."

"Is Preston OK?" she asked.

"Yes, I think he is still blasting at the enemy. The parachutists are going in and we are heading back to base. Now sleep and my guys will cover you with blankets and keep you warm. I still don't trust Buck flying my new baby."

"Our injured is doing fine and nothing broken," reported Carlos as he took over flying *Puff*. Preston was relieved as a now quiet *Blue Moon* headed out of the area.

They hadn't got one round off at the enemy but Carlos felt good going in to save a good friend. "*Pity about the other five pilots who didn't make it,*" he thought to himself.

One after the other the aircraft were helped northwards by the growing winds from the south. Dyess was reached within 30 minutes of leaving the scene.

General Patterson was worried about this storm. He knew

there was something bigger than just 30 to 40 mile an hour winds now behind him. While he was on the ground the air was so still that it was eerie, and suddenly the first gust had hit him in the back as he bent over Martie, nearly pushing him over onto her. All the slower aircraft still had good reserves of fuel; and he landed his Super Tweet first to see how the other jets were doing, getting ready for a possible second mission.

"It is weird not to know what was out there," he stated to the F-4 and F-5 commanders as they came up and saluted him.

"I spent five years in south Florida and Louisiana training on jets," stated the mature and experienced F-4 Flight Commander. "I smell a hurricane, and I would put some money on it that she is a doozy! Several times we had to scramble out of these wind squalls that hit from nowhere. We could always see the squall lines on the weather systems we don't have any more, and the national weather reports we also don't have any more. We were always out of the area once the wind increased up to thirty knots. General Patterson, if that squall nearly knocked you over, that is the tell-tale sign to get the aircraft away from the coast."

"So, Colonel," replied the general. "I'm not from a hurricane area; Washington State is where I learned to fly. Can your team do another mission into the area before whatever's coming gets here?"

"Sure, we will be ready to go in an hour and I recommend bombs, we can nail them hard with nine bombs per aircraft. General, I would recommend eight 750-pounders or whatever they have here at Dyess, and a napalm or fuel gel under the belly this time. I would aim to hit and destroy the outer buildings around where these guys went in. If I had just been hit with what we gave them, I would be heading into the built-up areas for safety like a bunch of hound dogs. My gut feeling is that we have about six hours before things get bad towards the coast. Here, we are far enough away from the coast to ride out the storm, but we'd better tie all the aircraft down, or get ready to base further north. It's going to take a couple of days before anybody can do anything after tonight."

General Patterson agreed with the man and asked the Dyess commander what he had stored. Within twenty minutes the men were bringing out their supplies of older bombs.

"We have looked in every corner and this is what we have. First, we have forty-two old M117 750-pounders. They are perfect for the F-4s, eight to an aircraft if need be. We have twenty-eight of the Mark 82 500-pounders for the F-5s. Everything else is pretty useless but I did find a dozen old MK 77 fuel gel 750-pounders and ten even older napalm 1,000-pounders. They are so old I think they will burn forever. If I may, General, since I spent seven years in Nam, I would suggest four Mark 82s under the wings of the 5s and a 1,000-pound napalm under the belly. For the F-4s, I recommend six of the M17s and two MK 77 fuel gels under the wings and again a 1,000-pound napalm under the belly."

The F-4 colonel who had also flown in Vietnam nodded his agreement. General Patterson was still a few years younger than the two more experienced pilots and had only risen to the rank of general from major a few months earlier when the president had crazily promoted him twice in two months.

"Who could I ask for a better plan?" he replied to the two men smiling. "Get your aircraft ready. Because the Super Tweets can also only carry 2 500-pounders in their current configurations and, it will take too long to remove their fuel pods, get all six armed and ready to go. We might as well throw what we can at the enemy before we are grounded by this weather. I have *Blue Moon* being refueled, and she will head out ASAP to give us an infra-red view of what is moving where down on the ground. We can't do much without her eyes."

He headed towards the terminal when, to his surprise, he saw three C-130s and two other aircraft coming in from the northwest. He hadn't ordered this flight and knew nothing about it. He stopped and waited. As the C-130s and the other two he wasn't familiar with taxied onto the half-empty apron, he saw the white and red markings of a Coast Guard aircraft and four U.S. Navy aircraft.

CHAPTER 5

Seal Team Six

THEY WERE PARKED IN A LINE by ground personnel under the apron lights run by six generators when, to his surprise, Admiral Rogers walked out of the first aircraft with a mass of men.

"Good to see you, Admiral. I'm glad you have some aircraft at your disposal," stated General Patterson seeing a good friend again.

"Yes, General, we navy boys are slow but sure. We also have two more 70s frigates nearly operational, and we have given up on the USS *Yorktown* in Charleston, but will have the *Midway* operational in a year. Also one of my ships reported bad sea conditions off Florida two days ago; and I've brought my two Lockheed Orion Hurricane Hunters, operational from yesterday. I know they look pretty old, but after refueling they are heading off to see what this storm is. I put my money on an early season hurricane, but they will tell us in a couple of hours. I have also brought you a gift from the navy, the best gift I can. I hear you are having problems in Houston. I will loan you our best Seal team, Seal Team Six. They have just returned from an outreach location in Africa. We had to wait for them to surface, and it took two months for them to get into Germany so that we could fly them back here. They arrived two days ago on the lone 747 you have operating out of Ramstein."

"Are you the guys who took out Bin Laden and got those hostages out of Somalia?" General Patterson asked with respect.

"My guys did Bin Laden, and those guys in the second aircraft did the hostages, Sir," stated a lieutenant who looked like he would kill if you looked at him too hard. "We were all deep in Somalia again in December after an American ship's crew of sixteen were captured and held hostage back in November. We were told to get ready to be extracted, and then nothing. We couldn't get communications when we called for the choppers on January 1st, so we just killed all the bad guys and walked north to the Med. We caught a lift on a fishing boat to Greece a month later, and we made friends with Greek soldiers who helped us travel to Germany. A long story, but we flew back with the hostages two days ago and are ready, Sir. What do you want us to do, General?"

General Patterson counted the men; there were ninety-three in all. "Is this all Seal Team Six?" he asked.

"That's right, sir, three platoons run by us three lieutenants. The only people we take orders from are Admiral Rogers here and then the Chief of Staff, Secretary of Defense and the president.

"Unfortunately we found the body of the Secretary of Defense in his house in January; the whole street had been attacked and ransacked. I'm the current Chief of Staff, and I would like to know how many of your men are Hispanic or Latino, Lieutenant."

"I'm Lieutenant Joe Paul, I have Mendez and Chavez; the second platoon, under Lieutenant Murphy, has Rodriquez and Santana," he replied.

"I have three," stated the third lieutenant, "I'm Lieutenant Charlie Meyers, and Joe and I, and several others easily passed as Latinos in Colombia when we were there two years ago."

"We could muster a dozen Latino-looking men, Sir, as long as our other guys are nearby if we need them, why?" ended the first mean-looking lieutenant.

General Patterson noticed that both the officers could easily appear to be Latinos as both men had brown eyes, skin and hair.

"Go get something to eat and drink, men," directed General Patterson. "Admiral, we will have a briefing once my angels of death and I get airborne and back in three hours. Also I want to know what we are dealing with, with this storm I mean."

The wind was beginning to howl as the jet aircraft left for Houston an hour later and forty minutes behind one of the Hurricane Hunters and *Blue Moon*. General Patterson was thinking up a grand plan as he led all the Super Tweets off, except Martie, who was being tended by medics from *Blue Moon's* tired crew; a fresh crew was in *Blue Moon*.

It was time to strike a new arrow into the heart of the enemy: Seal Team Six.

* * *

Manuel Calderón woke up in what looked like a school building with Alberto looking down at him.

"What happened, Alberto?" he asked, his memory slow to come back to him.

"Your Second-in-Command here got on the radio and told me you looked like you were dead so I came forward and with his help got you in his jeep, and we drove into Houston with the rest of your men. Manuel, we are getting all the men off the highway and into the city as fast as possible. They are spread out and as many as possible are coming overland. It is a bad sight out there; the highway is a mass of dead and broken vehicles but we are getting all the men under cover as you ordered. I got into contact with Pedro; he is entering the outskirts of Houston right now. He and his men went south to the next highway and are coming in on another road. We only need another few hours and then the weather—I'm sure a hurricane is coming—will protect us. We came north off the highway in case the hurricane hits this area, and I think we are in a school in North Houston. Pedro is going to come north and join us."

How many men have we lost?" asked Manuel groggily.

"Many thousands Manuel, but we met up with 5,000 guys from the Gonzalez Cartel that Sanchez told us about. Carlos Sanchez has not come on the radio since the attacks so I think he was hit.

Manuel heard Pedro's voice come over the radio close by and state that, by his map, he was in a place called Mission Bend and the road was getting wider.

"Pedro, go east until you get to the interchange with the Beltway and come north. Manuel is OK and we are waiting for you. I will guide you in," Alberto replied.

"The wind is bad, Alberto, and I will tell my men to head for the Beltway. Glad we passed out all those maps from San Antonio. I think I have contact with only a quarter of my men."

"How long have I been out?" asked Manuel.

"Three hours, and the doctor here says nothing is broken, just your pride!" laughed Alberto. As he laughed he heard screams from Pedro over the radio to tell his men to take cover and suddenly Alberto felt the ground vibrate slightly beneath his feet. The wind was too noisy to hear anything but he looked out of the window and began to see the horizon glow to the south-west.

"It looks like the Gringos are back, Manuel," Alberto stated simply.

* * *

"My crew doesn't see any movement on Interstate 10 apart from at the rear where the Marines are going through the

debris," stated the commander of *Blue Moon* over the radio to the jets circling a few thousand feet overhead. His AC-130 had only taken on ten minutes of fast fuel, and he had 30 minutes over the target area before he would have to head back to Dyess. It was the same with the faster jets, and he had his men searching for infra-red movement on the black strips of road.

They had packed a hundred HE rounds for the aircraft's 105-MM howitzer and he was hoping to return empty.

"Mike Task Force here, we got through about a mile of damage here on I-10. There are hundreds and hundreds of bodies. This place is going to become a cesspool of disease once this hurricane passes. They are all from south of the border and I've found odd information on a couple of bodies. One guy is from Venezuela, one guy is Brazilian and three so far look like they have papers from Colombia. Another one is from Mexico City and another from Panama. It certainly looks like South America is trying to do a number on us. Over."

"Thanks," replied General Patterson. "I have a C-130 about 30 minutes out, he is monitoring this communication; throw up a flare in 30 seconds; he has three pallets aboard to drop to you. It's the best we can do to help you ride out this storm. Mike, get as far as you can and then take shelter. We are searching for groups of bad guys and will be out of here in 30 minutes. Good luck and we will be back as soon as the weather lets us. Out."

"Blue Moon here, I have heavy movement of the next high-way further south and all over the rural areas south of I-10."

"Roger, *Blue Moon*, check out the densest groups and coordinate with the Foxtrot Fours, and Fours, use your HE first, keep the hot stuff for later."

Several voices acknowledged the commands, and thirty seconds later a large area of the western outskirts of the Mission Bend area erupted into large explosions as several bombs and one large Napalm bomb went in from the jets.

There were groups of men everywhere on *Blue Moon's* scanners, and they did their best to pinpoint the bomb drops. It didn't really matter where they were dropped; there were blobs of movement everywhere.

Within ten minutes the area west of Mission Bend was a hot place to be.

"There is dense movement around the same highway inter-section and the western Beltway heading north," stated *Blue Moon's* infra-red operator a minute later. *"It looks like there are thousands of bodies in the actual intersection. We need to head in closer but it looks like this group is heading off the west-east highway and going north... hold on... let me check my map. OK! I got it. The intersection is the Westpark Tollway and the Sam Houston Tollway North."*

"I see the lead group about two miles in front of that group," added a second radar operator in *Blue Moon*. *"Save some heat and I can get you a second really large group about a mile further north. Actually if you start at the intersection and lay down heat for a mile north, you should fry a lot of army."*

"Roger that," stated the F-4 commander. *"Lead us in and we will follow your line. I suggest a few howitzers HE's into the area from you guys, and we will cover the area around the blasts. Our heat will fry the guys under the bridges as well*

"Sounds like Thanksgiving is coming early this year for a few illegal immigrants," replied General Patterson giving his orders to all the aircraft.

The choreographed attack went in fast.

The Super Tweets followed the general in. They flew in at 5,000 feet in a tight arrowhead formation the girls had practiced every day during their month of non-stop training. They had great seats and watched the battle light up a couple of miles west of them.

Blue Moon was first in, heading north directly over the center aisle of the highway and lit up the two heavily populated intersections with dozens of white phosphorus flares before turning away to starboard.

As the general had ordered, the F-5s went in next, a thousand feet above and two miles behind *Blue Moon,* emptied their bellies into the first intersection and turned to starboard, climbed to 5,000 feet and headed home, out of the way of the F-4s behind them.

As the Super Tweets turned north over the highway, several miles south of the erupting battle scene in front of them, the F-4 leader warned that he was two miles out and in a tight arrowhead formation of three aircraft at 1,500 feet, with the second arrowhead of three F-4s twenty seconds behind him, 1,000 feet higher. He warned those behind that "heat" or Napalm was part of his load.

"Super Tweets, our target is the second intersection," stated General Patterson calmly. "Stay above 2,500 feet, that Napalm will burn your tires off and drop everything we have on the bridge across. Then we are heading home."

The Super Tweets, at 400 miles an hour came in tight formation and twelve, 500 pound HE bombs went into a dense area between the gas stations and the tarmac stretching over Westheimer Road. As the Tweets veered off to port one at a time, the heavy blasts hit their aircraft from the rear and pushed them forward like leaves in a breeze.

"*Wow!*" stated the F-4 commander already heading home. "*There was fuel in those gas tanks. It's like daylight down there.*"

General Patterson turned and dropped down to a thousand feet and headed south a mile away from the lit up highway. The commander was right; he needed sunglasses to look straight at the second intersection. The Napalm and fuel gel had now gone down and connected with the exploding fuel. It was like looking into the sun, it was so bright.

* * *

Martie was sleeping with Preston holding her hand and sitting by her bed. She stirred and her big blue and bloodshot eyes looked at him. She coughed and Preston wiped her mouth.

"I can still taste that smoke in the cockpit," she stated weakly to Preston.

"It won't kill you and I'll try not to kiss you for awhile," he retorted smiling. "The doc stitched up your arm and told me to ground you for two weeks until he checks you again and takes out the stitches."

"Two weeks," she replied still coughing. "I'm heading home to get my P-51."

"Oh, no, you are not!" replied Preston. "It looks like a hurricane coming in and we will all be grounded by early tomorrow."

"But it's only May! What day is it?" she asked. "It's too early for hurricane season."

"May 17th, you've been asleep for six hours. Well, I suppose General Patterson forgot to tell Mother Nature about our little war here in the south," he explained sarcastically. "We might have to move the aircraft back to McConnell. Admiral Rogers arrived an hour or two ago and he sent out one of his Hurricane aircraft to find out what's out there and where it's going to hit.

"Have the girls gone back to Houston?" Martie asked.

"Yep! They are doing a night-bombing run and should be back in thirty minutes. We are to be on standby in case we need to get out of here. The 130s headed off three hours ago to get more troops out of another base in Arkansas and will be dropping them into the area north of Houston at midnight. General Patterson wanted to divert a couple of the 747s to bring in troops, but decided that the winds are getting too strong."

"Are the girls alright?" she asked.

"They came in to see you before they left and ordered me to look after you until they get back and can give you real motherly care," stated Preston, cleaning her sweating face with a cloth. "They were all excited to go on the second night run, especially Sally and Jennifer. They have trained for this type of air-fighting for years. Admiral Rogers brought in Seal Team Six, and they are leaving to go somewhere once Patterson gets back and figures out what to do with them. They had been stuck in North Africa for three months."

"I was wondering when they would show up," added Martie.

* * *

"Pedro, Pedro. What's going on? I felt the ground vibrate," stated Manuel into his radio mike. "Pedro, Pedro can you hear me?" Manuel tried several times before he heard Pedro's voice.

"It's like daylight here behind me," he shouted very loudly into his mike. They hit us again with bombs I think. I was a couple of hundred yards in front of where the closest bombs hit. It looks like they hit a gas station; the first blast knocked me over and then the whole world lit up! It looks like more bombs increased the explosion into a massive fireball. I could feel the heat from here. My men counted over a dozen aircraft fly over-head. Manuel, there were a lot of fast jets everywhere. It's now starting to rain really heavy, and I'll tell you more when we get there. We lost a lot of men, brother."

Twenty-four hours later, at midnight on May 18th, Pedro finally reached Manuel and Alberto; they were waiting for him at Bush Intercontinental Airport, where Manuel had decided to get all the men together to ride out the storm. The remnants of Pedro's army were still slowly shuffling forward in heavy wind and rain squalls on the highway in a line five miles behind him.

Pedro didn't know it, but the burned and blackened bodies of over 11,000 men lay just over a mile and a half of highway to his south. Also, over two hundred vehicles and seven fuel tankers had gone up, increasing the flames and killing hundreds around them. The escape areas underneath the highway had become hot, blast ovens, incinerating the hundreds who scrambled under them for safety. Several hundred more were injured, blind or disorientated and would never see their colleagues again.

The three brothers set up camp in the vast area of the airport. It was the only location in Houston that could accommodate so many men.

As the storm grew worse and began rattling the buildings and hangars in which they were sheltering, Manuel and Alberto's commanders reported in with their numbers.

The totals rose as over 500 men stood in lines to report, several men taking down numbers of men, arms and vehicles. Pedro's commanders and what was left of Carlos Sanchez's men were ordered to do the same as they arrived.

"Our army doesn't look so good," stated Alberto to Manuel two hours after midnight as he waited, dozing every now and again, but awakened every few minutes to wind gusts hitting the terminal building. There were several fires in the broken-down terminal where men were cooking and several areas had rain coming in where windows had been broken before they got there. They also had to eject several old and decomposing bodies before the long buildings became semi-habitable. Pedro's men were still coming in, many helping wounded soldiers.

"What do you and I have in numbers?" asked Manuel, looking around for the half-empty bottle of American Bourbon he found at one of the bases they had ransacked.

In Laredo, we each had 25,000 men," replied Alberto looking at a vast list of numbers on a scrap of cardboard in front of him. We were joined by 5,000 fresh men, the Gonzalez Cartel, here in Houston. I believe you and I had 20,000 other men join us between Laredo, San Antonio and here. That is 75,000 men we used to have Manuel, now we have only about 55,000 men. We had more than 2,000 vehicles of all types between us, now we have less than 1,250, mostly smaller vehicles. In those lost vehicles they destroyed over 400 troop transporters and thirty-four fuel tankers. We still have our five howitzers from San Antonio, tons of ammo and three ground-to-air missiles and one launcher left. We lost most of our rations and we have food for our men for two more days."

By morning the storm was intensifying when Pedro's men gave their numbers. They hadn't slept a wink. "Manuel, out of the 60,000 men I started with in Laredo, I had 4,000 men join me and left 10,000 good men in San Antonio. After San Antonio more joined. Then Carlos Sanchez met us at the intersection with his Cartel of 15,000. That should have increased my numbers to 93,000 men.

"Manuel, Alberto, I don't know how many men and vehicles I have. Many hundreds were blown up and destroyed; even my own jeep took bullets, but still runs. Maybe more men are coming. I think I lost over 25,000 men just today. Manuel, my men have one aircraft missile, one launcher and three howitzers and 21 undamaged heavy machine guns from Fort Houston in San Antonio. I have one day's food in two trucks; they hit over 30 of my trucks carrying food when one of their aircraft exploded and obliterated the road."

"Well, any number over 100,000 well-armed men is still an army," stated Manuel. "Let's wait for our 50 trucks to arrive from the naval base in Corpus Christi. This little storm will blow over, and then we go and blow those Americans to pieces. What do you think about that?"

CHAPTER 6

The Hurricane With No Name

WITH A HEAVY TAILWIND, the first Orion Hurricane Hunter returned at 05:15 on May 18th, and the crew didn't need to wake up the admiral or the general. The wind and rain squalls were keeping them from a restful sleep. The rest of the pilots were still fast asleep; they were due at the 06:00 briefing. The wind squalls were now coming in from the north and, a lot of the pilots watching the weather had never seen drastic changes like this. The temperature outside had dropped twenty degrees in the last ten hours.

The flight crew reported back at 02:30 that they had found the storm. It was 120 miles off the Texas coast, a big one by the look of it, and they would report again once they had flown through the eye and out the other side. Their equipment was thirty years old and not as exact as the more modern equipment normally used, and there was no satellite help to guide them through, but they found the eye wall and thirty minutes later passed through the main body of the storm.

The second Orion was an hour behind them and followed a different route 50 miles closer to the coast to attempt to record the wind measurements of the frontal area of the storm. They were scheduled to land at 05:30, and during the flight home both aircraft could compare readings and have a report for the 06:00 briefing.

"It's a big hurricane alright," stated the commander of the first aircraft once all the dreary-eyed pilots and crew met in the briefing room. "I also believe that a cold front went over us from the northwest yesterday and, if that happened, then we have a perfect storm down there about 120 miles off the Texas coast."

The C-130 pilots had dropped the 93 members of the Seals with the second group of 3,000 Marines and full kit at 01:30 several miles north of the outskirts of Houston; it was just south of a small town called Spring, which General Patterson thought an appropriately named place to drop the men. At the drop point, there were less severe gusts when the men jumped at 1,000 feet, 10 aircraft at a time, into a clear area between two railway depots. The railway trucks could shield the men during the hurricane if need be, as well as give them a defensible position if enemy troops were in the vicinity. Also, it was a couple of miles to Houston's main airport which could be a second shelter position from which to scour the city for enemy.

The Seals were dressed in civilian clothes and carried mercenary-type weapons like shotguns and AK-47s. Their aim was to find the enemy and infiltrate as members of the rebel army.

"I don't believe you are going to get any more flights into Houston for the next 48 to 72 hours," continued the Hurricane Hunter's commander at the briefing. "Our read-outs show a full-fledged hurricane 300 miles wide and we have rated it as a Category Three. The hurricane eye looks like it is heading into the area east of Houston, somewhere between Galveston and Beaumont and will land in about ten to twelve hours. We can only gauge its forward movement on our second pass, but a hurricane of this size would normally average 12 to 17 miles an hour. At 03:05 this morning the eye was 91 miles off the coast, directly north of High Island. We are heading out again once our aircraft are refueled. I don't believe Dyess is in any danger, but I would move your aircraft back to McConnell just in case, General."

"You stated a cold front?" asked Admiral Rogers. "If it is a cold front that passed over this area yesterday —and I agree with you, I know a cold front when I smell one—then it must be either halting the forward movement of the hurricane, or the hurricane could possibly push it back over us, or both; just stop dead and pour rain down until the hurricane is consumed by the front. That could cause really destructive weather in Houston and the surrounding coastal areas."

"Correct," replied the commander. "That's why we need to get back to measure how far the eye has moved and in which direction."

"Pilots, head all aircraft back to McConnell. I want everybody out of here by midday. I will leave last in the Super Tweet at 11:59," ordered General Patterson and the pilots got up to prepare.

"I'm going to do some hurricane and weather surveillance of the area in the Coast Guard C-130," added Admiral Rogers. "She has old weather equipment on board, and I can monitor the area around Houston and relay any messages from my Seal Team. General Patterson, please fly some 130s into Camp Lejeune to pick up a third parachute drop of men and load a couple of the Gunships with extra ammo and supplies for the men already on the ground. We now have 6,000 Marines in and around Houston; and even with my 93 guys, that isn't very many against a couple of hundred thousand rebels."

General Patterson acknowledged and wanted a report on equipment movements from Harbin. He got on the phone to Mo Wang, still in China.

"It is going well here, General, we are working around the clock," stated Mo, once the general had asked him for his progress. "I have completed a timeline for the equipment at the factory where I'm currently standing, and will have the first of approximately 500 aircraft-loads ready in 14 days. The three Airbuses and all twenty 747s are flying out the food stocks and electronics from the airfield. The 747 Transporter is taking out munitions and loads of helicopter parts from the factory and all the weapons and ammunition you asked for from Colonel Zhing's location."

"Then it will take two months to move the entire factory? Is that correct, Mo?" asked the general.

"That is correct," Mo answered. "The airfield still has several outgoing flights with all the aircraft to go, counting two days per flight, before the storage depot is empty. Could I ask that you return my good friend Colonel Rhu who is still in Hawaii? He can help me with the inventory," asked Mo.

General Patterson said that he would send orders to Misawa.

"Do you need any more help: men or heavy duty machinery?" asked the general. Mo stated that he didn't. "Those other four partially completed helicopters I saw in the factory. What has happened to those?"

"We decided that you might need them due to the new problems you are facing," replied Mo. "So I ordered the factory to complete the helicopters. Two will be ready for testing tomorrow and the other two in a week."

General Patterson thanked Mo and told him to get the four completed Zhi-10s to Edwards Air Force Base as soon as their tests were done.

"Preston, Buck, Carlos, come with me. Carlos, I want you back at "The Cube" helping to get that satellite repositioned over us. How many more days do we need?"

"A week," replied Carlos. "We can see the western area of Texas and maybe the Dyess area in six days and the Houston area several hours after that. I believe May 25th is our day. There is no way I can direct the satellite any faster."

"Well, there is no flying here for a few days, so let's go and check on what is happening in California."

The other aircraft were already leaving; the winds were becoming stronger and the rain more constant instead of squalls. It looked like the whole of southern Texas was in for a lot of rain.

General Patterson gave new orders for an Air Force crew to fly out the twin-seat Super Tweet he was supposed to pilot. He, Preston, Buck, Carlos and Martie, who wasn't going to be left behind, loaded their gear aboard *Blue Moon* to take off in dark and windy weather towards Travis Air Force Base.

* * *

"What do you think?" Lieutenant Colonel Clarke asked his five majors reporting in and whose men were going through the blackened and rain-drenched Mission Bend intersection. At midday on May 18th, it looked like dusk and the rain was coming down hard. Counting the dead was dirty, wet work, especially checking for any identification.

"My men just can't keep up with the numbers," declared a couple of the men together. "There are just too many. It would be easier without this weather."

"I think a cleanup team of thousands should head in to both these locations as soon as this all blows over, and then we can get an accurate count," suggested the major.

At the Interstate-10 battleground, the carnage was very bad with thousands of dead bodies and body parts everywhere. Several badly wounded men were dealt with in accordance with their orders to take no prisoners. They counted seven thousand bodies and a thousand vehicles before they just gave up on I-10 and headed into Houston. They had been ordered to head to the area of the second attack on the highway south and the two intersections.

It was nearly impossible to count the dead and remains of

bodies and vehicles; the wind and rain made visibility bad, and it was impossible for the men to take accurate numbers. The wind was cold, colder than when they began the previous day.

Colonel Clarke was happy to hear Admiral Rogers's voice come faintly over his radio.

The colonel reported his numbers and stated that if it got any worse, he and his men would need to find shelter. Admiral Rogers told him of several large warehouses around and north of the second intersection where the last attack had taken place, but to be careful in case the enemy was still in the area. Admiral Rogers also told Colonel Clarke through a coded message that a second group of 3,000 Marines under Lieutenant Colonel Catlin were about seven miles north of the city airport, and Seal Team Six had also gone in and were heading for the airport in civilian dress. From now on the Marines had to be more careful about shooting on sight.

Lieutenant Colonel Clarke transmitted the urgent need for cleanup teams, and the admiral acknowledged. He had a good man to sort out this big problem, Mike Mallory.

* * *

The three Seal Team lieutenants were making good time to the intercontinental airport. They had consumed a quick meal inside several dry boxcars, and after a six hour nap, were still dry underneath their rain gear, and had a mile to go. None of them had seen any life. Even the dogs had disappeared to survive the heavy rain pelting everything. It was beginning to rain very hard and visibility was down to less than a hundred feet.

Their orders were to find the enemy. Once that was done, the non-Spanish-speaking men would set up a base of operations, and the two squads of six men would head into the melee of enemy and search out the commanders, whoever they were. Based on identification found on many of the dead bodies, they already knew the rebels were from Colombia, Mexico, Venezuela, and every country in Central America.

Lieutenant Colonel Clarke had earlier reported from the first scene of attack that several of the Hispanics carried U.S. papers such as Green Cards and even U.S. Passports. There had not been a black or white body in the whole search to date, and the Seal Team had been told that any whites or blacks they came across would probably be harmless civilians and should be given help.

Lieutenant Paul's men were the first to reach the outer-perimeter fence to Houston's Bush Intercontinental Airport. They reached the northwestern tip of the airfield and couldn't see past the first runway. Within a minute they had three holes cut into the fence, and the men slipped into the grassy verge around the runway tarmac heading out in a easterly direction as far as visibility would allow.

All three platoons had checked maps once they landed and mentally visualized the airport area. They had very little trouble staying hidden. The Seals didn't expect anybody to be on guard, and their next job was to radio the Marines behind them to move south into what they hoped were drier and better accommodations at the airport terminals than the ransacked railway box cars.

The other two Seal platoons arrived at the opened fence holes, marked with a small white ribbon a minute later and found Lieutenant Paul and his men.

"We are lucky the weather is so bad," shouted Lieutenant Paul to the whole group once all 93 men had congregated in the airport grounds. They were totally hidden from any prying eyes and were confident in standing around in the open. "We would have needed to wait until dark before we could get across the open runways. There is the taxiway, which has a flyover, or a bridge that goes over a road a hundred yards to our south. Why don't the rest of you take cover while we go forward and check out the first terminals? If it's all clear we'll come back for you guys to join us. Stay put until you hear from one of us, understand? We won't take a radio in case there are enemy there and somebody wants to search us."

The rest of the men nodded and quickly headed under the bridge to get out of the pelting rain. Now it was just the twelve men, and they moved forward, looking like they were patrolling the area.

Half a mile later they reached the second east/west set of two runways and walked straight into six poncho-covered men trying to stay dry in a covered jeep at the beginning of the front apron to the closest terminal. The Seals had been briefed on the battles during the last 24 hours and were ready for any questions fired at them.

The visibility was now down to twenty feet, the wind was wailing and even the Seal squads couldn't have seen the jeep before they almost walked into it.

"Where have you come from?" was the first question in Spanish from the passenger side, the man aiming his AK-47 at the Seals without even getting out of his dry seat.

"The first battle on the highway; we were at the back, and we lost several men. We were waiting in a ditch for someone to give us orders," Lieutenant Meyers, the lead Seal, replied in fluent Spanish.

"Whose cartel are you from?" the man asked.

"We are Panamanians living in America. We joined your army in San Antonio, twenty of us, and there are only have twelve of us left. I am the commander, Charlie Mendoza. We were supposed to be given a commander but nobody told us who our new commander is yet." Charlie Meyers/Mendoza replied calmly just standing there trying to look lost. "Are the others around here?"

"We are all here at this airport. You must have been with the rear army; they are staying in the last terminals to the south. If you follow this runway southeast," the man pointed to a taxiway heading directly south, "it's about half a mile. Ask for Pedro's army. Somebody will show you where to go. Do you have any missiles, launchers or any RPGs?"

"No, we were never given any. Why?" asked Paul.

"The army commanders need all of them, and if you see anyone else with missiles or launchers, tell them to head to the lead army. They are sleeping in the second terminal to the east of there," he stated, pointing in the direction the men had been previously heading.

Charlie Meyers thanked the man and headed to where they had been told to go to find the rear army. The weather had cleared slightly, and they now could see to the bridge where the rest of the men were hidden and, the others would have seen the confrontation with the men in the jeep. They could report back when the weather came in again.

There were jeeps every fifty yards or so and, casually walking past the second jeep, the Seals waved at the shapes inside. The third jeep was the same, except the rain was slight and a man shouted to them asking where they were heading. Lieutenant Paul shouted back, "Pedro's men," and an arm pointed to several cargo hangars including UPS, FedEx, and a couple of private looking terminals parallel with the runways.

"Who are you?" asked a guard at the hangar's small entrance door. All the large buildings were closed except this one door.

"Charlie Mendoza family out of Panama. We got lost on the highway when the gringos attacked," stated Lieutenant Paul using their Spanish secret name to communicate with each other.

"Go find a place to sleep," he replied, picking his teeth with a toothpick and pretty much uninterested in the men in front of him.

"Where's Pedro?" Paul asked.

"Why do you want to know?" the dirty guard replied relishing his toothpick more than talking to the man in front of him.

"We were told by the guards on the corner that Pedro was interested in any launchers or missiles his men have. We don't have one, but we saw a dead man with a missile launcher at the last intersection where the gringos had bombed."

"Pedro is in the front terminal talking to his brothers. I will tell him when he returns," and the man waved them away to get out of his face.

"It looks like we need to move up in the world from the rear army to the front army. What do you guys think?" asked Lieutenant Paul once they had moved away to a darker area where thousands of men were sleeping. They nodded their agreement.

"I don't think I would like to have these guys as my fighting comrades," added Lieutenant Charlie Meyers. "I think advancement in comrade-quality is the best way forward, or I could fold up and die in this stench."

The men always found Charlie Meyers to be the joker of the group, and even when they were in tense situations he was always had something stupid to say.

They saw a man exit the large cargo terminal building using a small door on the opposite side of where they had come in and they followed him outside. They exited into a parking area at the front of the building which had hundreds upon hundreds of ragged vehicles of all types in the parking lots and on the roadway where the fencing had been torn down for more room. They squeezed between the vehicles, which felt more like a Walmart parking lot at its busiest time, and headed back to buildings to their north.

"Where are you going?" asked a guard in one vehicle sheltering from the growing rain shower.

"Pedro and his brothers want to see us about a missile launcher," replied Lieutenant Mendoza slouching up to the vehicle. "What are his brothers' names? I have never met them."

"I don't know, but I think one's called Alberto. He is in charge of the second army, and the other brother is in charge of the lead army."

Charlie Mendoza thanked the man and they moved on. They got to within a hundred yards of the main terminal buildings and control tower in the middle of two massive terminals before they were questioned again. This time the guard was alert and braved the rain to find out who the men were.

"We have some news for Pedro and Alberto about a couple of missiles and a missile launcher. We were told that they were asking if anybody had them," replied Lieutenant Paul.

"I don't see them. You are not carrying them?" the guard asked. This time several of the men recognized an accent they hadn't heard for two years, a Colombian accent.

"We don't have them but we saw them back at the first attack on a broken vehicle, and we wondered if Pedro and Alberto wanted us to go all the way back to get them."

"It's not Pedro or Alberto who wants to know, it's Manuel, and he gave orders to find every missile. Go in and ask Alberto to ask his brother."

"Alberto who?" questioned Charlie Mendoza, never thinking twice about asking a stupid question.

"Alberto Calderón, you stupid mule, he is second-in-command to Manuel Calderón, your leader. Are you so stupid, you don't even know who is running this army? Go into that door there and be careful, amigo, they shoot stupid people like you in there." The man shook his head and, not wanting to cause trouble just yet, the two lieutenants apologized for being so stupid, backed away, and headed for the door.

Inside the smell was the same; dirty bodies littered the floors everywhere. It was dark and the terminal was at least half a mile long. This was the main terminal for the airport; there were dozens of broken and burned aircraft with hundreds of vehicles everywhere underneath the bent and mostly broken walkways to the dozens of aircraft.

Then they reached the main inner-terminal, where inside, a sea of bodies were sprawled everywhere.

"Looking for Alberto Calderón," stated Lieutenant Paul several times, and when asked why, he always had to reply that they had information on missiles. They moved through the thousands of sleeping people, and finally they got within a hundred feet of a lit-up area where there was a meeting going on.

* * *

Manuel, Alberto and Pedro were being bandaged up by the best medic they had, a doctor that had been with them and who had kept them whole for two decades.

"Ow! That stuff hurts!" exclaimed Pedro and was laughed at by his older brothers as the doctor tended his wounds. This bad cut was on the top of his head and needed a couple of stitches, and all the old doctor had to cleanse and sterilize the wound was Tequila. "I should drink it, not waste it on my head!"

The two older brothers had already had their wounds cleaned, and the doctor was down to a half a bottle of Tequila. Pedro noticed that and helped empty the bottle by taking two large swigs before it was pulled out of his hands by Alberto who took a swig and passed it on to Manuel.

"It's not worth wasting the stuff on Pedro. Let him scream with pain, it will give us a show while we wait for this storm to pass," laughed Alberto.

"I want a meeting of my section commanders, Luiz, in ten minutes," Manuel shouted to one of his top men across the extra distance. "After that I want to see Alberto's commanders and then Pedro's. I want all the other cartel commanders we have picked up in Pedro's meeting. You know what I have to say and while I speak with the men, I want you to go outside to check on things behind this terminal. Keep an eye on any movement. Also, change the outside guards every two hours, I don't want any guards sleeping, or I will personally cut off their ears and give them to their wives gift-wrapped if they are caught."

Luiz acknowledged his orders and headed for the closest rear exit to the walkway connecting the aircraft behind the terminal. He wasn't too happy to be on guard in the rain, but he was used to it, being a Colombian.

The first meeting started half an hour later, and several men were seated in front of the table where two powerful kerosene lamps gave Manuel and the men light to see each other.

"Everybody here?" asked Manuel and there was silence.

A couple of minutes after he started, the edge of his vision caught movement towards the rear of the terminal; a lightning bolt helped him see men moving, and he saw several shadows approaching the lit up area.

Suddenly there was a brilliant shaft of blue lightning outside the front windows which lit up the whole inner area of the terminal for a split second, followed by a crash of thunder enough to vibrate eardrums.

The twelve Seals froze; they were the only ones standing in that area and people suddenly noticed them.

"Who are you? Come over here now!" shouted one of the men standing around the table and who had noticed the twelve men standing there. The Seals walked over to the area. There was a map of Texas displayed on a square table and several men had been studying it when the lightning struck. "Why are you coming over here? Can't you see we are in a meeting?" He was tall, thick-shouldered, and injured with dried blood in several areas of his face; one eye looked half-closed and he was pretty mean-looking.

"I'm sorry, Señor," stated Lieutenant Paul looking as humble as an ugly guy like him could, "but we were told to come over to tell you about three missiles and a launcher which we saw undamaged in the first attack with the American fighter jets."

"Si, Señor, we wanted permission to take a jeep and go back to get them," added Charlie Meyers also nearly bowing and also looking as humble as he could.

"What do you think, Alberto? Should these guys go all the way back to Interstate-10? Can they make it in this weather?" Paul and Meyers saw the resemblance of brothers in the men and knew that they had hit pay dirt.

"Manuel, if they want to go back, let them. They look mean enough to look after themselves. Where are you from?" asked Alberto Calderón getting interested in the men.

The three Colombian leaders in front of the two lieutenants were tired, dirty and covered in dried blood from multiple cuts, scratches and bruises. The brother who had ordered them over, Manuel, by the sound of it, looked the worst, having a closed and swollen black eye and a deep gash down the same left side of his face.

"Panama, but we live in America, in San Antonio, and we joined Pedro's army there. I'm also Pedro, this is my brother, Charlie, and my other brother Antonio..."

"Thank you for joining us," interrupted Manuel, not wanting to really know their names. "Go back to the guard you met outside; he is one of my commanders and get him to give you a good jeep with a roof. It is worth the effort, three missiles. Now go; and I want you back in twelve hours and bring them directly to me."

"Hold on!" stated Alberto interrupting his brother. "You look familiar to me. Charlie, now that's a funny name for a Pana-manian. Also you and your men are pretty clean and even clean-shaven compared to us. Am I missing anything here, Señor Charlie?"

"I think we fought together in Medellin, Colombia in 2010 against those American soldiers. My friends in America call me Charlie. Remember, the American soldiers, they attacked us at that coffee company when we had their hostages and when we all left, I got out over the back wall," stated Charlie Meyers.

He was actually right. Seal Team Six had gone into the coffee company to capture two CIA hostages in 2010, who were being held there by an unknown cartel. He didn't know if these were the same people but he was sure they knew about the attack by the American Special Forces. The hostages were already dead.

"We are always clean-shaven for the ladies, Señor Alberto. You never know these days when you might come across a nice girl and me and my brothers consider that the cleanest and smartest one of us might win the poor girl's heart," Charlie joked getting the response he was looking for and showing that he certainly wasn't scared to stand up to the leaders. He knew that a joke always eased discussions amongst men.

"That wasn't me, Charlie Mendoza, that was my younger brother Pedro, who was there. You must have been one of the lucky ones to escape. Not many did. Now go and get these missiles, and we can talk about bringing you and your mean-looking brothers into the forward army when you return. And I hope you fight as good as you chase women, Señor Charlie, or you might not see many more women in your lifetime!" Alberto and his brothers laughed at this one as well as the dozens of men listening in to the rhetoric.

"Si, Señor," answered Charlie, looking down like a naughty kid in class.

The three Calderón brothers were a mean-looking bunch with their scratches and bruises. The Seal Team put the three enemy faces into memory and figured out who was who. They knew that the meanest-looking one who had asked the first question was the leader, Manuel. He was extremely dirty, looking like he had been in several muddy ditches in the last day or so.

They now knew that Alberto was in charge of the second

group and the youngest brother Pedro was in charge of the larger rear army.

The dozen Seals, half of whom had stayed behind their leaders to hide their faces in the dimly lit area surrounding the meeting, bowed out of the meeting to follow orders. Alberto shouted at one man to guide them to the outside man and tell him to give them a jeep.

Outside the weather had returned, the rain was dense and the two rebels had to shout at each other to get their words across. The order was given to find a jeep, and the outside guard nodded to the inside guard and headed underneath the terminal to the baggage area, beckoning the twelve men to follow him.

"How you fat load of men are going to fit into one jeep, I don't know," he shouted smiling at Charlie walking next to him "I have a good Mexican troop transporter that has a good roof and it might be better to get through the destruction on the highways. It has four-wheel drive, a full fuel tank, and is very old but in good condition," he stated, sounding more like a car salesman than a Colombian cartel commander.

They reached dry air inside the baggage area which had several hundred of the best vehicles they had yet seen. It seemed that these vehicles must belong to the first group, Manuel's group, as there were Panamanian, Honduran, Mexican, several American vehicles and even a line of civilian four-wheel drive trucks with Colombian number plates. They all had very bald tires, showing that they had certainly travelled a far distance.

Charlie Meyers/Mendoza and Lieutenant Paul jumped into the cab, and Charlie started up the troop carrier; the rest of the men jumped into the rear, thanked the guard who was lighting a cigarette in the dryness of the protected area, and drove out into the semi-blindness of the drenching, side-swept rain storm.

"We need to get back to the other guys and use the radio to contact the Marines further north," shouted Lieutenant Paul to Charlie Meyers.

"I think we drive straight up to the jeep on the corner and tell them what we are doing. That should keep them from becoming inquisitive," Charlie replied. Paul nodded and they drove slowly to where they had found the first jeep on the corner of the northern terminal.

The jeep was gone, but there was an American troop carrier on guard with a cloth roof fighting the wind and the rain. They drove up to the other vehicle and sided in as close as they could.

A new man looked out from the half open window and waited for Charlie to speak.

"We have orders from Manuel and Alberto Calderón to head back to the Interstate to pick up some missile launchers!" Charlie shouted in Spanish at the top of his voice.

"You are going the wrong way, this is north and you need to go west and then south!" the ugly face shouted back.

"This is the direction we came in after we found the airport fence. We should go the way we came in, or we will get lost in this weather!" Charlie shouted back.

The man nodded and closed his window, and Charlie drove forward, losing sight of the American truck within a hundred feet. It just disappeared into the lousy weather.

As soon as they were hidden by the weather, Charlie stopped the truck and switched off the engine. It was doubtful that the other members of Seal Team Six had heard the truck's movement; they were still a couple of hundred feet south of the bridge. On foot the two lieutenants found the bridge. It was easily reached, and the weather was now so bad that it didn't look like a bridge at all.

"The whole bloody South American population is in the terminals three hundred yards south of here!" shouted Lieutenant Paul to Lieutenant Murphy and the rest of the men. The noise of the wind and rain was deafening. "I need to see if we can get anybody on the radio."

"We already have," replied Murphy. "There is some nut up

there flying around in an airplane in this weather. I'm sure I recognized the admiral's voice. That guy is sure taking a chance."

"Charlie Six, Charlie Six here, requesting to give information to any friends listening. Over!" shouted Charlie Meyers into the headset.

"Hi, Charlie Six. This is a friend. It's a crappy day. Over!" came a voice Charlie Meyers knew was Admiral Rogers. Even though he recognized the voice he still had to go through the daily code system. If his reply was also that it was a crappy day, then he was being coerced into the radio communications as a captive. If he said it was a beautiful day, then he was talking freely.

"It's a beautiful day down here, friend," he replied.

"Well, it's getting bad up here, Charlie Six, and I was about to return north. What have you got for me? You have friends a couple of miles north and a second group ten miles west of you who are listening in; confirm, please?"

"Mike Two, reading you loud and clear," stated a Marine in the railway yard.

"Mike One, reading you faint, but OK," stated Lieutenant Colonel Clarke now at the first attack intersection."

"Mike One, we are coming towards you, will be leaving our location immediately for your position. Look out for us in one Mexican-painted M35, a "deuce and a half" troop transporter; I repeat one Mexican troop vehicle only. We need to find any unused ground-to-air missiles and any launchers your men might have found in their searches of the combat areas. We are on a delicate mission, and you may disarm them if you wish as we need to hand them over to the enemy to gain favor."

"Roger that, Charlie Six. We have found a shoulder launcher and one missile so far. I will check to see if any of my squads have found or seen any more. I will tell my men about your approach, I assume from our north?"

"Roger, from your north on the highway, Mike One. Friend in

the sky and all friends on the ground, I believe the whole rebel force is in the Intercontinental airport, thousands and thousands of men and vehicles. We introduced ourselves to their leaders, pretty decent, but very dirty fellows with good upbringings!" smiled Charlie Meyers into the headset. This was always appreciated by the people listening to him and was his signature that it was really him.

"*How many do you guess?*" asked Admiral Rogers.

Charlie shouted to the men around him for estimates on how many they had seen and he took the average.

"We saw at least 10,000 to 20,000, and considering the size of the covered areas, there must be 100,000 to 150,000. I counted over 1,000 vehicles, 20-odd howitzers behind old Mexican and American camouflaged M35s, hundreds of heavy machine guns, and truckloads of weapons. We didn't see much food stocks but there were a couple of dozen Mexican-painted M35s set off to one side. One had cases of jerky, corned beef and friendly U.S. MRE rations on the ground behind it. We saw only a third of the whole under-terminal area and two warehouses. The leaders and commanders are pretty beat up but still well armed..."

"*...Mike One, here,*" interrupted Lieutenant Colonel Clarke. "*I have reports of trucks incoming from our south, looks like 40 to 50 troop carriers. Orders please?*"

"*Suggestion, Charlie Six?*" asked the admiral.

"Depends on what you want us to do," replied Charlie. "It will be suicide to take the leaders out. We don't have enough men on the ground, and we'll be toast with their numbers. Extraction might be possible in the future, and if that is what you want, friend, then we think the trucks should be left alone, unless they have seen you, Mike One."

"*They haven't seen us; I left a surveillance group with a radio a few miles behind us. We can disappear if you want. It's not that difficult in this weather.*"

"Do you believe an extraction is possible, Charlie Six? And who are the leaders?" asked the admiral.

"What do you think we are, friend, green behind the ears? Of course extraction is possible! It will just take a little time. Extraction is three bad boys: Manuel, Alberto and Pedro Calderón out of Colombia who are the head of operations. That should cut the head off the snake, and make it easier for others to tread on it if we extract them."

"Extraction is a go, Charlie Six. Extraction is confirmed, but I cannot get you out by air until this weather blows over. Mike One, get hidden and allow their vehicles through. Charlie Six, if you can extract before we can get to you, I will leave Mike Two in place and Mike One will join them. Mike One, head for the town of Spring; Mike Two, guide Mike One in to your location when necessary. I have to leave, there are no more aircraft dropping friends until this hurricane heads out. By the way, you are to be hit by a Hurricane Three in about six hours and it should last at least 24 hours. Get down and get covered. Out!"

Towards the end, Charlie Meyers could hardly hear the admiral. The weather was getting worse, and they needed to get the equipment from Lieutenant Colonel Clarke's team ASAP.

* * *

The admiral's pilots were fighting the aircraft, which was hitting painful up and down turbulence constantly. They were happy to get the nod to turn the aircraft northwards from a smiling admiral. Judging from the smile on his face, they understood that the news they had all heard must have been good.

An hour later and 300 miles north of Houston and halfway to McConnell Air Force Base in Wichita, Admiral Rogers got into contact with the radio operator on duty. The winds had certainly died down and they were flying out of the really bad weather.

"Get me PattersonKey on set," demanded the admiral, sipping a hot cup of coffee now that it was possible.

"*Wait one,*" replied the operator and several minutes later General Patterson's voice came over the radio.

"*PattersonKey here.*"

"Is our friend Carlos anywhere close? He needs to hear what I have to say," stated the admiral. It took several more minutes and the general acknowledged that they were both listening.

"Enemy rebel force holed up at Houston Intercontinental, approximately 150,000 men and 3,000 vehicles. They are heavily armed and dangerous. Head of rebel army is Manuel, Alberto and Pedro Calderón from your part of the woods, Carlos. I've confirmed a possible extraction and will brief you more once I get back in an hour. Out."

* * *

Carlos smiled at the news as Admiral Rogers had done. It didn't surprise him to find out the Calderón Cartel was behind this attack. His uncle and his father had both suggested that the ugly head of the Calderón family could appear at any time. There weren't many other factions with the men or intelligence to attack another country, other than the whole Venezuelan army, and that was doubtful.

It was not a sensible hour to call family, but he immediately got on the phone to his Uncle Philippe, still holed up at the Colombian Embassy in Washington.

"I would assume that your news is good at this time of the morning, Carlos?" Uncle Philippe, the Colombian Ambassador to the United States stated answering the satellite phone given to him at the beginning of the year.

"I wouldn't call you unless you wanted to hear the information, Uncle Philippe," Carlos replied and told him what he had just heard from the admiral.

"And you say Admiral Rogers just told you this a few minutes ago, and there is a hurricane about to hit the U.S.? How come your satellite didn't detect this storm?"

"The satellite was repositioned over Hawaii a few weeks ago for the mission into China by General Patterson and the rest of us. It is still returning to its original orbit over Colorado, Uncle," replied Carlos.

"So, Senator Calderón is now directly implicated in an attack on America by his sons. I have never met the three brothers, but I thought that they would be up to something when I heard about the senator's ship arriving from Honduras, and the attack at the Panama Canal leaving all the dead Chinese soldiers. So these brothers have literally invaded Texas and are holed up in Houston in the middle of a hurricane?" Carlos acknowledged that his uncle was correct. "I will call Admiral Rodriquez on his satellite phone and my brother in Colombia. I don't think we have enough proof to get him taken in by our men just yet, plus if Admiral Rogers has ordered an extraction, like the one his team did in Medellin for those dead CIA agents in 2010, then we can pin a lot more on his head and get rid of his family and all his other government infiltrators at one time. That will be a good day for our country, Carlos. Tell my friend the admiral to take their captives alive this time. I need as much information as possible out of them. Tell him for me, Carlos. Your father is fine. He was worried about you and where you were. I will tell him that you are still alive and kicking.

"Keep me informed, and gracias."

* * *

Martie was still feeling groggy. She had slept a little and Preston wouldn't move from her side.

"I want to go home, Preston. There isn't much to do here, I'm not keen on hurricanes. Maybe Carlos will fly us home?"

"I'll go and talk to him," Preston replied, kissed her on the cheek and headed out to find his friend.

As usual Carlos was in the main control room and General Patterson was there too. Both were heavy in conversation, Carlos on his phone and the general on the radio to Admiral Rogers by the sounds of the voice at the other end.

Carlos said goodbye to the person he was speaking to and told Preston that he had been talking to his uncle. General Patterson ended his radio conversation with the admiral and got on his satellite phone. Carlos brought Preston up-to-date on the latest news, and Preston was impressed with how fast the Seals got in and out. He also overheard the general calling a Marine base somewhere on the east coast and ordered out every C-130 he had within the hour; they were to be filled up with troops, and he wanted a third flight of troops into Spring, Texas ASAP.

His next satellite call was to Andrews telling the base commander to divert the lone incoming 747 full of troops from Europe directly into McConnell; the pilot should have sufficient reserves for the extra hour of flight from Ramstein. The 747 was only an hour out of Ramstein and could be at McConnell in nine hours.

The third and last call was to California, telling all the pilots and weapon systems operators who could fly the 17 Chinese helicopters to get them into McConnell within 24 hours. They would need to refuel in Hill.

"That's great. I'm running a war here and the techies at Edwards told me that the recommended U.S. Air Force paint jobs on the Chinese helicopters would not be dry in 24 hours. I don't care if the helicopters are pink with purple polka dots; I want them ready to fight a war. Who ordered them to be painted anyway? It will totally freak out the enemy when they are being fired on by Chinese aircraft. Carlos, I think you would put the wind in their sails when the Calderón brothers see your Colombian aircraft flying around the skies. That reminds me!"

He spoke so fast that neither Preston nor Carlos got a word in. "Base commander, sorry to wake you at this lousy hour, when are those Colombian gunships ready to fly?" he questioned the Travis base commander. "Two days for the first five, great. We can test them out down here. We have a new war to fight; get them into Dyess ASAP. Bye!" He hung up on the poor guy who probably wasn't even awake before the conversation was terminated. "I need every aircraft I can get to blast these 150,000 rebels out of our country. Preston, you wanted to see me?"

"Martie wants to go back to North Carolina for a day or so. I thought that we could return in our own aircraft, it will help give you numbers. Buck is fine flying Carlos' Colombian DC-3 and I'm sure Carlos would like to collect his Mustang as the same time. I heard you sending out C-130s to the east coast. Can we hitch a ride?"

"All thirty C-130s are leaving in twenty minutes for Camp Lejeune. I want 4,000 more Marines and all the other men I can get into the Houston area before this hurricane fizzles out in three days. I think that you should be back here in 72 hours or at least in the air by then. Also I want your P-38 Lightning here. Preston, can I loan you a pilot to fly it over?"

"As long as you give me a 747 once they finish transferring cargo to the U.S.," suggested Preston.

"A what! A 747-400! What the hell are you going to do with that? You can't even fly it or even get it anywhere near your airfield!" stated the general looking directly at Preston with a look of total shock.

"Martie also wants one and so does Carlos, as payment for the use of our aircraft," added Preston.

"I do?" asked Carlos, also looking at Preston as if he had totally lost it.

"Why?" asked General Patterson.

"Well, I've been thinking about the future. I don't know if you know, but my father, Mike Strong, was the co-pilot for the Pan Am 747 Flight 103 that went down over Lockerbie, Scotland."

"No, I didn't know that, Preston. I'm sorry for your loss," replied General Patterson, his mind trying feverishly to solve the riddle Preston presented him.

"Well, after this war, I might have the opportunity to form the first new international airline in the world. I was thinking of calling it Mike's Airline, after my father. You could be a shareholder if you want, General Patterson," stated Preston with a straight face. The general could see that he wasn't playing with him.

Carlos laughed out loud and slapped Preston on the back. "Now I know why we normal humans don't think like you, Preston. You are always one step ahead of everybody.

"I could pay you the first installment of $50 million dollars, and Martie has another $50 million for the down payment if we can ever get our investment accounts up and running again."

"Is that how much you guys lost on New Year's Eve?" General Patterson asked seriously.

"I'm sure Martie's money from her grandfather's estate would easily treble our deposit, but who knows if money will be worth anything for a while? I would prefer to have my money in aircraft, especially an airline like that British airline mogul had. He was the only guy I was ever jealous of."

It took several moments for the general to answer Preston's request.

"Once this war is over, Mr. Strong, send me or the president an invoice and I'll see what I can do. Now piss off and leave me to my bloody war," he stated, shaking his head.

"Pretty good move there, Preston," Carlos stated, putting his arm around his friend's shoulders as they went to get packed up and tell a C-130 pilot that he should expect a flight-load of passengers bound for Apex, North Carolina. "Our own airline, huh? Now that's one for the record books. Three whole beautiful

747-400s! I can sure get excited to learn to fly one of those babies."

"I was thinking of asking for the ownership of RDU airport for our home base, but thought it too much to ask all at once!" Preston smiled.

Carlos just shook his head.

Since there was this hurricane brewing, and all fighter aircraft were grounded until further notice, all of the friends decided to join him and Martie for two days of rest at his farm in North Carolina.

The C-130 touched down several hours later and a couple of hours after Oliver and Puppy had done their morning ritual of checking out the perimeter fences.

Little Beth and Clint were being looked after by Will who was in control of the farm with Ben and Oprah, Marie, Beatrice and their daughters, as well as Mo's sister and two children.

The farm had been a peaceful place since the aircraft had headed west. Only a single FedEx Cargomaster arrived once a week with a fresh guard crew and any supplies on offer from Seymour Johnson.

An arriving C-130 was a welcome sight for the people at the farm to know somebody was returning. News was not getting out about what was happening, and the lovely spring weather was getting hot.

The group, with the kids' help, had tilled a large vegetable garden under the guidance of Will in their absence; Preston even noticed it in the right hand seat of the C-130 as he brought her in to his new airstrip.

A mass of brown and healthy bodies erupted from several of the buildings as Preston taxied the aircraft onto his apron in front of the original hangar next to the main house.

The rear cargo door was lowered and the group of sleepy pilots were rushed at and hugged by the excited crowd. Clint was first to the back of the aircraft, Little Beth pushing him as fast as her little legs could run and not thinking about possible wheel-chair accidents on the way.

Martie was now walking by herself with one bandage on her upper arm and one over her forehead covering a smaller cut. She was hit hard by Little Beth who nearly blew out the wind in her lungs.

"Martie, Martie! You're home. We've missed you so much!" she shouted, not noticing the injuries until she pulled away to look at Martie. "What happened? Oh! I'm sorry I didn't know you were hurt. Did I hurt you?" she asked, her face going white.

"No, I'm not that bad," Martie replied. "Nothing a cold beer won't fix, Little Beth. Hello, Will," she said, giving him, Oprah, and Ben a hug after Maggie was done being twirled around.

"Shall I get you one?" Little Beth asked.

"No, it's a little early but come and tell me what you guys have done since I've been away," she added, bending over and giving Clint a special hug.

Sally was happy to be with Carlos; they exchanged hugs all around and then headed off to their usual hangar bedroom. Jennifer and Pam looked towards the farm entrance and saw what they were expecting, a Rat Patrol jeep with Joe and David, coming to see who had arrived.

Preston thanked the pilots who were readying the aircraft for its short flight into Cherry Point and got attacked by the kids as he was the last to exit.

"The general busy?" asked Marie as Preston pushed Clint in his wheelchair back to the house, and the first engine behind him began its whine.

"I'm afraid so. There is a large battle with rebels going on in Houston, but a hurricane is coming through so we have been grounded for a few days."

"And Mo?" asked Beatrice.

"He's still in China, Beatrice, and will be for quite some time.

I think he should be done there in a couple of months. I'm sorry to be the bearer of lousy news."

"That's OK, he said he would be a while," she replied. "We have a big surprise for you and Martie behind the house. The whole team here, under Will's guidance, has worked on it for three weeks, since you left."

"I didn't know you had green fingers, Will," stated Preston smiling. "I saw your workmanship from the air."

Martie was led there first by Little Beth who was proud of the group's achievement. Martie was shocked to see nearly a quarter-acre vegetable garden already full of growing plants. She counted five rows of fifty plants. The lettuce was beautiful, big and ready. Then there were tomato plants by the dozens, still a week or so from producing little tomatoes, and a special herb area where a couple of dozen herb plants already looked like they were ready for picking.

Martie and Preston were impressed; over 50 rows of corn, sunflowers, rows of beans, carrots and squash, and certainly this garden would add to the farm's vegetable needs.

"Will decided that we needed to grow enough crops for at least 30 to 40 people," stated Little Beth still holding Martie's hand. "I have scolded Oliver and Puppy several times for digging in here, and I'm thinking of having the first vegetable garden to ever have a barbed wire fence around it."

"That should keep the dogs and any visiting terrorists out of your vegetable garden. Great idea, Little Beth," Martie laughed.

Joe came up with David and shook hands.

"I assume a BBQ could be the way to go tonight. Y'all look like you need a good feeding. Meat and beer for fifty by the look of it," stated Joe.

"And don't forget a nice big salad, Joe. I have been dreaming of a real salad for months now," added Martie. "I'm going to lie down for an hour, my heads hurts and I need an aspirin."

The farm settled down as many decided that Martie had the

best idea and an early siesta was in order. Little Beth and Clint headed into the hangar to continue their discussion with the Air Force guards about several hundred feet of new barbed wire being needed from Seymour Johnson for the vegetable garden. And since the church was finished, when was a swimming pool going to be built? Couldn't they see that it was summer and a pool would be the next most important thing on the list!

Anybody could guess who the people in charge of the farm were and the adults let them be.

* * *

Colonel Garrote, Commander of the 2nd Marine Division, was trying to hold onto his stomach as the C-130 tossed him and 99 squashed men in the aircraft meant for 90. He was in the lead C-130 of 30 from Camp Lejeune going into weather that wasn't fit to live in, never mind hang from a parachute in.

This was certainly not the luxurious 747 flight he had enjoyed two weeks earlier flying home from Ramstein. They were twenty miles away from the drop zone as the red light in the aircraft came on, and the pilot stated five minutes to drop time.

The second group of Marines already on the ground under Lieutenant Colonel Catlin who were part of his 2nd Marine Division had gone out from the railway yard to find a larger open field for a big LZ (Landing Zone) and had found one a mile east in fifty acres of barren farmland with no power lines or other obstacles that might injure the parachutists.

The winds were now steady at around forty-five miles an hour with gusts up to sixty and the men would be dropped with the aircraft flying at just over stall speed and against the wind's direction. This would slow down the aircraft's forward speed and allow the 100 men to exit tightly.

The danger would be the T-10 parachutes being swept out of the landing area by the wind and the men were jumping in low and as light as possible with no packs, weapons or food. Three of the gunships, having a much smaller area for cargo, only a quarter of what the transporters had, each carried a pallet of equipment with everything aboard the men needed. They were also to drop in extremely low and allow five seconds for the parachutes to open; they were packed to protect an extremely hard landing seconds later.

Hurricane No-Name was still two hundred miles to their south, and the winds were now directly out of the east. They were rapidly growing in intensity and this would be the last drop before it would be impossible to land a parachute. In these conditions, the injuries could be high, but the best men had been picked for the drop.

CHAPTER 7

We Need More Men!

AFTER SEVERAL HOURS ON THE PHONE, General Patterson found recently returned soldiers at Fort Hood outside Killeen, Texas, which also had vehicles to transport a decent number of soldiers.

Fort Hood was home to the 1st Cavalry Division, of which 6,000 men had returned from Europe a week earlier. The transportation of the entire 1st Cavalry Division of 50,000 men in Europe had been halted due to the general's decision to send the aircraft into China instead of Europe. They currently had 7,000 men on base. The general was also told that the base commander, a Major Deale, had just completed an inventory of mobile vehicles.

Fort Hood had thirty-one old, usable M35 troop transporters, twenty Vietnam-era Mutts with rocket launchers, several odd jeeps, fifty fuel tanker-trailers and three 5,000-gallon tanker trucks. What really excited General Patterson was that the base had dozens of old and rusty tanks and armored-vehicle carriers in storage, which were fully operational and reserved to be blasted as targets in the field. The old trucks had dozens of flat-bed trailers and each trailer could haul as many soldiers as a C-130.

"Major Deale, you say you can transport 4,000 men in the usable vehicles you have there at Hood?"

"Yes, Sir. A couple need oil and a good service, but I think we could have 30 of these old target vehicles coupled to flatbeds and sent to Houston within six hours. We also have a couple of tanks —old girls—and a truck-load of HE (High Explosive) projectiles in storage. We could have them packed up and on the road in six to twelve hours."

"Major Deale, do you have anybody to command the base in your absence?"

"Yes, Sir, my base commander is due in on this week's 747 flight out of Ramstein."

"Good. Get the base to active battle readiness and leave somebody in temporary command. I want you to get as many men as you can into the Houston area. Destination is Spring, a small town several miles north of Houston. There are 12,000 Marines already there or heading there. Major, I want you there in twelve hours, and then return your empty vehicles to Fort Hood for a second load ASAP. I'm sending in 4,000 Marines in C-130s which will arrive at Fort Hood in about fifteen to twenty hours. That will give us 20,000 men and machines to defend our country. Major, the C-130s will continue to fly in troops into Fort Hood until we win our war, so I want whatever your guys can fight with: men, machinery, and supplies. Send in your first delivery and tell the drivers to stay fueled up. Take tanker-trailers if needed, but I want 24-hour troop transportation until further notice, understand?"

The major acknowledged and suggested that the general call the 1st Armored Division in Fort Bliss, El Paso. Their troops, about 18,000, were also returning from Ramstein when the 747s were diverted but he knew that at least several thousand men had been flown over. He was friends with a Major Mike Johnson at "Old Ironsides" who had also been given a satellite phone upon his return to McGuire a week earlier. General Patterson thanked the major, asked him if he understood his orders, and hung up on him.

Major Johnson was happy that somebody wanted the use of his men. He had 5,000 currently on base and 3,000 who were on leave and looking after their families and farms around El Paso. Over 2,000 of them were from farming families. Under Captain Mike Mallory's instructions, a Southwest Airlines captain, they had left the military until further notice to help with the area's farming needs. Many others were helping. No, he hadn't seen any border crossings in the El Paso area, but he had constant surveillance and needed 600 to 800 men to keep up the 200 mile border patrols he was running 24/7.

General Patterson told the major that he knew Mallory and would be contacting him next to begin possible cleanup operations on Interstate-10 outside Houston.

"Major, what mobile vehicles can you spare for troop deployment to Houston ASAP?"

"Hell, General, I have many of my jeeps and smaller vehicles on border patrol. As you know, we have very few vehicles that are operational, but I have one old Abrams tank operational. She does our main gate guard duty and is there to offer her mean presence."

"Get her oiled, armed and on a transporter, Major. How many M35 transporters do you have operational?"

"Only six, sir, but we have several old tractors with tank-trailers. That is the only other vehicle here that works, apart from two 150mm howitzers standing outside headquarters."

"Get the howitzers behind transporters and a truck of projectiles. How many men can you get aboard your mobile trailers at a push, Major?"

"Gee, General, with food, ammo and provisions, about 2,000 on twenty vehicles with two old fuel tankers and a couple of fuel trailers. That will clean my vehicles out."

"You get everything you can on the road, without causing

problems with your border duty. I want them in Houston in twenty-four hours. It's seven hundred miles from El Paso to Houston, the highways are clear and they will liaise with ingoing troops from your friend at Hood, Major Deale, who will be 500 miles ahead of you. He also has a satellite phone and you have his number. He can guide you and your guys in, understand?"

The major did.

* * *

Manuel Calderón concluded his meeting and hit the sack for a few hours of sleep. This storm was getting really bad; many areas of the terminal were leaking rain water and the place was cold and damp.

Alberto had argued with Manuel for two hours not to keep all the men in one place. The Air Force could return at any minute and bomb the place if they knew they were there.

His older brother had laughed at him and told him to go outside and see for himself if aircraft could fly in this weather, let alone pinpoint bomb drops without visibility. Manuel respected the U.S. military, but even they couldn't work in such terrible conditions. He also knew a hurricane when he smelled one, and this one was either going to drown them or keep them safe for as long as it was in the vicinity. They would stay put at this airfield for as long as the storm grew, and would then disperse northwards towards Dallas as soon as the winds began to dissipate.

* * *

Charlie Meyers was having a hard time driving. It was hard enough to see out of the windshield with the wipers working as fast as they could, but now he was trying to get around bodies all over the road and felt every one the truck tires went over; they were scattered everywhere.

He gave up trying to dodge them as their numbers mounted and were too much for the truck to negotiate, and he turned back and headed for the highway exit they had passed a mile earlier. At least they could by-pass the carnage.

"The aircraft had certainly done a number on this lot!" he shouted to Lieutenant Paul sitting on the other seat and Corporal Rodriquez who was now front gunner. He had seen, stopped the truck, and picked up the beautiful undamaged tripod machine gun and several hundred rounds from a broken jeep as they had approached the carnage.

"I'm sure the guys will see us on the side road just as easily," added Lieutenant Paul and, several minutes after turning onto the side road, they saw men in front waving them down.

"You guys look like a bunch of drowned rats," stated Charlie, winding his window down and smiling at the Marines.

"You guys are sure roughing it in a limo, I see," replied a very wet lieutenant. "Mommy not allowing her babies to get wet, poor little dears," he joked, smiling at the face in the truck with rain-drops streaming down his face.

"Good news for you: clean dry accommodation a few miles north at Bush Intercontinental, but bad news is that a whole rebel army already has the lease. You are more than welcome to go and throw them out anytime you want. I see you let their trucks go through. We passed them a few miles before the airport. Where's your boss man?" Charlie asked.

"About 300 yards behind. He told us you were coming and has some blow-up toys for you youngsters."

He signaled goodbye and the truck inched slowly through hundreds of men on guard who were protecting hundreds more on the highway below them to their left.

"We found two ground-to-air missiles and one launcher so far," stated a wet Colonel Clarke as they pulled up underneath the overhang of a gas station half a mile further on. He and a hundred men were trying to heat up some food. The Seal Team left the truck in the rain and went to join them.

"I have already had their guidance systems disarmed, so if they are fired towards our aircraft, they will go straight past, unless they hit them head on."

"At least we have something to bribe them to be our friends," replied Lieutenant Paul, being offered a tin plate with a hot biscuit drenched with "SOS" sauce.

"What are your plans and how can we help? I've heard that the rest of our men with the 2nd Marine Division from Lejeune are coming in later with my commander and more are to be trucked in within twenty-four hours."

"How many men expected in total?" asked Paul, taking a good bite out of the biscuit after drowning it in the hot sauce.

"It looks like we will have 12,000 more Marines north of here in twenty-four hours, and we even heard of Chinese attack choppers and gunships as back-up. The Air Force lost three jet aircraft to those damn missiles yesterday so we are hoping that the bastards don't have many left."

"We counted two when we talked to the Calderón brothers, and we didn't see any more during our walk-about of their base," added Lieutenant Meyers.

"Cookie, get these guys some more food. I'm sure they haven't eaten for a while!" Colonel Clarke shouted over to the group of men boiling a large container on a massive gas ring. "We got in a pallet of cooking supplies with the last drop a couple of hours ago and have five stations cooking the men up some food. I believe there is no rush to get anywhere just yet and any place dry is good right now. There is a large, broken but still dry Walmart on the other side of the highway, and the other four cooking stations are feeding our men in there right now. The bodies down there take your appetite away, especially the napalmed dead. That old Vietnam stuff burns like a crematorium."

"We are going to bed in with the guys and might need back-up once we are ready to go. I know the admiral will place a Jolly Green Giant or an extraction chopper pretty close, and we will have to work by ear. Just tell the boss to try and warn us when he sends in the jets or choppers. I don't want to be taken by our own bullets. It might ruin my appetite," Lieutenant Paul replied. "Thanks for the missiles. We will give them to the enemy and will maybe suggest coming out and looking for more once the weather dries out a little."

"At least twenty-four hours, maybe forty-eight. We haven't even seen the worst of this storm yet," added the colonel.

"We can meet again in the town of Spring, whenever. Just call. Colonel, if you locate any more missiles, sort out their innards and we'll come and find you."

The Marines were thanked for the hot food, and Lieutenant Paul and his team got back into the truck and headed back to the airport, picking up another two good-looking machine guns and dozens of cases of ammo from the same Marine lieutenant they had met on the way in.

"No harm in having a little back-up for the boys," laughed Charlie Meyers as he drove towards the airport.

* * *

It was close to midnight the next evening, May 21st, when Admiral Rogers received word from the first Orion, which had gone out for the third time. The weather had been bad now for 72 hours and the hurricane's eye had only moved thirty miles north-eastwards, less than half a mile an hour. It was virtually dead still. "The cold front is destroying the hurricane bit by bit," he told General Patterson.

General Mark Watson, the current Commandant of the Marine Corps, had just flown in from Europe with the latest 747 delivery, straight into McConnell Air Force Base with General

Mike Austin, Commandant of the Army, who was on the same aircraft. The president also flew in at the same time to meet with the two new generals who, in December, had been directed to get the troops home from Europe, and had stayed there as long as necessary.

Now that there were very few soldiers left, only 70,000, they were able to return a month early at the request of General Patterson, who needed their expertise in this next battle.

Up to now, General Patterson and the U.S. Air Force had been in charge of the defense of the United States, but he felt that since he needed to use Marines and Army soldiers in this upcoming battle, he should at least bring in their commanders to help with the battle plans.

"General Patterson has worked 24/7 to keep our country safe since February 1st," stated the president. "He was actually in combat himself in China only a week or two ago. Admiral Rogers, in charge of our naval forces, has worked just as hard and I know you men have done the same for your country overseas. General Watson and General Austin, we are now the five men who control the entire United States of America. We need to work together to solve this next problem of border incursion before we start rebuilding this land of ours from scratch. Do all of you understand?" The four men nodded, and the president thought for a few moments before carrying on.

"I want you four to be the Joint Chiefs of Staff until further notice. I know that this is a promotion for all of you. The previous members have all been found and their bodies identified. General Patterson, who has been at the forefront of our country's defense, will be the new Chief and you three generals part of the Staff. We need to work together to end this battle against our country once and for all and, if we destroy this massive army from the south, I believe word will get out that we are still a strong nation and not to be played with. Once this battle is over General Watson and General Austin, you will both become the men in charge to help form and set up our new police force across the country. The idea I have, and both General Patterson and Admiral Rogers agree, is that all of our country's Military Policemen from all branches of service will become our new nation's police force. How many men can each of your departments offer for this new military police force?"

"My men are ready; only yesterday I confirmed that the Navy can supply 12,000 MPs to the new police force," stated Admiral Rogers.

"My second-in-command also checked yesterday, Mr. President," added General Patterson. "We have 9,000 active MPs who can join the new force. I also checked the latest numbers with Captain Mike Mallory who, for you guys who have just arrived back, is in charge of food, population numbers, and nearly everything civilian. He has 6,500 still-active policemen from across the country who are already working the beat. Not many, but they are already doing a stellar job in certain areas. I believe that ex-LAPD Detective Will Smart will certainly be a good man to help with the formation and then running of the new force. Don't forget him, Mr. President."

"Since I have only been back a couple of hours, Mr. President," stated General Austin, "I need to exact my numbers; but in Europe I had a force of 17,000 MPs dealing with getting the men ready to travel. I believe that I could increase my total to 20,000 given a few weeks."

"The Marines still have 7,000 MPs over in Europe and I have another 2,000 here stateside. That is what the Marines can offer, Mr. President: 9,000 men and women in total."

"Well, it's a start. Something you don't know, gentlemen, our latest numbers from Mallory's computer system that is counting our population. As of last night, we have 54,575,512 U.S. civilians registered alive. Our total military forces number 1,185,909 personnel and we have, as of yesterday, combed 79 percent of the country looking for civilians who are still alive. We still have low-population areas like Wyoming, the Dakotas, Idaho and a few other northern areas to check, as well as several large city centers, but that is it gentleman. Mallory tells me that we could add another five to eight percent to our numbers by year-end. Our U.S. population has dropped from 323 million to a possible 60 million. So, with the numbers from you men, we could have a new police force of 55,000 men to look after 60 million civilians."

"Is that all the people we have left in this country?" asked General Watson, shock written all over his face.

"Unfortunately, we have lost five-sixths of this country, General. A lot has happened here since you've been overseas. Our teams of hundreds of thousands of helpers have been cremating over 500,000 bodies a day, and we are still not halfway finished. Disease is now rampant in dozens of areas of this country. General Patterson is shipping captured supplies back from China. We believe, and the Surgeon General of the Air force stated to me a few days ago, that there are enough electronic supplies in these loads to get hundreds of hospitals operational within months. Disease and then food are our two most important factors to deal with after this darn battle, which is taking up too much time and effort by all of you valuable people. I'm ready just to pull out our troops and nuke Houston and be done with it, but the winds will blow radiation all over the East Coast and kill the few people we have left!"

This time all four military men looked at the president in awe.

"We still have nukes?" asked General Austin.

"Yes, and so did the Chinese, General Austin. General Patterson managed to capture a multi-warhead Russian M-36 nuke, I think it's called, aimed for Washington and a dozen other cities. It was ready for launch in Harbin, China. Gentlemen, many thanks to all of you, and also many thanks to your Marines, General Watson. We were maybe twenty minutes away from some Chinese officer sending this Russian missile over here. We were this close to total East Coast annihilation. You two just don't understand."

There was silence for a couple of moments as the two new men realized that it had been touch and go over here. While in Europe, they had been complaining to the president over their satellite phones about the 747s not arriving to get the military troops back home.

"I'm ready to work and to help," stated General Watson. "What do you want of me and my men?"

"Me too. I reviewed and admired General Patterson's battle plan for New York City. In Europe, we heard all about it several days after the end of the invasion," added General Austin. "The U.S. Army is ready to defend our country, Mr. President."

"Thank you, gentlemen," replied General Patterson. "Now what is the best way to destroy this army of 150,000 well-armed rebels?"

For an hour the four men planned. The weather at McConnell wasn't bad enough for the president to head back to Andrews in *Blue Moon*. With no expertise as a soldier, he wanted to return to Washington where he could be most effective aiding the civilian rebuild.

We must not let them retreat back into the city of Houston. If that happens, we would end up with months of building-to-building combat," stated General Watson.

"I agree," murmured each of the four men, all looking at a large map of Houston and its surrounding areas.

"I will have 12,000 Marines ready in the town of Spring to the north, and we have another 4,000 Marines here at McConnell ready to parachute in at the first opportunity. That will give us a good force of 16,000 Marines under my best leadership to halt their forward advance. It looks like their leaders might be anticipating capturing the state of Texas, and I believe will try to head north very soon. General Austin, I agree that if they run into my guys, plus choppers and attack gunships, they will retreat and go hide in the inner city, and we will have to go in and get them."

"What about an old-fashioned siege, like Genghis Khan did in Beijing, and starve them out by surrounding the city? For your information, next month the president will write into law that all cities north of Washington, in a line across the country, and a similar line from Dallas, Texas, except coastal cities, are to be off limits to civilians and patrolled by our soldiers as war zones, especially in the south. You men must understand that we cannot support the whole country. With only fifty-plus million people, the entire country is too large to police until our population grows and with it a need to naturally increase our living space. Cities like Houston, San Antonio, Philadelphia, and Chicago are now useless and disease-ridden, and are going to crumble and die before we breed enough people to fill them up again. By that time, we feel that they will need to be destroyed and rebuilt from scratch. That is why we looked at nuking Houston before this hurricane reminded us that it is in the wrong place due to fallout."

"A siege will take too much time, Patterson. I think that we should attack them from north and south," suggested General Austin. "Let's fortify an area around the highways they will need to use, wait for them to retreat into our strong defensive positions, and simply ambush them. They are rebels and will retreat when heavily attacked. It's like playing pinball; if we can get them to bounce backwards and forwards into different masses of soldiers, we can whittle their numbers away. General Patterson already has a large number of my men from Texas on the move, and they have a few tanks and howitzers to reinforce a southern position here on the North Sam Houston Parkway, between Interstate 45 and Highway 59," the general suggested, pointing to the map laid out in front of them. "That will stop any retreat into the inner city. I don't think a siege will work due to the time scale. It will take weeks or months, with us sitting around and waiting for them to get hungry enough to come out and attack."

The other two agreed and General Austin's and Patterson's suggestion was forgotten.

"It's a pretty open area on this piece of North Sam Houston Parkway I would like to defend," stated the army commander. "The open ground will give armor and artillery good aiming possibilities. Any area south of the Beltway begins to have buildings, and I believe not advisable to defend. I hope to have 6,000 to 8,000 men there in twenty-four hours and, we must cover and ambush on these five major north-south roads. I know of another 10,000 men and weapons I can get into this area from neighboring states within seventy-two hours. Patterson, there is a group from Alabama who fought with you in New York. They have a pretty powerful array of several tanks and the remaining howitzers you used around New York harbor in January; I believe there are 10,000 troops who are ready to move."

"Excellent. Get them moving," replied General Patterson. "Those guys were fantastic in the defense of New York, and I'll be glad to have them around."

If I cover the ten to twelve mile area of the same two major roads north of Spring and have heavy ambush positions on the highways themselves," added General Watkins, "General Austin and I should be able to surround the entire airport areas within forty-eight hours. I reckon that this storm has another twenty-four hours of momentum before the cold front picks it apart, and then those rebels will move north. I can have my current men positioned on the main routes north and, as General Austin stated, hit them and push them back to the airport to rethink their plan of attack. I bet they will then head south and bang straight into Austin's Army boys. By that time the Air Force will have better weather to pound the stinky meat off their asses."

"Plus, if Seal Team Six can extract their leaders, the Calderón brothers," added Admiral Rogers, "then their men should be leaderless for a time and factions of them will jump around inside their corral like wild horses. Then, as General Austin said, we can whittle down their numbers even more."

"And one more thing, they will not get any reinforcements corralled up like this, so their numbers should quickly reduce once the aircraft go in. Boy! Do I have a surprise for you guys!" laughed General Patterson and explained to the new men about the seventeen Chinese helicopter gunships about ready to fly into McConnell.

CHAPTER 8

The Battle Of Houston – May-June

HURRICANE NO-NAME WAS THE FIRST hurricane of the 2013 season. The formation of the initial tropical storm was a hundred miles west of Belize, and the lousy weather had missed Cuba, traveling northwards and passing westward and on the same path Mo Wang had taken northwards a month earlier in his ship.

The tropical storm had hit warmer than usual water east of Cancun and had turned in a Category One. It continued its forward movement at 12 miles an hour in a northwest direction until the winds increased to become a Category Two Hurricane, three hundred miles south of Corpus Christi.

The strong cold front coming the south began to affect the hurricane's direction, and the storm began to move from northwest to north and then northeast as it did its best to push the cold front northwards out of its way. The winds had just increased to a Category Three, winds above 111 miles an hour, when the two Orion Hurricane Hunters passed through on their first run several hours later.

With warmer than usual Gulf water for May, and the cold air sent southwards by the cold front, the 300-mile-wide hurricane with no name stalled a hundred miles off the coast of Port Arthur, Texas.

The cold front was strong. The two mighty weather patterns equaled each other for three days and stayed stationary fighting a battle one would lose.

Over time and still over warm water, the hurricane's winds slowly diminished to ninety miles an hour and the cold front, still a stable air mass, picked away at the storm's strength and warmth.

Meanwhile, weather over Houston was lousy with heavy wind and rain bands hitting the area from east to west in gusts of a hundred miles an hour. In this weather very few could stay dry. If they were dry, they stayed where they were.

* * *

Manuel was worried. He did not like having all of his men in one basket at the airport, and constantly had men go outside and check the weather. Every time they returned with the same answer: nothing had changed.

The Seals had returned to the terminal and had been ordered by Manuel's men to find a corner and wait out the storm. Manuel had eyed their gifts with thanks, and he had allowed them to stay in his terminal.

The rest of the Seal team had returned to the railway yard and located enclosed rail cars which kept them dry for the next 48 hours while the storm raged outside.

The temperature wasn't cold, it hovered just over sixty-five degrees, which was cold for southern Texas, but not cold enough to bring down vital body temperatures.

* * *

General Patterson and the other two generals couldn't do much more than monitor troop movements and fly men into Kansas, far enough away from the storm to still have sunshine and low winds.

The soldiers heading into the Houston area from Fort Bliss felt the storm's strength first; they hunkered down in their vehicles and the wind and rain increased as they drove closer at a good twenty-five miles an hour. They entered the Houston Beltway area and prepared to set up camp in buildings until the storm abated slightly.

The group from El Paso was twelve hours behind and had just entered the far-reaching bands of Hurricane No-Name.

* * *

North Carolina weather was hot and beautiful, so Preston understood the children's wishes for a swimming pool. Nobody could figure out how to actually build one, and the first trial was a simple hole in the ground dug by a back-hoe which was a dismal failure; the water just disappeared.

One of the technical sergeants remembered seeing several pallets of bags of cement and, on the second day, hitched a ride on a passing C-130 going into Seymour Johnson from Andrews to go and see if the bags were still in storage. He arrived back the next day in a C-130 with fifty bags of cement on two pallets and the soldiers and kids set about turning the hole into a shallow circular pool thirty feet across and five feet deep at the center.

There were still several bags of cement left over from installing floor slabs in the new buildings and, with a cement mixer, the kids and a couple of the female adults began the fun of becoming dirty and laying a six-inch thick cement layer from one end of the hole to the other.

Preston was amused at the antics of the builders. Every now and again a mud-throwing fight would break out as several smoothed the dirt in readiness for the cement; often it was Little Beth or Clint who started the fights.

Preston was going over his Mustang and P-38 Lightning with several Air Force technicians and mechanics flown in from Andrews. Carlos and Martie, now rested, were doing the same. Carlos was often on the phone to Mo Wang in Harbin and Lee Wang still working at *The Cube*.

It was fascinating what Mo Wang was finding in the storage areas, as he was packing up the factory for transportation.

It seemed to Preston that Mo and Carlos had put away their differences and were working together. Lee didn't have much to do but watch the satellite slowly change orbits, and he estimated three more days until the first visuals of western Texas.

Preston called two people during his visit to the farm. On his second day at home, his first call was to General Patterson asking for an update on the weather over Houston. He was told that nothing had changed and that the Hurricane Hunters had estimated forty-eight more hours before anything would change. He could stay a third day.

The second call was to Michael Roebels who was in Silicon Valley, using over 3,000 military engineers and civilian scientists to exchange new parts and spares arriving from Harbin, and installing them into the nearest hospital to connect the 300-bed facility to the now-working local Silicon Valley electrical grid. He told Preston that they expected to have the first civilian hospital fully operational, including all operating rooms and ICU units, within forty-eight hours, and then he could send out several teams to direct power and setup other hospitals. A small nuclear power station in the San Francisco area was now under power and would be at full capacity within a month.

Preston told him that it was certainly good news and reminded Martie's father that they had a nuclear power station within twenty miles of the farm. Michael Roebels replied that all the planning was already done across the country, and that they would have enough electrical parts and spares for ten small operational grids across the U.S. Preston's area was fifth in line for the revitalization of a fifty-mile-wide power grid.

Martie was feeling better and called her father every day to find how he was doing. Michael Roebels was a busy man; Mo Wang was sending in so many parts that all they could do was to offload the aircraft, categorize the parts on each pallet and send them into storage warehouses until they were needed.

He was enjoying his work and had hundreds of electrical engineers in ten teams working on designing and building new product. He had listened to his daughter, and set up plans to rebuild several hybrid cars found scattered around the streets and highways. One team was turning them into purely electric cars; they worked well, had a top speed of 40 miles an hour and a charge powerful enough for 160 miles.

A second team was using parts from China to build new vehicle recharging stations, and once the small electrical grid became live around Silicon Valley, they would start distributing several of them around the area. They needed to work on ramping up the charge rate and decreasing the charge time, and figured out that four to five hours would be needed to get a vehicle fully charged for a second 160 mile range.

Martie laughed at this idea, told her father what Preston had asked General Patterson for—the three 747s—and suggested to her father that he build the recharging stations next to motels and then upgrade all the overnight accommodations in California and go into the motel business. "We'll leave the car charger on for you!" got a good laugh from her father.

* * *

Manuel had had enough of sitting around for three solid days. Every hour meant that the Americans could attack them at any moment. Manuel Calderón didn't like having his men at the airport and finally, the next morning, May 22nd, three days before the satellite would be over the area, one of his men stated that he felt there was less power in the wind, and the rain seemed not to be penetrating the terminal building as it had done the day before.

"Get me my commanders!" he ordered men close to him. "I want vehicles ready in 30 minutes, packed and moving out. It's time to leave this lousy dammed airport and this crappy Houston weather!"

* * *

The first U.S. Army units had arrived several hours earlier and were setting up their howitzers a couple miles south of the airport.

The second group from El Paso was still a couple of hours away. Travel had been slow going, sometimes the wind so strong that drivers of the Mutts thought that their jeeps could be swept up and turned over. They had been drenched by the pelting rain for the last twenty-four hours, and all the vehicles had stopped a couple of times over underpasses to refuel and heat a quick meal.

The 12,000 Marines were ready and positioned across a ten-mile strip, on and between two major highways running north. With winds still topping 80 miles an hour, visibility was down to less than a hundred yards, and the men had dug in around the five exits leading north from the airport area. They were not that heavily armed, but had a dozen large mortars on each of the roads north as well as several machine-gun nests built behind wet and dripping sandbags, which the men had filled over the three days they had nothing to do apart from trying to keep dry. Many of the defensive positions were in second-story windows of broken houses, with open firing positions to the roads. Several positions were even a couple hundred yards away from the roads and under gas station roofs or any other overhangs, where it was drier than being directly under the pelting rain.

An AC-130 gunship, *Easy Girl,* was at 5,000 feet, fifty miles north of their position and had been circling for the last twelve hours, with a second gunship, *Pave Pronto,* flying south to take over guard duty. The men would be happy to be relieved as it had been a lousy flight; bumpy and stomach wrenching for twelve solid hours.

* * *

Charlie Meyers sat with his men in a corner of the expansive terminal and out of the way for the last three days. He was asleep when Lieutenant Paul nudged him awake and whispered that orders were being shouted out a couple of hundred feet from them at the command table.

Awake in an instant, he immediately got up and headed over to the command table where men were slowly gathering. He was smaller than Paul and would be less conspicuous.

"Luiz, get all the large troop vehicles loaded first," shouted Manuel, giving orders at a rapid rate. "Have the fifty trucks returned with our third load of food from Corpus Christi?"

"No, Señor, they are expected in about three hours," shouted Luiz.

"Luiz, I want the most recent American ration packs loaded on the drier trucks. The men can sit on top of the food and help keep it dry. We are not coming back here. I want somebody to go and tell Pedro to stay here and wait for the food trucks and then head north behind us!"

"I can do that, Señor!" shouted Charlie instinctively, now only several yards from Manuel and the growing group.

"Charlie Manéz... Montano... Mendoza, or whatever your name is, go and tell my brother Pedro to get ready to move out, but tell him he is to wait for the trucks from Corpus Christi!"

"Si, Señor!" Charlie shouted back and promptly headed for the rear door where he and the Seals had initially come into the building. The other eleven men were already heading for the same exit.

"Charlie, tell Pedro that his brother wants him and only him. Walk back towards this building and we will hide in the area and grab him," whispered Lieutenant Paul, meeting Charlie at the exit. He had heard the orders given.

"My sentiments exactly, amigo Paul, I'll go alone so that Pedro doesn't feel threatened!" Charlie replied, not halting his stride. He walked out of the building alone, the others not wanting to make their exit noticeable.

"Señor Pedro, Señor Pedro, your brother is very ill and wants you immediately," stated Charlie ten minutes later, walking up to the man who was the same height and who looked him straight in the eyes. "He wants to move out and told me to tell you to order your commanders to get ready. You must wait for the food trucks arriving in three hours before you leave the airport. Pedro, he is not well, puking everywhere, and I think you had better get the orders directly from him yourself!"

"Diego! Costa! Miguel! Antonio! Jorge! Get your men up and ready. We are moving out in three hours. Philippe! Come with me, we are wanted by Manuel!" Without even noticing or thanking the messenger, he picked up an AK-47 and headed for the door Charlie had just walked through into the rear terminal. A massive bear of a man nearly seven feet tall followed Pedro with a machine gun and several belts of ammo slung over his shoulder.

"The bigger they are, the harder they fall," Charlie thought to himself, smiling at the size of the man. He also noticed that the weapon was loaded, cocked and ready for use. *"Pedro is still limping and is walking slowly, his injuries must be hurting,"* Charlie noticed, as he followed the two men who had completely ignored him. *"Being ignored is a beautiful thing!"*

The weather was still pretty bad; the wind was howling and the rain drenching. Charlie put his head down, wrapped his waterproof poncho around himself and followed the two men out the door.

It was an 800-yard walk back to the rear of the northern terminals where he knew there would be guards and men running around getting personnel and machinery ready to move. He walked a few steps behind the big man and watched for movement coming out of the visibility curtain a hundred feet in front.

Charlie noticed three figures merge out of the drenching rain as they walked forward. They were standing still in their path, and one seemed to be gesturing to the other two, turning and pointing in different directions.

Pedro and Philippe headed off at a tangent to bypass the men. The one who was gesturing saw the three men approaching and shouted at them in an insulting way to walk over to him. Who were they?

"And who are you to order me around, amigo?" asked Pedro nastily, walking up to the bad-mannered man who, Charlie noticed, was Lieutenant Paul.

"Your worst nightmare, Pedro Calderón," laughed Lieutenant Paul as he swung the Glock Seal-Issue 21 and silencer he was hiding under his poncho and connected Pedro's head with its butt, hard. The surprised man dropped and didn't see two long, sharp and deadly knife blades enter the slow-moving Philippe, one in the neck and one underneath his ribcage, as the two men next to Paul did their job.

Paul shouted and three more men ran out of the visibility curtain and grabbed hold of the bodies before they hit the ground. Charlie had Philippe's trigger finger in his strong hand, and it had snapped at the same time the knives had gone in.

The bigger man was heavy and it took all three of the men to drag his body, still upright, off into the shadows of a building.

The unconscious Pedro was easier, and three more men ran out to take him away. Paul and Charlie were left standing next to a pool of blood which the rain was diluting by the second. They decided that peeing into the puddle would help color the blood as two men they didn't recognize ran up from the direction of Pedro's terminal.

"You have to piss everywhere, you dogs?" admonished the front man running up from the northern terminal. "Where is Pedro? We have heard from the trucks. They are still five hours away, the weather is bad, worse than yesterday on the highway, and the drivers thought they saw an American jeep on the road going the other way. We need to give him the new information immed—" Three rounds from Charlie's silenced Glock hit the man, still mouthing his next word, right between the eyes at point-blank range. The sound of the shots was as dull as a twig snapping. Paul whistled for backup as Charlie terminated the second man; three light taps with his trigger finger and four more men ran up and dragged the bodies away before more blood had to be diluted with pee.

"Charlie, you go back inside and tell Manuel that Pedro is in the toilet. He is sick or something and he should come. Maybe we could be lucky again."

"I did that old trick to get Pedro. Twice in one day is a little too much to ask," smiled Charlie Meyers. "But what the hell; it could be my lucky day!"

"I'll get four men to take Señor Pedro to our team outside the wire, and the rest can hide these bodies somewhere safe. The men can tell Clarke that they could see some action pretty soon. I'll wait behind the terminal for your exit.

"Señor Manuel, Señor Manuel! Señor Pedro is puking outside the last terminal," stated Charlie "His man, Philippe, says that he has a high temperature and needs a doctor!" Charlie was working on his best Oscar-winning performance to date when he reached the table. While he was shouting at Manuel, he even pushed several men who were around the map out of the way to get his message of urgency across. One happened to be Alberto, who slapped the bad-mannered "Panamanian" across the head hard for his bad attitude as he stood next to him.

"Mierda! Pedro is always slowing me down. Alberto, I'm heading out right now. Go and see what is wrong with Pedro, then get your men on the move. Wrap him up in blankets and tell Diego and Costa to take over his command. Tell them to wait for the trucks. Also tell them that we will all meet in Huntsville, about fifty miles north of here. We will spend the night there."

Alberto slapped three men on the heads, like he had done to Charlie, turned and they followed him to the rear entrance. "He had better be very sick, Charlie Panamanian, or you are going to feel sicker than he is!" he stated to Charlie angrily, as Charlie got into step next to him and was immediately pushed out of the way by Alberto's three men behind him. They reached the exit door, pushed it open for Alberto to walk through, and Charlie slipped out behind them.

He still had seven .45 caliber rounds in his Glock. Leaning forward and pulling the poncho over his body, he grabbed the Glock in his belt and pulled it out in his left hand to wet the silencer in the rain while grabbing his Bowie-style knife hilt, his favorite weapon of choice, in his right hand. He couldn't take all four men silently, but he knew there would be help out there. He also reminded himself that Alberto needed to be taken alive, so he would grab for Alberto first.

The weather had cleared slightly and the visibility was a little better. There was still a curtain of cloud and rain around the group as they passed outside the area of moving vehicles and men running everywhere. They reached halfway when Charlie saw several men coming towards them from the terminal in front of where Pedro was supposed to be. He could not recognize the men, but Alberto did and began giving orders.

"Oscar! Get the food packed underneath the men on the

trucks. Try and keep it as dry as possible. Jesús! I want the machine gunners in front in all the jeeps and as many standing through the openings in the roofs as possible. I want mortar teams ready to jump out as soon as we hear gunfire. Get the men ready and loaded. We are leaving in fifty-five minutes. I'll be back shortly. I need to go and see Pedro. Now, move!"

The group continued towards the last terminal as the weather let up even more and they could just about see the terminal they were heading towards, three hundred feet away. Charlie noticed three men peeing in a line on the outer wall of the terminal, close to where the northern exit door was. One glanced over his shoulder and saw the group heading for the door, finished his mission, zipped up his pants, and moved his poncho into a normal position. The three men then headed over to the arriving group looking like actors in a spaghetti western.

Charlie, still at the back raised his left arm into the air and pointed his Glock at Alberto so the other three knew who to keep alive. There was nobody else about, and this area of the airport was quiet.

The distance closed and one of the men shouted at the approaching group of men.

"Where's Pedro?" shouted Alberto, still needing to shout as loud as he could above the wind. One of the men pointed to the rear of the terminal/warehouse building where there were boxes and broken cases everywhere.

The group was now only twenty yards from the building as the rain began to drop in earnest again and a wind gust pulled heavily at Charlie's poncho.

"Why is he outside?" questioned Alberto angrily as he felt the large man next to him miss a step and lean against him. Charlie's blade had entered the back of his neck with extreme force and severed everything in there. Charlie pulled the knife through and back as Alberto turned, his mouth opening to shout something. His hand with the knife in it was still moving with momentum as

Charlie expertly flipped his hand over and smashed the heavy, blunt end of the knife across the side of Alberto's head, several times harder than Alberto had done to him minutes earlier.

Blood spurted everywhere from the first man, and the other two were already falling, their heads blown apart at the same time from several silenced rounds fired by the three men walking towards them. The shots were so close to Charlie that he felt the air vibrate and thump as the slugs hit bone on the men's foreheads and went straight through, missing him by less than two feet.

"Shit!" shouted Charlie as he kept the unconscious Alberto from hitting the ground. "Get them hidden fast. Anybody could arrive at any minute. Get them over your shoulders and run. I'll carry this guy!"

The three men picked up the bleeding bodies and ran for a smaller building which looked like it housed aircraft fuel tanker-trucks. Three more men ran out to help as they reached the door.

Charlie, running last, followed the rest towards the open door in the smaller building. He suddenly felt the hair on his back stiffen and saw a shape move in his peripheral vision. He threw the unconscious Alberto into hands through the open door, shouted to catch the body and that he needed back-up ASAP. He violently threw off his bloody poncho, turned as the door closed behind him and headed back the way he had run. It was raining hard and now he was getting wet; visibility had dropped somewhat but he could see what had caught his eye.

The wind was making a screaming noise again. Charlie felt to make sure his Glock was in his waistband, in position, and the rain-cleansed knife in his hand was pointing downwards. He looked forward to see a troop transporter coming towards him behind the warehouse they had just left. He also noticed that the blood hadn't diluted itself enough yet and would be easily visible.

Charlie waved at the truck which was coming straight

towards him. It was still fifty feet away when he pointed to the blood pool growing several yards in front of the approaching truck and put his hand in front of his mouth to signal eating food.

The truck carried on towards him, and he hoped that some of his men had heard his call for back-up.

"What is all this blood, amigo?" stated a passenger in the cab.

"I shot a large deer, it was standing right here and we are cutting it up in that building!" he shouted, pointing to where he had just thrown the body. "We want to skin it and cut it before we leave! Do you want some meat?" Charlie asked, noticing that he was totally alone. The men hadn't heard his request.

"Si!" replied the man. Charlie hopped onto the step as the truck continued towards the building he had just walked away from.

"How many men in the back?" Charlie asked the man, taking out his Glock and keeping it hidden behind the outside door panel. "We don't want to give away too much meat!"

"A dozen. We are going to get the rest of our men in the other terminal. We don't have to tell the other men about the meat, amigo," the man smiled while replying.

"That's good," replied Charlie as the driver stopped the truck, put on the park brake and both men caught a single bullet each from Charlie's Glock through the head. The silencer did its job; nobody would have heard the shots in the rear of the truck.

Charlie looked around and saw one of his men looking at him through the slit in the door waiting for orders. Charlie pointed to his Glock, showed two fingers for two men and then held up the four fingers of his free hand twice and pointed to the rear of the truck.

Immediately two men rushed out and headed for the rear of the truck on the driver's side.

Charlie jumped off the step and did the same. They met at the rear where all three men jumped up, held onto the closed rear gate, and simultaneously took aim and fired a dozen rounds into the rear with their silenced Glocks before Charlie ran out of ammo.

It sounded like somebody walking through a forest of twigs as the rebels inside the bed of the dark truck saw the movement at the rear and noticed three ugly men calmly and gracefully shooting them. There were a couple of screams as bullets didn't kill, but they were quickly followed up by a second shot which did.

Within seconds there was silence and Charlie told the men to go and inspect to make sure everyone was dead. "I will turn the truck around and we can offload the cargo," he shouted to the men. Already others had cleared the front of the cab. Charlie jumped in, felt warm blood soak through his trousers as he sat in it, and proceeded to turn the truck around.

One by one they dragged the bodies in. The death toll inside the building was growing rapidly and once the truck was clear, a tarp was placed over the dead pile.

"The front door is locked. These tankers don't work but we can make sure nobody gets in here for a while," shouted one of his men.

"Our work here at Bush Intercontinental Airport is done, guys, for round one. The first army is leaving and we should ride with our new Calderón buddy here, in the truck to visit our friends. I'm sure our guys have left the airport area after seeing increasing troop movements. I know that the radio will still be hidden under the bridge, so let's go and join the battle."

Calmly, they locked down the building making sure it would need heavy tools to get in, then started the truck with the unconscious Alberto in the company of six smiling Seals in the rear, and headed towards the northern area of the airport they had come in on. They joined the tail of a mass movement of vehicles heading in the same direction from underneath the northern terminals and stopped just after the bridge where the other Seals had hidden six hours earlier.

Two men retrieved the hidden radio, and they drove off to catch up with the front army.

"Charlie Six to anybody out there," called Mike.

"Mike Three here, Charlie Six," came a clear response.

"Hi, Mike Three, we are leaving the airport fence, and we are behind their forward army coming your way. It looks like they are heading northwest. We have extraction number two aboard and extraction number three is a few miles ahead of us. Three-quarters of their men are still in the airport and ready for an air show. Over."

"Roger that. We have a buddy, Pave Pronto, *incoming and two of her sisters about ten minutes behind her. We have the forward enemy unit visual and will start court proceedings in about five minutes. I recommend you head on foot towards the railway yard. Paul Six is already on his way in and Mike One, who is listening in, will meet and greet you. I hope you can return to the airport once the air show is over. Hopefully, Extraction Three will rejoin you there soon."*

"Roger that. Say hi to them from us. Send them back and we'll work out a new plan. It will take us about three hours to get our cargo delivered and then return to the outer airport perimeter fence. We will leave our limo-ride close by, so don't blow it up. Out!" he ended.

"I hope they don't find our body pile before we get back," suggested Charlie to the driver as they sped through the gaping hole in the fence where hundreds of vehicles had passed through the holes they had cut a few days earlier.

* * *

At the same time, *Blue Moon* was landing at McConnell. The weather was wet and rainy and the temperature cold enough to wear a jacket, as the North Carolina crowd deplaned and got ready for flying. Preston, Carlos, Martie, and an Air Force pilot had landed an hour earlier, flying in the Mustangs and the P-8 Lightning.

"They got two of the brothers, Carlos," stated General Patterson excitedly as the earlier pilots, now fed and ready for battle, walked into the control tower where the general had made his center of operations.

"Excellent! I'll tell my Uncle Philippe. He will certainly want to get them back to Bogotá for trial. There are many political implications getting them back there. I'm sure you and the president will understand," replied Carlos pulling out his satellite phone.

"I'm sure the president will agree once I put it to him," replied General Patterson. "We have a Jolly Green Giant going in to collect and resupply. Also, Preston, Buck's Huey is being retired as Air Force One as of today. You had better tell him. We have the president's old VH-3A Sea King, the one on display at the Nixon Library, now operational and it will be Marine One again until further notice. Buck is currently at Edwards getting ready to deliver your gunships to Colombia tomorrow. I asked him to go over and hold the delivery until we know we don't need them here. Only so many aircraft can blast one airport to pieces, and the first flight of Chinese helicopters, the ones we saved from Harbin, are arriving in an hour."

"We have more U.S. helicopters operational?" asked Preston.

"Yes, we are at desperate measures. We have pulled all the C-130s away from food distribution and have had every technician in all the forces working 24/7 to get as many choppers in the air as possible. The Coast Guard has three of their older Sea Kings in the air, the Navy has managed another dozen, mostly their SH-3Gs, the Air Force has seven more 70s-era Jolly Green Giants airborne, and the Marines have given us our biggest fleet yet: twenty-two of their Sea Stallions. We currently have 200 helicopters and the same amount of civilian fixed-wing aircraft helping Mike Mallory with his food program and a dozen newly revamped Sikorskys flying in for body-cleaning operations. They will be heading into the Interstate-10 area later today."

"What about the jets going in to Houston?" asked Martie.

"Weather is still too bad for flight operations for the faster jets for at least another hour, but you guys are heading out in thirty minutes with four air-to-ground rockets and two MK-77 napalm bombs per P-51. Your bomb weight is 552 pounds each and they are the smaller-sized MK-77 napalms. You will have four rockets per aircraft, two under each wing. We found a supply of these old World War II "Holy Moses" rockets. These High Velocity Aircraft unguided models are pretty old, but were used up to 1955. We have enough for two attacks and they are being fitted to your aircraft as we speak. Your P-38 Lightning, Preston, will have two larger 1,000-pound HE bombs and eight of these rockets underneath her wings. We will use up this old stuff until either they surrender, or they are gone. Our bomb loads are light enough for quick maneuvering. We already have three gunships on their way in, and *Blue Moon* will head in within five minutes.

"You guys are faster, so catch up to protect *Blue Moon,* and go in once *Blue Moon* and the other three gunships are done. Your mission is to open the terminal roofs or roadways, depending on where the rebels are, with your rockets and then drop in the napalm. Once done, you leave only after the gunships are safely on their way home. Of course you are free to use your gun ammo on anything moving, but there is a M35 troop transport the Seals are calling their limo, so if you see one vehicle by itself, leave it alone. The Seals wouldn't appreciate it and they get real mean when they are angry!" General Patterson smiled. "Also return to Dyess after this mission and Dyess will get our F-4s and F-5s back into a closer range once again."

"And the Super Tweets, General?" asked Martie.

"Martie, the Tweets are going in two hours after you guys return this afternoon. We will first have the gunships return and then you guys will be refueled and re-armed, and you will be air support for them on the next attack. We have a busy day and we had better get down to the briefing room."

The weather was letting up. The Orion Hurricane Hunters had reported to the men on the ground that Hurricane No-Name was no more; she had decreased down to a tropical storm, winds less than seventy miles an hour, was being pushed eastwards, and the storm center was 50 miles out and directly south of the Texas-Louisiana border. General Patterson gave orders for all aircraft not yet on flight operations to get airborne.

Lieutenant Paul reached the railway yard an hour later and twenty minutes after the McConnell briefing started. He handed his prize over to the Marines. The Jolly Green Giant was still an hour out, and so was Pedro. He had begun to regain consciousness halfway to Spring, but had been quickly given a sleeping pill: a blow to the head to put him back to sleep.

Lieutenant Meyers arrived an hour later. Now awake, bound and gagged, Pedro's bloodshot eyes showed shock as his brother's still unconscious body was placed next to him and was also bound and gagged.

Visibility was still bad in Spring, Texas, several miles north of downtown Houston, where the helicopter was been guided in by radio to an open landing zone between several railway cars. The rain was still heavy when the squalls hit and she came directly from the north and then turned eastwards to land into the wind.

Large cases of food and munitions supplies were hauled out, the two captives thrown in, had M-16s pointed at them by six men inside the large helicopter, and within two minutes, the Jolly Green Giant brushed over railcars to the east as her rotors bit into the wind and lifted her slowly up and away. She stayed low to compensate for any unnecessary noise.

* * *

The large Marine force covering the wide twelve-lane I-45 highway north of the airport could now see the enemy army several hundred yards to their south. The whole army had stopped as if it was a starting line for a vehicle race, and the Marines were wondering what was going on.

* * *

"Where is Alberto?" screamed Manuel into his radio. He had stopped the northward direction of every one of 25,000 men to ask where his brother was. Unbeknown to him, Alberto was being placed into a helicopter a mile south and four miles east of his position. A quarter of his men had traveled up the second highway, the Hardy Toll Road and had joined his group as they merged onto Interstate-45. The weather was bad, and the helicopter had gone in low and well out of hearing range, additionally obscured by the ground wind and rain.

This bottleneck had slowed down his forward movement, even though he had four roads stretching north—two four-lane highways and two two-lane side roads. This had happened every work day the previous year, when this area of highway was jammed with homeward-bound rush hour traffic traveling north out of the city.

They traveled slowly through desolate highway searching for any signs of life. Even the dogs had disappeared and this worried Manuel. He passed by a large empty and fire-destroyed mall on his left. "The Woodlands Mall" was noted on his American-made map and he decided to stop and find out where Alberto's and Pedro's men were. The weather was clearing and he wanted them out of the airport before an air attack could take place. He didn't know what was going on around him, but he knew never to stay in one place too long.

"Carlo, get me Pedro on the radio," he shouted into the mike, frustrated that Alberto's men did not know where his brother was.

"He disappeared to talk to you four hours ago, Señor. He never returned. We are waiting for him at the airport," answered Carlo, one of Pedro's commanders.

"Victor, where is your commander, my brother?" Manuel demanded asking Alberto's commander.

"Maybe he is with Pedro somewhere in the terminals. We have had men looking for him for hours in and around the empty terminals you stayed in, Señ... Señor!"

"I will wait for ten minutes and you radio me back when you find them. Tell them, Victor, Carlo, that I'm crazy mad!" shouted Manuel over the mike and handed it back to his operator sitting behind him in the lead jeep. "Mierda, Mierda!" he shouted. It wasn't like his brothers to act like this. He thought he heard a thudding of a helicopter blade to his east for a couple of seconds, but the wind gust fell, and so did the faint noise with it.

* * *

"What do you think is happening?" asked Lieutenant Colonel Mathews to his commander, Colonel Garrote. They were both over a mile north of the Mall on the highest roof of St. Luke's Woodland Hospital on Needham Road or Highway 242. Their men were all north of Needham Road and looking at the advancing army through binoculars.

"Hell, they could be having a bathroom break for all I know. I wanted them at least another 800 yards closer to the intersection before we let out the rabbit," replied Colonel Garrote. The "rabbit" was four jeeps, Marine Mutts with a forward machine gun and a rocket launcher standing up rear. They were to drive south on command to the center of the intersection from the north to become visual to the advancing rebels. The idea was to make them look like a U.S. army patrol that suddenly spots the advancing army from the intersection below the two colonels. As would be expected, when soldiers see an enemy patrol, the leader certainly would want to give chase and silence the enemy patrol before they radioed information to their headquarters.

Both men had estimated that this major thoroughfare, I-45, would be the one used to head north, if north was the direction the rebels wanted to go. The colonels had 5,000 men, mortars, heavy machine guns and two howitzers within range of this intersection. Also, Highway 242 was closed off by several more mortar and machine gun locations 200 yards off each side of the intersection in case the rebels decided to change direction.

They knew 5,000 wasn't much against the 30,000 to 50,000 rebels they estimated to be coming their way, but, Marines versus rebels, then add ambush and air support to the mix, and the odds should be evened a bit. There were three AC-130s ready and circling a mile or two north at 8,000 feet for air support. They hadn't seen the end of the vanguard army; their position and weather wasn't high or clear enough to see much further than a mile past the mall.

"Mike Two, Alpha, Bravo or Charlie, this is Mike Three; we have rebel movements one mile to our south. Have you seen any movement on your 1314 road? Over."

"Mike Two Alpha here, Negative Mike Three."

Colonel Garrote checked the command points of the other three roads heading north and got the same answer.

"Mike Two Bravo, leave Alpha and Charlie and head towards my direction. I count large numbers of enemy, and we might need some backup. All Mike teams, I need immediate warning of any enemy movement. All Mike teams and all aircraft, we will have "friendlies" mobile from east to west on Highway 242. Over." Several radios responded, acknowledging the information.

Colonel Garrote had just ordered a major and a thousand men to head westwards towards him along Needham Road.

"That will give the men in the western barricade a little backup if they need it," he stated to Colonel Mathews.

"Mike One here, extractions one and two are out of here. We have picked up their channel frequency and we are monitoring it. Over," stated Colonel Clarke at the railway depot, and who was fluent in Spanish.

"Mike Three to Mike One, they have halted their progress north. Any ideas? Over."

"Roger that, Mike Three. I think Extraction Three is looking for his brothers. We overheard him call a halt and give his brothers ten minutes to surface. Hold on; he is shouting verbal abuse to others we believe are still at the airport. I think he is getting ready to move out. Charlie Six and Paul Six will be back at Bush in 30 minutes. Over."

"Two, zero minutes!" interrupted Charlie Six heading back. *"We are ahead of schedule."*

"Easy Girl *here, Charlie and Paul, estimate aircraft attack on airport terminals beginning in two to five minutes,"* added the radio operator in Easy Girl, two miles north. *"We are waiting for a few friends. Mike Three, do you want us to take out your intersection at the same time? Over."*

"Only when I ask for assistance, *Easy Girl*; I think you could give us a hand on your way out of here. We want first blood. Over," smiled Colonel Garrote into his headset.

* * *

"Alberto, Pedro!" Manuel shouted into his radio. "I'm moving out. Get your armies on the road now. I mean now! Army Two and Army Three, get your men moving, forget my brothers. The weather is clearing fast, and I want your men out of the airfield in 30 minutes. Comprehend?" He got a dozen acknowledgments and he waved his hand to start engines. "Get this jeep moving!" he ordered his driver angrily.

* * *

Information moved fast from Colonel Clarke listening in to all the patiently waiting U.S. troops. Colonel Garrote ordered the four jeeps forward; it would take his vehicles 20 seconds to reach the intersection, at least 800 yards in front of the approaching rebels.

"Easy Girl *here, our two girlfriends have arrived;* Blue Moon *is five minutes behind and four fixed-wing bad boys five minutes behind her. We are starting our approach into Bush. We are coming in five minutes early to catch the exit rush, and will be approaching from the east across the northern perimeter of the airfield.*"

"Charlie Six, *Roger that. Leave our lone M35 alone. It's a block north of the northern perimeter fence. We'll be there in fifteen. Out.*"

* * *

Manuel Calderón didn't know that the enemy now knew what he was doing. He was too angry to care, and he desperately wanted to shoot something! He was going to beat the living daylights out of his brothers when he saw them again, and he really wanted to shoot something! He grabbed for his M16 and looked towards the intersection.

To his utter amazement, he saw four jeeps coming towards him three-quarters of a mile away and he immediately knew they were Americans. As the shapes rose up the intersection's slight incline and above the line of asphalt stretching north he saw a rear rocket launcher and a machine gunner. The light contrast was now perfect to see American camouflage, and he shouted into his radio that there was enemy in front and to charge forward as fast as possible. "Kill! Kill the gringos in front!" he shouted to the three radios of his forward vehicles on both sides of the wide highway, and the "dogs" leapt forward after the "rabbit"."

* * *

The Americans saw and heard the rev of vehicles on the highway to their south and, as planned, stopped. They sat there and waited for nearly 30 seconds before Colonel Garotte gave the order to fire.

"Mutts on Highway only, remember to leave the front jeeps alone. Open fire with everything you have, now!"

Four machine guns began their clattering and four rockets headed out of the launchers seconds later. The Mutts still looked down at the surging army now less than a quarter of a mile in front of them, and they easily fired into vehicles three to four rows behind the front jeeps which were gaining ground and speeding forward faster than the troop transporters. Several civilian trucks of all types were behind the jeeps and three took direct hits as the rockets slammed into them. A troop transporter on Manuel's side and a hundred yards behind him took a direct hit, which made him even angrier upon hearing the explosion, and he slapped his driver over the head to get his chariot moving faster.

It took the launchers thirty seconds to reload and fire off four more rockets. The machine guns had already emptied a case each of 7.62 rounds and were reloading. They hit several more vehicles, one of which exploded causing a second one to stop, cause a small pileup and then explode as well. One went up in smoke. The rockets this time went into four troop transporters three hundred yards behind Manuel's position, two trucks on each side of the highway, which made the headlong frontal push slow down slightly.

Manuel was oblivious to what was happening behind him as he saw the jeeps, now 200 yards in front of him begin taking fire themselves and head back the way they had come. With his momentum he would get close behind them.

It was interesting to watch the proceedings from the top of the hospital as Colonel Garrote gave orders for several mortars placed on roofs around the area to begin to bomb the highway. The lead rebel vehicles, a couple of dozen of them, were too close now for the mortars, and the bombs popped out of the tubes to drop into the positions where the later vehicles had to slow down to get around the burning debris.

"Manuel! Manuel! We are being hit by mortars, It is an ambush!" shouted somebody over his radio, and he looked behind for the first time and saw explosions riddling his vehicles half a mile behind his position.

"Retreat! Retreat! Take cover! Use the exit ramps. Turn down the exit ramps, get underneath the intersection. There are Americans all around us!" he shouted over his radio as his jeep continued. Several vehicles immediately took the exit ramps off the highway. There were already rebel vehicles on these side roads and as usual, exiting traffic had to slow down. He and several men continued after the jeeps, and he was away from the ambush. He was gaining on the American jeeps in front of him and began firing at the enemy now only a hundred yards in front of him.

* * *

As if in a ballet routine, the four jeeps screamed to a stop and spun around to face the oncoming rush. They were now abreast of the ramps north of the intersection, and a couple of armored vehicles drove out of the ramps to join the jeeps. All at once they began firing at the oncoming rebels.

* * *

"Turn, turn around! Get out of here, It's another ambush!" screamed Manuel over the radio as his vehicles now a dozen on both sides of the highway screeched into turns, the drivers spinning the wheels as hard as they could. One vehicle behind literally toppled over and began somersaulting down the highway missing Manuel's skidding jeep by inches. He fired at the enemy and emptied his banana magazine of thirty rounds, pulled it out and fitted the second magazine strapped to the empty one and began firing; his driver slammed the jeep into first and nearly threw his passengers out, as he smoked the tires and turned to retreat. Manuel and the radio man held on for dear life as the panicked driver did his best to push the accelerator through the steel floor.

They reached the top of the intersection and Manuel ordered his men to take side roads and head west, directly west. His driver screeched the brakes again as he approached the southern exit ramp and sped around the corner and down the ramp northwards. There were several men in front. It looked like they had fallen, or had jumped out of the rear of a truck and were right in the way of the fast moving jeep. The driver didn't flinch as he applied full brakes and turned the jeep left and scythed through the half dozen men, throwing bodies and guns in all directions. He expertly got the jeep facing west; there was a break in the line of turning vehicles, and he sped through a hole and down a side street.

Many of the men in the forward vehicles had done this often in Colombia to escape Colombian forces, and managed to escape the ambushes. Like Manuel's driver, they exited the intersection and headed onto side roads for a block and then were forced southwards by enemy fire. Some headed a block too far and straight into a Marine barricade which made them quickly turn and head through alleyways and even broken doors of buildings. The enemy vehicles all ended up moving in a southward direction.

* * *

It was the colonel's plan to leave three blocks of escape routes open for the enemy to lure them into believing they were escaping, right into the hands of the U.S. Army five miles south.

"Keep firing until all moving vehicles are out of the kill zones," Colonel Garrote ordered as he heard *Easy Girl* stating that she was going in.

The killing zones now stretched a mile south of the intersection; the mortars with him on top of the hospital had the furthest sight to the south, and kept firing. Mortars are reasonably quiet weapons and his hearing was still in one piece. Colonel Garrote hated to be near loud guns like artillery, which deafened people around them and halted the delivery of orders. His three mortars were fifty feet away from him and aiming southwards along the highway.

The highway south of the intersection had hundreds of burning vehicles and thousands of men running south on foot. There were fires for over a mile, and he looked down both sides of 242 to see the same thing. Slowly the rebel force, five times larger than the total number of his troops, were being routed southward, thousands already dead, and the living were heading into the arms of an even more powerful force to the south.

* * *

"Easy Girl *here, we are beginning our attack,*" Preston heard over his radio as he saw plumes of smoke rising into the air from a highway twenty miles in front of him, Carlos, Martie and Colonel Wright, the P-38 pilot. "Pave Pronto *and* Pave Spectre, *keep 300 yards distance between aircraft and stay above 500 feet. I want howitzer fire into the rear terminal buildings and cannon fire into visual enemy rebels leaving the airport. There is a long line of vehicles heading out through the northwestern corner, I want those taken out. Do not fire on any lone trucks! I repeat do not fire on any single vehicles, could be friendlies. We will do two passes and then let in* Blue Moon *and, after her, the fixed-wing guys. Boys, the fixed-wing have heat and it will burn. Here we go. Good hunting.*"

Preston was commander of his flight of four aircraft and knew what to do. They had all studied a map of the airport during their briefing and knew which buildings to hit. So did *Blue Moon* and, even Charlie Six had asked her nicely to destroy a single fuel depot building, a small refueling building he had stated was already full of dead bodies.

Seconds later he heard more orders from *Easy Girl's* weapons operator. She only carried three powerful 20-mm cannons and *Easy Girl* worked her way down the two northern terminals before causing havoc to the army trying to get out of the airport.

"OK, guys, Pronto *and* Spectre, *a change of pattern on second run*," heard Preston as his wing lost altitude and was getting nearer to the battle below. He could see smoke rising from the airport as well now. "Pronto *and* Spectre, *head north behind me. There is a mass of vehicles heading southwards on the highway south of the airport. It's called JFK Boulevard I believe. The enemy vehicles already extend all the way down to the Sam Houston Parkway and there are hundreds of trucks already on the Parkway itself heading west.* Blue Moon, *once you are done with your first run follow us; we are heading south. Over.*"

"*Roger that,*" Preston heard *Blue Moon's* pilot.

Preston gave orders for his wing to turn east and head out for a minute or two and then slowly turn west for their first bombing run. That would give *Blue Moon* time to do her thing and get out of their way. He was close enough now to see the first three gunships turning north just above the ground. He was still at 5,000 feet and high above the carnage being dealt out below. He saw *Blue Moon* a mile west of the airport. It was now her turn.

There was clear visibility, the storm had completely disappeared and sunlight was covering Bush Intercontinental Airport, or what remained of it. The long northern terminal had several fires glowing through holes in the roof and there wasn't much ground movement.

"All aircraft! Foxtrot Fours ten minutes out, Foxtrot Fives five minutes behind us and Tweets behind them. Suggestions and fresh information on best possible views for crowd control? Over." Preston heard this as he was going in, so did the three aircraft behind him.

"Highway running east to west a couple miles south of airport is your best bet for a good show, Foxtrot Four," replied the commander of *Easy Girl*. He was in charge of the battle below. *"I believe the airport is now empty of enemy, and all munitions should now be directed towards open highways south of the airport. Remember, we have friendlies in all areas so don't fire outside a three-mile area around the airport. Fixed Wing aircraft, I suggest you follow us; sweep left at the western edge of the terminal, head southeast, you will see a highway north of the main beltway; turn west over that highway and set up your runs. A mass of enemy has just turned down that road. Blue Moon, head west until you reach I-45. There are a large number of enemy heading southwards; that's now your area. Foxtrot Fours, you have the east/west beltway which is full of targets. All aircraft including Foxtrot Fives, after your first runs, hold off until the air is clear for a second*

attack. Tweets, stay twenty miles north and wait for further instructions."

The air got busy as Preston and the three aircraft followed him in. "Martie, Carlos, rockets only this pass. P-38 you are a go to drop hot sauce. All aircraft up to 1,500 feet and stagger your height a couple of hundred feet higher than the aircraft in front of you and remember our briefing; two miles distance between aircraft. I don't want you to blow each other out of the sky."

It wasn't necessary to fire into the terminals as he sped past north of them at 800 feet and 350 miles an hour. He swept his aircraft left and climbed rapidly as he reached the end of the northern terminals and pulled her around hard to begin a "Z" movement which would bring him into line to turn westwards again over their new target. Preston loved this type of flying and his P-51 was like a wild Mustang at this speed and altitude.

He saw the western highway branch off from the southern road and he prepared his rockets for release. "Arming now!" Preston stated as he leveled out above the highway at 1,500 feet, saw a mass of trucks and people running in the same direction, pushed his joystick forward, and went in to fire all four of his rockets. He fired the first two at 900 feet, and counted two seconds before he fired the second set at 700 feet, before heading out of the area. As he flew over I-45 he noticed *Blue Moon* several hundred yards south of him and a few hundred feet below his altitude.

Preston suddenly saw the smoke trail of a rocket or missile rise quickly up from the ground to meet her, and take out her outer port engine. The engine literally blew up in the air and part of her outer right wing sailed down into the masses of people on the highway.

"I'm hit! I'm hit!" shouted *Blue Moon's* pilot.

"Swing right and lazy, turn around to head over to the airport. You can make it with your height. Carlos, take over!" ordered Preston. "*Blue Moon*, I'll cover you."

"All aircraft stay away from the western area of the airport," shouted *Easy Girl's* commander over the radio.

Preston turned south in a 180 degree turn and curved around to follow the damaged aircraft now heading north directly in front of him. He knew that he still had a minute or so before the F-4s would arrive and he rose up to 2,000 feet to stay out of her way. He saw *Blue Moon* below him slowly curve to the east. He also saw Martie and Carlos flying in with explosions all the way down the mile and a half of highway they had just attacked. Suddenly the highway behind them lit up as a line of napalm followed the P-38 and spread in a rapid forward movement. He couldn't believe his eyes as he saw a second rocket plume rise out from exactly where he had seen the first one come from, and his P-38, which had just dropped its two bombs, disappeared in a massive explosion.

Preston immediately felt numbness go through him as he forced his attention back to the crippled AC-130.

It seemed that the rest of her wing was staying in one piece. Her pilot was very experienced and had brought her around 270 degrees gently and was lining her up with the most northern runway of the airport.

The damaged aircraft was still a mile or so out when Preston closed in to the side of the aircraft and saw her wheels go down. Fire was beginning to envelope the rest of the wing.

"You need to use your inner-port engine extinguisher, Dave," stated Preston concentrating on the aircraft getting closer and closer.

"We are ready to collect you guys at the western end of the runway. Extraction chopper incoming!" stated somebody over the radio, but Preston was busy willing *Blue Moon* on.

She had a hundred yards to go when he saw her second engine catch fire and the flames spread to the fuselage.

"Dave, open your rear door, your whole aircraft is nearly on fire. You are going to need to get out quickly," stated Preston, and he saw the rear door begin to open.

As the pilot put the aircraft down hard on the runway, pieces of the undercarriage flew out in all directions. The door continued to open as the aircraft, now a mass of flames on one side scraped nose-down down the tarmac and began to veer off the runway and onto the grass verge. Preston noticed a single troop transporter rushing down the runway from the east and towards *Blue Moon*.

She slowed her scraping as she hit the dirt and grass on the northern side of the runway and shapes began rolling out of the aircraft's rear.

The flaming aircraft finally came to a sliding halt and several more shapes scrambled out of the rear. He also noticed a dozen vehicles detaching themselves from the closest terminal, less than a mile away; he pulled up and seconds later and on full power, he dropped his aircraft into a tight left turn.

Moments later *Blue Moon* erupted into a massive fireball, and he felt his aircraft jump as the shock wave hit him hard. He hoped that the crew got far enough away.

Due to his hundreds of hours flying low to the ground in his crop sprayer aircraft, Preston was used to low-level flight, and he screamed down a couple of hundred yards north of the airfield and went in fast and steep aiming for the first one of several vehicles directly in front of him. He released his two 500-pound napalm bombs at the first vehicle, an old American Dodge Ram. It was a horrible green color he noticed as he pulled back hard on the stick, felt the seat he was sitting on want to crush him from below and he pulled the Mustang into a steep vertical climb at maximum revs to get away from the blast. He didn't know napalm bombs very well, but had learned to react fast to High Explosive bombs a few months earlier.

The two bombs hit several yards behind the lead vehicle and a stream of hot fire enveloped the several trucks and jeeps behind it. The lead vehicle was hit by the blast, but carried on towards the blossoming fireball that was once the pride of the U.S. Air Force.

It took Preston several seconds to climb and bank again, go into a near-vertical dive, and swing down to aim the P-51 towards the airfield again. He caught the lead vehicle in his sights and let go with his four cannons. Blobs of material rained off the old Dodge and he kept on firing until the gas tank exploded and bits of green bodywork blew out in all directions. He pulled away and looked at the scene below him.

"Easy Girl *here. All aircraft resume your attack positions and runs. Stay away from the eastern edge of the airport, extraction chopper going in.*"

* * *

Charlie Meyers was in the front seat of their M35 Mexican troop transporter, which was hiding between the closest buildings, across the way from the northern perimeter of the airport.

He and his men, mostly on the roof of the truck and surrounding buildings which were nothing more than burnt out houses, watched as the old propeller aircraft gracefully swept in from the east one at a time, swept around the end of the terminals and then south to line up with the highway just out of their view. It was like watching an air show.

First, three graceful P-51s came in a mile apart, left the terminal buildings alone and then a lone P-38 Lightning followed behind them. It was the most beautiful aircraft he had ever seen, and Charlie was one of the last to ever see it.

Lieutenant Meyers shouted for the men to get aboard, and then told the driver to head through a gaping hole in the fence after the pilot of *Blue Moon* came over the radio saying that his aircraft was hit. He heard another pilot tell the crippled aircraft to head for the airfield, and he told the driver to halt the truck in the fence break and wait.

It wasn't 30 seconds later when he saw the smoking aircraft coming in slowly towards the runway from the west a couple of miles away and directly in front of them.

"We are ready to collect you guys at the western end of the runway. Extraction chopper incoming!" Charlie stated over his radio as he heard the faint throbbing of an incoming helicopter from the north. He knew that there would always be one in the vicinity of the battle just in case. "Head in slowly and stay off the tarmac," he stated to his driver as they headed forward.

They watched as the aircraft came in and zigzagged from side to side; her wheels went down and Charlie saw that flames were eating up her starboard wing badly. He then saw the tail door begin to open as some pilot overhead gave the crippled aircraft advice.

The flaming aircraft hit the runway hard, and Charlie's driver slowly accelerated as they still had at least a mile to go before he judged where the aircraft would stop.

The troop transporter was halfway there when the aircraft came to a grinding halt, grass and dirt spewing everywhere. Men began running and rolling out of the rear door and seconds later a massive fireball went up; her munitions inside exploded, igniting her remaining fuel tanks on the other wing. The blast hit their truck hard but the driver kept on going forward.

"Vehicles coming out of the terminal a mile away," shouted Charlie to the men in the rear as they closed. He also saw a lone P-51 swoop up vertically, turn on a dime and come down in a fast dive towards the approaching vehicles. Two black shapes released themselves from under its wings; the aircraft went vertical again, and the whole area behind the lead truck enveloped itself into a running fireball of napalm. Lieutenant Meyers had seen this often and was extremely glad he wasn't in that group.

The driver was aiming for the closest group of airmen lying still on the ground as Charlie watched the P-51 go into a climb, roll and then for the second time, come down vertically, like an acrobatic aircraft, and head towards the last remaining enemy truck. Within seconds it was also a fireball, and he scanned the area to make sure that there were no more.

His driver came to a sliding halt a hundred feet away from the closest men. There could be more explosions, and the area was already extremely hot.

"Everybody out!" Lieutenant Meyers screamed and exited the door. "I want a perimeter for a chopper LZ! Eight men make a perimeter, the rest help with the closest men to the aircraft first. Pull them away from the burning aircraft!"

Charlie headed for the five bodies still lying still on the ground. He could see blackened flight suits and he reached the first one and began dragging him away from the fire. The man was unconscious and looked red and sunburned. He heard the Jolly Green Giant coming in behind him, and seconds later several men arrived from the helicopter and help drag away the remaining bodies.

Within a minute the entire crew of *Blue Moon* was in the chopper and it lifted off.

"Back to our limo. Let's go and see what remains in the terminals. This fight isn't over yet," Charlie Meyers shouted, running back to the truck as three P-51s flew low overhead.

* * *

Manuel Calderón had been shocked at the quick and extremely heavy reception they received once his vehicles began moving again. His anger quickly changed to cold fear as he realized that his blind anger had led his men into a massive trap.

His driver, obeying his fast and implicit orders, drove like a drunk on Saturday night, careening around burning vehicles and over burning men, and finally, with tires screaming, swung off the closet exit way. He immediately looked for an opening to head south or west.

There were dead everywhere as they flew off the highway; they hit and killed several of his own men as the driver braked and swung the wheel to the left to get around the tight corner at the bottom of the exit. Manuel was purely a passenger and he trusted Oscar, his driver, to get him out of tight situations.

He hung on for his life as the driver swerved around fires and over bodies on the ground, found a road to the west, and headed down and out of the ambush for a couple of blocks until several rounds began to hit the jeep from the front, one taking off Manuel's right ear lobe. The driver slid the jeep left and began heading southwards as the shots behind them faded.

"We are being attacked from the air and from the south, Manuel!" shouted a voice over the radio he recognized from Pedro's army. Manuel tapped his driver on the shoulder and the driver bought the jeep to a halt. *"Manuel, there are hundreds of American soldiers cutting off all the roads, even the road we came in on. My men are taking heavy fire. Orders, please!"*

"Attack the Americans!" he ordered. "Charge into their lines and kill them!" Manuel shouted back. He was in a burnt-down area of old buildings and gas stations and he couldn't see anything.

"We can't. They are everywhere, on top of buildings, and I see aircraft in the area. We only have four missiles left, Manuel!"

Manuel asked and got the man's location from him and he ordered his driver to head south again. Within three minutes he had found the man who was on top of an overpass on the highway and hiding behind the southern concrete wall. There were shots coming from everywhere: the buildings hundreds of yards on the southern side of the east-west highway, artillery fire raining down on certain areas of the highway, a tank rumbling up the road in the distance, and mortars blowing holes in the mass of vehicles, many of which were already masses of flames. There were thousands of bodies everywhere, and he realized that it would be suicide to mount an attack from the open highway.

The first aircraft came in, and he ran to find the man with the shoulder rocket-launcher. He was a hundred yards behind and he was ready on one knee and with the launcher loaded. Manuel noticed three more missiles ready in a line next to the man. A large C-130 came into view low and was shooting his men on one of the highways. He tapped his man on the shoulder who took aim on the aircraft as it swung in front of them less than half a mile away. The missile went straight into one of its engines and it flew directly overhead with pieces of hot metal raining down on the men around him. Three smaller propeller fighters came in next, a mile or two east of his position, and threw rockets down at the highway as they flew over The launcher was ready as the fourth aircraft approached a mile east, and the missile went straight into the nose of the aircraft as it flew over, blowing it into a million pieces.

"Return fire to the south, we are now winning the war!" shouted Manuel into the radio mike and his men seeing the death of two of the American aircraft renewed their firing into the buildings to the south of the highway.

The noise was bad on the ears, and Manuel's driver pointed to southeast of their position. There was another highway, the one they had arrived on, about half a mile to their south, and he saw what the driver had pointed at: two fast jets screaming in from the east and he tapped the man with the launcher and pointed to the incoming jets. The man swung around and fired at the first one, less than a mile away.

As with all the missiles they had used up to now, it wasn't necessary to aim exactly at the aircraft, the missiles locked onto the heat of the incoming aircraft and that was that. This time, and even though the man with the launcher was extremely accurate, the missile sped past the second jet and the plume of smoke behind it, and headed away from the target as if it hadn't seen it.

The rebel commander was shocked and his mouth hung open, blood still dripping from his ear. "Here come more! Fire again, fire again!" he shouted to the launcher who was being loaded by his assistant helping him. They missed the next F-4, and he released his last missile at the fourth F-4 a mile behind.

Manuel's face went white, and he knew that he was now in trouble as the last missile acted the same as the one before and missed the incoming aircraft by less than fifty feet and headed out of the combat area in a straight line. It was the first time in his life he suddenly didn't know what to do. He just sat in his seat and watched as two more aircraft, the same Mexican aircraft he had seen in his battles further south, came in and blew the troops around him into oblivion.

"We are being massacred! We are being murdered! We can't hold out against the firing from the buildings! We are being hit by artillery, mortars, aircraft, napalm, bullets! We are dying, Manuel! Orders, Manuel, Orders!" shouted several commanders over his radio and, he was at a loss what to do.

"Head back to the airport! Leave the wounded, leave the highways, go back to the airport and regroup immediately!" he shouted over the radio. "Get us back to the airport, now!" shouted Manuel to his driver, who crashed the jeep into gear and sped off the nearest exit ramp.

The carnage was bad on the way. There were napalm fires still burning, and men screaming and burning everywhere. He ignored them and sat in the jeep surveying the remnants of his armies. There were fires and dead everywhere; thousands and thousands of bodies and vehicles in flames, but there was a movement back to the airport. His driver must have driven over a hundred bodies before he got on the side road to the highway going north to the airport. Again the highway was not drivable.

The fires and exploding trucks were extreme and there were still projectiles coming in from the south.

A mile north of the highway the fires and bodies gave way to clear roads, and here there were vehicles and men heading north and following orders. Manuel saw somebody he knew from Alberto's men.

"Where is your commander? Where is Alberto?" he shouted to them as he passed, and all he got were shrugs that they didn't know. He entered the southern area of the airport and saw several of Pedro's men. Again, they shrugged their soldiers. The airport wasn't that badly damaged, the northern buildings anyway, and he shouted orders to get to the buildings and terminals to search for his brothers. He didn't care much for the war any more.

His driver rushed him to the rear of the terminal where he had sat out the hurricane and rushed inside the empty expanse of area which had several new fires and gaping holes everywhere in the roof and walls.

"We will hold this airport and fight until these dogs of Americans are dead, every last one of them!" he shouted to the group of men gathering around him as the terminal filled up. "Get vehicles ready to defend and attack underneath, they will be safe from attack down here in the baggage areas. I want tons of ammo in all vehicles and we will attack the armies when they arrive. This is our Alamo and we will defend it! We have destroyed most of their aircraft; it will be hard for their soldiers to cross the runways and open area of the airport. I want every man loaded and ready to fire back once all our men have arrived. I'm sure the Americans are following our last men in. Give them cover when they run through the entrances! I want machine guns on the roof of every building. Their airplanes will be back! Get all the buildings heavily fortified, we still have a chance to win this war!" shouted Manuel trying to convince himself as much as the dirty and bloody group of men around him. "I want numbers of men, and I want somebody to go and find Alberto and Pedro, my brothers!" he ordered.

"I think I saw your brother, Alberto, when I left the airport," stated a man who was absolutely filthy and had dried blood all over him. He was with three other dirty and bloody men Manuel did not recognize.

Sergeant Mendez, this time, was standing in front of three of the other Seals, Sergeant Chavez and Corporals Rodriquez and Santana. They had made themselves as dirty as possible, and had dirtied and bloodied their ponchos and clothing from a generous selection of hundreds of dead bodies.

They had been waiting in case "Extraction Three" returned to this building and they were in luck. Charlie Meyers and Paul didn't want to be recognized again so soon after the disappearance of the two brothers.

"He was sitting next to a man I didn't recognize. It could have been your brother," Sergeant Mendez suggested.

"Where? Where did you see my brother?" Manuel asked.

"Over there and in front of the terminal, there are dozens of dead bodies from the air attack," Sergeant Mendez replied pointing to the front terminal exit door from which they came in, and where the Mexican troop transporter was waiting with its engine running underneath.

The balance of Seal Team Six had set up an ambush point around the hole in the northern perimeter they had used to enter the airport.

"Oscar, Miguel, Carlo, come with me, bring your men." Manuel headed for the door. The area between his old command table, which was still standing, and the exit door a hundred feet away had filled up with men, and they were all looking at Manuel who was moving through them.

"Manuel, Manuel," called a man as he passed. "I've seen these men before. They were with the Panamanian men who walked off with Alberto. I was right there—" His head blew apart.

Corporal Santana fired three rounds from his AK-47, point blank, from three feet away.

All hell broke loose as three of the Seals fired into the crowd around them, piling dozens of rounds point blank that went through more than one person, the crowd was so thick.

"Cover me!" shouted Sergeant Mendez, a big guy at six foot three and weighing in at 250 pounds. He grabbed the collar of Manuel's leather jacket and pulled him off balance towards him and swung his AK-47 to connect hard with the shorter man's head. At the same time, he swiveled around, humped the falling man's body into a fireman's lift and began to run for the door, firing his weapon at anybody in front of him.

The Seal team was so fast that many couldn't get out of the way of the shower of bullets spraying in all directions, or Manuel's now inert body swung over the dirty man's shoulder. Sergeant Mendez was within twenty feet of the exit ramp door when it opened and four more AK-47s began blasting at the crowd.

Few got rounds off and one hit Manuel himself in the arm hanging loosely down the side of the running Mendez and made a gash in the Seal's side. He didn't lose pace, and he and the three men close behind him made it through the door, the Seals' fire enabling their escape.

"Into the truck, fast!" shouted Charlie Meyers as he turned back through the still open door and fired off the last of his rounds from his thirty-round banana magazine. He flipped the magazine out and over, shoving a fresh magazine into the weapon as did Lieutenant Paul, and they fired another sixty rounds into the mass of people falling in front of them.

Both men emptied their second magazines as they heard the horn of the truck below them blast. The Seals in the building, now out of ammo, caught up with the guys giving them covering fire from the door. They threw away the empty magazines, were thrown fresh magazines, shoved them into their hot weapons, headed down the exit ramp, and jumped ten feet onto the apron below.

A Seal began firing from the roof of the truck's cab with a heavy machine gun as Charlie, the last man, jumped up and clambered inside the rear and over the closed gate. There were vehicles being started up everywhere under the building as the driver floored the truck, and it lurched forward with Lieutenant Meyers nearly being knocked out as his head hit the rear gate.

"Head for the perimeter, we have vehicles coming at us from everywhere!" shouted Lieutenant Paul as the men in the truck began firing in all directions.

They left the terminal area and the driver slammed the screaming truck into second as bullets began hitting the protective steel sides from everywhere. He got it into third and headed over the apron as vehicles of all sorts headed out onto the apron behind them, weapons firing.

An M35 isn't the fastest vehicle in the world, and they reached the first taxiway when the faster jeeps began to gain on them. There was so much lead being shot at them that it was nearly impossible to fire back.

Three P-51 Mustangs screamed over, firing at the lead enemy vehicles which literally exploded and somersaulted over, spewing men in all directions.

This gave the cumbersome M35's driver a chance to double-clutch and loudly grind the gear lever into fourth, as the speedometer climbed through forty miles an hour. They passed by where the remains of *Blue Moon* were still burning. Charlie looked over the rear gate to count more than forty vehicles still gaining on them a hundred yards behind. They still had several hundred yards to go as the men firing through the cab's turret shouted "Choppers incoming" from the front of the truck.

"Hold your fire!" shouted Lieutenant Paul as the vehicles behind began slowing down; he looked outside and around the tarp over the rear bed to see a beautiful sight: a dozen of what looked like modern attack helicopters coming in low over the perimeter fence, and the lead chopper flew straight over the truck.

He looked back and saw the vehicles all turning and trying to head back as a dozen rockets went into the mass of vehicles. Within seconds he lost sight of the enemy and the whole terminal area of Bush Intercontinental Airport as massive explosions and smoke obliterated his entire view.

Charlie Meyers leaned back against the rear gate of the bouncing truck. His head hurt like hell, but he had a broad smile on his face.

CHAPTER 9

The End Of The Battle For Houston

THE INVASION OF THE U.S. by the rebels went downhill from there. With their three leaders gone and seventeen armed and deadly Chinese Zhi-10 helicopters, as well as every aircraft the Air Force could muster, blasting the remains of Houston's Bush Intercontinental Airport twice that day, there wasn't much the survivors could do.

Over two hundred powerful Chinese missiles and dozens of napalm bombs rocked the entire airport down to rubble.

When the helicopters left, ten AC-130 gunships arrived and flattened what was left of the northern buildings and then began to crumble the southern cargo and terminal buildings. General Patterson was achieving good tests on the seven newly fitted Colombian gunships, and they were escorted into the attack by three of the remaining U.S. AC-130s.

Then the Tweets came in and added to the carnage, followed by the remaining F-4s and the two F-5s. Finally the helicopters on their second run six hours later, and just before dusk, destroyed anything left standing.

General Patterson, now flying *Easy Girl*, which had returned for him, watched for five hours overhead as the airport slowly crumbled under the force of the firepower going into it.

Any escaping rebels were beaten back or shot at by the advancing Marines from the north and the U.S. Army from the south. They had the entire area surrounded, were closing in fast and, orders had been given that none of these invaders were to survive.

Finally, the soldiers on the ground had to take a few rebels as prisoners, as dirty white tee-shirts appeared on poles. The trickle began just before the helicopters came in for their second round and the wave of surrendering men to the south became a torrent as the final buildings of the airport disappeared.

"Well done to all pilots of the United States Air Force, civilian pilots, our country's brave Marines and U.S. Army soldiers. I would especially like to thank the Navy's Seal Team Six who bravely went in and cut off the head of the snake," stated General Patterson two days later at the battle briefing at McConnell Air Force Base.

The president had arrived in *Easy Girl*, which had flown into Andrews to pick him up.

Every man or woman from the Air Force who had taken part in the attack was still on base, as were the commanders of all the ground troops, whose men were still mopping up. Civilian personnel under the command of Captain Mike Mallory had been arriving in the area for twenty-four hours, driving into Houston with the most amazing collection of old drivable vehicles one could imagine.

Massive columns of smoke, miles high could now be seen twenty miles from the airport's grassy areas where large open pits a hundred yards long, fifty feet wide and thirty feet deep were being dug by military bulldozers, flown in under Jolly Green Giants, and piles of bodies were being cremated with napalm bombs dropped by helicopters.

Once the flames died down over the holes, one after the other was filled in. It would take nearly fifty of these trenches to bury the enemy's dead.

"The "No-Go Law" is the name of the new law in effect as of today. The whole of the southern United States of America, south of Dallas and across the entire country," continued General Patterson, "is to be completely locked down to anybody, except military personnel until further notice. Only those states that border the Atlantic and Pacific Oceans are excluded from this law. The same "No-Go Law" will apply in the northern areas, where people have already been relocated. All areas in a line across the country from Denver, Colorado, have the same new Martial Law applying to civilians. Only military personnel are to be allowed into these areas to patrol and secure these massive swaths of ground for our future generations. As you know, the latest and, hopefully last, attack on our country is over. But, we will not let our guard down; thankfully, our one and only satellite is back in place and giving us constant-feed pictures of the entire country, and two hundred miles out from all of our four borders. If the satellite had been in place a couple of weeks ago, we would have seen this attack coming.

Now, to bring you all up-to-date: the U.S. army is clearing San Antonio of 10,000 rebels which have held the city for over a week. The Marines are clearing the border area around Laredo, where the rebels entered and, anybody found in and around the border city is being picked up or shot.

"I spoke with the two generals now in charge of our armed forces, and a new Army/Air Force base will be built at every border town or city along our southern border. A maximum distance of 200 miles will separate each new base. Patrols by ground and air along our southern border will begin from today, 24/7, and we will never be blindsided by an attack from the south ever again. For your information, ladies and gentlemen, the enemy was a large army of rebels from several different countries. From our latest figures compiled last night, we have counted 121,445 rebel bodies in the remains of the airport. We believe the final number will be around 160,000 in and around

Houston's Bush Intercontinental Airport alone. Many of these bodies have no identification on them, and we don't know where they came from. As for prisoners of war, we have 7,780 men being held in the area, and they are doing most of the work cremating and burying their colleagues.

"We can add another 10,000 men in San Antonio, and we believe 5,000 in Laredo, where several have already retreated over the border into the hands of the Mexican army stationed there. We have been told from south of the border that the Mexican army had fought and followed this army from their southern border and were hungry to have a chance to attack the rebels. We killed over 21,000 in the first air attack on Interstate-10 and a further 19,000 on the Houston Beltway. All together, we destroyed an army of nearly 240,000 men, of which we believe more than 30,000 of the dead have been involved in terrorizing our internal and southern areas of Texas, Louisiana, and Arizona since January 1st. Our forces suffered as we do in any war. I would like to remember the brave who died in this struggle for freedom."

General Patterson read out the names of the twelve pilots who lost their lives in the battles for Houston. Three of the eleven of *Blue Moon's* crew hadn't survived their horrific wounds, and the pilot of Preston's P-38 all joined the names of the Air Force personnel read out. General Patterson also read out the names of 47 Marines killed in action and fifty-one U.S. Army soldiers. Over 200 soldiers were injured in the Battle for Houston. A minute of silence was observed for the dead.

"As a result of their attack on our country, the Calderón brothers have done us two favors," he continued. "First, they returned our attention to defending our southern border and second, it helped us annihilate entire bands of internal rebels and bad actors we would have had to fight over the next few years to bring peace to our civilian population. Now, it is time for us to regroup and help our population of the United States of

America to grow and become the nation it once was." He sat down and Admiral Rogers took his place.

"Ladies and gentlemen, we have the Calderón brothers in custody. We will get every bit of information from them and then send them back to Colombia for trial. Thanks to my team, who has already left for a bit of R and R, we have the best results to this fiasco we could ask for, and we will let you know the results of our interrogations at our next meeting in Washington. I now give you the President of The United States."

The president walked up and stood there for a minute before speaking. "This country always astounds me with its people, their bravery in times of duress, the way we handle ourselves under pressure and the successful end-results we always seem to achieve. I want to thank every one of you for your help coming to the aid of your country. Every one of you has given all you could at every needed moment, and I thank you and feel so proud to be your president. Thank you so very much."

Preston heard the speeches and felt for the victims, the pilots and men who hadn't survived. He could have been in the seat of the P-38 when it exploded into the fireball; he could have been the co-pilot of *Blue Moon*. Both pilots and one engineer died in the explosion. Martie, Carlos, Sally and so many of his friends could have been the victims being remembered right now. Thinking about what had happened while listening to the speeches, he realized how lucky they had been. Martie was feeling better and now over her crash landing. She still limped a little and needed to be checked out at a hospital sometime soon, but she and his close friends were still alive and there was still so much work to do.

He felt tired and drained, like he had just gone through a nail-biting movie and it had finally come to an end. Martie was holding his hand and Carlos was sitting on his other side and next to Sally. For Sally, the Air Force was over for the time being.

It was time to look after her parents and get the people she knew back on their feet.

"What do we do now for seven whole weeks? We have no more wars or orders!" Preston asked his friends as they stood outside the hangar where the briefing had taken place. "Do you guys realize that less than six months ago, we were having our fly-in at my farm in North Carolina?"

"It feels like a lifetime ago," added Martie.

"I feel so old," stated Sally. "I don't want to see the inside of an aircraft cockpit for at least a month."

"Well, you can have lover-boy Carlos chauffeur you around in his latest toy, whatever he has going for him at that moment, maybe his top open and cool DC-3?" Martie laughed.

"He can chauffeur me back to California," stated Maggie. "I feel like I've been flying in my sleep I'm so tired."

"I reckon we should go back to North Carolina, finish off the fly-in party, and extend it for another week. Then we can get back to work, whatever work is in this new day and age," added Preston.

They all felt bad for Preston, losing his beautiful P-38 Lightning. She had been a pure piece of history, and they had all wanted to fly her at one time or another.

"Well, let's all grab our aircraft and fly back together to North Carolina," suggested Carlos. "The Air Force can come and collect them when they want."

They did just that. Carlos headed for his Mustang; his DC-3 was in California and was being flown by Buck. Buck was left orders to return to Preston's farm when he arrived back the next day. Maggie, Sally Jennifer, Pam Wallace and Barbara headed for their Super Tweets, Preston and Martie for their Mustangs.

They flew back from McConnell non-stop in flight formation, and enjoyed the blue sky and the beautifully clear weather that Hurricane No-Name had left behind.

CHAPTER 10

What To Do Next?

FOR THE NEXT FEW DAYS, the group's aim was to relax and party at the farm. The crew at the farm was glad to see their friends return. The first thing Preston saw when he came into land was a new blue hole next to his house, behind his original hangar; a couple of small bodies were swimming around in it.

"We got a filter system from the Air Force and a large above ground pool cover which we placed in the hole!" stated Little Beth excitedly as the adults went over to view the completed make-shift swimming pool after they landed.

The temperature was hot, well over eighty degrees, when they had touched down, with the summer-shimmer of hot air over the tarmac at just before four in the afternoon, North Carolina time. The pool was basic, but nevertheless looked inviting. It was pretty deep, over five feet in the center, and thirty feet across. The filter had been wired up to the house generator and was pumping water into the pool from a piped filter unit which looked like a white, horizontal fountain. A small and simple electric motor sucked the water out of the pool and fed it through the new-looking pool filter.

"They even gave us some chemicals to keep it clear," added Clint, smiling, dripping wet and standing, pretty strongly, next to Preston. He was already brown and contentment showed on his face, accentuated by a massive grin. Preston noticed that his own one and only bathing costume was being put to good use.

Several sun loungers had been set up on concrete bricks next to the pool, which was now a sun-deck and all of the older girls had waved as the aircraft had taxied in. The girls were all in bikinis and in total sunbathe-mode when the aircraft had arrived.

"I would prefer to stay here than at a Hilton Hotel," laughed Martie getting a wet hug from Little Beth. "I think we have run out of ideas to add to this old place. It is beginning to look like vacation town."

"You could call it Prestonville," suggested Carlos being showered by Sally, dipping her hand into the make-shift fountain and spraying the hot pilots.

"Let's get out of this flight gear and pour several cases of cold Yuenglings down our throats, while sitting in the pool. I think we need to commandeer the pool from the younger set," suggested Preston heading for the house. Flying was thirsty work in this heat.

He was still upset about the loss of his magical aircraft, the P-38 Lightning; it had been really hard watching it die in a fireball. It had cost thousands of hours of work and nearly a million dollars to perfect and, now it was in billions of pieces over southern Texas.

Carlos brought him out of his reminiscing by handing him a cold beer from the hangar. They popped the tops and drank thirstily.

"Let's rest for a couple of days and then begin learning to fly a 747," suggested Carlos, and that sounded pretty sweet to Preston. He had always wanted to get behind the controls of a 747, ever since his father had been murdered flying one decades earlier. "I need to get over to China to see the three satellites they have over there. We can take Mo Wang some good American Yuenglings and help out with the flying."

"Sounds perfect to me," replied Preston, noticing that Mo seemed to be now completely forgiven by Carlos. "Martie will certainly want to come along and I'm sure Little Beth and Clint would enjoy the travel."

"Well, Sally is on unpaid leave and doesn't really want to go back to the Air Force just yet," added Carlos, taking a good chug of the ice-cold beverage. "And I'm sure a few others would like to go and see China, especially Lee and his family. Maybe also Mo's niece, Lu, and her kids. And I'm sure Beatrice would be keen."

"Sounds like a good idea," Preston replied, seeing Joe and David in a jeep heading down the runway towards the house.

Joe and David were welcomed by the crowd. As they were passed beers an aircraft could be heard approaching.

"I hope another war hasn't started!" sighed Preston as *Easy Girl* came into view from the west. She lazily turned in from the southwest over Jordan Lake and touched down a couple of minutes later. Everybody watched her slow approach, slightly worried that something new had started, as she taxied onto one of the aprons abreast of the new runway. Preston's old apron was still full of aircraft, so many that it looked like a military air show.

Marie was happy to see General Patterson, then Admiral Rogers, and finally the president step out from her rear cargo door.

"They just couldn't stay away from good meat and good beer," stated Preston, leading the crowd out to greet the three men.

"Just what I was thinking about on the way in, Preston," smiled the president, seeing the beer in Preston's hand.

"What kept you guys?" he asked in return.

"Just sorting out new soldiers to take on some of the work

load," replied General Patterson, shaking Preston's hand and then getting a hug from Marie.

"Nice to be invited!" added Admiral Rogers who also seemed to have somebody happy to see his arrival, Preston noted: Lee's cousin, Lu. She was at least twenty years younger than the admiral, but in this new world, nobody really cared anymore.

"Mike Mallory is an hour behind us. He is totally exhausted and I ordered him to get some rest. Buck is flying him in your Colombian DC-3. I thought to return your aircraft, Carlos, before the Air Force asks for the couple you guys commandeered," smiled the general.

Beers were quickly handed out and all the freezers on both farms were raided for a large BBQ that evening. Dozens of frozen chicken, pork chops and steaks were laid out on the hot porch to defrost. Mo's frozen fish would be left for his return.

It was time to celebrate the end of the American Wars.

An extremely tired and haggard-looking Mike Mallory arrived on schedule, and Barbara flew into Buck's arms.

Preston was surprised how a couple of cold beers made a man freshen up pretty quickly, and he was shocked how much weight the Southwest captain had lost. Preston looked around and realized that nobody was overweight in the crowd. Everybody had lost weight and looked extremely fit and healthy; even Joe looked twenty pounds lighter. He had never seen so many healthy people; there wasn't an ounce of extra weight anywhere.

"Found a couple of dozen cattle running around my farm a week ago, Preston," Joe stated, helping Preston and a couple of others turn the meat on the BBQ.

"We went and helped round them up," added Clint, thirstily drinking an iced can of Coke.

"I rode one, but couldn't get it to gallop," stated Little Beth.

"It's a bleeding cow, not a horse!" replied Preston. "Cows don't gallop, girl!"

"Oh!" replied Little Beth sheepishly.

Oliver and Puppy had been waiting for this day for some time now. They too could hardly remember when there were bones aplenty; the wild animals in the area could wait to be sniffed and searched out. The pool for them was also a new luxury and both dogs' coats were still wet from their last splash.

Buck also looked tired; Smokey the cat had appeared from somewhere and was happy in his arms, his eyes closed and purring. Smokey's serene face expressed what most of the people felt sitting around in chairs facing the mobile BBQ; it was half of a 55-gallon drum propped up on steel legs and had been placed close to the new pool.

The president's face also relaxed as his beer hit the spot. There was a large cooler with ice and it was full of beers and he was already eyeing his second. Summer was certainly in swing.

That night they partied and danced in the hangar. It was cool, the doors shut to keep out the insects, and finally after nearly six months of waiting, the New Year's Eve party was continued in style.

Oliver and Puppy did complete their morning tour of the airfield the next morning. This time they had three men walking with them around the perimeter.

"So what happens now?" asked Preston to the two men walking with him.

"I just don't know," replied the president feeling the beers from the night before. "I don't know how to run a country with no government, no infrastructure and no communications with the general population."

"Well, all good things have a "Day One," and I suppose this is one of them," commented General Patterson. "I feel we are miles along the road of advancement. Michael Roebels has the first small electrical grid running in Silicon Valley, he has a new electric vehicle he is testing, and there are already a million of these vehicles in collection compounds around the country. The first crops are being harvested across our nation; food is being produced by millions of famers and helpers. I think we have a good chance of survival for the foreseeable future. I also believe that the rebuild of a more modern civilization is a good possibility for this country."

"I think so too," agreed the other two men together.

They could not see the next problem looming over the horizon.

THE AFTERMATH

CHAPTER 1

August 1st

SEVERAL WEEKS AFTER THE THREE-DAY BREAK to relax and the ongoing party at the airfield in Apex, North Carolina, the first official meeting of the new United States of America was beginning in the repaired Capitol building.

The building had taken a little damage, mostly from a few citizens who had managed to get past the military containment and steal anything movable.

Over the last several weeks much had happened. Summer had finally blossomed, food was being produced, the dead were still being buried, and new energy was beginning to pump itself into the successes each new day brought.

August 1st was to be a celebration of the final flight of U.S. troops arriving home from Ramstein Air Force Base in Germany.

At Ramstein, there was a small group of Europeans, mostly German and English, saying goodbye to American friends. A few of the men were returning with European girlfriends—American wives-to-be, several of whom were pregnant.

Their long wait to be evacuated had produced new relationships and friends, with dozens staying behind. People like Michael O'Meara, a Scotsman who always dressed in a kilt, was bidding farewell to both of his pregnant younger sisters. Mary and Madeline were passengers on the last of the four 747s, each of which was transporting 600 men who were the last to leave the air base.

Also among the well-wishers were Martin and Helen Mackenzie, Major Paul Crotty and his private army of 300-odd men and women, Wing Commander Gordon Wade and his two pilot teams, the English film actor Peter Jefferies, German actress Michelle Moser and over a dozen other friends, all saying goodbye to the last group of the departing 1st Cavalry Division and the 7th Marine Regiment they had befriended, helped and aided in the battles Britain and Europe had gone through during the last seven months.

The troop evacuations had slowed over the last few weeks as more, and more aircraft were needed to fly electronics in from China and fresh food to the U.S. population, now living in a 500 mile-wide strip that stretched across the center of the country from the East to West Coast.

California, Oregon and Washington State on the West Coast were still inhabited, as well as much of the East Coast. Boston had a very limited population due to dangerous areas of disease in and around the city, and New York was nearly a ghost town.

Much of the north was on total lockdown. Disease was rampant, and few ventured into this forsaken land.

Cities like Chicago, Detroit, Milwaukee and Minneapolis were locked down tight. Body squads in sealed air-conditioned vehicles moved through the streets clearing away decomposed bodies, which never seemed to end. Rabid dogs and other animals were everywhere and immediately shot on sight. Buildings were gone through by men dressed in Hazmat suits and bodies were brought out to dump trucks waiting to cart them away to the nearest burn-pit. The numbers were staggering.

The authorities in charge of the body cleanup estimated that it would take another month or two before the mammoth task ended; then these areas would be closed to the public for a full year to make sure that any disease dissipated.

As usual, everybody who had been part of the invasion of the United States was invited to the Capitol for the August 1st meeting. The Capitol grounds had dozens of white painted helicopter landing zones across the green grass, and all were expected to be flown in from Andrews.

All of the surviving members of Congress had been ordered to attend by the president and, even with everybody expected, the House Chamber would still only be half full.

Barbara flew *Lady Dandy* while Buck and Preston flew Carlos' DC-3. Carlos, who had been shot and wounded while in Colombia, was still off active flying for a while and had around-the-clock protection for the first time Preston could remember. Carlos had only arrived late the evening before with a U.S. Air Force pilot flying his DC-3.

The North Carolina airfield had grown in population from just Preston and Martie a year earlier to now over two dozen people. Many were now permanent residents or used the airfield as a second home, going in to visit every now and again.

Lady Dandy carried sixteen, Barbara and fifteen others. Included were Joe and his five boys, Pam Wallace, David and Jennifer, Mo Wang, Beatrice and her daughter, and Marie and her two daughters. In the second DC-3 were Buck, Preston and Martie, the injured Carlos with his two bodyguards, Little Beth, Clint, and Lu, Lee Wang's niece, and her two children.

Everybody wore their best clothes, and they were all excited to see the inside of the Capitol, many for the first time.

All of the military personnel, like General Patterson, Admiral Rogers and the others, had visited North Carolina only a couple of times in the last several weeks. The first time was to help Preston take over command of RDU Airport. The broken buildings and interiors had been removed by dump trucks. The useless aircraft were all lined up in neat rows and stored on the grass around the runway. Michael Roebels had flown in for two days to repair the control tower and get all of the communications and directional flight equipment working again. RDU was now a military airfield, patrolled 24/7. Engineers had checked the aviation fuel tanks and decided that there were two million gallons of jet fuel and one million gallons of aviation fuel available for the use.

Several aircraft of assorted types were flying in and out daily to supply food to the local towns; it had become the main food-distribution point for a third of North Carolina, where three million people were now living. As with many of the now forty operational airports throughout the center area of the country, dozens of trucks of all types brought in food daily from the surrounding farms which was then airlifted out to dozens of smaller distribution points, usually military bases.

Carlos had returned from Bogotá late the night before, and nobody was allowed to visit with him. His bodyguards even refused Preston a short visit except to greet his friend. Carlos said that he had much to tell, and they would get together after the meeting in Washington.

Preston was surprised to see that Carlos was recuperating from a bullet wound in his hip and had a bandaged head injury, but he was still able to walk, although slowly. His head looked like he was wearing a turban. Preston noticed that Uncle Philippe and Carlos' father were absent and the pretty Colombian lady and Dani were very careful to protect his friend. Weird!

The two slow aircraft got into line for the final approach into Andrews Air Force Base where, with all of the past meetings, several aircraft were all arriving at once.

It was nice to feel a slight cool breeze compared to the hot muggy conditions further south. Everybody was tanned and healthy. The airfield's makeshift pool had been slowly modified and now was completed with tiled sunbathing areas, a BBQ hut, and shade gazebo; the pool itself had a newly laid cement bowl underneath the blue canopy. It didn't look as fancy as a hotel pool but, in the hot July weather, nobody really cared.

The Church would be the most important building on the airfield this coming weekend; it was booked out with a wedding on both Saturday and Sunday. Before Carlos left for Colombia, Preston and Carlos had tossed to see who would marry first and Carlos won.

August 1st fell on a Thursday and that gave the wedding parties time to get back and get ready for their grand day. Sally was flying in from Arizona with her parents for the meeting. During the three weeks Carlos was away she had spent the time with her parents making sure they were safe.

The airfield was busy with dozens of helicopters waiting to ferry the arriving people over to Capitol Hill. Estimates from General Patterson were that 200 people would be in attendance.

A crowded agenda included medals to be given out to the heroes in the Houston battle, a meeting with survivors of last year's cabinet, and then an unplanned meeting with four representatives from major corporations, who had suddenly arrived out of nowhere, and arrogantly demanded a meeting with the president immediately after his speech. These large corporate CEOs had sent a letter to the president in July demanding that their companies be given all help necessary to rebuild, immediately.

With military precision the groups were guided to the waiting helicopters, eight to an aircraft and, one after the other, they lifted off for the ten-minute flight to Washington.

Preston, walking next to the bodyguards who were helping Carlos, slowly walked over to the helicopter. He waved to Lee Wang and his family boarding one of the helicopters in front of them. Lee, his wife and daughter, were still working in Silicon Valley with Michael Roebels, They and Michael had flown over for today's meeting and the weddings this coming weekend.

Washington looked peaceful and empty. The buildings for several blocks around Capitol Hill and the White House had been cordoned off since June and many locals had headed out to live with family and friends outside the capital. It was not a pleasant city to live in any more. Little food and thousands of military patrols made a peaceful life in the capital city non-existent. The whole country had been under martial law since May and, Washington, D.C. was the worst hit area.

One by one the helicopters landed to drop off their passengers and took off once their cargo was out of the way. Soldiers on the ground helped show the incoming guests where to go and soon the pleasant cool of air-conditioning could be felt as they entered the building from the gardens.

Preston now had air-conditioning in all of his buildings as well; two of his Mann diesel engines had been returned to him with several military HVAC systems and, with the 5,000 gallons of diesel in his one underground fuel tank still intact, he and Joe had installed the systems just before the heat pounced at the end of June.

"I've always wanted to tour the Capitol," Martie commented to Preston as they entered the cool of the building. They both were helping Carlos who was looking for Sally; both of his wounds, although only flesh wounds, needed more time to heal.

"I did once, with my father, as a young kid. Think I was five, but I remember everything about our tour," replied Preston, walking into and remembering the Rotunda. "Just as I remembered it, Martie. Do you know several presidents have lain in state here? Gerald Ford and Ronald Reagan were a couple of them."

"I do know my history, Professor Strong," replied Martie, gazing up at the ceiling and taking in the massive area. "I can't remember if President Reagan lay here in the Rotunda or in another part of the building, but I remember watching people walk pass his coffin on television. The Rotunda is magnificent!"

Mo Wang and Lee and his family finally found them and they all happily greeted each other, then wandered around the building until slowly they were ushered into the House Chamber. Now, history really reached out to Preston. How many "State of the Union" speeches had he watched on television coming from this actual room? It was big. He looked up and noticed that the second level was empty of people, apart from dozens of military personnel.

"This must be the first time so many members of the public filled this room," Preston whispered to Martie as they were seated in the third row from the front and, as always, with people they knew. Mo Wang and then Beatrice sat on Preston's other side and looked around. Carlos had disappeared with his bodyguards. A colonel had come to escort him to an earlier meeting.

CHAPTER 2

Bogotá, Colombia – July

THIRTEEN MILITARY AIRCRAFT FLEW SOUTH on a warm July afternoon, three weeks before the Washington meeting. Carlos was flying his open-door DC-3 at high cruise, just keeping up with the seven refurbished Colombian Air Force AC-130 gunships with *Easy Girl* leading the way.

Three hours behind them were another twenty-four U.S. Air Force C-130s full of U.S. Marines; two thousand men ready for a fight.

The seven Colombian gunships were also full of men and ammo. Twenty-five members of Seal Team Six were in two of the gunships, recently renovated in the U.S. One of the AC-130s was full of the promised Miniguns, over one hundred of them, and the other one full of other bits and pieces Ambassador Rodriquez had requested, as well as several 80-mm mortars.

An hour ahead of the gunships were the twenty Zhi-10 Chinese Attack helicopters flying in formation, also at 10,000 feet, and with three HC-130 fuel tankers in attendance, ready to juice them up. They would make Colombian airspace before midnight, and they were all due to head into Santiago de Cali's International Airport, where the ambassador's brothers were ready to meet them.

The 747 transporter was due to leave Andrews later in the day and fly a belly-full of equipment into the same airport in Cali at about the same time; the city's international airport's tarmac was just long enough to take the massive beast. Inside the transporter were airport radio beacons, aircraft directional equipment from Michael Roebels, radios, several of the old Amiga computers as well as more mortars, bombs, and ammo for the Miniguns and pallets of projectiles for the new AC-130 gunships.

With twelve tons of ammo onboard, Carlos was glad he wasn't flying the monster into Colombian airspace; if hit by a missile the loaded 747 transporter would light up the sky for hundreds of miles.

The ambassador sat contently in the DC-3 with Carlos flying and his father sitting in the co-pilot's seat. Behind them sat Uncle Philippe's four bodyguards, Mannie, Manuela, Dani and Antonio, and five of Seal Team Six. The Seal Team members were all Spanish speaking and had captured the Calderón brothers. Carlos and the two older men had enjoyed the intricate details of how the brothers had been hoodwinked.

The three brothers were at the back of the aircraft, bound and in a tarp-covered steel cage. They looked tired and haggard after their capture, and not very comfortable with their arch-enemy, Ambassador Rodriquez, sitting twenty feet away from them.

The DC-3 and all the other aircraft were on auto-pilot and the open door at the back of Carlos' aircraft gave them a nice cool breeze which flowed through the aircraft. At 10,000 feet the temperature was only 10 degrees or so cooler than the sea below them, currently at 80 degrees. The captives had been told that if a noise was heard from them, out their cage would go, without a parachute.

"So, Uncle we are going to get the Calderón family once and for all?" asked Carlos taking a sip from a thermos of hot

Colombian coffee. "We must have really decreased their forces in Houston. Senator Calderón must have very few soldiers left."

"He is as slippery as a snake," replied Uncle Philippe. "I know that the men his sons had fighting with them are not the same men the old man has as protection. I've heard that he always has a couple of thousand men in secret locations around Bogotá when he is in the city. I have often thought of accidentally having a fight with his men, but not having much proof that he has ever done anything wrong or illegal, I've always let him be. During the time they are not needed in Bogotá, his men live in the mountains and cannot be easily flushed out by usual methods. Many lives would be lost if our men went in to get them in and around Florencia, where they normally stay when Senator Calderón is out of the country. He only spends a few months every year in Bogotá, and only when the government is in session. I've often tried to put a tail on him, or try to follow him to see where he holes up when he's not in the city, but he always goes through Venezuela, and he becomes invisible in that country."

"Will he be in Bogotá when we arrive?" asked Carlos checking his aircraft's panel gauges and looking at the other aircraft a mile or so in front of them in a very loose formation.

"Should be," Uncle Philippe replied. "I have convened an emergency meeting of Parliament. Parliament is always in session at this time anyway, from the end of May to mid-June, just before the summer break, and an emergency meeting of the government means that every government official should be there, whether they like it or not."

"Should be an interesting meeting," added Carlos' father. "Have you a plan of action yet, Philippe?"

"No, not yet, but I have one good idea forming. I just need to know that the senator is in town and then have our men and our allies who are flying with us, the Marines, position themselves around the governmental buildings, and position our new gunships in the air above; then, when his men attack, we are ready for them. I hope by taking all our U.S. friends into Cali after dark we will deter any radio or road messages getting to the old dog. My brothers have men clearing the buildings around the airport and setting up police roadblocks and army checkpoints on all the roads between Cali and Bogotá. If they try to tell him that we have arrived, I'm hoping we block the move."

"Do his bodyguards have good weapons?" asked Carlos.

"The very best," replied his uncle. Money was no problem for this man. At one time he was supposed to be worth over one billion U.S. dollars. We know that he has another army of men on San Andrés, the island he normally calls a stronghold. That is why the admiral and his three frigates are going to visit there tomorrow. We have 3,000 of our own loyal men, Colombian parachutists; ready to go in tomorrow and that should equal his men on the island. Luiz has always wanted that island; it was his wish when we were young boys. I told him not to flatten the Calderón estate or the main town, El Centro, with his frigates' guns, and he could take it as his own."

Two hours later, dusk arrived from the east as a black stripe of the coast was seen on the horizon; the pilots had already found the faint airport radio frequency from Cali's main radio station on their directional finders. It was all they had to direct themselves into the Alfonso Bonilla Aragón International Airport until the usual Colombian Kfirs, their now fully operational fighters, a dozen of them this time, came up to greet the incoming aircraft. They had to use the international airport this trip as all the protection was needed while the 747 transporter would be unloading in about 12 hours' time. Everything else needed for fire fights was in the cargo holds of the aircraft they were flying in.

With all aircraft engines on full power, and after climbing to 17,000 feet, they swept into Colombian air space with the formation of fighters around them; any higher and everybody would need oxygen. The pilots hoped the people on the ground would not hear the engines of dozens of aircraft above them.

Only on final approach, and with a five-mile line of aircraft, did the civilian airport's landing lights come on. They were the only lights allowed at the airport.

Carlos brought in his aircraft with the VIPs aboard second, *Easy Girl* going in thirty seconds before him. He could just see blackened remains of several buildings around the outside perimeter fence as they came in. This was his first visit to this locked down international airport. His last take-off had been at the military airfield several miles away.

"Philippe, it's so good to see you safe," General Miguel Rodriquez hugged his brother before hugging Carlos and his father. "Carlos you have been in the wars since we last met, I've been told," the general stated slapping him on the back and hugging him. "I'm going to have to employ you in our armed forces one of these days."

As the other aircraft came in to the heavily defended airport, the VIPS moved towards the safety of the command center.

Here, *bocas* and wine were ready for the visitors. The other brothers, apart from the admiral, Luiz Rodriquez, were all here ready for the visit: the always jovial Colonel Alberto Rodriquez, who was in charge of the Colombian Special Forces—Carlos had not been told this on his last visit—and, Commandant Alvarez Rodriquez, who was third-in-command of the country's police force

"We have two days before we must get you into Bogotá, Philippe, what do you want to do?" his younger brother Miguel Rodriquez asked once the last aircraft was on the ground.

"Unload your gifts from the American people, get all of our aircraft safe, and most importantly, get the 747 transporter out of here tomorrow night once she has been unloaded and reloaded," replied the ambassador, munching on a snack.

"We have ten tons of pineapples and mangoes, ten tons of

prime unfrozen Colombian beef, ten tons of fresh vegetables and a ton of coffee ready to be loaded. Can this aircraft take all that?" Police Commissioner Alvarez Rodriquez asked.

"She can handle up to thirty-two tons on this length of runway and such a short flight, Uncle Alvarez, so there also will be room for dancing girls and a rumba band," joked Carlos. "I have a plan. Can Colombia deliver a 32-ton load of food, meat, and produce once a week in return for new electrical parts and arms from America?"

"It will take a few weeks to set it up, but I think Colombia could manage that pretty easily. Who is going to eat our food?" Alvarez, who seemed to be the brother in the know, replied. "For supplies of aviation fuel, we could do this once a day if you wish, as long as the transporter doesn't use our valuable jet fuel on this side."

"The aircraft will fly into North Carolina and then Andrews Air Force Base on this flight and off-load half its load at each stop," replied Carlos. "The food will go into the main food distribution system. If you could find more coffee, or just make up 32-ton loads, then at least she will fly out full every time. She won't need refueling when she comes in later tonight. I'm just worried about a rocket or missile going up to meet her while she is in Colombian air space."

"We have 20,000 of our men within a ten-mile area around this airfield, and they have been in position for a month now. I feel it will be very difficult for our enemy to be in the area. Our plan is to have a fifteen-mile area cordoned off soon and only allow the local inhabitants in. We are even thinking of building a new and secret air force base in a very rural area south of here and actually make it no-man's land for a twenty-mile area," added General Miguel Rodriquez. "I'm sure whatever you send us will be valuable enough to build this new Air Force base. What other aircraft do we have incoming tonight? I need to make sure we have enough Kfirs up there as protection, and also enough accommodation for your American Marines."

Carlos told him about the twenty gunships, three tankers and second flight of C-130s with 2,000 Marines aboard, and the general's eyebrows rose at the mention of 20 Chinese incoming attack helicopters. Carlos could see his mind working.

"Don't get any ideas about the Zhi-10s," he stated smiling. "I had to get on my knees and beg to borrow them for this operation and if any are shot down, I'd better take you up on that job offer, Uncle."

"Sounds good to me," the general smiled back. "We win both ways."

"By the way, I would like to introduce you to a few friends of mine," Carlos continued. "General Rodriquez, may I introduce you to some men who have been here often, mostly to Medellin and Bogotá helping you with your undercover battles." Carlos introduced his uncle to the Seal Team members who had captured the Calderón brothers.

"Lieutenant Charlie Meyers at your service, General." Charlie stated, saluting. "These are my buddies, Lieutenants Joe Paul and Sean Murphy, and Sergeants Mendez, Chavez, Santana and Miguel Rodriquez, A family member of yours, I believe?" he stated in perfect Spanish.

"Ah! Miguel Junior, I was wondering when we would meet again," replied the general.

"Yes, Papa, I was looking forward to coming back home again," replied the sergeant, hugging his father. Sergeant Rodriquez was usually very quiet. The others, including Carlos, his father, and Uncle Philippe looked on, total surprise written all over their faces.

"I sent Miguel Junior to the States fifteen years ago at eighteen to get his citizenship and to see if he was good enough for the US Navy Seals," stated the Colombian Air Force Commander to the still-shocked group around him. Philippe, you never met Miguel, my second-born son. My first-born, Alfonso, was murdered by the cartels a couple of years after Miguel left for America. He returned for the funeral, after just completing his selection course for the Navy Seals. He was young, fit, and handsome when he left and he is still that today. And I am very proud of him."

"Why the Seals?" asked Charlie Meyers, thinking for a few seconds. "Now it all fits together. When we were completing the Coffee-Cartel sweep and termination mission in Medellin, what... five or so years ago, Miguel seemed to know the area like the back of his hand. For us that was a real plus, and we never normally ask questions."

"He went to high school in that area of Medellin, only a mile or so away from the coffee-selling houses, the same houses you guys cleaned out for us," replied the general. "Once he became a U.S. citizen, it was important to wipe his past Colombian history clean, so that there were no connections from the cartels to him. There are millions of Latin Americans with the same family name throughout Central and South America, so it wasn't difficult. It was necessary to get my son into a good group of military men, who General Pete Allen and Admiral Martin Rogers, both friends of the family, could send over to help us doing our weeding and cleaning up every now and again. How did you know he was family, Lieutenant Meyers?"

"Just a hunch, General," Lieutenant Meyers replied. "First we meet Carlos here who is a Rodriquez with fancy connections, then we are met at the airport by a whole bunch of the same Rodriquez family, then I took a guess from Miguel's knowledge of Colombia every time we entered this country over the last decade. General, I just put two and two together. That's what keeps us Seals alive, hey Miguel?" Sergeant Rodriquez nodded without saying a word.

"General Rodriquez, Sir, the second wave of aircraft is asking for finals, and the 747 is exactly an hour behind them," stated a soldier walking up to the group several minutes later while they still stood around the snacks table and chatted.

Thirty minutes later a long line of helicopters came in to land, swooping in from high altitude above the airfield as the general had ordered, once he was told they were in the airport area.

The last aircraft came in an hour later, minutes before midnight. The 747 transporter came in dark, her external lights off, and only the shape outlined by the runway landing lights showed her massive structure and her oval forward area. Other than that, anybody in the nearby area would have needed night glasses to see her black silhouette against the lighter night sky.

An aircraft of her size couldn't be stealthy and quiet, and the ground vibrated slightly as her engines were put into full reverse thrust; Carlos was sure that the noise could be heard as far as Bogotá, hundreds of miles away. She swept past the terminals several hundred yards away and, ten minutes later and still blacked out; her shape could be seen entering the terminal apron in front of the main building.

Carlos guessed who was flying her—only the best—and once the ladders were up, and her engines quiet, the nose opened for unloading. Majors Wong and Chong came down the stairs to be welcomed.

General Rodriquez was more interested in the two lines of ten Chinese attack helicopters to greet the incoming pilots. Carlos went with him. "Don't get any ideas, Uncle!" stated Carlos. "America will not give you a nut or a bolt from one of these. General Patterson knows, and so do all of us who are stateside, that these Zhi-10s are the most powerful force of aircraft in the world, and you have no chance, not even a little bit of no chance."

"Not even one, for everything we can produce?" asked General Rodriquez, already knowing that he was barking up the wrong tree. "How about a lifetime supply of our best coffees?"

Carlos smiled and looked at his uncle, silently telling him, "No!" They returned to the larger aircraft to inspect the gifts from America.

With a heavy guard, the airfield rested for the remainder of the night; the only activity was the unloading of the transporter.

Early the next morning, trucks began to arrive with produce already packed in boxes on pallets ready to be loaded, bound for the U.S.

For most of the day truck after truck had its cargo fork-lifted off and transported onto the special flat-loaders the aircraft had brought to raise the cargo up to the nose for self-loading. The transporter didn't fly anywhere without this well-designed system.

By midnight that evening, she took off on her return flight, first to RDU and then further north to Andrews. Majors Wong and Chong bid farewell to their friends and headed back with an aircraft full of valuable food.

The second morning was also the day before the group was to fly up to Bogotá for the government meeting. Plans were made using maps of the area around the government buildings and the best locations to attack or defend the buildings, whatever came first. Being a rest day, both countries' military rested, cleaned their weapons, refueled and armed all aircraft, and made ready for combat.

The C-130s with the Marines aboard took off first, an hour before midnight, for the short one-hour flight into Bogotá's El Dorado International Airport. Thousands of Colombian troops were ready for their arrival in Bogotá at the Catam Air Force Base inside the international airport. The Rodriquez brothers weren't taking any chances. The helicopters left an hour later and, at 3:00 a.m., the second wave of C 130 troop transporters took off for their short flight.

No problems were encountered, and once he had closed his aircraft down, Carlos decided to head back to bed in a new room.

This was to be the final day of rest and he was going to make full use of it.

Early the next morning, the ground transportation arrived to take the officials into the city, three separate convoys of dark limousines. Carlos was asked to get into the second of the first convoy's limousines, with Charlie Meyers and several of the Seal Team members, now dressed in Colombian military fatigues, to be driven to the Nariño Palace. They chatted, as did his father and Uncle Philippe in the car ahead of them, protected by their four guards.

Colombian police, army soldiers, and the same tank were there protecting the entrance to the Palace's main entrance when they swept through. Several miles behind them the Marines, with Colombian support, were being driven into the areas where they would be ready to attack the buildings. The attack helicopters were ready to lift off if needed.

Everybody in Carlos' vehicle was now quiet and all eyes scanned the open areas and buildings for angles and opportunities. Carlos noted that there were far fewer soldiers encamped around the area than on his first visit and he mentioned that to the men with him.

"Weird," he stated to the others. "Last time there were hundreds of men with everything from heavy machine-gun placements to mortars. Today it looks like a picnic in the park. I've only counted thirty soldiers, the tank, and one machine gun over there backing up the tank," he stated pointed to the only visible machine gun post.

"Better for us!" replied Lieutenant Paul. "Fewer soldiers to get in our way if trouble is brewing."

"Maybe they don't expect any trouble today. How many days is this government get-together?" asked Charlie Meyers.

"Three days," replied Carlos. *"If Senator Calderón wanted his men in here, he certainly doesn't want to show them to us,"* Carlos thought to himself.

"There are many places to hide many soldiers," added Lieutenant Murphy, sitting with them. Sergeant Miguel Rodriquez was the fourth bodyguard in Carlos' car. There was a third and fourth limousine behind them full of Navy Seals. The same was true of the other two convoys. One had General Rodriquez and the third would be twenty minutes behind as Admiral Luiz Rodriquez had just flown in from the coast in a navy helicopter.

Twenty of Seal Team Six, all the Spanish-speaking men, were included in the cars being driven into the government buildings, all with Colombian Special Forces uniforms given to them by Colonel Alberto Rodriquez, who was in command of the 10,000 loyal Colombian soldiers and the 2,000 U.S. Marines coming into the city.

"When are the three captives going to be presented to the meeting?" Charlie asked Carlos.

"Only tomorrow after lunch," replied Carlos. "The Ambassador wanted a full day and a half to lead everybody in the meeting to think that nothing out the ordinary had happened regarding the Calderón family, and the emergency meeting was purely to bring the Colombian government up to date on the latest world affairs. It was the only way to make sure everybody important would attend. That is why Admiral Rodriquez had to fly in."

One by one the cars stopped in front of the same entrance Carlos had used on his last trip. The men were ushered in in front of them and then it was their turn. Mannie, the ambassador's bodyguard, waited for the cars to show the visiting Seals where to go and how to act.

Carlos caught up to his father and Uncle Philippe as they waited for him inside the doorway and out of harm's way.

"Nothing has changed," Uncle Philippe said to Carlos. Once again they were in the large room where dozens of officials congregated around a long table helping themselves to *bocas* and soft drinks. This time Carlos recognized the short military man who came up to greet them.

"Ambassador Rodriquez, aides, I am happy to see you safe. Did you have a good flight in? How is the United States? I'm sure you have much to tell us."

"Yes, to all three, Mr. President. How is your grandson?" replied Uncle Philippe shaking the president's hand and bowing slightly at the same time. Manuel and Carlos just bowed.

"Fine, and now I have a second and a third grandchild on the way, Ambassador. I'm sure you must have much to tell us, convening an emergency meeting, no?" the president asked.

"It is important that every member of the Colombian government knows and understands what is going on outside of our borders," Philippe replied.

"Of course, of course, I look forward to your speech." The president saw General Rodriquez enter the room with Senator Calderón; both men seemed to be laughing at something. "Glad to see your families enjoying each other's company, Ambassador Rodriquez. Please excuse me, I must welcome them." He headed towards the two men, more like a salesman than a president.

"He is the only president we have ever had who deems it necessary to welcome every member on the first day to the government meetings. It is one of the small things he does which makes me want to trust him," whispered Philippe to Manuel and Carlos.

Philippe decided to follow the president to see what was so funny between his brother and the enemy, and they slowly wandered over, allowing the head of state the opportunity to greet them, and then move on to the next entering members.

"Ah! Philippe," stated the general as his older brother approached. "I was discussing how lax the guards are out there with Senator Calderón, here, and he agreed with me, adding that there is possibly little to worry about on the first day."

"Ambassador Rodriquez," acknowledged the senator.

"Senator Calderón," replied Philippe keeping his manners

impeccable and even giving his arch-enemy a kindly smile. Carlos noted that neither man offered a hand shake.

"Nothing much ever happens at the beginning of these government meetings," added the senator looking straight into Philippe's eyes and smiling. "It is always Day Two or later when our arguments get heated that fireworks could happen."

"What do we have to disagree about, Senator? The country has been going forward in these bad times, our citizens have food, and Americans don't need drugs anymore; I'm sure that helps the world's balance.

"Of course, Ambassador, now if you will excuse me," and the senator went off to meet others.

"Today is a day everybody wants to listen, not to fight," added Philippe to the two younger men.

Carlos didn't know how anybody armed could enter the main chambers when the time came to start. There were three different stations next to the defunct metal detectors where everybody was searched from head to foot. Small military metal detectors still worked and three times Carlos and his family members were checked for anything metal. At the third area, they were expertly patted down by men wearing plastic gloves and sniffer dogs were in attendance.

"They must be explosive sniffer dogs, very few would get through if they were drug sniffer dogs," joked Manuel to Carlos in a whisper. Carlos nodded and smiled in agreement.

They sat in the same chairs he and his father had last time, in the line of chairs against the wall, and he watched General Rodriquez and the Ambassador take their usual seats. Still munching on a snack as he was patted down, the admiral made a late appearance as everyone was taking their seats. The long table still had its forty-two chairs and Luiz Rodriquez was the last to take his seat nodding at everybody around the table.

The roll call was taken and Carlos noted that all forty-two

chairs had a person in them again; only two chairs around the walls were empty, directly behind the senator.

The meeting began with a speech by the president, and Carlos recalled what he had seen since he entered the Nariño Palace. The only real security was at the front and only entrance where guards checked everybody's name off a list. Then there was little security in the room where the snacks were. Only when everybody entered the main conference room, was everything checked. He had carefully counted the guards around the three separate security points. The first was the set of very large, dark wooden double doors which opened into a large palatial-style decorated, but empty room. Here, six well-dressed guards stood at attention. The large doors were built with thick mahogany; Carlos had tapped them as he had passed through, and they were thick enough to stop most bullets and small arms.

The second checkpoint was at a second set of doors leading into a second room with another six guards, the room much the same size as the first one. The third checkpoint was at the third set of doors leading out of the empty room and into the main chamber.

"It would be hard to get armed men into this inner chamber, which has no other doors leading in," he thought to himself.

The time came for everybody to introduce themselves and as he had done on his previous visit, he said, "Carlos Rodriquez, Second Aide to U.S. Ambassador Rodriquez," after his father had spoken his one-liner.

Carlos realized that there were new members where the empty seats had been last time and was quite surprised how young some of the governmental heads were.

For three hours the section-heads gave reports on the current situations inside the country.

Food was in good supply, farms and cross-border trade was doing well with all the countries around Colombia. Electricity was the main problem facing the country and help was needed to get it up and running. Ambassador Rodriquez was looked at often by the men speaking; the U.S. would be the most important country to ask for many of the current problems facing Colombia.

Carlos suddenly had a reason he and Preston could ask General Patterson to learn to fly a 747. The transporter, he realized could be doing this flight between these two countries on a daily basis.

Senator Calderón was quiet, he took notes and the two aides' chairs behind him stayed empty.

Lunch was served in the outer room and for the second time Carlos took note of the security. The officials headed out to the first room where tables had been set up to serve lunch and he sat at a round table with his father, three uncles, and the four Colombian bodyguards filling the other chairs so nobody else could sit with them. Senator Calderón, as expected joined the police commissioner's table, and Carlos observed that a couple of times through the meal, eyes were directed to their table. The food was good, spicy, and tasty compared the food he was use to in the States.

He searched for the Seals he had driven in with, but they were nowhere to be seen, just the usual guards in the usual places. Something, he felt was wrong because everything looked so peaceful and perfect. He was sure it wasn't going to continue like this.

As the meal was being finished, the ambassador got up from his seat and headed over to a table to speak with others. Carlos watched through the corner of his eye. He realized that one of the men, at the table the ambassador was visiting, sat next to him in the chambers. The aide belonged to the Minister of Education. Then his uncle wandered across to another table. The aides at this table sat next to his father and he knew they belonged to the Ministry of Water and Land Development. Then Philippe wandered over to a couple of other tables speaking to several ministers along the way. Carlos saw that he stayed away from the president's table and the one next to it where Calderón and the police commissioner were sitting. Both tables also kept the travels of the ambassador in the corner of their eyes; the rest in the room ignored the several people walking around.

For the second time that day everybody had to go through the three security monitoring stations and Carlos was surprised when four new aides, well dressed in expensive business suits, sat on both sides of him and his father. Members of Seal Team Six, wearing fancy suits and carrying expensive briefcases, had entered the chamber. Charlie Meyers sat next to him, saying nothing.

The afternoon dragged on. Reports from ministers about their departments followed one after the other. The list of speakers, five for the afternoon, had been given out to each person in the room with the U.S. Ambassador in the last slot for the day, and forty-five minutes of speaking time, the longest for the day given to him.

Finally the house called on Ambassador to the U.S. Philippe Rodriquez to stand and, he did so, looking over a fist of notes before starting. Carlos didn't know what he was going to say and the room became quiet, waiting for the news from the U.S.A.

For the first twenty minutes the ambassador reported the latest news dealing with what he and the Colombian Embassy personnel had seen and heard from all their sources. Carlos knew most of what was being said. His uncle spoke about the movement of the population into the middle area of the country for the summer, and maybe until further notice. He gave them estimated population losses, given to him by Mike Mallory. Then he spoke about the army returning and the developments in the president's plan to enact martial law and protect the survivors against any threats.

He worked through his notes slowly, going from information already agreed upon by the U.S. president and General Patterson. He then talked about the Colombian navy helping the U.S. protect its sea borders with the three frigates under his brother. "A great opportunity to seal a lasting friendship with the U.S.A.!" he added

Finally he stated that he would continue with his report in the second session, planned just before lunch on the next day; he concluded his speech with a description of the work being done in Silicon Valley, and the information received from the U.S. Chief of Staff about the trip to China, and finding more Russian and Pakistani nuclear missiles, with the Russian one having the range and capacity to take out the whole East Coast. He explained that if it went off course and slightly southwards, the ten nuclear warheads could have taken out much of Central and South America, including Colombia. He stated that the people of Colombia had to thank the work done by U.S. troops to stop this final destruction of the world by the Chinese Communist Party.

"Ambassador Rodriquez, we will now have ten minutes of questions and then we will adjourn for the day," stated the House Speaker. "Chief of Police, you have the floor," he stated, acknowledging the first person who had raised his hand.

"Thank you for the latest information, Mr. Ambassador," said Pedro Gonzalez. "In your last report you stated that the army had set up martial law across the United States?"

"That is correct, Pedro," Philippe replied.

"What has changed since that report, and what has happened to possible lawlessness on America's southern border?"

"The latest information I have, Pedro, and I had a feeling you would ask a question like this, is that the U.S. Chief of Staff has decided to set up a new police force using the military police from all the American armed forces divisions. That is, I believe, a hundred thousand men who will join any police forces still in existence."

"So, they have soldiers and their new police force now

patrolling the borders?" the police chief asked. The ambassador nodded. "Can you give us any numbers?"

Carlos was quite surprised by the ambassador's reaction.

"Pedro, I am not told exact numbers, and I'm sure the U.S. government doesn't want you to know their numbers either. I cannot understand why you ask these questions. All I know is that there are about half a million soldiers on the southern border, a hundred thousand on the northern border and the American government has cleared all cities and towns of civilians for at least 200 miles of each border."

Carlos looked over to the senator and police chief as this was being said. His uncle was purely bringing the troop numbers out of thin air, but the looks on the faces of the two men were priceless.

"In addition to the U.S. soldiers, they have hundreds of air-craft, vehicles, jeeps, troop transporters, mortars and machine gun posts being dug in along the southern border especially." Now Carlos knew his uncle was putting fuel on the fire he had just started. The ambassador continued, "There has been a little violence on the southern border, nothing to worry the American president about, and the American and Mexican armed forces are working well together to keep any border violence and crossings down to a minimum."

What type of violence has been happening along the U.S.-Mexican border?" asked Senator Calderón.

"What has this to do with Colombia?" asked the president sharply. "Senator Calderón, Police Chief Gonzalez, it sounds like you have something going on over there?"

"Please excuse my questions, Mr. President," replied the police chief, "but it does help our matters of internal and external security to know what is going on elsewhere around us."

"I agree," added Senator Calderón. "Ambassador Rodriquez, please answer my question," the Senator asked curtly as if the ambassador was an insignificant member at the table.

"Of course, Senator," replied Philippe, smiling kindly at the senator. "There have been a few small problems in Mexico which spread into Texas. The U.S. military believes it was Venezuelan drug cartels trying to get a foot in the door. The Mexican army shot the first small group of banditos to shreds and the rest, who managed to boat across the Rio Grande, were quickly dealt with by the American soldiers. That's all, nothing significant, except that the Venezuelan cartels are fewer in number than before."

"Are you sure these gangsters were Venezuelan?" Senator Calderón asked, his face etched in stone and very composed.

"I don't know, I wasn't there, but I was told this information by the American Chief of Staff. He even offered me a few prisoners to bring back here for information purposes; they will arrive in Colombia tomorrow, and we can interrogate them here in Bogotá. Hopefully Pedro Gonzalez can see fit to give these prisoners accommodation?"

"Of course!" the chief of police returned.

There were one or two other questions from others at the table: the quality of food in the U.S.? Were they still drinking coffee? Could relations be put in place to transport needed items in both directions? The ambassador acknowledged that ideas were already in place to work on all possible needs for both countries.

Carlos could see that things were not good on the other side of the table, and both the senator and chief of police were itching to get out of the room.

Five minutes later the president thanked everybody and the House Speaker reminded everybody to return in the morning.

It had been a long day, and Carlos followed the others out. He wasn't rushing and Charlie Meyers stayed by his side. Suddenly it dawned on Carlos that the security details were gone. There were only the six fresh guards in each room standing at attention in their Presidential Troop uniforms.

"I think we need some firepower in there tomorrow," Carlos

said to Charlie. "Now is a good time if you can hide pistols or something in there, the security and metal detectors are down, and I'm sure they will be back in the morning. I think only a cleaning crew will be allowed in between sessions."

"Stay here," replied Charlie Meyers quietly. "Make sure I can get back in. Here, take my briefcase. We can say I left it in there. I will be a few minutes," and he quickly walked off towards the outer room.

Carlos returned to the room and placed the briefcase on his chair and returned to inspect the guard uniforms in the first security room, waiting for Charlie's return. The men were as silent as the Queen's guards he had visited once, outside Buckingham Palace in England. He tried to start a conversation with one man, but he stayed silent and stared forward.

His uniform was extremely colorful. He was one of the couple of hundred Presidential Guards always here at Palace Nariño. Much like the English Guards, he stood at attention and he didn't move. Carlos saw movement in the corner of his eye and saw Charlie Myers and young Miguel Rodriquez, both dressed in their fancy civilian suits waiting for him.

"Are you coming, Carlos?" Miguel Junior asked with a very Colombian accent.

"Yes, but I think I left my briefcase in the house chambers," Carlos replied.

"Well, hurry up, the drinks and the girls won't wait, Señor. Let's go and find it and then go party," Miguel replied loudly for the sake of the guards and the three men re-entered the government chamber. It was still empty, the last one or two aides were still talking and leaving the chamber, something about looking forward to seeing these Venezuelan prisoners tomorrow.

"Carlos, guard the door, don't let anybody in. Give us three minutes and we will be out of here," ordered Charlie and he and Miguel Junior headed for the seats they sat in that afternoon.

Nobody came towards Carlos who looked as official as possible standing outside the doors, still looking at the second set of guards. They still hadn't moved, and he was beginning to think that they were maybe models when he felt the two men arrive behind him.

"Señor Calderón, I have your briefcase, it was next to your chair. Now let us go and join the party," stated Sergeant Rodriquez and Carlos smiled at the false name being thrown around for the sake of the guards.

The outside room was nearly deserted as they left the building, and their waiting black car pulled up. Sergeant Paul looked curiously at the men as if they were school kids doing a school prank.

In silence they drove back to the airport and the safety of the air force base, just in case the car had been bugged while they were in the Palace.

"We strapped a silenced Glock underneath the seat of each of the four chairs we sat in this afternoon," stated Charlie as they entered the Air Force building. "Magazines are full and they are held underneath the seats with two pieces of duct tape, so pull hard when you need them, Joe. I'm sure we will have the need for them pretty soon. Carlos, a good bit of brain work, and it worked perfectly. I hope the cleaners don't look for gum under the chairs tonight. Well done, amigo!"

A short meeting was to be held for all the people who attended the meeting. Uncle Philippe wanted feedback from everybody for anything and everything: a small gesture, a raise of eyebrows or a suggestion he might have missed.

"We can see that Gonzalez and Calderón think in the same cesspool," stated the admiral. Nobody had briefed him since he had arrived late.

"Luiz, how did the negotiations for your new island San Andrés go?" General Rodriquez asked smiling.

"We arrived there to more than a hundred hungry tourists

trapped there, a thousand unhappy citizens and 2,000 of Calderón's men around his large estate just outside El Centro. Our first flight of 1,000 troops parachuted in five miles south of his estate at midnight the night before last, and was ready for the surprise attack at daybreak. I had our three frigates a mile offshore from his private beach to seal off any escapes by sea. The second flight of parachutists were circling ten miles out to sea and ready to go in

"Without a shot being fired our attacking force got within 800 meters of his stronghold, walled-in like a fort, before they were noticed. Then all hell broke loose and at least a dozen machine-gun emplacements opened up on the men from the thick wooden wall.

"Colonel Moreno, who was leading the first attack, radioed in the gun positions and our frigates literally flattened the wall for a couple of hundred yards. Then I ordered in the second wave, dropping the parachutes along the wall area and inside the estate while peppering any machine gun emplacements around the large grounds with the first group advancing."

"A well mapped-out surprise attack, Luiz," said Philippe.

"Yes, thank you ,Philippe. I believe it was a good attack. The ongoing battles lasted most of the day as we found several underground tunnels leading to military command posts, even a couple of underground sleeping areas for over 100 men. It took the whole day to flush all of Calderón's guards out, but we completed the mission by midnight last evening. I left Colonel Moreno in charge to clean up the rest of the island, help the injured and get a list together of supplies needed for the islanders."

"And the tourists?" asked Carlos.

"Mostly German and Scandinavian tourists, and after hearing about the news of the rest of the world, they all decided to stay. I was a few minutes late this morning due to getting several of our

C-130s full of doctors, medical supplies and food supplies over to San Andrés."

"Casualties?" asked General Rodriquez.

"When I left, under forty men killed, approximately a hundred badly wounded and another hundred slightly wounded. On their side we counted over 700 dead, many hundreds wounded and about 500 captured. I believe that we will find another few hundred men or more before we have completely cleared the island. I intend to return as soon as we are finished with this emergency meeting you, Philippe, got me into."

"Sorry, just another two days, Luiz. Do you think Calderón knows?" asked Philippe.

"I'm sure he knows everything. I looked at him often in the meeting to see if he looked concerned. I only saw a slight bit of worry in his face when that aide walked into the chambers and gave him a note about an hour before we were done for the day. From then on he and Gonzalez were pretty keen to get out of there."

"Radio Moreno, Luiz, tell him and his men to be cautious," added the air force commander. "I'll get one of our new gunships into the airport there fully armed, just in case. Our friend Pedro Gonzalez and even that fat slob from over the border, the obese Venezuelan friend of Calderón might have his own protected little corner of our Colombian heaven. I think I should send in a wing of Kfirs to be ready for an air attack from our neighbors. Our Venezuelan friend could have his own little protected base on our island."

"You could airlift in the two U.S. jeeps we left here on our last trip and a couple of the mortars we brought with us. A C-130 belly-full of extras might come in handy," suggested Carlos and both the admiral and the general nodded and excused themselves to sort matters out. They could have just started a bad war on the island hundreds of miles from the mainland.

"At least air superiority will be the main benefit in this

operation, Luiz, since you already have the three frigates there. I would get one of them closer to the mainland and you could use it as an early warning system for extra air and shipping in the area," stated the general to the admiral as they left the table.

"How do we act tomorrow, Uncle Philippe?" asked Carlos as the rest resumed the main meeting.

Early the next morning, with the thousands of loyal Colombian and U.S. soldiers embedded and hidden in buildings around the Palace Nariño, most within a couple of miles of the grounds, the limousines headed out in a different order than the first day. This time Carlos and his father rode in the fourth vehicle in the second convoy, while Uncle Philippe, the general and the admiral sat together in the third vehicle in the third convoy. The first convoy was full of Seal Team members dressed in smart business suits, twenty of them, and the four vehicles squeaked with the heavy weights of whatever the Seals had stashed in the large vehicles.

The three captives were going to be delivered during the lunch break in a second motor convoy of all the vehicles together, twelve limousines with military armored troop carriers as protection in front and behind the convoy. This time the tank protecting the gate would be ordered to let the whole party through and this time Colombian Special Forces would be in the vehicles as guards.

Carlos had the feeling that today there was going to be fireworks and everyone was issued thin, modern, bullet-proof vests under their suits. Philippe tried to refuse, until the general told him that he and Luiz would undress him and get the vest on him themselves if he didn't comply.

The vest was hot under his suit as he walked into the outer room where there was always the *bocas*, soft drinks, gallons of coffee, and the president to welcome them. Only the two extra "aides" were unloaded at the door with the VIPs. The others were driven around back to work out their own way to get in.

Philippe had suggested one or two of the Seals join other groups as they entered and separate from the groups before the president made his usual introductions.

"Ambassador, you rested well and enjoyed fresh Colombian cuisine for a change. Far better than Washington, I'm sure," the president welcomed his group as they entered.

"Yes, Mr. President. It is surprising how much one misses home when one is away," Philippe replied.

You have a few new members in your entourage, Ambassador?" queried the president shaking hands with Manuel and then Carlos, but interested in the two large men with the group.

"Ah, yes, they belong to the Minister of Education and also Water and Land Development. They live by the international airport and asked if they could catch a ride with us this morning," the ambassador responded.

Lieutenant Meyers and Sergeant Rodriquez had been warned this could happen and, bowing, began to give their stories. The president noticed more ministers entering the door and was already away and nodding his acceptance before the first sentence was complete.

Carlos watched him head towards the door and saw Paul and a second Seal move away from the group that had just entered. The president, with his eyes on the Minister of Roads did not see the two men head away from the group and skirt around the wall and then over to Carlos. For Carlos, it was interesting to watch the goings on.

By the time they headed into the main chamber, and Senator Calderón and Police Chief Gonzalez entered, six more Seals had disappeared into the building somewhere.

"Could be a boring morning and exciting afternoon," Manuel whispered to Carlos as they went through the third round of security. The two Seals were ahead of them and took the same seats they had yesterday. It seemed that the ambassador had asked each of the two Ministries to bring one aide less for the day's business.

Carlos sat down in his usual seat and looked around the room. It looked clean and certainly the cleaners had gone through the room since they had left. He carefully felt underneath his chair and the butt of a pistol entered his hand. He looked up at Charlie Meyers sitting next to him and got a smile back in return. He then pretended to whisper in his father's ear and felt under his chair. This time a rounded barrel of a silencer was there facing him, tight under the chair. He felt better. With the vest and the weapons in the room they were ready for any trouble, and he began to relax.

Carlos then checked out his uncles on the main table. Uncle Philippe was directly in front of them, General Rodriquez had moved a space to Philippe's right to allow for the Minister of Education to sit between them. Carlos thought this a good move as it would have been easier to shoot the two men sitting next to each other. As Calderón and Gonzalez reached their chairs, he noticed that the admiral was still sitting next to the chief of police, and Lieutenant Paul was one of his aides sitting behind him. He then noticed Miguel Rodriquez, the Seal sitting on the other side of his father, get up and with his briefcase walk around the table and over to the admiral's aides. There were handshakes and greetings as if the two aides were good friends, and the young Colombian returned to his seat just as the House Speaker banged the mallet.

Senator Calderón looked a little more tired and pale than the day before, but his stone-faced features persisted throughout the morning. Also the two empty chairs behind the senator had been filled with two large mean-looking men, who, like Charlie Meyers, didn't resemble anything like what a mousy aide should look like.

The police chief looked more edgy and his aides had also changed overnight. Gonzalez was sitting next to the Admiral of the navy, the man who was in command of the frigates which had bombarded San Andrés a day or two earlier. They certainly knew what had happened. Carlos noted that all three Rodriquez brothers at the main table smiled at Calderón and Gonzalez when their eyes wandered in their directions.

The Minister of Agriculture had just finished his 30-minute speech, the fourth and last before lunch, telling the table the abilities of the farming community to feed the population, his worry about coffee not being sold to anybody outside Colombia, and the world grain and beef prices now held no value, when it came time for the last question and answer session before lunch. Senator Calderón was the first to fire away and it wasn't at the Agriculture Minister.

"I have a question for the Ambassador to the United States, Mr. Speaker." Before permission was given or refused, Senator Calderón carried on. "When are we going to see these so-called captives from the government of the United States of America... and what rights do the ambassador, a Rodriquez, the chief of the air force, a Rodriquez, and the admiral of the navy, another Rodriquez, have to attack an island belonging to our nation... as if it was an enemy country?"

There was absolute horror and silence from the room as everyone waited for the ambassador to answer. He first looked at papers in front of him for a few seconds, then took off his glasses, rubbed his eyes, replaced his glasses and finally looked straight at the senator; this time he wasn't smiling.

Senator Calderón... first, that was two questions, but I will answer both for you. We will see these captives in this room after lunch. They are already in this building and have been since early this morning. Where I don't know, but they are being guarded by our Colombian Special Forces," he replied. Carlos knew that it wasn't exactly the truth. "I received these men's names from the U.S. government late last night when they arrived in the country. All I will say for now, and since you have mentioned our Rodriquez name three times, I will let the cat out of the bag that one of the names of the prisoners is Calderón!"

There was a gasp in the room. "Yes, Calderón is a name found all over the Latin world, but this Señor Calderón is a Colombian Calderón, and we think he might be one of your family members." Again there were gasps and sounds of shock around the room.

"To answer your second question, Senator Calderón, we heard from reliable sources in the United States and our spies in our neighboring country, that a coup was taking place on the island of San Andrés, one of our most valuable islands. We didn't believe it, but the admiral, chief of the air force, and I decided to find out for ourselves and put men on the ground, just in case the rumors were true. Funny, our men—our own Colombian soldiers—arrived on our own island to find out that there were thousands of armed soldiers suddenly shooting back at them. Now, Senator Calderón, is that a possible coup or not? It took us less than twenty-four hours to kill the enemy forces, which were well over 1,000 soldiers mainly around a couple of prominent villas outside El Centro and we are checking to see who those villas belong to. That should tell the Government of Colombia who was trying to take over its territory. Personally I believe it is somebody from Venezuela, but we don't know yet."

There was absolute silence in the room. Uncle Philippe just sat there and looked at the senator and for the first time Carlos saw a twitch on the senator's face. It was the first time the usually stone-faced man had shown any emotion.

"Is this all true, Ambassador Rodriquez?" asked the president in shock, and Carlos then knew that this poor man knew little about the country he "governed."

"I'm afraid so, Mr. President," the ambassador responded. "I need to discuss how we will bring these prisoners into Chambers with you and your Presidential Guards during lunch, if you don't mind. I speak first after lunch, and I will elaborate on these important topics."

The House Speaker awkwardly banged down the mallet for lunch. Lunch was a pretty quiet affair. Nobody laughed or joked as they usually did between colleagues and the room had a dark cloud about it.

The ambassador sat with the president explaining how dangerous the next part of the meeting would be. He suggested that all guards with guns should not be present in case they might be spies or in the employment of a possible "dark side".

The president couldn't believe his ears, that there could be so much potential trouble inside the actual Government Chambers. He refused to order the guards to leave until Ambassador Rodriquez told him that if there were men with guns in the room, he could not bring in the captives. Any bad soldier with a weapon could easily take out the whole government, if given the chance.

Slowly, and wanting to see these so-called gangsters from America, he relented and stated that he would give orders for the room to be cleared of the Presidential Guard, as long as the men bringing in the captives were also unarmed. Ambassador Rodriquez agreed.

Carlos counted the decreasing minutes to the end of lunch. He noticed that Calderón and Gonzalez were nowhere to be seen.

"When the crap hits the fan, duck and get under the table, Carlos," ordered Manuel, his father. "I'm sure that there will be more hardware in the Chambers than in the military armory by the time we show the captives. Keep eyes on the aides sitting behind Calderon and Gonzalez. Also check every face in the room to see if it is a new face. I've tried to commit every face around the room into memory and I will nudge you if I see any fresh faces." Carlos nodded.

The three security positions were slow and methodical in

their searches as the members entered the large room. Security checks included total body patdowns this time, except for the president who was the only person who wouldn't be checked. Even shoes were removed.

Carlos was to wait until the very end while his father went in first to check for any changes.

When he entered the large room Manuel was surprised to see one man had beaten him in, a thin, mousy-looking man with thick glasses, who was already sitting several chairs down on the opposite side of the room. He had a briefcase with him and wouldn't make eye contact when Manuel looked at him.

Manuel had been first in line and couldn't figure out how this man had entered before him. The doors had been closed until he was allowed in. He immediately returned to the closest security point and ordered the six guards standing there to evict the man from the room, or at least make sure he had nothing on him or in his briefcase. The man was unceremoniously escorted out of the room, briefcase and all.

Manuel returned and sat down, working on whether he had seen the man before. He was sure he hadn't, and missed noticing a lone briefcase that blended into the shadow of one of the chairs against the wall, one chair away from Calderon's aides and where the evicted man was sitting.

Slowly the room filled. Carlos was to be the last man in and looked for the two men he was watching for. As he was about to stand and move towards the door, the ambassador and president returned and went in. Carlos rose to join them. He and the ambassador were patted down and their briefcases gone through. All the aides had already gone in. The president was not checked.

"I haven't seen our targets yet," he stated in a whisper to his uncle, who nodded. As they were checked at the third security point, Carlos noted that the first security check point was about to start packing its scanners up. Carlos nudged his uncle who turned and noticed as well.

"We still have more people to come. Stay alert until the prisoners are checked through with their bodyguards. There will be nine guards with three prisoners!" Uncle Philippe shouted back to the men at the first and second checkpoints. The president shouted to the security points that they were to stand on duty until the prisoners entered, and then they were to leave.

Carlos had surmised that Calderón and his partner-in-crime would be late and they were; the members were seated and waited five minutes before the two men and their aides arrived, maybe hoping to miss the security inspections. There were shouts and orders given; the noise could be heard through the still open Chamber doors.

Finally, the two men appeared, both looking angry, with their aides close behind and all without their briefcases. The four aides were the same men who sat behind them during the morning session.

Charlie Meyers and three of the Seal team were sitting in the same chairs as in the morning session, behind the Ministries. Two of the admiral's bodyguards sat behind him and right next to Gonzalez's aides. To Carlos the six men sitting behind the three members looked more like a football defense line than diplomatic aides.

"We start the afternoon session with a report from the Ambassador to the United States, and the lead-up to these Colombian prisoners being captured inside the United States. Then these prisoners will be brought in and viewed," stated the Speaker of the House.

"Mr. President, members of the Colombian government, what I am about to tell you came straight from the President of the United States, his Chief of Staff and information from the Mexican Armed Forces who tracked these men through Mexican General Miguel Ortez."

For twenty minutes, the Ambassador told a rapt room the movements of this army of nearly 250,000 men from nearly every country in South and Central America. He described the capture of the Panama Canal by 10,000 Chinese soldiers, who also weren't meant to be there, to the final battle in Houston and the capture of the three leaders. He did not say anything about Seal Team Six and during the report Carlos kept his eyes directed in Senator Calderón's direction, and looked for any movement around his area.

Only towards the end of the twenty-minute report, and when the Ambassador stated that the three men would shortly be brought in, did Carlos notice slight movements from behind the area. One of the aides sitting behind the senator quietly got up, walked forward, bent carefully over the senator and whispered into his ear. The same had happened several minutes earlier when Gonzalez signaled one of his aides to get up and, as if to pass on information, whispered into his ear.

"Be ready, son," whispered his father. "I'm sure everybody in that group is now armed."

The ambassador looked at Senator Calderón and smiled, then he nodded towards the armed guards securing the closed doors and they opened them and exited. Three bedraggled men, with their hands tied behind their backs and cloth hoods over their heads were brought in one by one. Three Special Forces guards helped each man in and were ordered by Philippe to stand with their backs in the corner furthest from the door.

Only one member had to turn to view the prisoners; the rest of the main table just turned their heads to the left of the president.

"These men were handed over by the United States government and their president," began the Ambassador, "and asked that a trial be held here in Bogotá for their attack on the soil of two foreign countries, Mexico and the United States of America. Of course, these criminals did not act alone and the governments of both of these countries would like their leaders to be found and prosecuted as well."

There was total silence in the room and even Carlos couldn't help but look at the three dirty men standing there, about thirty feet from where he sat.

Uncle Philippe nodded and one of the Seals undid the hood from the first prisoner; there was a loud gasp from many in the room when Pedro Calderón's dirty face was shown. Carlos fixed his eyes on the aides behind the senator and then on the senator's face. He didn't show any emotion. Carlos was aware of Charlie Meyers moving slightly near his right shoulder, but didn't look. He already knew what the Seal was doing.

"Señor Pedro Calderón, for you members who have never seen this man before, is a Colombian drug cartel member and was born in Bogotá in 1975."

Carlos moved his eyes towards Pedro and noticed that he didn't look in the senator's direction, but in the ambassador's direction and then spat on the floor.

"Senator Calderón, could this be one of your family?" Ambassador Rodriquez asked blatantly.

"Never saw this gangster in my life!" The senator smiled calmly at the ambassador. "But, Ambassador Rodriquez, he seems to know you well."

There was still silence and a sort of relief went through the members, thinking that any danger had passed. This Calderón wasn't the senator's family. Ambassador Rodriquez nodded a second time and the hood was lifted from the second man's head.

"Our second captive, Alberto Calderón, born in El Centro on San Andrés in 1971," the ambassador stated calmly, looking directly at the senator this time. "Maybe since your villa is on San Andrés, maybe this Calderón is a member of your family, Senator?"

"There must be a dozen Calderón families living in San

Andrés and another 100 families on the mainland. How am I supposed to know them all? Do you think I was a father to all these children?" the senator replied.

Carlos saw this time that the second Calderón had certainly surprised the senator, and even more so, Gonzalez. Both men had reacted this time, sitting straight up.

"Well, maybe the third man might be known to you," and the Ambassador nodded for the third time and the hood came off revealing Manuel Calderón's face. This time there was a gasp from certain members sitting around the table and suddenly all hell broke loose. Many knew this Calderón!

Carlos was watching the senator's face, which froze at seeing his first-born son staring back at him and he didn't make a movement but Police Chief Gonzalez suddenly moved next to him, a small pistol in his hand and pointed it at the admiral sitting right next to him.

Before a warning could get out of Carlos' mouth, he felt movement next to him and he saw the police chief pull the trigger twice. Then the pistol was turned rapidly, and its third shot hit the ambassador in the forehead as three holes suddenly opened up the police chief's own forehead.

The senator had now risen, as had the four men behind him; he, too, had a small pistol in his hand and Senator Calderón shot the President of Colombia twice before turning his aim towards the ambassador who was already hit. Senator Calderón got off a third shot at the minister sitting next to the president before the silenced weapon in Charlie Meyers' hand fired three times, taking off the senator's entire shooting arm, from the hand upwards.

By now nearly everybody was clearing their chairs and trying to get under the table. Two of the aides behind Gonzalez went down, but not before shooting many of the ministers trying to get out of harm's way. Calderon's "aides" were already standing on their chairs, and helping to mow down ministers with one man, Carlos saw, aiming at his own father and the second one about to aim directly at Air Force General Rodriquez.

Carlos rammed his father sideways and tried to push him onto the ground to cover him. He felt a bullet slice through the side of his body, just above the right hip and an inch below the Kevlar jacket as he turned and a second furrowed across his forehead, right above both eyes as his attention was on his father's moving body. He watched as another bullet entered his father's arm, just outside the protected area and he felt warm blood gush over his face as his body fell onto the older man beneath him. His head hit the floor hard and that was the last he remembered.

He came to with a nurse looking over him. Seeing his eyelids flutter, she smiled at him then disappeared from his view and called somebody. His head felt heavily bandaged and he couldn't feel his left arm. Actually he couldn't feel anything, Carlos felt no pain; the room looked fuzzy, and a new face appeared in front of him, a man with a white coat.

"Señor, you are alive, but you need rest. You have lost much blood and need to sleep. Here is something to knock you out."

When he again regained consciousness, his arm hurt and he managed to move his fingers to make sure they worked. There were a couple of machines around him beeping, and slowly he moved the fingers on his other hand and then the toes of both feet.

"You have not lost any body movement, Señor," said a nurse, who must have been sitting next to his bed but out of his view. "You have two bad flesh wounds and were pretty much out of blood when you arrived."

'Where is my father, Manuel Rodriquez?" he asked weakly.

"He is about the same as you, also one non-lethal wound, lost a lot of blood and is in the next room," she answered.

"And my uncles?" he asked.

"I cannot say anymore. It is five in the morning and you will have visitors in about eight hours time. Now sleep and let your body heal, Señor," the nurse responded.

Carlos was sitting up, his head feeling like he had hit a train head on, when Air Force General Rodriquez walked into his room eight hours later. He had awakened an hour earlier and the nurse, a new one with a different voice, raised the top of the bed so that he could take a drink of water. A pain pill came with the water and she told him to only move when necessary; his hip wound was too fresh to hold its stitches with any sudden and abrupt movement.

His head hurt like hell, like a migraine, and his right hip and whole leg felt stiff and sore. He didn't really want to move, but felt a little better when his eyes focused on the room; he could now see.

The same doctor had entered a few minutes earlier than his uncle. "Good to see you feeling a little better, Señor Rodriquez. You are very lucky the bullets didn't hit any important parts of your body; the loss of blood from the hole above your hip was the main problem with your being shot."

"And my father?" he asked.

"The president is doing fine and is in the next room to yours..." the doctor replied being interrupted.

"I don't care about the president. What about my father?" Carlos asked.

"As I said, Señor, the new president, your father, is slightly better than you, took only one bullet in the under arm and is already in a meeting in the room next to yours," the doctor smiled.

"My father is the President of Colombia?" Carlos asked, shutting his eyes and hoping the pain pill would hurry up.

"I cannot say anymore; you will be visited soon, and that pill will help your head in a few minutes," the doctor replied and left the room. He shut his eyes until he heard more people enter his room.

"Good to see you have managed to sit up, Carlos," General Rodriquez stated as he entered the room.

"What about the others?" Carlos asked.

"A bad day yesterday, young Carlos, for the Rodriquez family, but maybe a good day for Colombia," he responded pulling up a chair and sitting down. "I have a slight wound, one bullet grazed me slightly, nothing like yours and, somebody has to keep the country together."

"What happened, Uncle?" Carlos asked. "All I remember is falling on my father and that was it until I woke up in this bed."

"You saved your father's life, Carlos. One of the bullets that hit you would have killed him if you hadn't pushed him out of the way. Manuel is alive, thanks to your fast and brave work."

"And the others?" Carlos asked. "I saw Uncle Luiz get shot, twice I think, and then I pushed my father down.

"Yes, Luiz was actually shot four times; three of the shots hit his bulletproof jacket, one didn't. He is still alive and on life support. He is in the ICU, and we are hoping he will recover; it is touch and go with poor Luiz. Unfortunately, Philippe was killed, two shots from different pistols. The president and six of the highest ministers were also killed. Gonzalez looked like a colander with so many holes in him. The senator was shot in his right arm and is still alive to face trial. Their aides were all killed by the American Seal Team."

"And my father?" Carlos asked.

"Your father, the new President of Colombia. He was elected late last night once the Chambers had been cleaned and the remaining ministers voted to have a Rodriquez in the hot seat. They wanted me, but I refused and suggested a man who had very few ties with any remaining drug lords or cartel members here in Colombia. Your father was the first choice and you the second. In absentia, we gave the job to your father who has reluctantly agreed and is now keen to help get our country back on its feet."

CHAPTER 3

The Meeting On Capitol Hill

THE MEETING AT CAPITOL HILL finally got underway. Carlos returned to his seat a minute or so before the entrance of the president. Sally was with him and they took their seats as the president's entrance was announced and everyone stood.

Preston noticed that the president still looked fit as he passed; his hair was graying, but the man looked healthy and had his usual glow about him.

Instead of shaking many people's hands, he smiled as he moved forward and headed for his seat. The Speaker of the House was a congressman standing in for the former Speaker, and he worked his way through the opening procedures. The vice-president's chair and the chair of the leader of the opposition were both empty.

"Ladies and gentlemen, the President of the United States," the Speaker stated and sat down.

"Thank you, Mr. Speaker. Members of Congress, members of the armed forces, citizens, and guests of the United States, I welcome you to Capitol Hill. So much water has passed under the bridge since I stood here more than a year ago," began the president, "so many people have died since then, here in the United States, North America and around the world. We will not know the full details of this worldwide atrocity for a long time to come. We do have limited communications with our bases in Europe and Japan. We also have limited communications with the countries of Australia, New Zealand, and Colombia. I have been on the phone with the leaders of these countries, many of whom are new leaders filling in for others. They, themselves, need years to get their countries back on their feet and do not yet know the total devastation in their countries. We, the United States of America, are now the most modern country in the world. We have the best communications, the only reasonably sophisticated air force, the only satellite system and one of two operative railway systems. Thanks go to so many who helped keep this country on its feet and kept the survivors safe and fed. We are so lucky to have Americans and non-Americans who have helped in their way to keep this country alive and victorious in the face of invasions. There were two invasions—one from Zedong Electronics in China and the second, a collection of drug cartels from Central and South America.

"Thanks to our men and women, we beat these invasions back, worked with the limited resources we had, and kept our country and our land in one piece. It is not possible to thank everyone, but many will be thanked in different ways. Today, I would like to thank members of our armed forces and civilians for their distinctive service to our country."

Nobody knew who would be getting medals today, but it was well known that several medals were to be awarded.

"I will start with our armed forces. I have the honor to award the Air Force Congressional Medal of Honor for the second time, posthumously, to General Peter J. Allen, United States Air Force, for his leadership and command in thwarting the first invasion against the U.S.A. Everyone please stand and observe a minute of silence for the general." Everybody did. "General Pete Allen leaves no family and his two medals, both designed on a metal plaque from an AC-130 gunship will be hung in the Oval Office." There was silence.

"Now, I would like to award the Congressional Medal of Honor to the following recipients here with us today. Air Force Medal of Honor to General William B. Patterson, Navy Congressional Medals of Honor to Admiral Martin J. Rogers, Lieutenant Charles H. Meyers and, Lieutenant Joseph A. Paul."

The men rose and headed forward, each receiving his medal over his head to hang around the neck. They stood in a line as everybody stood and applauded.

"Second, I would like to award four Air Force personnel the Air Force Cross for bravery in the face of the enemy: Majors Sally M. Powers, Jennifer S. Watkins, Joseph M. Chong and Lee D. Wong. Please come forward."

The four airmen received their medals. It was a proud day for Sally's parents who had been flown in for the ceremony.

"Now I would like to give out ten Presidential Medals of Freedom, all awarded with Distinction, to U.S. civilians, in or not in the service industries, who helped keep our country stay free before and during our conflict. First, I would like to give the Presidential Medal of Freedom posthumously to Wolfgang D. Von Roebels, a German immigrant who, after the Second World War became an American citizen. I would also like to award the Presidential Medal of Honor with Distinction to his son, Michael W. Von Roebels, and his granddaughter, Martie A. Von Roebels. This one family has been instrumental in keeping our country safe for over four decades. Michael, Martie, please come up and receive your family's three medals."

Preston felt Martie rise next to him and felt proud of his soon to be wife.

With a standing ovation, they were presented with their medals.

"I would next like to award the following U.S. citizens the Medal of Freedom, also all with Distinction: Barbara B. Metcalf,

Margaret B. Smart, Michael R. Mallory, Buck A. McKinnon, Carlos M. Rodriquez, Detective William A. Smart, and Preston M. Strong."

Again there was much applause as the medal recipients had their medals placed over their heads and stood in a line facing the chamber. Preston felt good and could see both Little Beth jumping up and down, and Clint standing and waving several rows back, as excited as he and Martie. They returned to their seats.

"Thank you all. Now we need to move to the more somber part of this first Congressional meeting since the fateful day, January 1st," continued the president. Preston looked over at Martie, saw her face had a tear halfway down it and he felt for her hand and held it. "We have just about completed the clearing of bodies in and around our twenty main cities, many to the north of us and many to the south. We still have over 300 crematoriums working across the country, but the burning pits are now complete. After seven months of counting our population, we have 47,568,990 citizens alive and well in the United State of America." There was a gasp from many in the chamber. So few people! "We will never know how many Americans died. We estimate 273 million people did not survive this attack on our country for many reasons. Please rise and observe a moment of silence for our fallen family members, friends, citizens of the United States of America, and citizens of the world who did not survive this terrible catastrophe."

"The two main causes of death were exposure to cold and gunshot wounds," continued the president a couple of minutes later as the silent chamber sat down. "As far as the rest of the world is concerned, we believe that over four billion people have died because of the ideas of one man. Nobody on earth has ever caused as many deaths as this one man, Chinese CEO of Zedong Electronics, Chairman Wang Chunqiao. This man will be remembered throughout history as the man who nearly rid the earth of mankind. His actions have put the world back into the dark ages, and I'm afraid we will be "dark" for decades to come.

"Moving forward, I can say one positive thing: At this moment there is probably not one war being waged between any people or factions on earth. It is the first time in our history that the world is completely clear of war, and I hope, for God's sake, it stays that way for the rest of my life."

There was much agreement about that.

"Now we need to rebuild. We need to rebuild our complete infrastructure and, this effort started within days after the New Year. We have some of the best engineers in the world, thousands of them, working on new ideas to bring our country back to the grandness we knew last year. It is going to take time, but we will see these advancements through and win. We have enough food for our people. It must have been God's work, as there was no way our systems could have fed 300 million people. It was a struggle to feed that number before this happened. All our citizens have been placed on farms, or in positions of work to feed, aid and advance our country. For the first time in our lives, money does not rule. I'm sure that in the future people will again be seduced by the power that money can bring, but until that happens we are doing OK. Electricity is being generated to small areas. Many hospitals are up and running across the country and the remaining population is strong and ready to work. I'm more proud to be the President of the United States this year, with what we have achieved, than at any earlier time in office."

There was loud applause.

"As I promised, we need to form a new House of Representatives and Senate, and I will be sending out letters of invitation to people who I believe will be an asset to our country. They will join the current remaining members of Congress, and we will have a complete and running system of government by Christmas this year. I must admit, it has been peaceful for the last

couple of months as president not having the House of Representatives to fight, but all good things must come to an end."

There was much laughter and applause.

"Our new police force is going through training. We have
200,000 military police from all the armed forces joining the
22,000 remaining police officers who will from January 1st, keep
the rule of law across our land. Our armed forces will keep our
country free and democratic until the military hands over
control to the new police force on January 1st. Amtrak is
working well, and we have the complete country under workable
rail. Our farms and farm communities are doing well; a total of
ten million people are working to feed the population and
already preparing for winter. We have collected as many vaccines and medical treatments for illness and disease as we can
and are prepared if any disease spreads into our mid-country
living areas. We plan to open up the southern areas in the next
year or two, depending on many safety factors and the northern
areas after that."

"Lastly, I will organize presidential elections as soon as
possible to do so and then I can hand over the administration of
the country to a duly elected president. Thank you all for your
individual services to your country. Thank you all!" The
president left the chamber.

At the president's exit the Speaker made a final announce-
ment, "Please join the president and members of Congress for
refreshments in the Rotunda. We would like to hear from
anybody who would like to make any suggestions to everyone
congregated here. Afterwards, we will adjourn and the helicopters will take you back to Andrews. Thank you."

"So, Carlos, when are we going to hear about your Colombian
battles?" inquired Martie as they got up to leave.

Sally joined them and inspected him from head to foot and
gently gave him a hug. "See, I let you out of my sight for a couple
of weeks and you come back looking like somebody used you for

target practice! Once we are married, lover boy, you will not be trusted to travel back to Colombia without me. What's wrong with you guys, not looking after my man here?" she stated, looking sternly at Manuela, who was standing by.

"He will tell you, Senorita Sally. We were not in a position to protect him. Even the American Seal Team couldn't protect him," she replied smiling back sweetly.

"We all look pretty medaled up here. I wonder where they found all these medals?" Preston asked. "I'm sure there were more soldiers who should have received medals."

"I was told that these were all they had in stock," commented Buck, coming up to see if Carlos was alright. "The president has a hundred people on his list who are going to get medals, but more medals have to be made first."

"I heard there are fresh doughnuts and fresh Colombian coffee," added Maggie, coming up to join them with Will, Ben and Oprah.

Everybody congratulated each other on the new medals hanging around their necks.

"We have lost the world's coffee market for our Colombian coffee," added Carlos as the group made their way towards the Rotunda. "Colombia is hoping to swap coffee and other items for electronics and, Preston, I think I found a way we can get our 747 licenses."

"Now, that is something I'm looking forward to," replied Preston. "And flying that transporter as well as Majors Wong and Chong will make my day."

"I asked the president to meet with us over the weekend. He is coming down for the weddings, and I think those two majors should be our instructors," replied Carlos. "This is something even Sally can't teach us."

"I'm officially retired after getting my medal. Jennifer and I will be civilians tomorrow, but we might like to fly right seat at least, lover boy," added Sally. "We aren't married yet, but I'm working on my husband-domination protocols as we speak."

"I'm thinking Colombia could be safer than being married... and don't you hit an injured person, Major, or I'll get Manuela to sort you out," replied Carlos, smiling at Preston.

The coffee, doughnuts and Danish were excellent, and it seemed that there wasn't much going on. The president wasn't in the Rotunda and didn't make an appearance.

After half an hour the Speaker apologized and said that the schedule had been changed, the day had come to an end and the helicopters were ready.

CHAPTER 4

Wedding Days

OLIVER AND PUPPY WERE HAPPY to hear the first aircraft returning. The sun was getting low, they had missed the kids in the pool, chewed and broken the only plastic pool bed and fell asleep in the shade of the porch in late afternoon.

One by one the aircraft arrived. Both DC-3s came in first with a lone C-130 bringing in more people.

The late afternoon heat hit everyone as they deplaned and headed for several of the buildings where the air conditioners were doing their job.

"I'm going to get my wound dressed and I'll see you by the pool, Preston," said Carlos, heading towards the hangar. Sally stayed next to him in case he needed help.

Joe, David, and their group wanted to head back to their house, get out of their fancy clothes, grab some meat and come back to get the BBQ started. Martie and the two young ones headed inside to get swimsuits on. Preston hit the closest fridge for a cold Yuengling and made himself comfortable on the porch.

Mike Mallory arrived in his Cessna 210, in formation with Michael Roebels' Beechcraft, and they headed towards the largest building once they closed their aircraft down. Preston noted that Mike Mallory had a large suitcase with him, waved as he closed his aircraft's door, and headed to the large building with Martie's father.

Nobody else was due to arrive. The general, the admiral, the president, and others wanting to attend the two weddings would arrive the next day, Friday, for the festivities. It was beer time in North Carolina, and he was really looking forward to hearing how his friend had been injured. It all seemed rather hush-hush!

The noise from the direction of the swimming pool began as Preston, his medal now on the table next to him, dozed eyes closed; he first heard Little Beth's screams and then the barking of the two dogs. He smiled, envisioning what was going on.

"Asleep already?" asked Carlos mounting the steps onto the porch alone. "Sally wanted to swim and since I cannot, I decided to bring you up-to-date on Colombia."

"Don't you want to tell everybody at once?" Preston asked, his eyes still shut as he heard Carlos take the white rocking chair next to him.

"Much is still top secret, and on a need-to-know basis," Carlos replied. "I just had a weird call from the president while I was changing. He had some sort of meeting with a group of corporate CEOs who seemed to have survived this catastrophe unscathed, and they are beginning to demand a few things he doesn't want to give."

"What things?" asked Preston, opening his eyes and looking at Carlos.

"He wants to have a private meeting with a few of us here, tomorrow—General Patterson, Admiral Rogers, and Mo Wang, of all people. It sounds important and he sounded worried. I've got this weird, uncomfortable feeling that there could be another attack on our country."

"So, what's new?" replied Preston. "It seems everybody wants a slice of this country."

"Preston, before we get company, I'll fill you in on Colombia," continued Carlos. "The reason I am wounded is that we, the

Rodriquez family, were attacked inside the main governmental room by Senator Calderón, the Police Chief Pedro Gonzalez, and four of their men posing as aides."

"You told me there was very heavy security to get into the government chamber," Preston cut in.

"Yes, but we also had four Seals in there, also with guns, before the firefight. Everything happened in a split second, and it wasn't good," continued Carlos. "The first people shot were my uncles, the admiral, and Uncle Philippe. The admiral was hit by four bullets at point-blank range from the police chief and his aides. Luckily only one shot penetrated down the arm hole of his bulletproof jacket and missed most of his vital organs. He is still in intensive care, but he will live, and will continue as Admiral of the Colombian Navy. Uncle Philippe was shot in the head twice from across the table, a shot each from Gonzalez and Calderón, and was dead before he hit the ground. The damage was already done with one uncle dead and one badly wounded."

Preston said nothing, but looked at his friend in shock. He had liked the ambassador; he was a straightforward and honest man.

"Unfortunately, they had the element of surprise, and six shooters against four. Once Gonzalez shot Uncle Philippe, he, as well as one of Calderon's "aides" aimed at my father who was standing next to me. I pushed him out of the way and I got the bullets meant for him. By this time, Charlie Meyers, who was standing next to me, disintegrated Pedro Gonzalez's head. On my father's other side, Sergeant Rodriquez was firing, but I think my father, pushed into him by me, ruined his aim for a split second. This second gave the four "aides" behind Calderón and Gonzalez, on the other side of the table, time to shoot the president and six of the most important government ministers before Lieutenant Paul and a fourth Seal sitting on the other side of the room blew the four "aides" to bits, I believe before I even hit the floor. As I said, it was all over in a second or two."

"The whole Colombian government in one second!" exclaimed Preston.

"Pretty close," replied Carlos. "The most important and most powerful government ministers always sat on either side of the president."

"What were Calderón's sons doing?" asked Preston.

"Nothing. They didn't move. The senator collapsed back into his chair, his right arm spewing blood from three shots from our side of the room. I was told that he just sat there looking triumphant with a broad smile on his face. The guards in charge of the captives were slow to act and by the time they moved, two Seals, Manuela, and Dani crashed through the door offering to shoot them all if there was any movement from them or the captives."

"I'm sorry to hear about Philippe. He was a good man," Preston replied.

"He would have become the next president, that is why both men shot him," continued Carlos. "The president is now dead, and the vice-president has been missing for a couple of weeks, so Uncle Philippe was sure to be the first choice to become president. While I was being rushed to the hospital, the remaining government officials decided right there and then, and with all the blood on the floor and walls, to elect my father as president... which means that now I am the son of the President of Colombia. Unbelievable!" Carlos exclaimed.

Preston was totally silent, and again in shock. It was as hard for him to believe as it was for Carlos.

"I was released from the hospital four days later. Even though it was only a flesh wound of sorts, the bullet hit a blood vessel or something, so much of the blood on the floor was mine."

"It must have been close, you reaching the hospital and getting blood into you?" Preston asked.

"Yes, but don't tell anybody. I am O-Positive, and they had me connected and were pumping blood into me minutes after the ambulance got me to the hospital. Sergeant Rodriquez and Manuela, I was told, held my wound to halt the bleeding all the way. Thanks to them I'm alive today. Please, Preston, don't tell Sally any of this. I will tell her in my own good time in a few days when we have time to talk. Let's get this meeting with the president over tomorrow morning, and our weddings behind us on Saturday, and then I think things will come together."

Preston silently agreed. "What happened to the Calderóns?" he asked.

"They managed to keep the senator alive for a week, while I regained enough strength to leave the hospital. My father wanted to wait for my uncle, the admiral, to regain strength, but he was and still is in the ICU, so they decided to go ahead with the trial. The court was convened the day after I was discharged and the trial lasted two days..."

"Preston! Preston, Carlos, come and swim?" asked a dripping Little Beth from below the stairs to the porch looking up at them, her eyes pleading.

"Sorry, little girl, Carlos and I are having a meeting," replied Preston. "I will be there shortly. Now go and play and I'll join you when we are finished."

"Why are grown-ups always having meetings?" Little Beth complained, shaking her head and running back to the cool water.

Carlos smiled. He wasn't able to swim yet, but the thought of it was pleasant.

"The justice system took two days to conclude the trial. Senator Calderón knew he was done for, and his sons never said a word during the two days. The Senator lambasted the government for listening to my uncles. He stated to the court that the assassinated president was a puppet of the Rodriquez family and he and the government officials should be on trial, not him. He reminded the court how his father was killed by my grandmother, shot at point-blank range. When the court asked him about his father shooting farmers and other innocent victims decades ago, he just smiled and told the entire room that his father was just cleaning the trash out of the country."

"Innocent farmers are trash?" Preston asked.

"He happily stated that anybody who wasn't a Calderón today, or in the Calderón Cartel, or other family cartels, was totally unimportant to the country. He reminded us Colombians that three of his ancestors ruled this area of South America for 40 out of 120 years, and the Calderón family still had a say in the running of the country with him as senator."

"They did?" Preston asked.

"Yes, but the judge reminded the senator that the last time the senator's family had ruled Colombia was over 150 years ago, and the man was called Arboleda. He had taken over power in a coup and didn't have a very productive history, nor did any of Calderón's earlier ancestors. There was much laughter in the courtroom. The judge certainly knew his history. He even mentioned that my ancestor, Mariano Ospina Rodríguez, ruled well for six years before Arboleda, I think, and men from several other good and prominent Colombian families had been president since then. And the judge reminded the senator that, although he may have forgotten, the president he had personally shot also had the last name Calderón, but that didn't seem to matter!"

Preston looked at Carlos in shock. "The president was also a Calderón?" He shook his head. Latin America was a hard region to understand.

"That was why my uncles were always careful around the president. They didn't know what side he was on, but now we now know he wasn't aiding the other Calderón family."

"So, what happened?" asked Preston urgently.

"They were all found guilty of treason. Colombia did away with executions years ago because Colombia used some of the worst ways to kill people, and it was important to stop all forms of execution; but several of the ministers who had survived the chamber massacre wanted it back, forcing my father to temporarily reinstate death by firing squad."

"Tell me one," requested Preston.

"Ever hear of the *Colombian Necktie*?" Carlos replied. Preston stated that he hadn't. "It is believed to have been introduced by Escobar in the fifties. In this method of killing someone, especially someone you don't like, the victim's throat is slit with a knife or a sharp object, and the tongue is drawn through the open wound." Carlos imitated the act, showing Preston how and where. "The tongue is pulled towards the sternum rendering the name necktie. The victim dies of blood loss or of asphyxiation. The killing method is very disturbing and is meant to warn others, such as informers of illegal activities. I had heard of it, but never saw it myself, and don't know anyone else who ever witnessed a victim."

Preston wanted to be sick and looked at Carlos with his face whiter than usual.

"Unfortunately, my uncles and most of the government ministers still alive thought it necessary to bring back state executions in this new world for as long as necessary. They passed a new law the same day the Calderóns were found guilty of treason. The senator had a smile on his face up to this point, knowing that he would be looked after in prison. Everyone was sure that half of the men in the prison system, inmates and guards, would certainly see that he got everything he wished for, hence the need to bring back executions. Preston, you should have seen the senator's smile disappear when the judge was approached by the rest of the government ministers with a Decree stating that Death by Firing Squad was now available to him as a sentence."

"They announced this new law in court in front of everybody?" Preston asked.

Carlos nodded. "The smile left Calderón's face and was suddenly on most of the faces in the gallery. Then he went berserk, shouting obscenities at the judge and everybody. He was then gagged so that he couldn't speak. The judge passed sentence, stating that five days later the four men would be shot at dawn in public by military firing squad. That happened two days before I returned."

"Didn't anybody try to rescue him?" was Preston's next question.

"My uncle, the Air Force General, had 50,000 loyal troops brought into Bogotá, and nobody was allowed in or out until the executions were over. The senator was shot writhing and screaming for mercy. He was worse than a rabid dog. His sons, Manuel, Alberto and Pedro were much braver. They stood there, refusing blindfolds, smoking their last cigarettes and even tried to ignore the screaming senator, now bound to a post next to them."

The next morning the usual flights brought in the president and several military brass, including General Patterson and Admiral Rogers.

Preston was surprised that it was to be such a small meeting, less than a dozen people, in the president's log cabin lounge.

Only he and Carlos were asked for. Everyone else continued to enjoy the swimming and preparing the church for the Saturday weddings. Preston and Carlos had decided to get married in one ceremony, and the girls had agreed.

Preston walked in helping Carlos; Carlos' bodyguards, ever close behind, stayed out as the doors were closed. He looked around and saw a couple of guys he did not see land earlier, Lieutenants Charlie Meyers and Joe Paul, both in their Seal uniforms. As expected, Mo and Lee Wang were there, as well as Patterson, Rogers and Mike Mallory. Three other military guards were in attendance.

Everyone sat down around the long dining room table, and the president began the session.

"I had a very strange meeting with several men yesterday after the meeting in the Capitol," he began. The room was quiet and everyone looked at the man speaking. "This meeting had been prearranged through one of my staff working at the White House. Peter Westbrook, whom many of you know, ran the agricultural company *MonteDiablo* up to last year. He called the White House on a satellite phone and wanted to speak to me. I was actually here in North Carolina at the time and he was surprised to find out I was not available; he wanted to know where I was, but was not told. Three days later I received a call from Bill Bowers, head of the pharmaceutical group *Bruche*, who many of you know was the biggest drug company in the U.S. and, I believe the world, up to last year. He wanted a meeting to discuss matters of extreme urgency and I asked him to come to Washington the following day, if it was that urgent. I was informed by the Air Force that he arrived at Andrews in a fully-operational ten-year-old Gulfstream jet. The engineers at Andrews wanted to go over it, but the pilots and an armed guard refused them entry; however, they found the exterior of the aircraft to be original and fully operational."

"How could that be?" Carlos asked. "General Allen's private aircraft was about the same age, and it had less than ten percent of its electrical equipment working."

"I was told afterwards that Bowers was pretty upset that Air Force personnel had inspected his aircraft. It was the same lousy attitude he had when he and a couple of his cronies talked to me —Mark Weinstein and Paul Proker, the CEOs from the drug companies, *Hearst* and *Decibel*. They were emphatic that since their three drug companies, and *MonteDiablo,* the agricultural company, had lost nearly a trillion dollars each in assets and business since New Year's Eve, that they should receive the help of the entire country's infrastructure to rebuild so they can supply the United States with their products."

"Why?" asked Mike Mallory. "Look around this airfield. Look at all the healthy people around here. We know the U.S. population is not as well off as the people who are living here at Preston's airfield, but I've seen hundreds of thousands of average civilians and military personnel over the last couple of months. I have always personally handed out food, and I always noticed that the survivors, the people who are still out there, are very strong and healthy; far healthier than the people I used to fly around for Southwest Airlines. I can't remember when I last noticed an overweight person. Remember the trouble Southwest got into when they used to ask extremely overweight people to leave our aircraft?" The Americans in the room nodded.

"Who still needs the drugs from these companies?" asked Preston. "I'm sure most of the people dependent on those drugs are no longer alive."

"That's exactly what I told them," continued the president. "I informed them that even the First Family hadn't taken so much as an aspirin since New Year's Eve."

"What about *MonteDiablo*? What did they have to do with the meeting?" asked Mike Mallory.

"We had been in the meeting for less than thirty minutes, and in walks Peter Westbrook. He had just landed at Andrews in the exact same type of Gulfstream as the three drug CEOs. I was told the only difference was the numbers on the tails."

"Very odd!" commented General Patterson. "Where did they fly in from? Did you ask, Mr. President?"

"I did and they weren't very forthcoming... What range do those Gulfstreams have, General?" the president asked. The general got on his satellite phone to Andrews and it took only a couple of minutes to get the answer he needed.

"They were Gulfstream Vs, range over 6,000 miles. They could have flown in from anywhere in North America, even

Europe or parts of Asia non-stop," the general replied. "But they should be pieces of junk with at least 90 percent of their electronics non-operational." He thought for a few seconds. "Mo Wang, could you enlighten us from Zedong's perspective on why these two jets are still flying?"

The room was silent.

"General, I don't know any more than you. I also cannot understand how these aircraft did not get produced with parts from Zedong Electronics, but we could look at similar parts in the Z-10 helicopters. Some parts could be fitted to both aircraft: directional systems, radar, communications. If we get a second chance, have a few of the Chinese engineers inspect the aircraft when they are available."

"Good idea," added Carlos, and Preston raised his eyebrows at Carlos' remark.

"They must have had Chinese parts fitted into their flight systems at some time, especially if they were made by Raytheon or Bendix King and especially Garmin. We know they used these defunct parts in everything they fitted into all modern aircraft worldwide. These jets began flying between 1997 and 1998 I believe, and if they are even the oldest Gulfstream Vs flying, they would have had Zedong parts in them."

"Or the parts were changed before New Year's Eve?" Preston offered, and everybody suddenly looked at him. There was again silence in the room.

"Could these companies be in cahoots with Zedong Electronics?" asked Admiral Rogers.

"And why would they flaunt their fancy jets right in front of our noses?" General Patterson asked.

"Unless they have more power and security than we know, and want us to realize they are a force to be reckoned with?" suggested Preston.

"What did they actually want from you, Mr. President?" Carlos asked.

"Very simple," he replied. "To halt all future production across the United States and go to their aid to rebuild their factories and supply them with labor. Also, re-introduce the dollar immediately, and get Wall Street and the banks up and running. Peter Westbrook simply wanted every farmer in the country to be forced to purchase his products, stocks of which, he declared, were enough to feed this country and most of the western world."

"And Westbrook and *MonteDiablo* have enough stockpiled to do this?" Admiral Rogers asked.

"It seems so, with the world's reduced population," the president responded.

"Isn't that good?" the admiral asked.

"I don't actually know," the president replied. "In the last several years they had invited, or persuaded farmers to purchase their GMO, genetically modified products. I've had so many conflicting reports from the USDA, farming groups and other interested parties in my term of office that I stayed away from the discussions. I had enough problems trying to get our troops home. Even closing Guantanamo was a never-ending fight with the Pentagon."

"There was a lot of controversy, I remember," General Patterson added. "It wasn't my line of interest. But, I think we are getting away from our immediate problem, which is, did they threaten you, Mr. President?"

"Not directly; they just made it clear that the U.S. would be far better off if medications were made Number One on the priority list and Westbrook's products Number Two. They were certainly very polite and direct and to the point. I felt much like a lamb being sized up for dinner by a tiger or a lion; which part to bite first. You know what I mean?"

"What was the final outcome of the meeting yesterday?" General Patterson asked.

"They want me to immediately send groups of electricians

and engineers to seven of their main production plants around the country and get them up and running again. Then they want troops to guard these production plants.

"Reintroduce the dollar into the economy and Westbrook wanted every farmer to purchase his products from locations he is supposed to be setting up across the country, on credit."

"Yes, I heard of one of these new locations, twenty miles north of Kansas City, where the farmers are being told to get their agricultural products on account and that they would not be charged for them until the economy gets going again," added Mike Mallory. "There was a report of a farmer who refused to accept their help, and he hasn't been seen since. This was only a week ago."

"Sounds bad to me," suggested Preston.

"I would like to have these new locations inspected by the new police force," stated General Patterson, and the others around the table nodded.

"I will get as much ground information as I can," added Mike.

"I think we should get these guys back for a meeting with you, Mr. President," suggested Carlos. "Say, in a week's time. I could search for any transponder use from the Gulfstreams as they fly towards Washington by bringing the Navistar satellite closer towards the atmosphere. That will take about 72 hours.

"General Patterson, maybe the gunships could be put out in a spider's web to monitor radio signals from unknown traffic heading towards Washington? Admiral Rogers, you have those two Hurricane Hunters. May I assume their weather instruments could source out unidentified flying aircraft up to a reasonable distance?"

"A good 500 to 600 miles," replied Admiral Rogers.

"If these guys have Gulfstreams flying, and they were in cahoots with Zedong Electronics, they could have an army of Chinese troops protecting them, a base of operations and modern weapons as protection... Hold on." Carlos thought for a couple of seconds. "General Patterson, the 747 transporter couldn't fly from Harbin, China to JFK nonstop. It doesn't have the range. We used Hawaii to refuel, they didn't. Where would they have refueled the transporter to get it into New York at the very beginning?"

Everybody thought this one out and General Patterson pulled a map of the United States and a map of the world out of his briefcase. Then he phoned Major Wong, who happened to be flying the 747 transporter towards Colombia. The general switched the phone on to speaker, so that everybody in the room could hear.

"Maximum range, fully loaded 4,970 miles, Sir. That is the absolute limit and I wouldn't fly it further than 4,800 miles with the loads we are carrying today. We have this baby full of very heavy electrical parts and motors, Miniguns and ammo, and I think we have exchanged at least a hundred miles of range for cargo weight."

"How heavy do you believe the aircraft was when we watched her fly into JFK for the first time in January?" The general asked.

"I would say at normal load, 4,900-mile range minus head winds and other weather problems. Since her end-station was only New York City, they must have allowed for problematic weather patterns, I would say a maximum range of 4,500 miles."

"Thank you, Wong, fly safe. Out," replied the general ending the phone conversation. "So, gentlemen, the Chinese pilots flying a heavy load into JFK with no alternate landing possibilities would have taken off from a base within 4,500 miles of New York. That's about a quarter of the globe."

"Didn't the transporter fly in with the other 747s, which could fly non-stop from Harbin, and possibly Shanghai?" asked Carlos.

"Your point, Carlos?" asked the general.

"Somewhere they joined into formation, so the transporter

would have had to fly in a direction to join them, which needed a second leg, and a shorter range. The aircraft could not have flown a straight leg into New York and the airfield it took off from must have been close to the polar route the 747s took."

"Good point!" replied the general. "Which means they must have another air base in Western Russia, Canada, or even Alaska? The 747 transporter must have taken off somewhere closer to the Arctic."

"Can we check its black box, or flight-recording data on board?" asked Preston.

"We tried months ago and found that the black box, transponder, and all recording devices were missing," replied General Patterson. "There was absolutely no recorded flight data at all anywhere on all the captured Chinese Airlines aircraft." There was silence as the general looked over the map.

"Canada would have been too cold. They would have headed pretty far north though, to get away from prying eyes, setting up their base," suggested Admiral Rogers.

"Russia, or Alaska, or its outlying islands sound like a good places?" suggested the president, and General Patterson worked out distances westwards from JFK.

"JFK to Anchorage is 3,336 miles. Japan and Vladivostok are too far, and they didn't go into Hawaii, so I think Alaska is in a good position for a refueling point, but where? Do you know how big Alaska is?" General Patterson asked.

"Yes, it would be like looking for a needle in a haystack," agreed Carlos. "But if we can catch their incoming flight direction into Andrews, we could backtrack the direction, and if we just so happen to have one of Admiral Rogers' Hurricane Hunters flying high out of Elmendorf Air Force Base, it might even see the aircraft's direction closer to its departure point. The second Hurricane Hunter could be directly north of Andrews, say over northern Canada if the Gulfstream flies in on a polar route."

"Great idea, Carlos," commended General Patterson. "We could, as you say, have a spider's web of outer aircraft, say 3,000 miles out over Anchorage and Canada, a middle sweep of AC-130 gunships, say, 2,000 miles out, and our radar capabilities will pick them up at 700 to 900 miles distance. They will have good pilots, and I'm sure will not fly in directly, but rather come in from different directions; when our radar picks them up, it will make us think they are arriving from Europe or somewhere. They have enough range to fly in circles around the U.S. if they want to, and I'm sure they will pick up our radar as soon as it finds them."

"I'll bet a Yuengling on Alaska," smiled the president.

"And what happens if you are wrong?" asked Preston.

"I'll give you my job, the Oval Office... and my comfortable bed at the White House," stated the president.

"Mo Wang, what can you tell us about this new information that you haven't told us already? Anything you can remember, something small that might be relevant to this discussion," General Patterson asked.

"I have been going over many things in my mind while you were discussing the problem," answered Mo. "The private jet aircraft of the Chairman was also a Gulfstream. I remember seeing it in Harbin, a white one and I thought it a very expensive aircraft. Once, I saw two of the same aircraft together, in December 2011, I think. I wondered why the Chairman needed two aircraft. Both aircraft were only there for a matter of hours.

"I did have a conversation with my friend Colonel Rhu, who was the base commander at Harbin. I met with him in Hawaii a few days after we left China to attack the South Americans. He was quite surprised about the nuclear missiles at the second base."

"He didn't know about them?" General Patterson asked.

"No, he was surprised we only found the big one. He remembered the smaller nuclear missiles which came into his airfield beginning in 2010. I told him three of the Pakistani missiles had been fired on China, and he was surprised that we didn't find more at the location."

"More of the Pakistani missiles?" asked General Patterson, his face slowly going white.

"Yes, he was sure that he had seen more than three of the smaller missiles go through his base, but he thought he could have counted the same load twice. Colonel Rhu remembers the 747 transporter bringing in two of the missiles on one flight. They were not unloaded while he was on duty; the aircraft just sat there and was refueled. It was gone the next day. The next week it arrived again with 2 missiles, maybe the same ones, as he did not see the first two off-loaded. He told me that this time he did watch them being removed from the aircraft. They weren't very large, about 18 meters—50 feet—long, and in one piece. There was equipment inside the aircraft which helped roll the cigar-shaped missiles forward out of the large nose door. It took less than two hours to have both missiles inside a hangar. A few weeks later he was in the control tower when the 747 transporter landed and this time there was only one missile aboard and off-loaded the same way, and the two first missiles had disappeared from inside the hangar. The guards from the other base had been in control of the missile movement."

"Oh my God!" stated the general. "The enemy, whoever they are, could still have nuclear missiles aimed at the United States." There was now total silence in the room.

Carlos was the first to speak. "The range from anywhere in Alaska won't get to Washington D.C. The range of these missiles, you told me was what, 1,500 miles?"

"Correct," replied the general. "Maximum 1,500 miles, but that is a big chunk of the United States. Let's say they are in Anchorage, Alaska. 1,500 miles would put..." He studied the map again. "Would put the entire West Coast in range. Maybe the Russian multi-head was to terminate the East Coast and if

Zedong Electronics had more of these Pakistani Shaheen II rockets, they were meant for the West Coast, or even Hawaii?"

The meeting ended with a plan, which was top secret, and nobody would be told outside of that room. Even the guards had been asked to leave once the meeting had begun.

Early the next morning, after very little sleep, Preston walked alone around the airport with the two dogs. The wedding was the main reason he hadn't slept. It wasn't that marrying Martie was a problem, but it was all happening a little too fast.

He did not have a nice, new suit to get married in, just the one and only suit he had worn to Capitol Hill for the meeting. Martie and Sally had not been seen for a day. They were with all the other girls, using Martie's old sewing machine, he assumed, to make wedding dresses. While he was entertaining Little Beth and Clint the evening before, he noticed that the beige dining room curtains were missing. He didn't say anything but Little Beth saw that he had noticed the missing curtains, and sternly asked Preston not to ask about them.

"All this happening in the world, and now I'm about to get married!" he thought. The timing wasn't perfect, but at least they had a church, friends and enough food and drink for the occasion. Even their old friends, the initial Air Force guards, including his friend the tech sergeant who had worked on both his fighter aircraft, had flown in late the previous evening for the occasion.

Even with his unease, the day turned out to be very good for Preston.

He and Clint chatted while he dressed, and then helped Carlos, who was getting stronger every day, into his one and only suit. The weather was hot and sticky, and for the first time, he felt he would rather be swimming in the cool water of the pool instead of walking to the church on a muggy morning. Clint had on one of Joe's old suits, which was a size or two too large, but they made it work for him. He was wheeled to the church by Mike Mallory, who also had on an old suit.

To Preston, they looked like a bunch of dressed-up gun-slingers from the old days, or part of Al Capone's mob with handkerchiefs hanging out of their breast pockets. All they needed were hats and Tommy guns.

Carlos and Preston, together at the front of the new church, waited with the Air Force minister from Seymour Johnson. He looked inside and noticed that everybody had managed to squeeze into its small interior. He could hardly recognize many of the guests, now all dressed up, and saw that the president, Will Smart and oddly, Mo Wang, were the best dressed men out of the civilian males, their suits stylish and well-made. Joe still looked like a farmer with a suit on, and David wore a sports jacket and khaki slacks. Maybe he didn't own a suit? Joe's boys looked like a bunch of youngsters suited up from the Bronx. Only the military men, all in their best dress uniforms, looked comfortable in their attire.

The French girls all looked gorgeous. They were tanned and dressed in the European clothes they had arrived with. The First Family and the Smart family were elegant. Lee, his wife and daughter, as well as Lu and her family also looked good, but Preston could see the difference between their best clothes and the European models. He was still wondering what had happen-ed to the dining room curtains when both curtains suddenly shadowed the entrance to the church. An old record was put on the record player, which began playing an instrumental of the Wedding March, Martie's favorite, and the only piece of wedding music they had. This got Preston all emotional as he had often listened to it with Martie.

Both men looked towards their brides and Preston, with damp eyes, realized that he had never seen his dining room curtains so beautiful. The newly designed curtains had been transformed into identical dresses, simple, strapless gowns and looked like they had been purchased in a fine dress shop. He realized that Marie and Beatrice had certainly helped in their design.

Martie with her father, and Sally with hers, walked up the aisle slowly. The two fathers kissed their daughters and left the girls with their grooms.

Preston recalled a myriad of hazy memories while the Minister spoke, of his parents, his childhood, when he first met Martie, and the times they had discussed their wedding in a big church somewhere. Now he was getting married in a makeshift Air Force church in North Carolina with old aircraft all around, and the best bunch of people anybody getting married could ask for.

He got his words right. Clint gave him the ring and Little Beth gave Carlos Sally's ring, both donated by the French girls.

And then he was married. Both he and Carlos kissed their brides and the church was totally silent.

Together the four newlyweds walked down the aisle and into the heat, where two soldiers, each driving one of Joe's Rat Patrol jeeps all dressed out with flowers and greenery, took them the short fifty yards to the house porch.

It was a party to remember. The day blew past in a crazy ensemble of happy, smiling people, beer, and BBQ, and the four newlyweds were thrown, fully dressed, into the swimming pool.

CHAPTER 5

Who Are These Guys?

THREE DAYS LATER, with the weddings and festivities over, many of the attendees were heading back home. The latest information shared by the president the day before the wedding, was discussed at the airfield between Preston and Carlos. They had already discussed married life over a beer, and both agreed that a good escape, if ever needed, was to get invited aboard Mo's boat to go fishing.

"So, we now have three days before we go hunting for these guys. Where do you think they are, Carlos?"

"I'm siding with the president and saying somewhere in Alaska," replied Carlos, enjoying a second, ice-cold beer. Canada doesn't have many airfields long enough for a 747-ERF (extended-range freighter). Russia, I'm sure does, but the area around the Bering Sea, and where General Allen flew over on his flight to Japan would be my bet."

"Does Alaska have many long runways?" asked Martie, coming up with some freshly-made snacks with Sally a few steps behind.

"I'm not sure, but I did hear about several extended runways prepared for the old NASA program years ago."

"I'd sit on your lap, lover boy, but you are so fragile in your old age!" added Sally, sitting down next to her husband.

"Yes, how are your wounds doing, Carlos?" Martie asked.

"A couple of flesh wounds and he thinks he needs an army of pretty Colombian nurses to look after him," added Sally, punching him on the shoulder, although not as hard as she normally did.

"I think our secret escape location is getting more important," stated Carlos to Preston smiling innocently.

"We have only been married a couple of days and you guys already want to get away?" asked Sally, looking at Carlos sternly. "I assume you want to go fishing or something?"

Preston laughed. "Sal, you are so on the button every time!"

"Why are you guys talking about Alaska anyway?" Martie asked, sitting on the stairs in front of Preston and grabbing two beers from an ice bucket next to her husband. She handed one to Sally.

Preston, who had been given clearance over his satellite phone to bring Sally and Martie into the picture by the general earlier that morning, told the two girls the next problem facing America.

"That's a load of crap!" asserted Martie, hearing about the drug companies. "Why so many people were on these drugs, I will never know. I think that most of these new drugs invented by these horrible drug companies were designed to "cure" diseases that didn't even exist until the drug companies invented them as well! I don't have bad gas, constipation, bad bones, stomach problems, or suffer from any of the things they always advertised on television, and I don't know anybody who has!

"I can understand diabetes, or cancer, or heart disease, but within the last couple of decades they promoted bodily problems I never heard of; and they always used an acronym to name the disease like IFD, APR, or..."

"A four-hour erection?" added Carlos.

"Oh, shut up!" exclaimed Preston.

"Yeah! Just let me know when you have one of those, lover boy, and I'll give you some tablets for it!" laughed Sally, nudging Martie.

They then discussed how many people did not like Westbrook, head of *MonteDiablo* and how that company always seemed to be bullying small farmers.

"Now that's all we have, small farmers growing natural crops, and he wants to stop that and get the big GMO-supplied farms running again. I think I know where to put some of those bullets you got for me last year, Preston!" added Martie. "Up his Alpha Sierra Sierra!"

The girls were shocked when Carlos told them about their possible link to Zedong Electronics, and Martie replied that life in America would have been hell if the other side had won.

"Carlos, can you ever get the Navistar low enough for its cameras to actually get a visual on an aircraft?" Preston asked.

"The more modern models, which are now useless scrap metal up there, yes, but remember this was an experimental model and the first of its kind. Lee Wang and I have tried to define all the ways we could enhance the satellite's viewing capabilities: infra-red, heat-sourcing, X-ray, but this old girl just doesn't have the technology; plus, the screens we view the information on would have black and white dots bigger than any aircraft, even if we lowered her to within 70 to 80 miles above earth. One hope for the distant future is to rebuild more advanced technology into the three satellites aboard the second Russian rocket we found in Harbin, and get that up into space ASAP. I reckon that is up to Martie's father to come up with new electronic marvels and not Mr. Westbrook getting all the people in the world to fix his agricultural company."

For the rest of the day they sat and enjoyed each other's company, and discussed the world as they now knew it. All four understood that these CEOs lacked integrity; they had no interest in the common good or for the United States. Their only goal was to rebuild their own personal fortunes and the power that went with it.

Three days later and fully relaxed, the four headed up to Andrews for the scheduled meeting on Capitol Hill with the corporate CEOs. All of those staying at Preston's airfield had been invited to the meeting as potential new members of Congress. Buck and Barbara were doing the flying this day for the first group and left separately.

There would be several of the former House and Senate members in attendance. Overall, the president wanted the meeting to look like an official meeting of the new U.S. legislative and executive branches.

Lady Dandy, now fitted with several military-issue arm chairs and a couple of other luxuries, like an old refrigerator and coffee machine, was the transportation of choice. Buck had been hard at work with Michael Roebels; he had taken Grandpa Roebels' place and had flown across the country with Martie's dad for the wedding and then the meeting.

They arrived at Andrews and met Lee and Mo Wang in an empty hangar. The two Wangs had a couple of the best Chinese engineers with them and were trying to get a modern FBI tracking device, the size of a box of cigarettes to work. They didn't have replacement parts for such a modern device and were trying to improvise.

"That's a one in a million chance," stated Michael Roebels once he was shown what they were trying to achieve in the empty hangar the CEOs had demanded. "I thought of this when General Patterson explained the situation to me. It will take months to get any tracking device working. The only idea I've come up with to track an aircraft is to bypass the aircraft's own transponder on/off switch and make sure that it is beeping away to us when they leave. That won't show up on their radar and if the "on" light is disconnected, then the pilots shouldn't notice it giving us a position every few seconds.

"Great idea!" exclaimed Carlos. "I wish I had thought of that. We just need to get into their aircraft, but they want this hangar sealed and they are bringing in armed guards to make sure nobody gets in. Can they do that?"

"I doubt it," added Preston. "This is an American Air Force base for heaven's sake. They don't have diplomatic immunity. I'm sure someone will get into their aircraft somehow."

"They are even getting mobile fuel trucks in here, so they can refuel themselves," Lee Wang added.

"Mo, are there any parts we got out of Harbin that could help us with a tracking device, or this FBI bug to follow these guys? We have two massive warehouses full of your Chinese replacements," Michael asked.

"Those types of replacement parts, as far as the Chairman was concerned, would no longer be necessary in his new world," Mo Wang replied. "Remember the several Zedong Electronics open-door bugs the Cambridge University engineers found and studied back in England in May 2012, I think the month was?" Everybody nodded. "Once that news hit the papers, he decided that the only parts needed in his new world would be to get the infrastructure of the country going again, everything but devices for military software, aviation and nautical electronics. With his own fleet of Jumbo Jets and ten massive container ships, he would have the only import/export transportation fleet worldwide, and it would be sufficient to transport everything he would need in his new country. He wasn't at all interested in the rest of the world. They could all go and live in caves again for all he cared."

General Patterson walked in with a couple of men behind him.

"Good morning," he stated, shaking everybody's hand. "Got

any ideas on how we can track these guys? They are due to land in two hours and so far we have seen nothing on any radar screens."

"Nothing much so far," replied Martie's father. "It's a sort of impossible task. These guys, their pilots, and their connections would have had time to think out these problems months or even years ahead as a possible scenario. Somehow we need to get one person in here to play with their transponders and hopefully get them working. Are you going to adhere to their demands of privacy while their aircraft sit here? Why don't you just take them into custody and make them tell you where they are based? Guantanamo is still open, as of December last year."

A soldier ran into the empty hangar. "Radar connection with one aircraft over Newfoundland, approximately twelve hundred miles out, sir! The Hurricane Hunter noticed her several seconds ago."

"So they are not coming in together," stated the general "Excuse me, I want to check all our radar aircraft out there," and he left the hangar at a rapid walk.

Carlos and Preston followed him at a slower pace. They knew where his command center would be, in the Andrews' main communications room.

"I think we have something," General Patterson said to them as they entered a few minutes later. "The Canadian Hurricane Hunter over the U.S./Canadian border thought they saw an extremely faint blip of an aircraft over an hour ago on the extreme edge of their screen in the western area of the Labrador Sea; it was so faint that they didn't think to report it. It couldn't have been an aircraft, unless it was flying less than 2,000 feet above the terrain."

"At that low a cruise altitude, any jet will be literally burning through its fuel, even at slower cruise speeds," stated Carlos. "A Gulfstream could lose a third of its range."

"Correctly stated," replied General Patterson. "Even if they stayed over water, which they would have to do at that altitude, it would cause havoc to the jets flying conditions, not to mention the dense sea air going through the engines."

"Maybe they didn't fly the whole trip at that altitude, but just the last part," suggested Carlos looking at the extra-large map General Patterson was studying on a massive map table. "The other Hurricane Hunter hasn't reported anything?"

"One virtually unnoticeable blip, three hours ago, about 300 miles north of Alaska, well over the Beaufort Sea. One millisecond blip and it was gone," General Patterson replied.

"Sir, we have a new contact from the gunship over Seattle," stated a female Air Force soldier listening on a satellite phone. "Unidentified aircraft incoming from the direction of Hawaii, 200 miles from San Francisco, at 49,000 feet and at a fast cruise."

"It's weird that Hawaii didn't pick her up, or tell us of any aircraft movements in their area," stated Preston

"Radar coverage is only 500 miles out from the air force base," stated General Patterson. "The aircraft must have known this and headed at an angle further north than that. This one must have flown over the Bering Sea and then across the Pacific far to the north of Hawaii and then turned directly eastwards, always out of range of our Hawaiian, Alaskan and West Coast radars. These guys certainly know our limits without our satellite coverage. Sergeant, tell the Hurricane Hunter over Alaska to head into Hawaii to refuel and then take up a position west of Hawaii and directly on the International Dateline. That inbound aircraft will be at least three hours late for our meeting, if it is coming in our direction at all. Sergeant, tell our nearest West Coast base to get into contact and find out who it is."

"I wonder why they are so late?" asked Carlos.

They found out several minutes later from the air force base that it was indeed Westbrook, and he apologized to the meeting attendees saying that he had had aircraft problems and would be three hours late.

By this time they were also in contact with the aircraft incoming over the Labrador Sea. It carried the three drug CEOs, and they stated they were on time and were flying out of Scotland.

"Rubbish," commented General Patterson. "I know that route well. I've flown from Scotland to Andrews dozens of times and the usual civilian flight lane is at least 200 miles south of their current position. Nobody would be flying so low over the North Atlantic. I see they have already climbed up to a normal cruse altitude of 40,000 feet. Those Gulfstream Vs can sure climb fast. Ten minutes ago he was reported at close to sea level. They must be coming in from somewhere else." He began plotting times and ideas onto the map with a red marker and a long ruler. Carlos and Preston joined him.

"The flight over from the first blip northwest of Alaska would take two and a half hours at their current speed," continued the general talking loudly to himself, "and that blip was registered over three hours ago, which gives them an extra 30 minutes to maybe fly further north and stay well out of our radar range.

"Two-thirds of a 6,000-mile range is still 4,000 miles," suggested Carlos. "General, I think you should get a gunship somewhere around the Resolute Bay Airport, Northern Canada, here." He showed the location on the map to the general. "There is a complete open sea corridor which passes right by the airfield. I bet the jet was flown low through this corridor, which leads directly into the Labrador Sea and where the aircraft is currently. That is about 1,000 miles of low flying. I bet the pilots have to cut the corner to get into Andrews on their fuel reserves. I bet he has flown only a part of the way below 5,000 feet."

"Good thinking," replied General Patterson. "I actually did an emergency landing at Resolute about three years ago and was told by the locals that the runway was due to be extended to 3,000 meters. That could even be their base of operations."

"Not if that blip on the radar over the Beaufort Sea has anything to do with the same aircraft," Carlos replied.

"Well, let's say they thought they were out of range, they were, apart from the Hurricane Tracker, and it's totally different electronics to monitor wind speed and not your usual everyday gas-guzzler fancy jet. They could have kept low for another couple of hundred miles to cut the corner which would get them over the Beaufort Sea in the shortest possible route, then climb while flying through the McClure Strait, descend and fly low through the Viscount Melville and Lancaster Sounds in case the Canadians were tracking them, about 400 miles in distance. Once they got through to the Davis Strait, they might have headed over to Greenland and then thought it safe to climb back up to a normal cruise altitude once they were in the middle of nowhere. I have calculated 5,100 miles of which at least 700 to 800 miles were flown at low altitude and I believe, if they are coming from my scenario area, the pilots are going to land on fumes."

"Not impossible," commented Carlos.

"I agree," stated the general and got on two different satellite phones to order other aircraft to refuel and then to deploy further and over Canadian airspace. "Their fancy upgrades won't distinguish between Canadian aircraft and U.S. aircraft, and we fly the same planes. Maybe we should get pilots with Canadian accents."

An idea had been formed by the time the first Gulfstream came in and landed at Andrews two hours later. Mo and Lee Wang were to be hidden inside the hangar in a locked broom cupboard, wear captured Red Army uniforms, and have several other sets of captured Chinese civilian clothing available to try to blend in with the guards with whatever they were wearing.

The Gulfstream, which could carry a maximum of twenty

people, including pilots and necessary crew changes, was directed into the hangar, the doors closed and three small cameras connected to old television screens in the ops center showed the goings-on. Mo had his satellite phone on pulse and was quickly told that three men wore business suits, four men wore white coats and looked Chinese, and ten men who also looked Chinese wore civilian clothes and were armed with AK-47s. The three men in suits looked around the large hangar carefully while ordering the armed men to guard the doors. They were certainly looking for cameras and immediately saw two cameras—modern, normal, non-working cameras which had been placed there years earlier. Orders were given. There was no sound from the hangar but ladders were moved and the cameras smashed.

"I'm going out there to knock on their door and ruin their party," stated General Patterson angrily. "These SOBs come into a U.S. Air Force base and start destroying defunct equipment. It's time to find out who they think is running the country."

He headed out, signaling two guards to follow him.

"This ought to be fun to watch," stated Preston as Carlos got on the phone to Lee.

"Lee, our friend is heading to the door to give you your chance to move into the hangar. Wear your white coats. Confirm white coats, Lee?" Carlos asked.

"We are changing into our white coats, Carlos," Lee replied.

"I'll tell you when the general is outside the main hangar door, Lee," Carlos continued. Two thirty-year-old black and white cameras had been placed outside the hangar to view goings on there. Preston and Carlos watched as General Patterson, with only the two guards a few steps behind, walked up to the closed large doors and hit one hard with his fist.

The smaller door next to the hangar was opened by one of the men wearing a suit and he walked out to talk to the general. The general bypassed the man and tried to walk inside the hangar.

Here he was stopped by two of the men holding AK-47s. Immediately the two guards behind the General aimed and pointed their M4s at the two men inside the door. The men on both sides of the door could be seen shouting for back-up. Preston and Carlos could see both inside and outside the hangar and saw all the visitors looking at the confrontation by the side door.

"Lee, Mo, head towards the rear of the aircraft," ordered Carlos into his phone. "There is nobody looking in your direction. The rear aircraft door is wide open and the steps are down. Two pilots left the aircraft and are walking towards the door where the argument is happening. I think the aircraft is empty."

It didn't take them long to see Lee and Mo walk over and climb into the aircraft. The argument was still going on, and they could see that it was getting pretty heated. Several more Air Force guards arrived in a couple of jeeps and were brandishing machine guns directly at the doorway. General Patterson looked angry and now there were hundreds of air force soldiers running around the hangar to cordon it off.

"Mo, look where I showed you. Unscrew the bulb above the word "Transponder," now look for the Transponder control switch, it should be right above the bulb location," Carlos stated into his phone.

"*Carlos, Carlos, there is a hole where the transponder switch used to be. The bulb socket is also empty. I think they have removed the transponder system,*" Mo answered at the same time giving Lee directions.

"Crap! They are not stupid," Carlos replied. "Mo, look for any parts that you recognize. Something that has Chinese markings on it! Also get Lee to take the photos of the flight control systems with the camera. We need something that proves that there are working Chinese parts in that aircraft. You have less than a minute before the general will run out of ideas. There are soldiers ready at the side door waiting for you."

"*In the passenger compartment, there is a Chinese anti-*

radar jamming device," said Mo. *"I remember seeing the same on the Z-10 helicopters being built in Harbin. I don't think there is any other equipment, except for the jamming device strapped to a seat."*

Carlos and Preston watched the standoff at the door. The whole flight of visitors still had their faces turned towards the door. Finally a radio was asked for inside the hangar. One of the armed men walked to the door with a modern handheld walkie-talkie, and the man with the suit began talking into it. Carlos assumed that the president, in the White House, was being called.

The conversation was quite long and Carlos smiled, noticing that the phone used was a very modern communications device. The general was given the phone, and he listened for several seconds to the planned conversation with the president. The suited man seemed to be smiling. The walkie-talkie was then given to the general who listened and then nodded. Afterward harsh words were spoken by General Patterson to the suited man, whose smile quickly disappeared, and a scowl took its place.

"Mo and Lee are leaving the aircraft and walking towards the side offices," Preston told Carlos.

"Mo, head straight towards the door. Do not stop. Do not look at the other men, they are beginning to turn towards you." He then spoke into the second phone in his other hand. "Sergeant Perry, two Chinese men in white coming your way. Go in and get them when I say so. Remember, if asked they were coming in to help with refueling

Preston and Mo watched as Mo and Lee walked across a half empty hangar in full sight and finally reached the door which would shield them from all the eyes in the hangar. They had just walked through the doors when it seemed that one of the Chinese engineers who flew in with the aircraft shouted out something. Several of the armed men ran towards the door Mo and Lee had just gone through. Mo and Lee had twenty yards to walk to get to the side exit door on the outer wall.

"Perry, enter now, get our men out of there, but don't, for heaven's sake, use your weapons. Go!"

This time no camera was in place, and Carlos and Preston could only watch as three armed men ran through the same door Mo and Lee had first walked into. There was also a mad rush by everybody in the hangar for the same door.

With relief, the two in the ops room watched as Mo and Le were escorted by Sergeant Perry out of the outer hangar door, and several soldiers barred the door so that nobody else could exit. Sergeant Perry left last and the door was closed behind him.

Fifteen minutes later, and still having to wait an hour for the second aircraft, which was now over Missouri, General Patterson, Mo, Lee, Carlos, Preston and Sergeant Perry met in the Ops Room.

"OK, that man has the weirdest idea that he thinks he is in control of the United States of America. All threats and no action! That darn fat cat!" said General Patterson, now cooled off from his confrontation with the man in the suit. "The president told me that I was to be barred from the Capitol Hill meeting, on orders from this twit, Bill Bowers. Mo, Lee what did you see? The film, from the old camera is being developed as we speak and will be ready in 30 minutes."

Mo dug into his pocket. "I have retrieved two fuses, and this little arming device I found sticking out from under the left pilot's seat. I have seen it before and designed a bomb-arming device much like this one twenty years ago."

"A bomb!?" asked several together.

"A bomb in the Gulfstream?" asked the general.

"Yes, a small but powerful device fitted under one of the pilot chairs. About three ounces of C4 would turn the cockpit and that jet into confetti at any altitude. This device was designed to work on a walkie-talkie or satellite phone frequency."

"So, if we stole their aircraft, they could destroy any evidence inside the electronics?" Carlos asked.

"Correct, I think," replied Mo.

"Glad they didn't arm the 747s the same way," added Preston.

"So they certainly don't want us to get inside their aircraft. Carlos, did you see if they wanted to inspect the aircraft once Mo and Lee left?" asked the general.

"It didn't seem so," Carlos replied. "I don't think anybody saw them close enough to think about it. The pilots disappeared into the second office where we had set up refreshments and still haven't come out. The engineers went about refueling and only the three men in suits stood around discussing what had happened. Nobody has entered the aircraft since Mo and Lee left and most are in the refreshments room. That jet is certainly thirsty; they are still pumping fuel in."

"What else do you have Mo? Lee?" General Patterson asked.

"Three small light fuses and the main fuse for the light in the toilet. They will have to use the toilet in the dark on their way home," Mo replied.

"Important parts of the aircraft," stated Carlos smiling.

"They are," added Lee. "These minute fuses are among hundreds which would have died aboard every aircraft in the world. These small parts would not have made the aircraft crash, but thousands of these were installed in all modern moving machines and, guess who produced them?"

"Zedong Electronics!" stated Carlos and Preston together. Mo and Lee nodded.

Twenty minutes later, and the second aircraft on final approach, the developed film was handed to the men in the ops room. Lee shot over 20 photos of every inch of the flight control systems, and every corner of the flight cockpit. He even took three pictures inside the passenger compartment, and Mo Wang immediately described what Lee was trying to get on film.

"See there! Tied to the seat, a recently installed radar jamming system, the same installed on the Z-10 helicopters," stated Mo. "I watched in Harbin while several of the helicopters had their final assembly completed. The staff at the factory was very helpful and explained every detail to me. I had never seen such small electronic boxes and so much equipment going into such small spaces."

"So we now have proof that they have Chinese parts and even bombs aboard these aircraft," stated General Patterson. "Also, they can jam all our air force and civilian radar following them; but we will know when their jamming devices do this, so I must get our web up before they leave and we can follow their direction when our radars are jammed. I will get the two Hurricane Hunters on the outbound route Carlos suggested and if they are jammed as well, which I think their equipment can do, at least we will have weather equipment to follow them as well as a destination area to find them."

The other parts Mo had removed were also Chinese, although he didn't know what they were for. General Patterson hoped that Mo hadn't actually disabled the whole aircraft. Only time would tell.

The second Gulfstream headed into the same hangar, and three more refueling tankers followed it. A flight of three helicopters was ready to transfer all invited personnel to Capitol Hill and the general, who hadn't planned to be at the meeting, told everyone to get airborne before the others came out of the hangar. Nobody seemed to care that the president had been made to wait three extra hours for the meeting.

Unseen by the men in the hangar, Preston, Carlos Mo and Lee were flown out, minutes after the second jet had disappeared behind closed doors. General Patterson had much to do before they returned.

Again, they all dressed in suits and planned to act as concerned American citizens. The four headed into the meeting room and chatted to the others already there. Preston remembered a dozen of the congressmen and senators from before New Year's Eve, long-standing men of authority. Several other familiar faces were also there—Mike Mallory, Michael Roebels, and, of course Barbara, Martie, and Sally. Then he saw Jennifer and Pam Wallace who must have had flown in separately from North Carolina; they were standing next to Joe and David, also suitably attired for the meeting. There were several other faces he didn't know.

Everyone was asked to head into the chamber. This time Preston was surprised that Mo Wang was included. Mo wasn't even a U.S. citizen.

Once everybody was seated, the president entered and walked directly to the podium where he usually delivered his speeches.

"Thank you all for coming. Before our guests arrive, I wanted to inform you there are sixteen current members of the House, seven members of the Senate and forty-two prospective people who I would like see as members of Congress in the near future. One friend is here purely as an advisor to me, on matters pertaining to our second meeting here today. I need to hear from our current members, how we can go about re-forming the Congress into two working bodies within a month of today. Our population and occupied land have decreased in size; we need to adjust the sizes of the House and Senate to accurately represent our reduced population, and they will implement necessary laws to govern the country. I plan to step down as president as soon as law and order are restored, but would still like my old senate seat back, and continue as an active member of the United States Senate. It will be up to us, here in this room, to elect a new president when the time comes. First, we have to finish what our enemy started on New Year's Eve and make sure that our country is safe, and can grow and prosper in peace and harmony for the next decades to come. This, I feel is close at hand."

For twenty minutes there was a question and answer session

from the still active members of Congress, suggesting what should take place in the near future and the meeting was recorded. Nobody else had the authority to speak.

The president received a note and put his hand up for silence. "Our friends have arrived, and we will start our second meeting after a short break for refreshments. Many of you do not know why this second meeting is scheduled, but I want you to make up your own minds up about what our next guests are going to demand. Everybody in this room will vote on whether we should give these men priority over and above the current programs for survival and growth that we have in place in our country. The voting will be held anonymously. Thank you."

* * *

Meanwhile, General Patterson was busy. He watched the four helicopters take off, each flying one man to Capitol Hill. He could monitor the inside of the hangar, but not much else, so he had several air force technicians watching the old screens and trying to detect any changes to Gulfstream V by comparing them to blueprints they had found.

The search aircraft were beginning to land. He had changed the flight plan of the closest Hurricane Hunter to Alaska, to not refuel in Hawaii, but at Elmendorf. He also ordered the second Hurricane Hunter into Resolute Bay to refuel and be prepared to sound Canadian if anybody called them on their radios.

He spent a long while on the satellite phone to Admiral Rogers. He found out that the navy could have its only two old, but operational, Tang Class submarines in the Pacific off the coast of Alaska within a week. They would be aided by the only destroyer in San Diego harbor, where the two submarines were stationed. Admiral Rogers said that he had been in contact with Admiral Rodriquez in Bogotá. The general was to tell Carlos that his uncle was out of hospital, in a wheelchair, but Admiral

Rodriquez had already ordered three of his light frigates to head through the Panama Canal and up to San Diego at full speed. They were fast, and once through the canal could catch up to the U.S. ships in 72 hours, by the time they reached Alaska.

It was a gamble to target Alaska as the enemy's base of operations, but he didn't have much choice. At any rate, he knew the enemy base would be somewhere in the cold north.

General Patterson had learned much from General Allen, and to be ahead of events was his number one priority. Nobody knew what this third threat on the U.S. homeland would entail, but he wasn't going to wait around to find out.

* * *

The second meeting began after coffee and snacks. The visitors entered and were seen greeting and shaking hands with the members of government they knew. Carlos whispered to Preston that the whole area was being taped, to look for evidence of collusion between current government officials and the visiting CEOs.

"I'm sure many of the people here had already been on the payroll of Westbrook and Bowers," Preston quietly shared with Carlos and Mike Mallory.

Martie and Sally were chatting with the other girls, and the former members of government certainly had no time or interest in the newcomers. Several members of both Houses had already looked disapprovingly at Preston and Carlos; they were not politicians.

Bowers, of *Bruche,* gave a 20-minute speech, describing how he, and America, had lost so much since New Year's Eve, and that with aid his company and the other drug companies could be up and producing within a year. He detailed what was needed in his several plants across the country, another dozen around the world, and what he wanted was a lot.

Westbrook took the floor after him and said much of the same thing; that he and *MonteDiablo* had proven to the world that their products were the best, and even reminded the listeners that the president himself was instrumental in getting *MonteDiablo* products into all of Africa only a year or so earlier. Without his modern agricultural products, the world would starve, and it was the job of the United States of America to feed themselves first, and the rest of the world second.

There was to be a question and answer session afterwards, but before the president concluded the meeting, he explained what he wanted. "We are still a free country and we have the right to vote. You have heard these two men give you reasons why their programs should be given priority as we proceed with reconstruction and of the list of advancements. Some of you know these men, some of you don't. Many did business together before the end of last year. Many of you don't know how big a job it is to reconstruct our country, nor have taken any interest in the reconstruction. Many of you have been hands-on. There is not one member of our armed forces in this room today. They will take orders from me and from you, the people in this room. Forty-eight million Americans have survived this international mega-disaster, and these are the people we must answer to, to help them survive and grow this country into the strong, powerful nation it used to be. If you feel these corporations here today proposed the best avenue for us, then vote for them to be at the top of the to-do list. If you feel these companies do not represent the best methods forward for the greater good, then vote against them. Before we vote, we will now have a short question and answer session of only ten questions, five from current members of congress and five from the new people in the room. You all have directions on how to use the still-working, I might add, voting buttons on your chairs. The "for" and "against" votes, as usual will come up on the screens afterward. I will let the temporary Speaker of the House decide who asks the questions."

It took a while before the first hands were raised.

"Congressman Elders, Montana. Mr. Westbrook, how will your products produce a better crop than what our farmers are currently using?"

"All our growing products, being genetically modified organisms, are more refined to resist disease and drought. We have designed all of our U.S. and international products to be hardy, with a greater chance to survive pest, droughts and most other conditions farmers have come up against for the last couple of centuries."

"Congressman Brown, California. Question for Mr. Bowers: The survivors in this country have not had the availability of drugs for six months now. Why would they need to take your drugs?"

"The American population is used to taking drugs. They might have weaned themselves off many drugs temporarily, but when disease and bodily malfunctions become rampant again, they will be glad the drug industry has been put back on top. Think of chicken pox, malaria, typhoid and other insect-carried or air-carried diseases that could destroy the rest of our population. Yes, my company didn't make any of these drugs or vaccinations, but it will be our first priority once we are given the necessary aid to manufacture life-saving drugs and vaccines."

The questions went on, there was little argument about positives or negatives. Martie managed to get in the ninth question. The speaker was being careful who to ask and had passed over Mike Mallory, Preston and Carlos for three questions.

"Martie Strong, North Carolina. A question for both of you men: if we vote to place your companies at the top of the list for reconstruction, are you going to repay the American people by giving all your new products to the population for free?" She sat down.

Bowers was the first to answer. "I will answer for my company, the other two drug companies represented here today, and Mr. Westbrook and his company. Prior to today's meeting, we met with the president to outline what we need to operate our four international corporations. First, the U.S. dollar must be brought back as the international currency of choice. Second, all banks must be reinstated to help farmers pay for agricultural supplies. Third, Medicare and Medicaid must be brought back to help our customers pay for needed drugs. Finally, every American should be paid a minimum wage so that they can purchase what they need. In other words the world's monetary system, its bartering system, and banking systems must be made live so that people can start paying for what they need."

There were many hands and again Mike Mallory, Preston and Carlos were overlooked. Michael Roebels wasn't going out without a fight and stood up to ask a question.

"Please sit down," the Speaker stated arrogantly. "I have not yet made a decision."

"Since several months ago the president asked me to oversee the country's reconstruction efforts. I think I have the right to ask a question, Mr. Speaker."

The House Speaker ignored him and picked another member of the Senate.

"Mr. Speaker," interrupted the president, "I think Mr. Roebels has a valid point. The members of the House have already had their five questions. Mr. Roebels, go ahead please."

"Michael Roebels, California. Mr. Bowers, it seems that you are far ahead in your ideas of our country's current reconstruction. To date we have Silicone Valley and one small part of San Francisco under electrical power. To power the entire United States could take anywhere from one to three decades. As you well know, Mr. Bowers, the government, the treasury, the banks and other financial institutions need electricity to operate. Second, the farmers already have enough growing crops to supply our reduced population for this summer and plan to have the country's food plants and bottling and canning operations operational before winter. These programs are at the top of the list. Surely getting your corporations up to speed should not be placed as a higher priority than our current actions."

Bowers answered, "Mr. Roebels has brought up some good points. First, yes, food is a priority and Mr. Westbrook's company can feed the world. Second, a point you didn't bring up— without electricity countrywide, hospitals won't work, the sick will not be cared for, people will continue to die and our population suffers. I hear you do have electricity and computers, and we feel that our companies should have everything you have to offer for at least the next few years to get us up and running so that we can help the world survive. I'm sure you, Mr. Roebels, will understand that our program is the right one and the president, the leader of this country, will aim this reconstruction program in the way it is supposed to be. That is his job, Mr. Roebels, not yours. It will be the job of the Congress, to make sure that people like you can survive. I have asked the president to prioritize the formation of a new House and Senate as soon as possible and that should take priority over anything else, other than keeping our fellow citizens alive." Unabated, he turned towards the President of the United States. "Mr. President, I think we are done with this line of questioning."

Preston was angry. He was really pissed off at this man's arrogant attitude toward the president and Martie's father, and stood up.

"And if we vote no, that your projects don't take priority, what happens next, Mr. Bowers?"

The Speaker banged his gravel and asked for the question to be ignored and that Preston sit down.

"No!" stated Martie standing up next to Preston. "Let him answer it, Mr. Politician. There was much agreement, and the

Speaker looked for guards to evict the trouble makers. There were none.

"I think Mr. Bowers should answer the question, Mr. Speaker," added Mike Mallory, standing up. There was agreement as a dozen more stood up muttering the same.

The gravel sounded, and for the second time the president intervened.

"I think that is a logical question, Mr. Speaker, and since Mr. Bowers just stated that as president, I am currently in charge of this country—and that includes this Chamber—I order you, Mr. Speaker, to allow the question."

Preston and Bowers were the only people left standing.

"Who are you, young man?" Bowers asked smiling.

"Preston Strong, North Carolina," Preston replied.

"I will say this once, Mr. Strong. We will not have another meeting about this issue whether you vote for or against our needs. We know that certain members of Congress will vote for us and most of you unelected citizens will vote against us. But I will give you one word of warning, Mr. Strong: if we don't get our companies up and running very soon, this country won't survive."

Preston noticed that the man's smile remained frozen on his face. He was sure of himself, and Preston realized that he didn't actually care.

"That sounds like Armageddon, Mr. Bowers," Preston countered.

There was absolute silence.

"Take it how you want, Mr. Strong. Mr. Westbrook and my other colleagues are not going to stay around to hear the vote. All we have done here today is to bring our message of reconstruction to Washington. If Washington doesn't hear us, then we will have to accept that. Mr. President, members of Congress, and public citizens, have a nice day. We are out of here."

Without another word the four men left the Chamber. There was absolute silence as they left.

The vote ended the way Preston knew it would. The president had ensured the outcome by inviting more members of the public than members of government. The vote ended with nine for and forty-seven against. Many in the meeting were shocked at how many politicians had actually voted for the corporations.

Not far behind the four visitors, Preston and several others headed out to be taxied over to Andrews. The four men were a speck in the distance once the helicopter Preston was in left the ground. General Patterson had already been told the four men were returning and they were already on their helicopter's radio finding out if both their aircraft had been refueled and were ready to depart.

Preston, Carlos, Martie and Sally were in the first helicopter to land, and it was directed close to the operations room where the general was waiting for them. They entered as the first Gulfstream trundled out of the hangar and was cleared for taxi and takeoff.

"It seems that Mark Weinstein and Paul Proker, the CEOs from the drug companies *Hearst* and *Decibel* are the first out of the door," stated General Patterson as the four entered. "Also, Westbrook and Bowers are having one long argument in the hangar. There was a slight problem with a small malfunction in their aircraft. And it is not the one Mo and Lee got into, so it's not our fault," he smiled.

"They must have swapped aircraft," stated Preston.

"It seems so. Bowers and Westbrook had a discussion with one of the Chinese engineers when they returned, and the cameras showed Westbrook telling Weinstein and Proker to get aboard, take half of their guards, and take off first. Bowers had a long conversation with the pilots while the luggage was switched around and I think they are onto us being inside that aircraft."

"So they are taking the safer one," stated Carlos. "No honor amongst thieves," he added.

"We have all aircraft refueled and airborne, except the Hurricane Hunter in Alaska," continued the general. "The aircraft is still an hour out from Elmendorf, and I was told would need 90 minutes to refuel. The Gulfstreams will take five hours to get there anyway, so I think our web is ready to keep our eyes on them. We have two AC-130s in Canadian airspace, one more on the U.S.-Canadian border, three C-130s over Greenland and Iceland in case they outwit us and head for Europe, and two more C-130s over the center of the country. I don't believe they can get out of our web without our knowledge."

"Where is the second Hurricane Tracker?" Preston asked.

"She is also in Canadian airspace about 50 miles northeast of Resolute Bay and in an hour will turn around and head in a southeasterly direction towards Vancouver. I want her to have as small a radar footprint as she can throw out, hopefully keep the two Gulfstreams on her higher frequency weather instruments, and look like a routine flight from northern Canada to western Canada. I heard about the arrogant way those two men strutted around talking to you guys, and I'm sure they will expect to see other aircraft in the skies. If they go through the same corridor where they came in, I want them to think that they are seeing routine flights around the country. They won't realize that our delicate weather instruments are watching them."

For three hours, tabs were kept on both aircraft. Mo and Lee arrived to join the men while Buck flew the rest of the North Carolina crowd back home in *Lady Dandy*.

The two Gulfstreams were 60 minutes apart and both flew out over St. John's, Newfoundland, as any of last year's civilian aircraft flying to Europe would have done. The first one disappeared off the Andrews radar twenty minutes before it reached the Icelandic coast, but was picked up by the radar of the C-130 fifty miles east of Iceland flying on a regular route from Europe which would take it into JFK.

"Gulfstream losing altitude rapidly, currently at 23,000 feet and turning east, directly towards us. I haven't got the visual on the second Gulfstream yet," one of the C-130 crew stated into a satellite phone, not the aircraft's radio.

"Stay on your course and keep the aircraft on radar. We still have the second Gulfstream on several other units," replied General Patterson, allowing the conversation to be on speaker.

"Roger that. Our altitude is Flight Level 21 and they have descended through 17,000 feet, 100 miles ahead of us."

"Turning slowly and I'm sure thinking that this is for our information, in case we are watching," General Patterson added.

"Aircraft is down to 10,000 feet and still heading due east, 9,000, 8,000, 7,000, 6,000, and looks like she is going to go below 5,000, 4,000, 3,500. She is starting to turn south at 2,500 feet and in a steep dive as her altitude is still dropping. She looks like she is leveling out at 1,000 feet. The Gulfstream is now heading south and twenty miles out from the Icelandic coast at a slow 350 knots. It looks like she has leveled at 900 feet, and about 40 miles north of the southern tip of Iceland. We can just keep her on our screens.

"Hold on, she is turning eastwards. The Gulfstream is turning towards the north, twelve miles out from Reykjavik and going even lower to 700 feet, still at 350 knots. If she gets any lower we will lose her."

"She will expect you guys to have seen her go down. Head towards her position where she began to descend and complete a dozen circles. What is the weather like?"

"Clear, beautiful day, high stratus clouds, visibility 100 miles," was the reply.

"OK! Charlie-130, act like you are worried where she is; complete a dozen circles. We want them to think you are looking for aircraft debris. Then resume your course into JFK. That should give you twenty minutes before the second Gulfstream gets to the same location and you will be only 50 miles west of them, if they try the same trick."

Much like playing a game of chess, General Patterson moved his web to tighten around the Canadian coast, so that if the Gulfstream did head in that direction at 700 feet, somebody would see them.

The second Gulfstream, seeing the C-130 on their radar screen, continued past Iceland and an hour later disappeared from view on all radars.

"We are about to lose her," stated the same airman in the C-130, now 300 miles west of Iceland, as the Gulfstream descended down through 2,000 feet a hundred miles east of Iceland and was heading south when it left their radar screen.

"Now it's wait time. I have a C-130 heading north over Hudson Bay for Cambridge Bay, a couple of hundred miles southwest of Resolute Bay. If they go through the sea corridor, they should be visible from both aircraft. We know they have radar-jamming devices aboard and if they use them, then we will lose radar from the C-130 but the Hurricane Hunter will still have them visual. Also I have an AC-130 gunship heading due north to Cambridge Bay. She will pick them up with infra-red or heat."

For the next couple of hours the two aircraft were spied on. As Carlos expected, they flew through the large, wide-open water lane from eastern Canada to western Canada, now forty-five minutes apart and at 3,000 feet above sea level. To reduce fuel consumption, both aircraft had throttled back to a low cruise of 330 knots. Over Greenland they rose higher to get better economy, but descended down near to sea level once they got closer to the Canadian coast.

South of Resolute Bay, the open-water corridor was close to 250 miles wide and both aircraft stayed 240 miles south of Resolute Bay. Here, the Hurricane Hunter lost them, high cliffs making their electronic systems go fuzzy, but twenty minutes later the aircraft moved into the more open water of the Viscount Melville Sound, and their extremely faint bleeps were picked up again.

It was dark. Dinner was served in the ops room as the lead aircraft left the McClure Strait, rose in altitude to 10,000 feet and headed westwards towards the Beaufort Sea. The second aircraft did the same forty-five minutes later.

"Happy Harry to base, we have lost visual on the first aircraft," reported the second Hurricane Hunter by satellite phone over southern Alaska three hours later.

"What!" stated General Patterson over the operations room satellite phone still on speaker-phone. "How could that happen? What were the last coordinates?"

"Don't know, Sir. She suddenly lost altitude. She was flying at 15,000 feet, and I heard a short radio transmission about changing to reserves, and seconds later the first Gulfstream went into a dive and I lost her going through 500 feet. She had just turned southwest and over the Chukchi Sea, fifty miles from the Alaskan shoreline. She was about to fly over the Bering Strait. Pilot thinks she went straight in, sir. He reckons that there was something wrong with her reserves."

"Roger that," replied General Patterson. "Head southwest towards Anchorage. The second aircraft should be on your system by now, about 500 miles behind the first one. Tell the pilot to get you into a position so that you can monitor the Bering Strait and south. I want to know if they are heading into Russian airspace, or our own."

"We are turning southwest, Sir."

"I think we must have taken out something important," stated Lee, Mo nodding in agreement.

"Well, they could still be flying below 500 feet, a jet fighter with the right equipment could do so, but with the photos you took of the cockpit interior, Lee, our technicians couldn't see any modern equipment added to do this."

The exact same thing happened with the second aircraft an hour later, except that there was a two-word radio transmission, "May Day," and fifty miles further south of the first one, the second Gulfstream disappeared from view.

"I've checked out their entire flight distance," stated General Patterson. "The second aircraft has flown 5,290 miles, of which 890 were at less than 5,000 feet, high fuel usage. With maximum reserves, they have less than 500 miles of fuel left. I checked what was pumped into their tanks here at Andrews, 400 pounds of fuel less than the aircraft's maximum fuel intake. That means that they were empty on arrival, maybe ten to fifteen minutes of safe flight time. If I add that to what they should have now, I reckon 600 miles is the maximum they can fly before going down. They were due west of Norton Sound, and that puts western Alaska and a very small amount of Russian terra firma into the possibilities. I think Carlos pinpointed it, somewhere in Alaska. Guys, it's time we headed up to Alaska."

CHAPTER 6

Alaska

BOTH GULFSTREAMS DID MAKE IT, unbeknownst to the group back at Andrews. Gulfstream I, short on fuel, headed down to below 500 feet and stayed there for the rest of its flight.

General Patterson hadn't logged the first aircraft's mileage and had forgotten that the first one had turned north on the U.S. side of Iceland, allowing for a shorter flight of 500 miles; this allowed the very experienced civilian American pilots to stay low for the final 1,000-mile throttled-back glide into their secret air base.

Gulfstream II dipped down later as her American pilots worked out distance and fuel usage and stayed under any radar surveillance for the final 600 miles of their flight.

Both aircraft were well into their reserve-fuel capabilities on final approach to the long, wide, American government-owned runway.

The second Gulfstream came in fifty minutes after the first, and just managed to land and taxi towards the hangar. The pilot killed the engines before the jet fumes gave out.

* * *

"Get your aircraft to your refueling base, and then I want a complete high altitude sweep of northern Alaska and 400 miles into western Russia," General Patterson was telling the pilot of the closest Hurricane Hunter. "Always try and make it look like you are on a food mission. Fly straight and photograph or monitor swaths of country as you go."

He had already told the second Hurricane Hunter to head towards Elmendorf, several flight hours west of its current position, where both aircraft would now be based.

"What can they look for?" Carlos asked the general.

"I think future aircraft movement is all these two aircraft might pick up. I don't think those guys can fly anywhere soon but you never know. A 747 with 300 Marines on board is two hours from taking off for a direct flight to Harbin, in case Bowers wants to return there. I phoned the colonel at Misawa and instructed him to fly radar search missions over northern Japan using anything he has to search for any identified radar transmissions.

"I have two AC-130 gunships going into Hill in Salt Lake to meet us and take us to Elmendorf. Preston, Carlos, Sally, Martie, get ready and please tell Mo Wang we are leaving in twenty minutes. By the way, Sally, you will be my co-pilot for the C-130 flight into Hill.

"I asked Buck to fly *Lady Dandy* up to Elmendorf. I want him to act like an old privately-owned Alaskan civilian aircraft. The visitors never saw Buck or *Lady Dandy*. He is unknown to them, and I want him and Barbara to help check out Alaska for any movement from a civilian's point of view.

"The AC-130 gunships will be able to pick up aircraft movement, heat trails, or infra-red signatures from a reasonable distance without causing alarm in the enemy camp. Of course, that depends on what they have in modern electronic surveillance equipment from our friends at Zedong Electronics."

Two hours later the group was in the air. Sleep was now a

necessity and most slept, except for General Patterson and Sally, who would get their sleep in the next leg from Hill up to Elmendorf.

It was midnight by the time they took off. The 747 was already outbound for China over the polar route and second and third 747s were being loaded with a couple of the Seal Teams and 800 Marines bound for Elmendorf. The 747 transporter would be returning in six hours from Bogotá, unloaded and then reloaded at Andrews with arms and ammo for Majors Wong and Chong. At the same time, the two submarines were about to leave San Diego for their long trip north with the lone destroyer as escort. The three faster, smaller frigates of the Colombian Navy were closing in and about to pass through the Panama Canal to catch up with the U.S. vessels en route.

Dawn raised its lazy head over the Rockies as the C-130 headed into Hill Air Force Base. Sally, who had caught three hours of sleep while General Patterson piloted the aircraft, brought her into a red-skied landing as the sun's rays shone through the clouds behind the mountains to their right. During most of his shift, the general had used the satellite phone to send messages around the country. Four of the remaining five F-4s were heading out of Edwards and would be refueled in an hour on their flight up to Elmendorf.

The general wasn't taking any chances at being caught with insufficient air and ground power, in case there was a formidable enemy. He had the feeling that, if the country thwarted this third attack on its sovereignty, there could be a peaceful life afterward. Being in the military system for over half of his life, he thought only of attack and defense and most other issues were of very little concern to him. Better to let the experts, people more knowledgeable in food, water and civilian populations, do their jobs. His meeting with Bill Bowers made his skin crawl. It was like seeing a rattler at close range. All the snake was interested in was getting its own way.

He detested this type of American people, only interested in their own agenda and screw the rest of society. In many ways he thought that Zedong Electronics had actually done the United States a favor by ridding the world of much of the greed and modern systems that he felt were polluting the civilians. He had seen it in the Air Force ranks—soldiers texting on their cell phones, instant and social communications giving personnel, who didn't think that somebody might be listening, opportunities to communicate valuable and often secret information to the enemy: where they were, what they were doing, even down to lousy military food. All this could be downloaded, listened to, or recorded to give a bigger picture of what the U.S. military machine was doing and their future intentions.

Now that was all gone. The whole world was in turmoil, and the U.S. had the upper hand with all the communication equipment in known hands. All he needed to do was to win this next game of chess. He wondered if they had any Shaheen II missiles, or worse, a Russian multi-head missile at their disposal. Then it occurred to him. They wouldn't know that the Chinese satellite system was out of their control, and that if they fired any GP-guided missiles towards the mainland, the missiles could go out of control and head in any direction. It didn't decrease the harm they could do, as there always would be fallout, but now that there were fewer people in the cities the missiles could be aimed at, if they went wild instead, they could actually kill more Americans. Could Carlos and Lee Wang direct those missiles if they were launched?

The two AC-130s and *Mother Goose*, the HC-130 tanker, were still being refueled when Sally landed the C-130. They had arrived an hour earlier and would take them nonstop to Elmendorf, being refueled in-flight if they had bad headwinds.

Thirty minutes later, five of the Z-10 Chinese Attack Helicopters came in. They flew in from Dyess and were the first of three flights on their way to Elmendorf.

"I now regret having these Z-10s painted in U.S. Air Force colors," stated a tired General Patterson over a breakfast of coffee, toast and scrambled eggs.

There was a newly erected chicken coop just outside the back of the Officers Mess with over 100 chickens; they had been found running wild around the outer areas of the base.

"It was a pretty funny operation to watch from the air," laughed the base commander. "Several chickens had been seen by low-flying aircraft while coming into land, and we decided to do a jeep roundup. Most of the chickens in and around the desert region around the Great Salt Lake were starving, and the water was not drinkable. I went up in a chopper and had three jeeps filled with men and old soccer netting at the ready. We would see a couple of chickens and the men would surround them as if to capture the enemy. In all, we caught 108 chickens, 43 pigs and 27 head of cattle. For the larger animals, we had horse trailers pulled behind the jeeps. Now we have our own farm on the base, and enough fresh eggs for the Officers Mess. We are trying to breed the chickens and pigs, but still need a rooster and a bull."

"I just don't know what this world is coming to," replied the general. "Now our bases sound like old third-world country bases, with more emphasis on farming than flying."

"The enlisted men have an interest in having fresh eggs for breakfast. I think one of the spotter jeeps saw a lone rooster over at Dugway, the old proving grounds, a day or so ago. It is great excitement across base right now. We were wondering where we could get some trackers to track this guy!" added the base commander.

"A couple of good-looking egg layers with lipstick should do the trick," stated Sally. There was much laughter from the table.

"Don't laugh, guys," added the colonel. "Seven of the cows we caught were milk cows, and the milk you are drinking is fresh non-pasteurized farm milk. Good for you, I was told as a kid!"

"Better not tell the authorities in California," laughed Martie. "That was a criminal offense in California last year, supplying raw milk."

"That's one of the good things I was thinking about when we were flying in here earlier," General Patterson added. "Have you noticed how much better the freshly farmed food tastes?" There was a nod from the table.

"One of the things that worries me with Westbrook and *MonteDiablo*," added Preston, "is they want us to go back to the mass-produced, non-natural and tasteless food we had last year."

"Not on my watch!" added the general.

"I'll stick to a fish diet once you are finished with my services," added Mo Wang.

Hill Air Force base was left to its new farming techniques once the gunships left the runway bound for Alaska. With full stomachs, the crews aboard settled down to a long flight. Sally and General Patterson were asleep before the aircraft left the runway.

Martie fell asleep and Preston, Carlos and Mo Wang were left to chat.

"What do you think the general has in store for us this time?" Preston asked Carlos. "With over a million troops back home, why do you think he is taking us civilians across the United States?"

"I suppose he feels less threatened by us," Carlos replied. "And after watching those politicians vote for anything that could be worth money or a kickback to them, I don't trust many of the 'old school' anymore either."

"Nobody really noticed my being there," added Mo. "I did see those company owners having pretty one-sided discussions with some of your American politicians. It seemed that there was much threatening going on. Lee showed me that Mr. Westbrook was pointing his finger at one of the politicians. I don't know his name, but the poor man's face was as white as a sheet."

Preston opened his satellite phone and pressed in a call number. "Mr. President, Preston Strong here." He listened for a few seconds. "I had a thought a few moments ago. During the time we spent outside the House chamber during the last meeting, Mr. Westbrook and Mr. Bowers seemed to be threatening some members of both the House and the Senate. There were certain members who voted for the acceptance of the plan given by Mr. Bowers. I would suggest that you get those men in and find out what they were threatened with, if they were at all. I'm sure that if a few colonels or generals sat in on the conversations it will encourage those men to share some inside information with you. It might help us with deal with the enemy this side.

"Yes, Mr. President, we are heading towards the west of the country. I don't want to tell you any more, I don't have the authority, but give the general several hours to rest, he is exhausted, and I'm sure he will back up what I just told you."

For the rest of the flight the men discussed fishing and other non-military-related topics, like marriage while the girls slept soundly.

Elmendorf Airfield was reached as the sun set. It had been a long flight from the East Coast, twenty hours of flying, and Preston and Mo were discussing whether salmon tasted better than tuna, when they flew over the Alaskan coast.

Mother Goose, carrying only a small amount of reserve fuel, wasn't needed on this trip, but would become important if search-flights started around the clock.

That night they indeed enjoyed freshly caught salmon. Mo thought it the best salmon he had ever tasted. Preston, Martie and Carlos, who had not spent much time in Alaska, thought so too. Sally had flown here often, knew several of the soldiers around base, and told her friends how she and Jennifer had always looked forward to a training flight this far north.

General Patterson joined them towards the end of the meal and sat down to a grand dinner.

"Did you speak to the president?" Preston asked, savoring a "Summer Ale" from the local Alaskan Brewing Company, which happened to still be operating with the help of a dozen large Air Force generators.

"Yes, and thank you for the suggestion, Preston. He and I agree that if the politicians were being threatened, then whatever information we can get out of them might give us some insight into the plans our new enemy has. The president has already talked to two of the members of Congress who voted for Bowers and Westbrook. One said that he firmly believed that the two CEOs were on the right track but the second said that he felt threatened. It was suggested that his family might suffer unfortunate accidents if he didn't side with Westbrook."

"Where does his family live?" Carlos asked the general.

"The president didn't say, but he was from Washington State or Oregon, I believe. I'll get the information tomorrow. It's already past midnight on the East Coast."

"What is going to be our role here?" Martie asked.

"We have a couple of Cessna 210s from the local airfields which we commandeered from their owners for fourteen days. With *Lady Dandy*, which is on her way and should be here by lunch tomorrow, you guys are going to pose as civilians looking for lost members of your family. For the next several days I want you guys to head out over designated areas of terrain we give you, and slowly go through every airfield across Alaska. You won't believe it but there are more than 500 airports or airfields in Alaska, of which maybe 60 have tarmac runways long enough to take jets. Several of those could have been extended over the last decade to take bigger aircraft."

"So many airports!" exclaimed Mo Wang in shock. "That's more than all the airports in the whole of China!"

"Mo, I think you are correct," answered the general. "We are going to work Alaska from east to west; your team will search along the south coast, while the two Hurricane Hunters and two AC-130s check out all the airfields further north with cameras. If they find any extended runways, they will let us know, but they have thousands of square miles to fly and only 200-odd runways to check out. That means with you checking out the warmer areas in small aircraft, we should complete the reconnaissance of 300 airfields within ten to fourteen days. Same with the larger aircraft.

"I don't believe the Gulfstreams will fly again once they see or monitor other aircraft within their area, and I believe that they are west of Elmendorf. I want you guys to start from the east, to give them a few days to maybe fly somewhere. Then we can pick them up and close in on their field. Also we have ten days before the navy arrives. They are going to get involved and emphasize that we are still a powerful country, even to enemies within our borders. The Seals and Marines are already here and resting. Once we find the enemy, I want them to go in and check out their facilities before we mount any form of attack. I have this sinking feeling in my gut that these rich and powerful men have far more arms than we expect, and possibly nuclear missiles aimed at the mainland."

For the next couple of days, the two Cessnas, under the control of Carlos and Martie, flew into a dozen dirt airstrips and five larger airports, Palmer, Valdez, Cordova, Yakutat, and met up for the second night in a small airport motel just outside the town of Haines.

There was a rowdy bar and the tired pilots and ground checkers were happy to grab a cold beer and listen to music from an old jukebox, with the always present sound of a generator close by.

They had asked over fifty people in and around the airports if they had seen anything out of the ordinary, and the answer was always the same: no.

The next morning they flew back to Elmendorf and were happy to see the Seals running around the airport perimeter, led by Charlie Meyers and Joe Paul.

Early the next morning General Patterson gave them another six airports and fourteen smaller dirt strips to check out, this time west of Anchorage. He warned the four that Dillingham Airport, their last stop, could have enemy, as it had a somewhat long tarmac runway and nobody had heard from this part of western Alaska for months.

CHAPTER 7

Mike Mallory – The Right Wing Threat

WITH HIS EVER-FLYING CESSNA 210, Mike Mallory and his new friend, Jenny, who had been one of his flight attendants on the Southwest flight, flew into Food Station 12, the newest food-dispensing airport in Oregon. It was situated in Medford, a small town just north of the California state line.

In this part of the country, although farming was still a primary occupation, new strain on the distribution was coming from the thousands of people who had moved west and then south from eastern Washington, northern Oregon, northern Idaho and even as far as Montana, a few weeks into the new year. Now that summer had arrived these people had no way to return or were not allowed back into their locked-down areas. Nearly 500,000 people had settled in several new makeshift "container towns," as they were now called and the farmers couldn't feed the area's four million people.

Mike Mallory was working out a plan to ship flights of food from the Mid-West and East Coast into Medford, calculating how much food one area could spare for the other.

A canning plant in Virginia had been given several military generators to re-establish its normally large operation, and it was working 24/7 to can any and all produce which could be delivered. Tomatoes and cucumbers from North Carolina, and onions and green vegetables from Kentucky, West Virginia and Ohio were flown in daily using a dozen C-130s. The canned goods were then flown out to many of the food stations that needed more supplies than the area around them could produce. Several now-empty Air Force warehouses were being used as food storage depots for the coming winter. Fifty percent of everything canned was being shipped by the new Amtrak system to the bases.

Mike Mallory's main job was to try and juggle the current food needs with the future needs over the first full winter period. There wouldn't be much to spare.

Coffee and fresh foodstuffs were arriving once a week from Bogotá and Mike decided to fly one shipment into the Medford airport. The Air Force personnel, now under the command of Captain Mallory and given to him by General Patterson to help plan flights in and out of areas, had explained that Medford airport was perfect as a food distribution point. The terminals had been increased in size a couple of years earlier and the 8,000-foot runway could easily accommodate the 747 transporter landing with a heavy load.

"OK, where can we steal enough food to feed how many, Lieutenant Shaw?" Mike asked the Air Force officer in charge of the 747 distribution flights.

"We have 4,270,000 people in an area that used to be home to 1,750,000. There are approximately 12,900 small to medium and 300 large farms, and they can feed about four million. We are about a quarter of a million stomachs short and need a dozen incoming 747-loads a week to equal our needs, Mike." The soldier responded.

"What about the Amtrak route through here?" Mike asked. "I cannot afford more than one flight a week into here.

"The old *Coast Starlight* route used to run straight through Medford from Sacramento to Portland. Currently we have a weekly route from Virginia through the mid-west, Salt Lake City, Sacramento and into San Francisco. We will have our tenth engine and train ready to run in the South Carolina refurbishment depot in a week. We could move it up to Virginia, load up as much as we can, and then get it over to our food distribution station in Iowa to see what is available there. It can pull its first load over to Sacramento and be the first train north in about fourteen days, as long as we have a full load for her at the two food points; that should be enough to feed this area for a month. Since we are only running two trains a day on our main line, there is plenty of railway room to get our new train back and forth on the Iowa/Virginia route once every two weeks. That will eliminate the need for 747s coming in."

The team of just over forty civilian and military personnel had taken over the airport only two weeks earlier and even the main guard detail hadn't yet arrived. They had six Air Force soldiers as a temporary unit helping set up the internal facilities when the attack came.

The airport was fenced and secured and only several dozen people knew of the newest food distribution point outside of the work force presently setting it up. The president had discussed the Oregon need with Mike Mallory a couple of weeks earlier in Washington and, for the first time the surviving members of both houses of Congress had been part of the discussions.

The attack was not large. At four the next morning, two of the Air Force soldiers walking the perimeter fence had their throats cut as five trucks, mostly old Fords and Dodges crashed through the closed airport gates and headed towards the main terminal. The airport tower which housed the communications was empty and dark, and the several generators turned off for the night.

The forty people had worked a full day and were all asleep. The first they heard of the attack was when the doors of their makeshift bedrooms, the old offices in the terminal building, were kicked open.

One by one each person was dragged out. The four remaining soldiers and several Air Force personnel were rounded up, and everybody was dragged or pushed into the main terminal area. Not a word was said by the attackers as most people asked what was going on.

Mike Mallory, already suffering from a bleeding head wound, when he had been aroused was pushed into the room. He was forced to sit in a line with his colleagues who were already there.

"What is going on here?" he asked a man who was dressed in black and wore a face mask. He was hit by the butt of the man's AK-47 and told to shut up. One soldier tried to tackle him and was shot through the head with an extremely loud pistol by another man, also dressed in black. This atrocity silenced the rest of the work team and the last remaining people were thrown into the room. There were several women in the group. Two were Air Force personnel and the rest civilian food-aid workers.

"Maybe you fine people will now listen to what we have to say, not that it really matters," said the man who was the only person who had a pistol and seemed to be in charge.

Mike Mallory heard an American accent and could see that the man was Caucasian by the skin showing around the eye holes in the face mask. His accent was also pretty local. He wasn't that good, but the man's accent sounded like he was from the Oregon/Idaho area.

"Who's in charge here?"

"I am," stated Mike Mallory, trying to stand up, which meant a third blow with the closest man's rifle butt.

"Are you military?" the leader asked.

"No, Flight Captain with Southwest Airlines," Mike Mallory replied.

"No, what? You piece of crap! You call me sir when you speak to me, understand?" Mike Mallory received another butt to the head, which really made his head bleed. Semiconscious, he slumped back and lay on the floor, face down.

"Leave the guy alone," demanded one of the uniformed Air Force soldiers and received a third eye for his bravery.

The leader who shot him smiled. He was really enjoying this.

"You bunch of capitalistic pigs better start behaving now. I've waited twenty years for this to happen and to get my own back from you and your crappy American government. I will be happy to shoot every one of you people. Now, shut up! Since the fancy airline captain is of no more use to me, who is second-in-command here?"

The Air Force lieutenant, who had been helping Mike Mallory the day earlier, and who was to be in command of this Food Distribution Station, stated that he was.

"Name, rank, and number, soldier," laughed the leader.

"Lieutenant Peter Shaw, United States Air Force," was his curt reply. The leader could see that he was angry and pointed his pistol at the man.

"There is nothing I hate more in this country than cops and soldiers. You had better get your attitude right, young man, or you will be next. Since you might hold the important information we are after, I will keep you alive a little longer, but your attitude towards your new country's leader pains me, so..." The man turned and looked at the frightened group in front of him. He picked out the pretty middle-aged woman kneeling and wiping blood away from the unconscious airline captain with a cloth, and shot the man next to her in the head.

There were screams from several of the women around the poor civilian, and three of them were shot by the same man. Silence reigned again.

"You people are really stupid. Now I have to reload. Daniel, give me one of my full magazines."

Mike Mallory felt the slim, light body of a woman fall across his back. He had just come back to the land of the living and his head was hurting bad. He was half under a table and a chair and, as his eyes focused, he saw in front of him a yellow stub of a nearly used-up and discarded pencil. In the pocket of his now-bloody shirt, hard against his breast, he felt a couple of pieces of paper he had used to take down notes the day before. He slowly pulled them out, inch by inch.

"OK, Mr. Lieutenant Shaw, it's time for you to tell me the names of the farmers around here you are working with and where they are located," ordered the leader, smiling and certainly enjoying his new role of judge and executioner. "I want the farms who intend to supply this warehouse and the names of the farmers who are your main suppliers, now!"

Mike felt the body on top of him move slightly giving him hope that Jenny was still alive. As the lieutenant shouted out a list of names he remembered, Mike began to write short bloody notes on the paper, keeping his head on the ground and facing sideways so that he could see. "White Americans, 30-40, killing our staff, well armed, sound right wing, accent Idaho area, not Canadian..."

Suddenly the radio above him atop the table squawked. *"Foxtrot Sierra Charlie (Food Supply Camp) 12, this is Foxtrot Sierra Charlie 7, are any of you awake? Over. I know it's still early for the West Coast but its dawn over here, and I thought to get patched through a couple of aircraft and check in. There are three Charlie 130s with your Marine guard detachment on the way to you guys. Your Marines should be there in a short while. Just thought to warn you of incoming aircraft. Anybody awake there...?"* And suddenly several rounds went into the radio still on the table above him.

"It looks like the cavalry is coming!" Four more rapid shots rang out. "Oh, crap! I'm out of ammo. We got what we were looking for. Get the missile launchers loaded and get out of here. We need to shoot those aircraft down before they land."

Then a scurry of footsteps was heard out of the office area by a still-alive Mike Mallory and silence reigned inside the terminal. He tried hard to not lose consciousness.

CHAPTER 8

Who Is In Control Of This?

LATER THE SAME DAY, PRESTON was doing the flying this time while Martie spent time looking out the right side of the old 1980s Cessna 210 for any signs of large runways not on the map.

They were flying over Lake Clark National Park and hadn't seen a sign of civilization for an hour. Preston had taken off from Elmendorf at dawn and their task for the day was to fly over the old, desolate and empty mining towns of Iditarod and Flat City, then down to the small town of Dillingham. The two old mining towns were still ghost towns, and showed no signs of new civilization, but could have been a well-planned secret location.

Sally was flying Carlos in the second Cessna 50 miles to their south, also towards Dillingham, but closer to the coast which was now full of debris, Carlos thought, from the Japanese Tsunami disaster a couple of years earlier. They spent an hour flying in long circles and then landing in Kodiak to ask the locals if they had seen any extra flight traffic or visitors in their community. The locals hadn't.

Buck and Barbara were further north of both Preston and Sally, aiming for Bethel, a town of about 6,000 inhabitants and the only detention center in that part of Alaska. Nobody had heard anything from this lone outpost, only reachable by sea or air, for several months.

One of the AC-130 gunships, *Easy Girl,* was twenty minutes further north of *Lady Dandy*, flying down the Kuskokwim River and checking out the small habitats down the river edges. On this day *Easy Girl* and *Lady Dandy* were packed with a dozen well-armed Marines in each aircraft. The AC-130, being faster, had flown a more northerly route than *Lady Dandy* to look out for ground movement and was scheduled to meet the DC-3 over the town.

None of the four aircraft had seen anything out of the ordinary on their first and second day of boring flying, so all were getting excited that the time to find something—anything—out of the ordinary, was getting closer.

Preston and Sally were being caught by a second, faster flying AC-130 gunship, thirty minutes behind them. Both gunships were to go into the larger town first and make the airports a safe landing point for the three unarmed civilian aircraft. All five aircraft were covering a lot of ground, visually checking for anything, and also scanning with the more sophisticated surveillance equipment on board the gunships. General Patterson was flying *Easy Girl* and would be heading into Bethel first. He was still able to talk to the base back in Anchorage using *Mother Goose,* fully-fueled and flying high 250 miles west of the Air Force base as a message relay station. Two F-4s were at Elmendorf, as well as a dozen C-130s full of Marines, ready to take off at a moment's notice.

Twenty minutes later, and after a sweep of the town and its surrounding areas, General Patterson lowered *Easy Girl* onto the 6,400-foot long, wide main runway at Bethel Airport. *Lady Dandy* went in ten minutes later, after the first load of Marines made a perimeter for her safety.

The airport was eerily quiet, Buck noticed, as he and Barbara, the last to leave the DC-3 climbed out of the rear cargo door and stretched.

"Something doesn't smell right here," Buck stated to General Patterson.

"I agree. I already scrambled two F-4s and one of the C-130s with machine guns, two jeeps, gunship ammo and a platoon of Marines before we came in. *Mother Goose* is also heading our way and will bring in fuel for the F-4s. The fighters should be here in twenty minutes and the C-130 in two hours. We need to get the airport secure ASAP."

There was nobody about at the airport. The first signs of trouble were that every small aircraft that Buck and Barbara opened and checked had been tampered with and were not flyable. Many had several bullet holes through the cockpit instrument panels and several were cold, old, and burnt-out skeletons with grass and weeds already covering the metal parts.

"Somebody didn't want anybody to fly out of here," General Patterson stated as the lead F-4 pilot came on the radio asking for instructions. "PattersonKey to Foxtrot leader. Do a swoop over the Yukon Kuskokwim Correction Center. Here are the coordinates," and the general read them from a map he was holding out on the runway. "Then fly down the town's main street to tell anybody we are in town and come in on runway 18, temperature 55 degrees, wind speed strong, 12 knots from the east. Out."

"Roger that," was the answer from the F-4, still thirty miles out. Only the incoming breeze could be heard.

Twenty minutes later, with the F-4s on the ground and protected by the Marines, General Patterson, Buck and Barbara still hadn't seen one local human being.

They were not going to move until the C-130 and back-up arrived and waited for any locals to show their heads.

A bunch of kids on bicycles did an hour later.

"What's going on here, boys?" General Patterson asked the

kids once he had shouted to the two Marines guarding the main gate to allow them in.

"We haven't seen visitors since January, seven or eight months ago," the oldest boy stated. Buck noticed that he looked clean, fed and healthy. "Not since the army of Chinese soldiers came in here and released all the prisoners from the jail and flew them out, just after New Year's Day."

"Chinese soldiers on American soil?" questioned the general.

"Yes, sir!" a smaller boy added.

"Real Chinese gooks, sir!" stated another boy.

"Is everybody in town okay?" asked Buck.

"Yes, sir!" stated the eldest boy. "The Chinese soldiers and several Americans in fancy clothes flew in on jets and took over the town. They left us civilians alone, but killed the dozen guards at the detention center and released all the prisoners and over a week flew them out from this airport."

"Weren't you guys snowed in?" asked General Patterson.

"Oh yes, sir, over three feet of snow on the runway and the airport staff, who were also murdered, were first forced to clear it for the jets. A helicopter, a Chinese helicopter came in before the jets and landed the first soldiers, about six mean Chinese dudes, who got our guys here to clear the runway. Then these fancy jets came in with a bigger Chinese propeller airplane full of men and a couple of jeeps, and sort of took over the whole town.

"We had a small base of army soldiers just outside town, and they didn't stand a chance. The Chinese killed all 20 of them, and then headed over to the prison. And, on their way through town they searched out every truck or car that was still working and shot its engine to pieces. They searched every house and business in the town and blew up all the radios people used to talk to others in the outer areas. Then they shot all the prison guards, took the prisoners, flew them out, and we never saw them again."

"How many prisoners," asked the general?

"About 225, Colonel," stated one boy.

"General to you, young man. I was a colonel a month or so ago," General Patterson smiled.

"Sorry, General," the young boy replied. "It took them about a week. My dad was a cook at the detention center and was not there when they murdered his friends."

Once the F-4s had been topped off with fuel they took off for Dillingham, 250 miles to their southeast, where the two Cessnas were soon due to land. General Patterson waited for the two jeeps and then did a complete surveillance of the town and detention center. The inhabitants were living well, with enough food and fuel for another few months. He told them that he would get a C-130 in with more generators, fuel and food before winter. He thanked the boys for their good information.

* * *

Preston was two miles behind the gunship and ahead of Sally, going in on finals for Dillingham airport when a new voice came over the radio.

"*Easy Girl, this is Foxtrot Four Leader. Do not, I repeat do not land until we check out the airport. We are at Foxtrot Lima (Flight Level/Altitude) 21, 900 knots and 150 miles out from your location. ETA, ten minutes. Over.*"

"*Roger, abort landing,*" replied the pilot of the gunship. "*Aircraft behind me, abort landing, climb, and follow me around. Out!*"

"Roger that," replied Preston and he retracted the undercarriage, decreased his wing flaps and increased the engine's revs as ordered.

Sally did the same and Preston climbed hard, following the dot of *Easy Girl* in front of him. She was climbing away rapidly and he had the Cessna's turbocharged engine on full power.

Minutes later, the F-4s swooped over the town of Dillingham, now a couple of miles ahead of them and *Easy Girl* headed down to also search, telling the two smaller aircraft to stay above 10,000 feet and wait for orders.

Twenty minutes later, with the F-4s heading back to Anchorage, Preston climbed out of the Cessna and headed towards the main terminal of Dillingham Airport.

A frightened voice in the airport tower, seeing the F-4s fly over a few hundred feet above the airport fully armed, stated the airport was safe, still under American civilian control, and nobody had seen anything odd since New Year's Day, when nothing worked anymore.

The enemy was not based here either.

* * *

Mike Mallory's head hurt badly, and he regained consciousness to feel a bandage being put around his head.

"How long have I been out?" he asked his Southwest flight attendant who was bandaging him.

"About eight minutes since those sods left. Twelve people dead and two still alive but won't make it. I think that radio communication stopped them from killing all of us. That guy shot people until he ran out of ammo and then left. I watched them. They are setting up some sort of shoulder rocket launcher outside, close to the main runway. The radio is dead. What do we do, Mike?"

"Get somebody up to the control tower. Those guys sounded pretty rural so hopefully they didn't think about destroying the control tower," he replied.

"We watched them enter the four aircraft out there, the FedEx Cargomaster, the two Red Cross aircraft, and the one we flew in on, and we heard gunfire. I think they destroyed all the aircraft's instrument panels."

"Okay, help me up. Let's get to the control tower."

It was quite a way, and they had to climb several flights of stairs to get up there. The door was locked so several of the men helping Mike up the stairs kicked it in.

"We always lock it down for the night," stated one of the men as they entered. Mike quickly checked the closest radio. It was still operational and he quickly found the frequency the C-130s would be using.

"Medford to incoming Charlie-130s, Medford airport to Charlie-130s, are you reading me? Come in. Over. "

"*Who are you? State your identity. Over,*" crackled the old radio.

"Mike Mallory, Southwest Captain under orders from Patter-sonKey. Do not go onto finals, enemy combatants on Medford runway with rocket launchers and you will be shot down! You need air support to clear the runway," Mike stated into the microphone.

"*Are you crazy, Captain, or whoever you are? But we will abort and circle. Do you have direct communications directly to PattersonKey? Over.*"

"*Charlies, abort long finals and stay low. Let's circle until we find out what's going on down there.*"

Mike Mallory breathed a sigh of relief. "Yes, Charlie 130, somebody has gone to get my phone. Do you have contact with any firepower? I believe these guys are American. They have modern weapons by what I can see, and heat-seeking or infra-red possibilities. Get somebody out here to clean them out. They have four civilian trucks mid-runway on the runway crossover, both left and right side, civilians and amateurs, but dangerous. They just executed a dozen of our staff. Twelve casualties down here. Over."

"*Wait one,*" the pilot responded and the radio went silent for several seconds. "*We have two Foxtrot Fives taking off from an air base to our south. ETA fifteen minutes, carrying heat for the guys on the ground. One Charlie 130 coming in closer to circle and keep them interested. We found an open section of highway about five miles north of the airport. Two jeeps are on board one of our aircraft and I will get them down and send them your way while I direct the heat onto target. I've been told Medivac Charlie 130 enroute to you now as well. Over."*

Mike Mallory sat in the air-traffic controller's chair, asked for a set of binoculars and looked along the horizon line from the control tower. He could just make out three flying dots west of the airport spreading out to do their thing.

Then he looked towards the men half a mile away on the main runway. They had pointed one truck facing southeast and one pointing northwest on either side of the longest runway and directly on the crossing point of the two main runways. Mike could see dozens of men dressed in civilian clothes around the four vehicles. Four had what looked like shoulder rocket launchers, modern-looking ones, at the ready. Boxes of rockets or missiles were being unloaded and made ready. Most of the men were using the vehicles as protection.

His head hurt like crazy. His eyes watered as he tried to focus, leaning on the desk to steady the glasses. Then he saw a military uniform, and it wasn't American. It was a foreign uniform with lots of red braiding on the breast and shoulders, and an odd-style military hat.

"Crap!" he said aloud, as a second and a third soldier wearing the same uniform climbed out of the front seat of the same black truck. It had a shell over the rear bed and a couple of the American civilians ran towards the vehicles and began lifting off the rear shell. Mike noticed that it was a 1970s or early 80s Ford with an extra-long bed. He held his breath at what he saw once the shell had been tossed away.

"Charlie 130s, I have just seen three Chinese soldiers climb out of a truck. Men have pulled the rear shell off one of the trucks, an old black Ford F-350, and there is some sort of anti-aircraft rocket launcher on the rear. It looks mean and deadly. Over!"

"Roger that. Confirm Chinese soldiers. Can you count how many missiles ready? Over."

"There are two missiles on two different gun-looking launchers. Four in total," Mike replied.

"Roger, that. Wait one." The radio went silent as the operator in the aircraft must have been checking with his control center. *"Charlie 130 to ground, they could be Chinese LY-60s. We are in trouble and pulling back. Out!"*

"All Charlie 130s get down low immediately. Possible Chinese Mach 3 missiles on the airport. Charlie 130 Leader to Foxtrot Five Leader, did you hear the conversation with base? Over."

"Loud and clear," came a new voice over Mike's radio. *"Foxtrot Five Leader to ground spotter, we are ten minutes out and incoming from the south. Which way are the rockets pointing over?"*

They are working on them now," replied Mike. "At the moment they are all pointing skywards, but I can see that they are mobile as one has just done a three-sixty. Over."

"Foxtrot Leader. Roger, nine minutes out. Charlie 130 Leader, can you begin long noisy finals onto main runway 32 from the south. Go in very low and keep just above the buildings. I want you to be a decoy. Over. Get their attention. In five minutes, we are going hot. Out."

Even Mike Mallory knew that going hot meant lighting their afterburners, and he watched the men below him. "Everybody get down. They also have binoculars and could look this way at any second." There was a rustle of body movement as bodies dropped just as one set of Chinese binoculars held by the high-ranking Chinese officer with lots of red braid turned towards the control tower.

He swept the tower for a whole minute. Mike watched the

man trying to look through the darkened glass. Then somebody shouted something and pointed towards the south. All the binoculars turned in that direction. So did Mike and he saw a lone C-130 turning in to set up for finals a couple of miles south of the airport. A second C-130 was visible a couple of miles behind the first one and he assumed that the men on the ground had heard the noise of the aircraft's engines as they were too low for the men on the ground to see the very low-flying aircraft.

"Charlie 130 Leader to Foxtrot Five Leader, we are at 400 feet, three miles from the airport and turning in on finals."

"Roger that. We are coming around and need 90 seconds. Stay low and we will go over the top of you. Out!"

"Foxtrot Leader to Ground Spotter, we need wind direction, speed, direction of aiming missiles and which way the target is focusing their attention. Over."

"Wind coming in directly from the west, windsock looks like about 3 to 5 miles an hour, missiles facing incoming Charlie 130s from the southeast and all targets facing south. Over."

"Roger that, Ground. You say four vehicles together on mid-runway crossover. Confirm final target please. Charlies, stay under 500 feet. Thirty seconds to target, will have visual in 15 seconds. Over."

Mike confirmed the target, which looked like they were ready to fire at the incoming C-130s. As he put his binoculars down, he saw two dots silently sweep over the runway from the north at about 500 feet and suddenly two lines of red fire erupted from several hundred feet to the north of the enemy trucks and sped towards the unsuspecting men who were beginning to look up. Then there was an almighty explosion as the flames engulfed the four trucks and all hell broke loose as the windows in the control tower shook and vibrated as explosion after explosion slammed against the reinforced glass.

Once Mike realized that the glass wasn't going to break he

looked over the window sill and was shocked at what was going on down there.

* * *

"Foxtrot Four to Charlie 130, the airfield looks safe. We will stay up here at 10,000 until you can confirm that. Over."

The C-130 went in followed by Preston and then Sally. The airport looked deserted and three blackened circles showed where three small aircraft had once stood.

The Marines were out and within ten minutes declared Dillingham Airport safe. The F-4s headed back to Elmendorf.

It began to get dark and rain looked pretty close. Preston's satellite phone rang.

"Preston, Patterson here. I've just had a message from Mike Mallory in Medford, Oregon. Something about an attack by Chinese soldiers in Oregon of all places. He seems badly beaten up and his team has had several casualties. I have a 747 passenger jet incoming with Marines here at Elmendorf in 75 minutes. Leave the soldiers to guard Dillingham. You guys get your Cessnas back here. I'll wait for you."

Within five minutes, Preston told Sally to follow him, gave orders to the soldiers on base and was pulling back slightly on the Cessna's throttle and retracting his undercarriage. It would take them at least ninety minutes to fly the 300-plus miles back to Elmendorf at a fast cruise.

Two hours later, and with soldiers converging on Medford, and Oregon in general, the 747, which did not need refueling, took off with an F-4 Phantom flying out to catch up to the larger aircraft.

Only one of the four F-4s that General Patterson had relocated to Elmendorf had all three of its extra under-wing fuel tanks fitted. *Mother Goose* was already heading 300 miles south of Elmendorf and would fly south so that the fighter jet could top off with enough fuel to fly the 1,600 miles into Medford, only 250 miles further than its already extended range.

A high-cruise flight of three hours got the 747 down on a blackened but cleaned-up Medford runway. General Patterson had stayed on his phone for the whole flight, putting the country on high alert.

With no national communications, a pattern of calling one phone user and telling them to put out the alert on all radios in his area and also call several nearby bases with satellite telephone communication was the only alert system in place.

It took over seventy calls and three hours to get the whole of the United States on "High Alert", where a year earlier it was virtually instantaneous. The general had ordered several C-130s to reinforce all the western air bases, in case there was more than one band of thugs or enemy soldiers.

By the time the two aircraft's engines whined down, General Patterson was talking to the Air Force medical crew which had come in three hours earlier and transferred a dozen injured personnel to Travis Air Force Base, the nearest air base with full operating facilities.

Preston, Carlos, Martie and Sally found Mike Mallory in the airport's small first aid center. He looked pretty bad. As he acknowledged their presence, the nurse tending him told Mike's friends that he had a bad concussion. He had been given a pint of blood and some Air Force clothing to replace his bloodied clothes, and needed sleep. They noticed that his girlfriend seemed sedated, had a drip running into her arm and was asleep in the bed next to his.

They were asked to leave, and Mike weakly told them to give him an hour or two of sleep.

The four returned to find General Patterson looking through the terminal area which, even cleaned up, looked like a massacre had taken place. There were blood stains everywhere—floor, glass walls, chairs and signs. A Marine captain was updating the general with the information he received when he arrived twenty minutes after the two F5s had blasted the runway with napalm.

"The Charlie 130 flight leader ordered us, the third C-130 in line, down onto a clean stretch of Pacific Coast Highway, about five miles from the northern airport boundary," the captain stated. "It took us several minutes to get down and out. As a dozen of us climbed into the two jeeps, we saw smoke coming from the direction of the airfield. We headed towards Rogue Valley International at top speed and crashed through the locked north gates to see half of the runway still lit up with napalm. We immediately headed towards the main terminal as the lead 130 came in on the northern section of the main runway. There was just enough room for her to land without getting her wings burned and we headed over to her to set up a secure perimeter. The runway smelled like cooked meat. It was bad. The Marines got out and Major Blakely ordered me to take my men to the terminal in the jeeps. There were no enemy in the terminal the civilian on the radio had reported. We got over there and it was horrible. Twelve people, including seven Air Force dead, bullets in the head execution-style. Then there were two civilian males and three civilian females, also murdered execution-style. The rest were huddled in the control tower. This airline captain, Mallory, totally bloody from head to foot from a large gash or two on his head, was still on the airport radio keeping lookout. We had three medics with us, and they started helping the wounded, another dozen with head wounds from rifle butts and boots, and two of them had less severe wounds."

"Let's go and see the enemy position," General Patterson ordered the captain.

"Yes, Sir. We haven't touched the enemy camp as you ordered, Sir. Major Blakely only cleared the runway for you guys to land."

They all walked out of the terminal into air which smelled as if a hundred barbeques were cooking meat for a large gathering.

Martie and Sally didn't want to go and said that they were going to see if anybody needed help.

It was a grisly scene. Four metal outlines of trucks could just be made out, as the ammo which must have exploded blew them to bits.

"General Patterson, Sir, over here please!" shouted a Marine major.

"Major Blakely, I presume," stated the general, saluting back to all the men who had stood at attention and saluted.

"Correct, Sir. We have the live remains of one of the enemy, an American citizen, a right-wing mercenary from northern Idaho who belonged to a group of about a hundred others from the same area who were recruited, trained, and paid well by some person he never saw."

They looked down at the blackened remains of half a man, who was alive purely by the medication being pumped into him. He was very badly burned. Most of his clothing that remained was also blackened cloth melted onto parts of his body. He had one leg missing and a tourniquet had been applied just above the remains of his left knee. Most of his left arm was also missing and a second tourniquet, just below his shoulder kept him from bleeding to death.

An Air Force doctor stood up and looked at General Patterson. "We are trying to keep him alive, but his vital signs are fading. For a terrorist he is going to die pretty happy, with the amount of morphine we have pumped into him, maximum allowed dosage. He is on the morphine drip and blood drip to keep him alive, but only for another few minutes, I believe, sir. He is not delirious and able to talk."

"What is your name, young man?" General Patterson knelt down, nearly retching from the smell of burnt flesh and looked the dying man in the eyes.

"Charles, Charlie Law. Born in Spokane Washington, live in Sandpoint, Idaho, and proud member of the "Freedom Forces against Total Government Control," headquartered in Coeur D'Alene. I'm proud to die fighting U.S. government soldiers!" he stated proudly.

"Oh, cut the bull crap!" replied General Patterson. "Without that morphine drip going in you, you would be hurting real bad, so tell me who killed all those people back there in the terminal or I'll pull your drip and you will die screaming."

"Our lieutenant, Joe Gibbs. He killed all those people back there, every one of them."

"Why?" asked the general. "All they were doing was feeding innocent civilians.

"We were told that they were under the control of the U.S. government in Washington and needed to be taken out." The man replied smiling, his pupils as small as pinheads from the drugs surging through his body.

"Who told you that?" the general continued quietly and showing no emotion.

"Lieutenant Gibbs told us that he had been given his orders from the guys in Alaska to take out the people at the terminal. They even sent in a cargo plane with some of the Chinese soldiers and modern weapons to help us out."

"In which airport did they fly in this aircraft?"

"Here, right onto this runway a week ago. We were..." The man stopped, his eyes went dull for a second and he coughed up a pool of blood. "We drove in here from Sandpoint a week earlier and were told to kill anybody we found here. There were three soldiers, National Guard guys, on duty here, and we killed and burned them. The next day a couple of civilians arrived, and we rocketed their truck. It blew up outside the main gate, and we didn't see anybody else until the aircraft and all these people began to arrive a couple of days ago..." Again he stopped and coughed up blood."

"I should decrease his morphine intake," the doctor interrupted.

"Captain, go and find somebody else to attend to. Increase his dosage so that he can still talk and buzz off!" stated General Patterson angrily. "You stated Alaska, do you know where?"

"No, we were all blindfolded in and out. It was on an island, or close to the sea. It smelled of fish," the man responded.

"Did all the 100 men from your club or group go with you?"

"Only fifty at a time for training. There wasn't much room with all the gooks over there, Chinese soldiers. Can you increase the stuff again doctor? The pain is starting to come back."

"Only once you have answered my questions," General Patterson replied.

"Well, hurry up, ask!" replied the man.

Preston could see he was slowly fading away.

"When did you go to Alaska, the first time?" was the next question.

"Only went once, 50 of us from August last year to November. The second group arrived on the same aircraft which took us out. We spent ten weeks doing basic military training. There was a second group, guys from Montana who were there too. We were crammed into two houses with bunk beds. The Chinese soldiers had the other houses, dozens of them and hundreds more in the large hangars around the airfield."

"How many Chinese did you see there?"

"I counted about a thousand at one time, but they came and went on Chinese aircraft once a week. At one time it was totally empty and another, there were thousands and thousands, maybe three or four thousand. Once they arrived on massive jets, dozens of them, just like the one you flew in on. I thought you were coming to save me." Again he coughed and was silent for several seconds trying to regain some strength to talk.

"Where are all your other men in your group, and what are they expected to do to complete their mission?"

"Everybody got different missions...... some are to attack... farmers and make them sign papers to buy stuff from this company............ a farming company, I think. I don't know its name. Others are heading to destroy food places... like this one...... but most of the men, about 300 of us in total are supposed to be heading south on horseback... or trucks... to poison water depots..., or......... make farmers sign the documents...... or kill the f... f...ood......" and the man's body gave up the will to live.

"Damn!" stated General Patterson getting up. "Let's go and see Mallory and get all the food locations that could be in danger."

"You can't go in there!" stated an Air Force doctor coming up to bar the men from Captain Mallory's room.

"Captain, go and tend to somebody's wounds. I'm busy!" The doctor was swept aside as the three men entered. "Nurse, please wake the captain up for me. I need some life-saving information, and then I will leave him to rest," he added to the army nurse tending him.

The nurse did as ordered and slowly Mike Mallory came to.

"Mike, I need every location you have, established or future. I think somebody in Washington has released information to a group to destroy these food stations."

Mike Mallory told them the two dozen towns across the western states that already had food depots as well as another six which were due to get them in the next couple of months.

General Patterson thanked him and returned outside and called a dozen air bases to get troops into these towns, over a thousand men in each food station within twenty-four hours. Then they went out to see the remains of the enemy position.

"Find anything unusual?" asked the general to a tech sergeant in charge of searching for objects with a metal detector.

"Very little ammo left, just an AK-47 round here and there. Most of everything was ignited or burned from the napalm. I have a pile of stuff over here," and he showed the three men to a selection of blackened items next to one of the burned-out trucks. "A Chinese military combat boot including foot," he stated pointing to a boot with a blackened mass still inside. We believe the next item is a barrel of a modern Chinese anti-aircraft weapon. It's hard to determine what it was but I would guess it is part of a radar-equipped non-GPS guidance system still intact, and about ten years old. Three Chinese coins, a part of a major's uniform, the medal strips on his breast didn't burn as bad as the rest, nor did his rank on one of the blackened epilates. Name on uniform is Choo. Other than that, one hell of a mess and not much more to go by, except a small silver metal mini-briefcase case found in the burned-out glove compartment of one of the other trucks. It's melted shut, but I have a guy trying to get it open."

They waited patiently for the corporal to jimmy the small case. He finally did, and General Patterson was handed the small, heavy case and he thanked the man. The smell of burnt flesh was becoming overpowering, and they retreated back to the terminal building as another C-130 came in with more troops and medics.

They checked on Mike Mallory. Both Martie and Sally were chatting softly next to his bed and the three men left the girls to head back up to the control tower and look over the airport while checking what was in the small silver case.

"Just slightly underdone papers," stated General Patterson, but I have a feeling I know where they are from. Preston, Carlos, look at the engraved emblem inside the top of the case. I've seen that emblem once or twice before."

"*MonteDiablo!*" stated Preston and Carlos together.

"Peter Westbrook had the same emblem on his jacket when he spoke to us the first time we met him at Andrews," added Carlos.

"Yes, I remember," continued the general. "When I was looking at the camera showing the inside of the closed hangar, both pilots had the same emblem on their flight jackets."

For several seconds, General Patterson flipped through the several pieces of paper. "Two pages with six copies all with *MonteDiablo's* emblem on the top. A signed letter, it's a contract actually, with Westbrook's signature at the end of page two and the other party's information left blank, I assume to be filled in."

A copy was passed to Preston and Carlos and they read the two-page contract.

"So this is what all these deaths are all about," Preston stated. "These are to be handed out by these gangsters to farmers in the area, and I would assume that the farmer signs it, or they kill him and his family. Mike Mallory was telling us about several farms being hit and whole families murdered in the last couple of weeks."

"I think you hit the nail on the head," replied General Patterson.

"This contract is between a farmer and *MonteDiablo*, to supply agricultural products for credit. It states here," continued Carlos, reading page two of the contract, "that once the U.S. dollar or any other form of currency including the Chinese Yuan is returned as a form of payment, then the above-mentioned farmer will begin paying *MonteDiablo* for all the farming supplies purchased by him."

"I find the last paragraph interesting," added General Patterson. "Product will only be purchased from *MonteDiablo*, by the farmer from the signing of this contract between the farmer and *MonteDiablo*. If the farmer is found purchasing or obtaining any other products for free from any other source including the U.S. government, U.S. military, or any other legal, or illegal source, then severe retributions will be held against the farmer and his family. It states here in black and white that his land will be seized by *MonteDiablo!*"

"Isn't a free society and capitalism a joy to behold!" stated Preston.

"So!" added Carlos. "The job of these banditos, or soldiers of

MonteDiablo, is to drive around to farms, heavily armed, ask the farmers nicely to sign a contract with no end date to purchase their products, and if the farmer decides that he doesn't want to, they shoot or torture his family and him until he signs?"

"I think that is what is happening out there," stated the general.

"I think our Colombian Cartels could come up here and learn a few lessons from these guys!" Carlos responded.

"I was up in Bethel, Alaska, north of you guys yesterday," continued General Patterson. "Some kids told me that a team of soldiers and aircraft cleared out the detention center up there. Around a couple of hundred inmates disappeared. I think this could have happened at several locations. We already know from the guy, Charlie, that 200 men, mostly right-wingers have been enlisted. Pretty ironic for right-wingers to be hired by the Chinese, but it seems that Westbrook, apart from a couple of thousand Chinese soldiers, has a second army of a thousand or more American civilians driving around or even riding on horse-back killing farmers, the guys we need more than anybody to keep this country alive."

"I think that the whole country's farming community could be at risk," added Preston.

"I think so too, but thank God we have all our troops back. I'm going to empty every military base in the country, save enough men to repel any attacks, as we learned from Carlos' Colombian cartel attacks, and get the guys mobile and on the ground to get these banditos, as you rightfully call them, Carlos."

"I think it's pretty important, as the old Calderón stated to my mother years ago to also 'cut the head off the snake'," replied Carlos. "That's what we did with the senator and Police Chief Gonzalez. I think you had better warn the president that he has enemies inside his government and he needs to clean house."

For the next hour, General Patterson was again on the satellite phone and made a couple of dozen calls. Preston and Carlos headed back to see the girls and saw that Mike was still asleep, his girlfriend sitting by his side.

"Now that we know who is to blame for this horrible massacre of innocent people, I think we should head back to North Carolina and get our three Mustangs," Preston suggested to Carlos and Martie. "What about you, Sally?"

"You guys head back. I'm happy going as the general's co-pilot in whatever he flies. I think the Mustangs and their good fuel range will be an asset for continuing the search and will save the jet fighters being scrambled every time we think we see something. This Westbrook guy is going to be found."

General Patterson agreed, adding that the 747 transporter with Wong and Chong flying was arriving in 90 minutes or so from Andrews, full of jeeps and men to begin looking for more of these bad guys. They could get a lift back to the East Coast, land at RDU, and fly over to Alaska to resume the search. He was going to spend the next couple of days of August in North Carolina and head back to Elmendorf on September 1st, a good day to meet up there.

After saying their goodbyes several hours later, and Sally giving Carlos a long goodbye kiss, they climbed aboard the loading door of the now empty 747 and joined the majors in the cockpit.

They both had ideas to help fly the aircraft over to the East Coast.

CHAPTER 9

We've Found Them!

A DAY AFTER THE TRIO HEADED BACK to North Carolina, Buck flew into Elmendorf to refuel. The two gunships were already there. He had been left alone to finish the northwestern area of Alaska above Bethel, and had finally completed his search pattern. For the first time he felt the air to be warm enough to say so. Where he had based in Bethel, the weather had been in the mid-fifties during the day and low forties at night. Upon landing at Elmendorf he learned the gruesome news about what had happened in Oregon and was glad to hear that Mike and his girlfriend were alive.

The local pub was a noisy affair, and he and Barbara relaxed for two good nights, enjoying Alaskan beer with some of the locals. The locals enjoyed the outside company and asked dozens of questions about what was happening in the rest of the world.

The next morning was the day he and the other search aircraft, the two AC-130 gunships, were to relocate to Dilling-ham. It was time to check out the Aleutian Islands and there was much flying to be done.

Information had been collected by the Air Force from several people who tried to go to the islands the previous few weeks. An important piece of information was that the Alaska Marine

334

Highway, a Marine ferry transportation system, had only two of its smallest modern ferry vessels working and, so far this year, had only ferried people as far as Kodiak and Port Lyons, halfway down the volcanic island chain and no further.

Over the usual meal of salmon and beer, Buck, Barbara, and the pilots of the gunships agreed that if the ferry had been to these ports, they were not being used by the bad guys. That left seven ports the ferry service had not been to since New Year's Day: Chignik, Sand Point, King Cove, Cold Bay, False Pass, Atukan and Unalaska.

They had vague information on airports and small airfields, and one of the Air Force pilots remembered hearing about the extended runway at Cold Bay, something about an extended runway that was built for the Apollo program, or by NASA for emergency shuttle landings.

Without much to back up the anecdotal stories, they decided to toss for the towns to be visited the next day, once they had flown into Dillingham. Because the AC-130s had double the speed and range of *Lady Dandy*, one pilot suggested that he fly out and check the farthest two towns, Atukan and Unalaska. The second gunship took the first three, Chignik, Sand Point and King Cove. Buck and Barbara would check out False Pass and then backtrack to Cold Bay.

Everyone agreed and then met up at Cold Bay for the night. There was supposed to be a motel in the town and they planned to use it.

"We are running out of places these guys could be. They could still be somewhere in Russia," suggested Air Force Major Harditz, the man in charge of the search operation while General Patterson was down south. "I'm a little worried about you and Barbara, Buck. You are unarmed and cannot defend yourselves."

"We fly a civilian aircraft and have flown around the country. Anybody could have shot at us. I think you guys are more in danger. You are slow and don't have the modern electronic defenses you are used to, just a thirty-year-old radar system," replied Buck. "I don't think many sane Americans are going to shoot at us. *Lady Dandy* has been flying for fifty years and can't harm anybody."

* * *

Meanwhile, Preston, Carlos—who was now cleared to fly by the doctors—and Martie had hours earlier in the day said goodbye to Little Beth, Clint and the team back at the farm and flown into Hill Air Force Base to overnight and refuel.

Carlos needed a couple of hours to head up to his mountain observatory, now "Number Two Satellite Control Center," above Salt Lake City to check out the satellites and pick up his team of a dozen astronomers, scientists and communication specialists stationed up there. He was to have a meeting at *The Cube* in California with his whole team the following day to design a plan of action to position the Chinese satellites into a simple U.S.-only Geostationary GPS/communications orbit. He also had to check how the old Navistar-P satellite was going.

He had given instructions to position Navistar-P 350 miles northwest of its 200-mile-high, central position over the middle of the United States to view more of Alaska, and lower it a hundred miles to try and get visuals on smaller ships and any other traffic.

The lower the height, the more of its lifespan was eroded away. The poor Navistar-P was not meant to be operating anymore, but it was, and he knew that the lower the altitude, the lower the lifespan the old test satellite had.

Navistar-P had only a year or two left in her and she wasn't designed to sit at the optimal altitude, 22,300 miles above the planet. At exactly 22,300 miles above the equator, Carlos and every other satellite expert knew that the force of gravity was cancelled by the centrifugal force of the rotating universe. This is the ideal spot to park a geostationary satellite instead of orbital satellites like the old military GPS system used. Also there was less space junk to worry about. Unfortunately, the pictures of earth from Navistar-P at the higher altitude would be beautiful, but of absolutely no use to anybody.

Carlos was itching to get back to China and help get the Russian missile launched with the three additional satellites. He had spent two days over there with the best men from various NASA locations around the country who had survived the catastrophe. He located them in the several Air Force bases and after hours of pure mathematics and calculations, realized that with a little luck and a few changes they could have a 20- to 30-year simple GPS/communication system above the United States for satellite phone and defense purposes.

Since there was no electricity, the old Internet, television and other communication systems were all unnecessary. Also, he knew that by the time the power across the country came on again, a couple of decades in the future, his simple satellite system might have already expired. The modern junk satellites in space had a ten- to thirty-year lifespan.

Early the next morning, after a breakfast of fresh ham and eggs, and admiring the newly-caught wild rooster the men had rounded up in jeeps, and with a C-130 to ferry Carlos' team, the three Mustangs headed towards California.

The Cube was surrounded by a mass of aircraft. The Onizuka Air Force Station was certainly a busy place. A couple of the 747s were on final approach, still moving electronics in from Harbin. Three 747s were being unloaded and the 747 transporter had arrived in from a flight to Alaska and was taking off for China, via Hawaii.

Three of the Z-10 helicopters were in a pattern for air protection, and an F-4 Phantom and a dozen more of the Chinese Z-10s were on the aprons and ready for action. An AC-130 gunship was in front of them as they were allocated landing numbers on final approach and the 747s slotted in behind them. Preston felt like it was the good old days with all this traffic going on.

Michael Roebels was happy to see their arrival. His daughter looked well and had seemed to have gotten over her crash landing down in Texas. He had been told of their imminent arrival and had gone out to meet them. He offered a grand tour which they eagerly accepted to see how the country's new electronics were getting on.

"As you know we have the first nuclear power station up and running, although it was a small test station," he began, walking into a separate warehouse from *The Cube* itself. "Here, we have 300 electrical engineers going through the daily cargo from Harbin, China and looking for parts for the grid. We have this base and twenty square miles of grid operational; that includes seven large hospital complexes in the surrounding area where any injured people from across the country are flown in for emergency operations. We are overstaffed with surgeons begging me daily to get electricity to more hospitals. These fine people are doing about 300 major surgeries daily, and the operating theatres are booked up for two weeks in advance, 24/7. Of course, when we get emergency injured in, as we did a couple of days ago from Medford, Oregon, they take preference and the wait list lengthens."

"When are you going to get more electricity? Surely the small power station can handle more than you are using," Preston asked.

"Yes, ten times more power, but it's taking time for the parts to be modified to fit our existing system. I think we will have a second grid, about thirty square miles, operational in a few weeks, and that will add another four major hospitals with operating rooms and Intensive Care Units."

"And the whole country?" Martie asked.

"From what we've been told by Mo Wang and a couple of my

specialists in China who are looking through the massive stocks over there for the parts we need in, there could be enough to get the whole of the San Francisco area, as well as the whole of Washington, D.C. up and running before we have to produce our own. We have several hundred men looking at the electrical manufacturing machinery coming in from that helicopter factory in Harbin, and, of course, what we can scrape together with new parts over here, I believe we can start adding to the grid within twenty-four months."

"Still, won't that take decades?" Carlos asked. "At least my satellites don't have to worry about Internet traffic for a while."

"No, for a long time," smiled Michael. "I doubt that Internet, Facebook, Twitter and any other forms of social media will ever work again, and by the time they do, our younger generations will have thought out a far better system. To answer your question, Carlos, now that the population has been compressed into a smaller land size, only a third of the whole country's land area, it will take about a decade to power the mid-swath of land; and, as I said at an earlier meetings, two more decades to get the whole country up and running."

"That means that cities like Houston, New York, and Chicago could be ruins by the time power is back on?" asked Preston.

"I think you could be right, Preston. The weather and lack of dry air because all of the millions of old air conditioners and winter heating systems are not working will cause rot, damp and mold to run riot. I cannot think of anything to prevent these problems. In some places it will be a couple of years before anybody is allowed back in. Disease is rampant in many cities and we have several aircraft, mostly old crop sprayers like yours, Preston, flying in chemicals to try to sterilize the areas, and I mean really powerful chemicals. No human illegally living in those areas will survive the disease and especially the bacteria-killing toxins the Air Force is spraying into those areas. I don't believe they have any choice, as emergencies are rising with people now contracting plague and other deadly diseases. We have dozens of new quarantined areas where anybody who is believed to have a contagious and deadly disease is placed, and these places are mostly full. I was told at a meeting last week that there are dozens of deaths a day of these infected people across the country. Now that we had the attack in Medford, over a 100,000 more troops are being deployed to the northern boundaries of the new population areas to set up road blocks and with these roadblocks go more and more quarantine and food stations."

They toured three more large warehouses full of people in white coats, and Michael explained what they were doing. Some were trying to get more modern electronic farming equipment working. One group was working on hundreds of electric cars which had been sourced from the San Francisco area. Another group was only working on modern hospital equipment, including dental chairs. The largest group, over a thousand men and women in white coats, were unpacking the daily shipments coming in and sending the parts to the different areas, as well as loading dozens of trucks of all sorts to send necessary parts to the main and larger operation in Silicon Valley.

"At last count we have 10,000 men and women wearing white coats, another 2,000 personnel in transportation, and we are growing by dozens a day. We have scouts in all the new container towns and the original towns looking for engineers to rehouse them in this area; hence 1,000 builders in the suburbs are refurbishing all the living accommodations around here, getting thousands of broken and empty houses and apartments ready for occupancy with all the old luxuries, electricity, sewer, and running water. This is the first area of the United States of America to be under normal conditions again, and we will work outwards from here until the whole country is back to normal."

"What about the people still living around here?" asked Martie.

"About 50 percent of the housing units are still occupied. Where the other people went, I don't know. There were a lot of malicious killings around here before we arrived, and I believe many others went to look for family and friends living somewhere else. We are fixing occupied houses as well and, if there is a spare bedroom or bed anywhere in any house, the deal is that we fix up the house for the owners as long as they give a roof to our incoming engineers. We have up to a dozen people living in the larger houses around here, and there is absolutely no crime."

"And the electronic vehicles I see running around here?" Preston asked.

"We have 900 newly-refitted electric cars running, and they are becoming the new rush hour traffic around here. We are offering each person working for us food, shelter, and transportation. There is an electric vehicle recharge station at the entrance to the airbase where we have installed 500 electric connections for these vehicles, and our new team here at the base is completing a dozen vehicles a day. Yes, we are far behind the numbers needed, but we have 8,000 vehicles ready for the work to be done and should have one per worker by the end of the year. Here, at *The Cube*, we are at maximum employment capacity, and it is nearly that at Silicon Valley; and, with our second vehicle plant putting out three to four dozen vehicles a day, we will soon be able to give each of our workers a vehicle. We are achieving great strides in a short time, and what we do and succeed in here will be the base of operations to produce the billions of parts we need for the whole country.

"By the way, Carlos, you must thank Mo Wang for me. These parts are the real advancement of this new country; if he had not told us about the storage depots in northern China, we would be years behind where we are today."

"How much is left over there?" Carlos asked.

"I spoke to Mo yesterday. He and a Colonel Rhu are doing a great job over there. I think he said we are about 90 percent done on the airport warehouse parts and only 10 percent done on the helicopter factory parts in a massive second storage warehouse; we want those parts and the factory's machinery here. Only the 747 transporter can carry the larger machinery over here from China, and our aircraft is always getting emergency orders to go somewhere else. Yesterday, General Patterson and I discussed turning Beale Air Force Base into the third engineering unit and, then maybe Camp Pendleton and its large area into the fourth depot early next year."

They travelled over to the Silicon Valley operations area in one of the electric cars. It was extremely weird for Preston, used to his old and noisy Ford truck, to travel in such a quiet vehicle. It was like a fancy golf cart and the car, a Japanese model with four adults aboard, headed down the empty roads at a good 60 miles an hour, Michael ignoring all the old 45 mile-an-hour speed signs.

"Here, we have 7,000 of the 10,000 white coats, I call them, working. This area is three times the size of the air base and has electricity, sewer, and running water. We don't really need heat and air here, but to practice on all the needs the country faces, I have a dozen people working to get those systems up and running here. Other parts of the country will require those systems as necessities, not luxuries, and I have a building of twenty engineers designing the necessary parts for future use. First we must design the parts, and then we must design and configure the machines to build the parts."

"So what about helping those corporate drug guys getting the whole banking infrastructure working?" asked Preston.

"Totally impossible," replied Michael pulling silently into a parking lot. "It won't happen in twenty years, even if we let everybody in this country die and only worked on what those twits wanted. It's the electricity they need and that is what is going to take the time. We give all the electricity to them, and we won't have any here. You understand the complexity of getting a nuclear plant under power, and powering a working grid, but they don't. One doesn't work without the other. You saw the dozens of guards and jeeps with machine guns. My two working facilities are the most heavily guarded places in this country. That is to stop these guys from trying to get in the way. We have dozens of Chinese ground-to-air missiles set up here; same with the airbase. The only dozen 80s-era working Abrams tanks the country owns are here, ready for action. The F-4 is stationed here and so are a dozen of the Chinese Z-10 attack helicopters to stop any interested parties. The rest are ready for transportation to other areas. I hear six more Z-10s are heading up to Elmendorf later today."

"How many do we have in total?" asked Carlos.

"Seventeen in the first group, a dozen more from the nuclear base over there; three arrived from the Harbin factory last week, and the last two yesterday. Carlos you are good at math!"

The factories tour was a real eye-opener. All three had degrees in engineering and understood the mammoth task the Unites States placed on one man's shoulders, Michael Roebels. And he was just breaking stride.

Martie was extremely proud of her father, and he was really enjoying himself, working at full speed.

They stayed overnight in a small cozy motel by the air base; there wasn't time to visit Michael's wine farm, and they left at dawn the next morning for the flight to Elmendorf. They didn't have the range and refueled at McChord Air Force Base, just outside Tacoma.

* * *

Buck and Barbara were taking off in *Lady Dandy* a day late. The D-3 had an engine problem and needed the Elmendorf air forces techs to put her right. The problem had been minor, a dirty fuel line, and the two gunships had decided to wait for her. Their plan was to be around if she needed backup. The air force major didn't want *Lady Dandy* to fly at all. If the enemy had fighter aircraft, the DC-3 was a sitting duck, but against modern fighter jets, the two AC-130 gunships would not fare much better.

Buck had to head towards Dillingham first. The long flight from Elmendorf to False Pass was close to a thousand miles and he would be short of fuel if there was no fuel at Cold Bay. He agreed to refuel, check on False Pass first, and then head back to Cold Bay, the overnight stop.

"There are supposed to be 60-odd people in False Pass, and the major hasn't done his homework for the first time since we met him," stated Barbara in the right seat. Buck switched the aircraft, now leveled out at 10,000 feet, to auto-pilot after taking off from Dillingham six hours earlier. "Runway is gravel and only 2,100 feet long, 600 feet shorter than Preston's. We are going to just scrape in and out of there."

"And Cold Bay?" asked Buck. They had done this a couple of dozen times in the last week. In and out of long tarred runways and shorter dirt ones. All the runways were too short for the gunships.

"A grand total of 108 people at last count," Barbara replied sipping a cup of warm coffee. "Twenty-odd buildings in town, one or two large hangars at the runway, maybe an office building and I would assume a couple of single aircraft hangars dotted around. The runway is long enough for a 747 and tarred. Remember the guys told us that it was a backup for NASA or something?"

Buck nodded. "We might as well fly over Cold Bay on our outward leg and give it a once over before we return later today."

It was still a three hour flight into False Pass from Dillingham and then another hour back to Cold Bay. Luckily the days were long. They would be in and out of radio contact with the two gunships once they spread out, but that was usual in this vast and rural area. Most aircraft radios worked up to about a 500-mile distance.

Buck flew south, southwest to get over Cold Bay, slightly south on a direct line from Dillingham to his first port of call.

Slowly and still at a cold 10,000 feet they saw the piece of land the small town of Cold Bay stood on facing eastwards. At that altitude they could just see the town ten miles ahead of them. The runway was easily visible, a long line of black stretching east to west across the bleak ground far below them.

"Town looks normal," suggested Buck looking out of his forward windshield at the town now a few miles ahead of them. He directed the nose of the aircraft slightly to the south so that Barbara on the right side could get a better view as they passed overhead and the autopilot did its job. "Airport looks much more built up than what you described earlier, Barb."

"Looks like it," she replied, checking back through the notes handed to her at Elmendorf. "This report, dated about eighteen months ago, states two larger hangars and half a dozen smaller hangars, a small terminal/office building, a fuel point on the port side of the second much shorter runway and one windsock. That doesn't look like the report to me down there. I'm counting nearly thirty long buildings, three extremely large hangars, several mid-sized hangars and the half dozen single aircraft hangars."

Buck got out of the left seat to walk back and view the airport now below them and just under their starboard wing. "That's about it, and I'm sure I saw an aircraft on the apron a couple of minutes ago, but it's not there now. It seems that either the report is old and outdated, or just plain wrong, or Cold Bay had one of those television makeovers before the networks went down," Barbara laughed. They would check it out on the way back.

False Pass was the opposite of what they had seen over Cold Bay. The landscape was empty of anything moving, the town looked desolate and lonely and after a couple of circles, Buck put her down on the short runway using every inch of gravel. There was cleared space at either end of the runway and he gauged that under full power he had more than enough room to get airborne again.

The afternoon was cloudless and even though the sun was still high in the sky, the wind was getting icy cold. Winter was certainly only a few weeks away.

There was nobody about and so they decided to walk the fifty yards or so into what would be the center of town.

It was desolate and empty, except for seagulls everywhere and the odd prowling dog or fox.

"Weird!" stated Buck. "It looks like everybody locked up shop and just left town. How could that be if the ferry didn't come this far?"

"Maybe they were airlifted out of here and that's why Cold Bay has more buildings than it was supposed to have?" Barbara surmised.

"Maybe Cold Bay has become a new center for all the small towns and inhabitants in the area?" Buck suggested. The buildings looked like they had been empty for months. They looked through several windows and found the insides neatly in place, as if people were expecting to return. The only store-type building was locked up and Buck didn't want to trespass. It wasn't their job.

Thirty minutes later they were airborne for the return flight to Cold Bay where they were both certain that they would be given answers.

Lima Delta (*Lady Dandy*'s call sign) to Charlie, are you in range? Over," Buck asked over the radio as they climbed up to 5,000 feet this time. At the higher altitude the air was getting chilly. They had enough time to reach their destination on time; actually they would be there first, twenty minutes ahead of the others, if they were on time.

There was no response and he waited another thirty minutes before trying again. This time he caught a scratchy noise of a voice. This told him that another twenty minutes would be needed for the closing aircraft to get closer to him and their far higher cruising speeds.

The day was breathtaking, the views over land and sea were rich in colors and they enjoyed their travels around Alaska immensely. Buck told Barbara that it had been some of the prettiest flying he had even seen.

Buck was descending into Cold Bay and had just spoken to one of the AC-130s who was now only thirty miles behind him and rapidly catching up. He switched radio usage to his second aircraft radio, already primed to the locally used radio frequency and asked for landing instructions when a powerful and unseen Chinese missile went into *Lady Dandy*'s port engine and 60 pounds of High Explosive blew the engine, the fuel tanks, and the old aircraft into a million pieces.

CHAPTER 10

Cold Bay, Alaska

THE SATELLITE PHONE RANG in the operations room at Elmendorf Air Force Base.

"Elmendorf," stated the airman on duty.

"Rogers for PattersonKey, is he there?" the man heard and he looked down his list of phone owners to see who this Rogers guy was.

"Sorry, Admiral, the general is on his way back from the mainland. His ETA Elmendorf is two hours."

"OK, tell him that my current position is three miles southeast of Kodiak, and in the area of Chiniak Bay. I have a shore tender I'm about to launch and head into the harbor to see what I can get in fresh provisions. What do you have there to supply us, young man?"

"Frozen salmon, Sir, about two tons on a couple of pallets in the freezer. Other than that, old frozen vegetables and frozen French fries, about a ton of each; that's all the entire base can spare at this time, Sir."

"I'll take whatever you have. I'm sure you have a C-130 on the ramp. Load the food aboard and get her into Kodiak. Do you have a heavy-lift chopper? Our Seahawks aboard the frigates don't have the underneath lift capabilities."

"We have two Jolly Green Giants here, Sir."

"Good. Ask a couple of pilots to fly one down here to Kodiak to lift the pallets aboard our ships offshore. She can't miss them. Oh, yes... Are the Seals with you?"

"Yes, bored to death, Sir!"

"Get a dozen of Lieutenant Paul's guys into the 130. They can help the Air Force men move the pallets around."

The radio operator hadn't put the phone down before the radio buzzed.

"This is Elmendorf," he stated into the receiver.

"Charlie, is that you?"

"Affirmative. Over," he replied to a voice he recognized—his older brother—Major Harditz, flying one of the AC-130s to Cold Bay.

"Charlie, get the airfield on High Alert. We just saw a single missile launch on our radars, in the vicinity of Cold Bay and I believe it took out Lady Dandy. *I think she's down. We saw a very faint explosion ahead of us and* Lady Dandy *is not responding on the radio."*

"The general is two hours out on a 747. Do you want me to call him? Over."

"Negative. I'll call on my satellite phone, but get the base on High Alert and a Foxtrot Four over Cold Bay ASAP. Get the fighter airborne, it will take her 30 minutes to get here."

"Not possible; the only Foxtrot Four with full drop tanks is on her way back with PattersonKey. The other one doesn't have the range."

"Damn. Get the Chinese helicopters to Dillingham for refueling and give Mother Goose *orders to fly there as well. We will circle out of range until we hear from the boss."*

The young operator did as he was told and suddenly the air base was busy.

"What!" shouted General Patterson once he was told what had happened by the major. "*Lady Dandy* got a missile? Those bastards are going to fry, slowly. Stay out of missile range; thirty miles and under 2,000 feet should suffice. Do you think the enemy saw you on radar?"

"I'm sure sir. *Pave Pronto* was to our northwest when it happened, at 10,000 feet and fifty miles out, too far for an accurate ground-to-air missile on a propeller aircraft. We were ten miles closer, at 5,000 feet and 30 miles behind *Lady Dandy* when she disappeared from our radar screens. I'm sure that if they are using modern Chinese radar, they must have seen us at least 100 miles out."

"Agreed! I have absolutely nothing to go in with and fry the bastards. The F-4 needs to refuel. Return to base, we need to launch a full attack. At least we know where they are." And the call abruptly ended.

For the next several minutes he called up several air bases on the mainland and ordered as many aircraft to head into Elmendorf as he could. Admiral Rogers called him and slowly a plan formed.

Several hours later, and with many unhappy and angry faces around the room, including Preston, Martie, Carlos and Sally, the meeting at Elmendorf started. Outside everybody could hear the noise of incoming aircraft, one after the other.

"OK, ladies and gentlemen," General Patterson began. "We have confirmed the downing of *Lady Dandy*. She has not returned to any of our bases. Their missile strike was effective and we are 100 percent sure *Lady Dandy* was hit." There was silence in the room.

Preston was still shocked; Buck, his close friend, unarmed and in a civilian aircraft, shot out of the sky. He felt a new, raw anger building up inside him. Preston felt it was time to teach these people a lesson, just like the others who had tried to invade the United States.

This time they were fellow countrymen, with greed and power as their main motivation for killing others. Buck and Barbara were good people and Buck was the only one of them who had never fired a bullet at anybody else in anger. He had always worked like a machine, flying people around and getting things done.

"We will have a funeral for our civilian pilots once the people who murdered them are brought to justice," continued the general. "Now is not the time. We must end this aggression against our country, now and forever." There were sounds of agreement from the forty people in the room. "I would go and bomb this little town until it fell off the map, but there could still be innocent civilians in Cold Bay, 108 of them at the last count. Plus, Mr. Westbrook and Mr. Bowers and their cronies might have Pakistani Shaheen II nuclear missiles aimed at the mainland. We will meet here again once Admiral Rogers is flown in. He has ordered supplies, and the chopper is already there and about to lift the food aboard ship. The admiral will return with the C-130.

Three hours later General Patterson called a second meeting. "Admiral Rogers, would you like to describe the plan we discussed upon your arrival an hour ago? Ladies and gentlemen, the admiral has a good plan to get our troops deployed in and around this town. Admiral?"

"Thanks, General. The remnants of our U.S. Pacific Fleet, namely one post-World War II destroyer and two post-World War II submarines, are in the Kodiak area. The submarines are preserved Tang Class diesel submarines from the 1950s, and are heading towards Cold Bay as we speak. With our fleet are three light, more modern frigates of the Colombian Navy, loaned to us by Admiral Rodriquez who has given me full authority to make use of his ships. He is in Colombia helping elect a new government.

"It is not much of a fleet, but we must use what we've got. I have with me a map of the land around Cold Bay. Often I thought it was an island, but this whole piece of land is actually connected to the mainland; unfortunately there are no roads to get a large army in there. We have to go in by sea and air, the old-fashioned way.

"We have 90 members of Seal Team Six here at Elmendorf and we have two more teams arriving tonight, Seal Teams Four and Five, 280 of the best men the navy has. The Marines are shipping out men with parachutes today from three of their bases in 747s. 1,500 men will arrive tomorrow and a second load of 1,500 the next day. The army is filling the 747 Transporter down at Fort Bragg with the longest-range artillery weapons we have. Every helicopter with lifting capacity is heading towards Elmendorf, working their way up the western United States, refueling as they go. We have a Chinese container ship leaving Hawaii in an hour and will get here at full speed to transfer all this hardware onto the land mass around Cold Bay if we need it. I don't think we will, but back-up is always part of a good battle plan.

"I'm flying in with a separate 747 with enough underwater equipment from San Diego to get our Seals onto land, under the cover of darkness. Now, you see here on the map, Mortensen's Lagoon, about five miles south of the Cold Bay runway?" He used a pointer to indicate the locations on the map now pegged onto the wall in front of everybody. "By the way, I will have extra maps here tomorrow. The sea charts show that the submarines will be able to get to within 300 yards of this beach here in about 60 hours' time. It's the deepest area with a sandy bottom, few rocks and only a couple hundred yards from the main ferry channel. I'm sure that the channel companies have dredged this area annually. I ordered our ships towards Cold Bay three hours ago and they are currently at 18 knots which is full speed for the slower submarines.

"I have arranged for our incoming supply ship, now five hours southwest of Kodiak, to change course and intercept our ships. Helicopters are transferring the first loads of men, food and equipment to the Colombian light frigates and will do so for the next three days. Distance is a problem, but we can ship needed supplies and helicopters into closer airports as the ships move westwards.

"The two submarines have the old World War II systems of internal/external evacuation chambers to allow men to leave ship while underwater; these chambers were often not designed into our more modern subs. Both submarines can release six men at a time through a pressure chamber while thirty feet underwater and the men can be ejected to the surface. Each sub can transport in fifty men or thirty men with supply packs and, this will also be done under the cover of darkness. Since we are going into fall, we have a seven-hour night window in which to operate close to shore.

"The navy is going to deploy the first sixty-two men of Seal Team Six onto the beach east of Mortensens Lagoon the first night and the rest of them the next night, weather permitting. Seal Team Five and Seal Team Four will parachute in with the Marines. That will give us nearly 100 men ready for anything and Seal Team Six will have two nights to check out the area and see if they can get into the hangars to find out if they have these missiles. Two miles south of the main runway is an old World War II runway." Admiral Rogers pointed to a vague outline of a dirt runway. "I was part of a team flown in on the darn thing thirty years ago to check the area out as a possible naval facility. I also remember reconnaissance photos of the old airport taken a decade or so back and noticed the semi-ruined buildings; they were occupied buildings on my last visit. Whatever remains is enough to hide 100 Seals from any detection equipment that may be installed at the modern airport to the north. I'm sure they will have patrols around the area 24/7; our idea is to dress in whatever they are wearing and get men inside their camp. Only if and when we get confirmation that they have nuclear capabilities, can we go forward."

"Thank you Admiral. With Seal Team Six on the ground, the rest of us can go home," quipped General Patterson, returning to the front of the room. For the first time in that meeting there were several smiles. "Once we know that they have nuclear capabilities and it has been dealt with by the Seals, the Marines and the air force will go in. We know that their missiles, if they have them, won't be as accurate without the old GPS system and, I believe the enemy doesn't even know that they don't have GPS guidance anymore. Unfortunately, with or without GPS, those missiles can still fly; where they fly, nobody knows and they may have been fitted with other manually-guided directional backup systems just in case. We cannot allow these missiles to go hot. I will have Z-10 helicopters with air-to-air missiles ready to shoot them down if they ever poke their noses above ground, or wherever they are. Once we are at this stage, we can flatten these guys once and for all. There are reports of up to 5,000 Chinese soldiers being housed in the area. Also, we know of a possible 250 U.S. civilian prisoners from the Bethel, Alaska area and approximately 300 right wing mercenaries from northern Idaho and Montana—the same guys who hit Medford, Oregon. I believe the last 400 to 500 civilians are not in Cold Bay, but in the States and visiting farmers. Within 72 hours every area on the mainland in which these anarchists could be operating will be teaming with U.S. troops and they will be found and taken out. Today alone three farmers and their entire families were murdered and their farm houses were burned; one in Washington State, one in southern Idaho and the third in central Colorado.

"I was informed that these farmers refused to sign paperwork put in front of them. We already know how and where these guys are operating; so far about 100 farms have been forced to sign these documents and we have a couple of Z-10 helicopters moving into these areas ready to blow these squads away. Latest reports are that these mercenaries are operating in truckloads of four, much like the Chinese hit squads seven months ago, and for all we know there could even be more Chinese hit squads helping them as well. It seems that Westbrook and Bowers had their men trained by the Chinese soldiers to act the same way as the first Chinese squads.

"So, it looks like these CEOs, Westbrook, Bowers and the other two are already responsible for dozens of deaths, including our pilot friends, and good U.S. farmers. I promise that while I breathe air, I'm going to get these guys. I'm going to follow Admiral Rogers' plan. He is in command of Phase One of this mission and once the information is gathered, Phase Two will be the destruction of this base by the air force and Marines. Questions?"

"Why don't we just nuke the area and be done with it?" asked an airman.

"Nothing I would like to do more, but we are west of the Continental United States, which I believe Westbrook and Bowers also know, due to the positioning of their base. That means radiation fallout will hit the jet stream and head over Alaska, areas of Canada and parts of the U.S. Also, we need to see who and what these guys are. Like a tumor, we need to isolate and exterminate the whole problem. This could just be a splinter group of another, even larger group. Last, these guys must have been working with Zedong Electronics before the end of last year, and if we can capture one or two alive, American or Chinese, we could extract vital information to find out if there are others out there. I want this to be the last attack on our country, so that we can rebuild in peace and not always have to watch our backs for bad guys for the rest of our lives."

"Was the attack on our country from South America also

Zedong Electronics related?" asked Captain Kohout, one of *Easy Girl's* regular pilots.

"No, we did our homework, covered every possibility, and know from our allies in Colombia that there was no connection at all, or they wouldn't have killed the 10,000 Chinese troops along the Panama Canal. Those Cartels, realized that money, their lifeline, was going to dry up; if there was no more money to be made in the drug business, then land, was the most valuable commodity. That is why I am opposed to immediately reinstituting a monetary system in our country. Yes, the ex-rich will bitch, and I'm sure the wannabe-rich and even the poor will bitch, but I believe it will suppress human greed, at least for a while; once we are a strong nation again, then maybe cash will be allowed to return, and be king."

With the meeting over, Preston and Martie headed off to their allotted room behind the Officers' Mess. Both were solemn contemplating the murder of Buck and Barbara. So were Carlos and Sally, until General Patterson came to find them and invite them for a drink in the bar.

"One thing I always enjoyed as a kid was reading flying stories from World War II," he started, as they headed in a group for the bar. "The downing of pilots became such a regular occurrence that they used to have a kitty, or pre-paid tab, at the bar and every day all the pilots put in small change or any money they had to spare into the kitty. When it was confirmed that one of their own went down, they took money out of the kitty and purchased a round of drinks in memory of the downed friend. I think we should do the same. There's no flying tomorrow and we might as well toast our flying friends the old-fashioned way."

They did. Tired after long hours of flying, the drinks were welcomed. The bar was made open with free drinks for all pilots and crew, and after several rounds, and an old upright piano being banged hard in the corner every now and again, names of recently downed pilots and friends were shouted out with the raising of dozens of glasses at the mention of each name.

Many names, over three dozen, were called out by different people. There had been a lot of downed pilots in the last several months.

Even General Patterson stayed and raised a glass, drink for drink with the rest, as many remembered good friends who no longer flew with them.

* * *

It was a different picture aboard the two Tang Class submarines slowly heading closer towards land, a couple of miles south of Cold Bay, two and a half days later.

Lieutenant Meyers and his thirty men had been first out of Elmendorf departing with full equipment in three large navy Seahawk helicopters; the U.S. Navy helicopters had hitched a ride north from San Diego on the helipads of the three Colombian frigates.

They were already fitted with external fuel tanks, added before they left San Diego to aid in the transfer of food and supplies to the Alaskan outlying areas. The extra fuel increased their range to 700 miles. Even with the added fuel weight, they could have ten men crammed into them with gear.

After two hours flying they caught up with the fleet; the helicopters transferred the men and headed back for the next two platoons of Seal Team Six before the ships got out of their range of Elmendorf, in twelve hours' time.

To the Seals, the submarines were a home away from home. They had spent time aboard larger, more modern craft for training and extraction, but these Tang class were much older and smaller, and one could feel the coldness of the water outside invading the entire, more tightly packed craft.

Flights with men and parachutes were arriving into Elmendorf from Quantico, Pendleton and Camp Lejeune in 747s, while C-130s were transferring supplies onto the shorter runway at Dillingham Airport 600 miles to the west, where General Patterson was setting up his forward headquarters. Dillingham was the closest he could get to Cold Bay; from the small outpost it was a shorter 300-mile flight.

The 2,000-odd townsfolk of Dillingham hadn't seen so much action for decades.

At full speed and meeting up with the supply ship, sailing due north to connect up with them, the submarines were refueled on the surface. They took on more than enough diesel fuel to get to their destination and dived to continue the journey.

Forty-eight hours later, it was time for the Seals to use their underwater equipment recently lined aboard the submarines from the frigates. The three helicopters had relocated to Dillingham a day earlier to be able to supply equipment aboard the frigates.

Up to this time, the frigates had stayed 120 miles out to sea, so that the enemy radar wouldn't notice the low-flying helicopters.

One of the frigates headed closer to shore, keeping a large island land mass between her and the Cold Bay airport. South of the island, the equipment was passed by rope and then lines to the submarines, thirty miles from the landing beach, and then underwater, the submarines aimed to get to within 300 yards of the beach at a 30-foot depth to allow the men to surface.

Charlie Meyers and Joe Paul would lead the first two groups of six men in their respective submarines to be "blown" to the surface. It was a simple affair. Each man had the use of a single scuba tank firmly attached to the wall of the escape chamber. The chamber was dimly lit and they sat around the chamber wearing rubber dry suits over their uniforms to keep out the cold water. Only their heads were outside the suits and the top of the suits tight around their necks. Each man placed a waterproof pack of equipment in his lap: weapons, ammo, food and, blankets for warmth. One held a radio.

The chamber door was closed and sea water pumped in. Each man breathed from his inverted scuba tank until their leader unscrewed the large, watertight, six-inch-thick steel hatch to the outside. Once the pressure had equalized, he pushed hard to open the hatch. Then, one by one, the men grabbed a piece of thick cloth tied to four different places on his pack and from his mouthpiece filled the cavity underneath the cloth with air, let the pack float out of the chamber and he, taking a last gulp of air, followed it upwards, breathing out all the way to the dark surface 30 feet above.

Within 40 seconds the soldier and the pack reached the surface three hundred yards offshore. The second to last man took the last man's pack, which left Charlie Meyers to take his last breath, leave the chamber and close it from the outside, screwing down the hatch so that the water could be pumped out for the next six guys. He took a small float with him as he left. This was to help anybody struggling on the surface.

The water was icy cold around their heads as each man kicked and reached the surface. Underwater goggles kept their eyes dry, snorkels helped them breathe, and flippers propelled them, as they waited for the entire team to surface, each man holding the inflated cloth with the heavy backpack next to him.

"Count off, men," ordered Charlie, and he heard five men respond. The water was still cold on the surface as they silently moved towards the black-lined beach.

The next load of six men would do exactly the same. They were lucky that the night was dark with little wind and the sea relatively calm. Three hours later sixty-three Seals and one air force pilot were accounted for on dry land, the last of them still climbing out of their dry suits.

The next night, when it was time for the next team, six men would swim bags of the suits back on a small black float and, with rope, the next team would pull them down back into the submarine to hide the evidence. The last suits would be swum back by a couple of sailors in suits, pulled into the submerged craft, and all evidence of any men swimming ashore would disappear.

"OK, guys," said Charlie quietly, as several of the men gathered around while the others were already on watch. The last men undid their packs and wrapped themselves in blankets to warm up after the swim in frigid water. "I will go forward to scout the area. You two guys get the couple of Chinese uniforms out and try to keep them from looking a mess. Those silly red uniforms are about ten sizes too small for me. Major Wong, did your quick scuba course help you? Sorry you couldn't practice in real water inside the submarine, but you seem to have survived."

"As I told you guys, we did a little downed aircraft evacuation in the Air Force and yes, Lieutenant Meyers, I am here and I'm alive! Were you guys taking bets on whether an Air Force pilot could handle it?" asked a smiling, but shivering Major Wong.

"Might have, Major," smiled Charlie back at him. He had seen this small guy fly several different aircraft already and had a lot of respect for the Air Force major. "Major Wong and Sergeant Rodriquez, I think you guys are the only ones small enough to fit into those clown uniforms. Get them on and we'll go with one more man watching our backs. Sergeant Mendez, you come with me as back-up and stay a hundred feet behind me. Grab your two silencers. I want the silencers on your Glocks and your sniper rifles in case we are expected. The boss said that it is three miles to the runway, so we will check that out first. I'll radio back to the rest of you. Joe, take command of our rear guard and get everything moved to whatever is good cover at the old airfield once we give the OK. My team will go on and scout the perimeter of the larger runway and we will be back at the first runway by dawn."

With orders given and clothing arranged, the four men set off in the northerly direction towards the airfield. The wind was from the north would help cancel out any noises made by them if someone was listening.

The first, older dirt airfield was barren and empty. Admiral Rogers was right when he had described ruins. There was not much left, only a few walls and a part of a roof on a couple of the smaller buildings. Enough to keep equipment dry if it rained and they were sure it would. It actually started twenty minutes later. As the night went darker, rain clouds passed overhead and a very light drizzle began to wet them.

There was an old path from the beach area north of where they came ashore and it led them to the old runway, and then further north towards the main town and airport at Cold Bay.

Charlie Meyers, a mile north of the dirt runway, radioed the rear group to tell them to move towards the first runway, warned that there wasn't much vegetation or hills to hide movement, and there was an old road to the west of the runway which had recent tire tracks, a Chinese jeep by the look of it, so hide all foot tracks.

He and his men had also begun to sweep their tracks, once they came across the larger road leading into the old runway.

Suddenly Charlie Myers crouched down and the three men behind him did the same. He heard a faint snore, a human snore, yards in front of him. With hand movements he told Rodriquez and Wong to stay down, their lighter uniforms were easier to see. After giving more hand signals, he headed left to flank the area in front and Mendez went to the right. A slight misty breeze had helped to send the noise south.

Fifty yards north, and directly on the path, they came across a heavily camouflaged anti-aircraft defense missile system on the rear of a Chinese jeep.

Both men crawled in as close as they could. The area had sparse ground cover, only grass a foot or so high. Charlie could see two men, both asleep, and they were wearing the same uniforms as Major Wong was wearing. He returned to the others.

"Major, there are two men just north of us manning a mobile missile launcher on the back of a jeep," whispered Charlie to the three men gathered around him. "You and Rodriquez head up the road and we will cover you from several yards to their south. The light is better against the darker north sky to see what is going on. They are Chinese, asleep, and I'm sure they are not meant to be. Sneak back like a Chinese officer would to catch them asleep and then ask them these questions. Mendez and I will cover you. Once done, leave them be. I don't want any alarm signals of missing men just yet. Rodriquez, you don't speak a word of Chinese, just grunt and look like you are the man's aide or something. Write notes. You don't need weapons."

Twenty minutes later Major Wong quietly sneaked up to the side of the jeep with Sergeant Rodriquez a step behind and had to literally shake the men awake.

"Both of you sleeping at your position! Didn't I hear orders last month that at least one man must always remain awake?" stated Major Wong in Chinese to the two surprised and sleepy men, both wrapped up in blankets, and who were trying to assemble themselves in a erect and proper guard position.

"Yes, Sir, Sergeant!" one man shouted out.

"No need to wake the others. I'm going to inspect them after you," stated Major Wong keeping his voice down. He suddenly realized he had to check his dark jacket to see what his rank and name was and realized that the former wearer's name, above the upper left breast pocket, was that of a lowly Sergeant Chee, so he acted like one. "You are lucky I'm only a sergeant and not an officer. They would not be as kind as I am." Then he remembered the questions he was to ask them.

"How long have you been guarding this launcher? Maybe it is time to move you to another one. How many of the launchers have you guarded in the last few weeks, Private?"

"Private Fung, Sergeant. Just the three south of the runway, Sergeant. We are scheduled to move to one of the northern jeeps tomorrow night, Sergeant."

"And the other placements?" he asked, immediately realizing that there weren't any. The man looked puzzled. "Just testing you! Who is your commander?"

Corporal Zeng and then Sergeant Ma, Sergeant," the private replied.

"And since you have been asleep for most of the night, can you remember your password for tomorrow morning to return to the airfield?"

"Yes, Sergeant! Tomorrow morning's password is 'turnip'."

"OK, I need to make a report, but I will not mention this misconduct. What building is your platoon in, Private Fung?"

"Block three, by the mess hall, Sergeant."

The two men left the worried-looking guards to man their jeep, and headed east along the length of the long runway, as if to head to the next missile emplacement.

Charlie Meyers sneaked up to them while they were walking and "Sergeant Chee" told them what he had learned.

Ten minutes later they silently found the second jeep, several hundred yards from the first one. Again the two guards were asleep and much the same happened. This time Wong had three different questions to ask.

Once the men were awake, he began. "Private, tomorrow's pass code is lettuce, tomato or turnip, which one is correct?"

"Turnip, Sergeant."

"Excellent, at least sleeping didn't deprive you of your intelligence. Maybe it has helped your memory. Let's see. How many American civilians are on base?"

"Only the one block of prisoners remains, Sergeant, and the VIPs. The rest left months ago."

"I know that, stupid!" How many Americans in that block was my question?"

"I don't know, Sergeant. We are never allowed to mix with them, but yesterday morning on parade, I saw about a hundred."

"Well done, Private. Let us see if your sleepy commander, the Lance Corporal is just as intelligent. How many of our glorious soldiers were on base today?"

"I have never counted, but at parade yesterday there were the usual three battalions, Sergeant!"

"I know that, you stupid soldier. How many soldiers in a battalion? That is a question you might be asked for your next promotion."

"I have been studying, Sergeant! Normal modern Chinese army battalions, 700, Sergeant. Our Zedong Red Army Battalions, 900 men, Sergeant!" the man responded proudly.

"Since you are good men, I will let this sleeping-on-guard misconduct pass. Now stay awake." He left.

Again the information was passed to Charlie Meyers as they moved along outside the perimeter of the southern side of the airport and found the third jeep, this time both men were awake.

"Well done, Privates. You are the first guards I found awake tonight. I will tell your superior, Sergeant Ma, I believe?" The men nodded looking tired. "Do you remember the password for the morning?" Both men were better than the last and nodded that they did, and also kept their mouths shut. "Turnip, right?" Again they nodded. "Let's see if you are really awake. How many missile emplacements are north of the runway, Private?" stated Wong peering at the man's name on his Zedong Electronics' military tunic. The weather had lightened slightly and he could just about see the man's name on his tunic.

"Two jeeps, Sergeant," the private replied.

"Private, how many machine gun, mortar or artillery emplacements are stationed outside the airport fence?"

"None, Sir, they are all inside the fence," the man responded thinking that he had been asked a trick question.

"You men are really awake. First, Private, if we have three missile emplacements south of the airport and two north, how many more are there?"

"A trick question again, Sergeant?" the Private replied, smiling and now at ease. "Five is the correct number, Sergeant."

"Well done, men. In my report I will mention to Sergeant Ma that his men at this missile emplacement were alert and ready for action. Now, don't forget your password tomorrow morning." He turned, with Sergeant Rodriquez following him into the darkness.

* * *

Back at Elmendorf, the last of the aircraft were preparing to head to Dillingham, which now looked like the whole U.S. Air Force had come to visit. The runway was long enough for all the aircraft, except the 747s. It hadn't been built to carry such large and heavy aircraft, so all the cargo and supplies came in on C-130s. Tents by the dozens, large, medium and small, went up within hours of the men arriving. The locals were excited to see two F-4 Phantoms arrive and a couple of hours later two F-5s come in, old and still very noisy jets.

The next day, two more F-4s arrived in between a constant stream of C-130s bringing in arms, fuel and supplies. Then six Z-10 helicopters arrived just before dark. These caused interest, as two of them still had their Chinese air force paintjobs and four had U.S. air force colors.

Now it was time for the three Mustangs to make an appearance. Early the next morning, Martie, Preston and Carlos landed and, this time many came out to see the old World War II aircraft. This was something the two oldest gentlemen hadn't seen at Dillingham for well over half a century.

Finally, the second group of six Z-10s arrived, and with them several different types of American helicopters; mostly old naval Seahawks, a Jolly Green Giant and two Hueys.

Overnight the town's population grew ten-fold as the Seals and Marines, a company of a hundred men per C-130, arrived and were dropped off with tents and equipment. Twenty aircraft worked all night to bring them in and by morning, two of the larger helicopters headed out and were to return throughout the day with pieces of artillery slung underneath.

The second load of Seal Team Six, commanded by Lieutenant Murphy, were waking up on the frigates, with the submarines now alongside and thirty miles offshore. The ships were now stationed south of the large island and due south of Cold Bay. The calm weather had changed somewhat in the area, the cloud layer had descended down to 1,000 feet and there was a non-stop windy drizzle.

* * *

"Hey, General, are you awake yet?" Charlie Meyers called into his satellite phone ten minutes before dawn.

"Yes, Lieutenant Meyers, I was awaiting your call," the general replied smiling. He was getting to like this ugly-looking Seal.

"Your Major Wong did a great job. Ok, got something to write with?" The general replied that he had.

"Five modern anti-aircraft missile emplacements on jeeps, three south of the runway and two locations north. They look like permanent fixtures as their tires haven't moved for days. I haven't studied Chinese crap for a while but believe them to be swivel HQ-7s, older models with four missiles per jeep. They are the only armaments outside the airport perimeter. I believe there is enough firepower to bring down your entire air force, General." Patterson agreed. "There are three battalions of 2,700 men inside the airport and I believe approximately 100 American prisoners inside, the town's residential population, I would assume."

"Sound like the right number," Patterson replied.

"That's it for now. I'm going to get Major Wong in there in an hour. He can give us a good idea of what to expect. He is the only guy who can go in during daylight. We might go in and visit after dark, depending if we can get in and out undetected."

"Wong is good. He has done this often, and I did get a Chinese colonel's uniform packed somewhere in your supplies. It has his real name on it and that should be enough to give him freedom to roam," added the general.

"Right, General. He seemed a little perplexed in a sergeant's uniform last night!" laughed Charlie.

"Landing tonight begins at 03:00 hours and the weather looks wet and windy. Call me same time tomorrow. Good luck, Lieutenant!" and the general ended the conversation.

Major Wong found a pressed and neatly packed colonel's uniform, a set of extremely powerful army-issued Chinese binoculars, and a swagger stick in one of the other men's packs and he happily increased his rank. They ate a cold meal of rations and three men held sheeting and kept the "colonel" dry. They were now stationed at the old runway and there wasn't much to keep the men dry, other than a couple of small 20-foot by 8-foot brick buildings with roof corners and parts of the walls still intact. The wind wasn't much help.

The drizzle eased as Wong was escorted as close as possible to the two jeeps on the dirt road without being seen. The clouds parted slightly and rays of sunshine dotted the sparse landscape. He thanked the men and meandered forward to walk up the road. It didn't take long for one of the Chinese soldiers, a new man, a sergeant this time, to run up to him and salute.

"We didn't see you come down the road, Sir," the perplexed Sergeant exclaimed.

"Of course you wouldn't, Ma. I came around from the eastern side of the airport, across the grass and up the road. I try to do this walk at least once a week, Sergeant."

"Yes, sir. May I ask you for today's password, sir? I must do my job, sir!"

"Of course, soldier, it is good that you are alert and saw me so quickly. Last week I nearly walked past the first jeep before they looked up and saw me. 'Turnip' is today's password, I think, Sergeant Ma, or let me see, is that tomorrow's?"

"No, no, you are correct, Sir! 'Turnip' is today, 'Mao' is tomorrow's password."

"Glad I got it right. Now let me get back before it starts to rain again. I was lucky to get my walk in today without getting wet." With that Wong returned the salute and continued up the road.

The second jeep didn't take any interest in him several hundred yards further east and on the road leading up to the closest main gate. There was good daylight visual between the three jeeps he had "inspected" before dawn and they had seen him waving his swagger stick at their sergeant in the first jeep.

He had been told that many Chinese officers enjoyed using these short riding crops as authority and had asked for one to be packed with the uniform. Thank God most of the stuff purchased in the USA was 'Made in China'.

At the main gate, two guards looking alert, watched him coming and saluted as he arrived.

"Turnip," he stated and without a word they opened the single smaller gate next to the larger gates, and he walked unopposed into the enemy camp.

The guards must have phoned for a jeep for him as one sped across the runway. The driver saluted and he got in, asking to be taken to the American prisoners' building, he couldn't think of any other place at that moment in time.

"I haven't seen you before, Colonel Wong," the driver, a lieutenant, commented as he drove across the airfield.

"I came in on the last flight," replied Wong, looking around the field.

"But that flight came in from Washington, Colonel," the man said. "I was on it!"

"Correct. We still do have several men still in Washington, mostly the hit squads and a few of the Chairman's secret service men," the colonel replied calmly, still taking in all he could see. "I must have been aboard the other aircraft."

"You have met our glorious Chairman, as well?" the driver asked in awe. "I met him at Shanghai harbor just before he left for America. He just happened to pick a few of us and he acknowledged me."

"I worked with Comrade Wang and his hit squads, and was in America when the tragedy happened," Wong continued.

"Yes, I heard about the death of our glorious Chairman. All the work he had done to change the world and it is now not so."

Yes, I agree," added Colonel Wong as the jeep pulled up to the first in a line of single-story barrack-like buildings with two guards standing outside. "Lieutenant Chun, that third large hangar over there. Was it here several months ago when I was last here? It looks new to me."

"No, it has always been here, but I arrived only four months ago. Maybe it was built after you left, Colonel. Hangar Three, the one we are not allowed near has always been off-limits to lower officers since I've been based here." He dropped off the colonel, waved to the two guards he seemed to know and waited for further orders.

"Thank you for the lift. I know my way around. I prefer to walk, as I usually do outside the perimeter every week." The lieutenant then saluted and drove off. The jeep had a Chinese license tag on the back and he memorized it.

"I'm here to check on the prisoners," he stated to the two sergeants standing outside the main doors to the prisoner building. They saluted and opened the door and let him into the smelly interior.

"Morning Parade is in ten minutes, Colonel. The prisoners should be dressed and ready," stated one of the guards.

Dozens of eyes looked at him as he entered the musty, hot room. Several American children under 10 years old looked scared as he returned their glares.

"Who is in charge here?" he asked, trying to sound like a Chinese soldier speaking bad English.

"Joe Mathews, our mayor. He's over there," stated one of the adults. He was led into a small private room where an older man was sitting on the single army-issue bed, already dressed and, Wong assumed, ready for parade.

"We had a quiet night and nobody didn't cause any problems, sir," the man stated, looking at the entering Chinese officer he hadn't seen before.

Wong shut the door behind him and looked at the man.

"Please don't beat me. I can't take much more. Get one of the others to be the leader," the man stated looking at the ground.

"Where are you from, Mathews?" Wong asked.

"Don't you know? Are you new here? This is our town and we have been locked up like this for ten months now, ever since October last year."

"How many of you left?" Wong asked trying to keep his cover.

"You shot Pete Smith and Mike Parkins in March, the two guys trying to escape. We are now 105 in here. One kid got away a month or two ago, we don't know how and I think the jeeps went out and shot him. We heard shots all the next day. Why are you asking all this? We have been perfect prisoners since the kid's escape. Please don't beat me up again with your stick, I can't take any more."

Colonel Wong left the room. He so wanted to tell the old man that help was soon at hand, but he knew that blowing his cover would not be very fruitful for the Seals at this moment.

He walked outside as sirens sounded and he thought to return and stay in the building as the Americans, all dressed in old dirty clothes, rushed out to the airport tarmac. The old man stumbled past him last, looking down at the ground as he shuffled by.

Sitting by a front window on the south side of the runway Wong looked onto the area where the Chinese soldiers in uniform were forming up. Looking through his binoculars he had a direct view of the three large hangars and he watched as one set of large hangar doors opened. It was the middle hangar, next to the one he had asked the driver about, and he saw two white Gulfstream Vs, several military jeeps and a couple of what looked like armored vehicles inside. He also saw several high-ranking Chinese officers walk out, he assumed to inspect the parade.

He trained the glasses on the inside and saw several engineers working on the two jets and a couple of the armored vehicles that were manned and ready. A band struck up a chord from somewhere he couldn't see and he recognized it as an old Communist Party song as all the Chinese soldiers began singing along with the band.

When the doors closed behind the officers, he focused on the approaching men. There were thousands of soldiers facing the approaching officers who slowly walked out of his view. He had seen several colonels and one general, by the look of the fancy red braid on the shoulders of the shorter, extremely overweight man leading the group.

There were a lot of shouted orders and he understood that the troops were being inspected. From his window he could see most of the Americans at the eastern end of the parade line and many of the soldiers in formations. The Americans were inspected last, the old man standing in front of the group. With much the same swagger stick as Wong had, the general finally got to the American prisoners, hit the old man hard on the top of a shoulder with the stick, shouted something at him and, as the man fell to the ground, headed back out of view.

Nobody left ranks to help the poor man who slowly got back to his feet. The band played a second tune and there were more orders shouted and the Americans began running down the runway and the soldiers headed off in different directions, mostly toward the buildings next to where he was watching.

The old man, too weak and old to run, headed towards the prisoners' building and the same two guards followed him and closed the door once he had entered.

"He does that to me every other day without fail," the old man said to Wong entering his room to lie down. It didn't seem to matter to the old man that he was talking to a Chinese colonel.

"Where are Americans running to?" Wong asked in bad English, and silently getting up.

"One lap around the airfield, then to the showers and finally over to the vegetable garden to tend the crops for the rest of the day. Mr. Westbrook likes his vegetables fresh." The old man looked around, but the colonel had already gone.

Wong now felt that he was free to move around and inspect the base. There were dozens of soldiers walking around the airfield and he became invisible as he blended in with them.

He checked the dozens of buildings next to the prison and then a second row in a line behind the first buildings. Inside were barracks, three beds high and he counted 300 beds per building.

"Not much more room than in that submarine. Glad it's cold around here," he thought to himself. Several men were about to

go to sleep, many awake and they saluted him as he walked through each one and then out the door at the other end.

The last three buildings in each line had slightly better quarters and a lieutenant was getting undressed as he entered.

"At ease," Wong said in Chinese, saluting back. He hit his swagger stick on several pieces of furniture and exited the other end.

He headed across to the northern buildings of the airport and counted about 100 guards patrolling the third large hangar. He thought it best to stay away from that building for the time being.

The first hangar was clear of guards as he entered. There was one large Chinese military transport aircraft, a modern four turboprop Shaanxi Y-9, the first he had ever seen. It was the most modern mid-sized transport aircraft the Chinese had and was slightly bigger than a C-130. Around the hangar walls and out of the aircraft's way were two dozen Chinese armored vehicles, three Chinese medium-sized tanks, a dozen jeeps of all sorts and a couple more jeeps with the same anti-aircraft missiles he had "inspected" outside the perimeter on the rear beds.

"This aircraft has been busy flying in all this stuff," he thought.

The hangar was empty of personnel and he did some calculations in his head. He worked out that Harbin, China to Cold Bay was approximately 3,000 miles. This transporter could do that non-stop. Suddenly a door opened and he realized that there were living quarters in the hangar. *"This might be where the general resided,"* he thought as the general himself walked up to him. He stood at attention and saluted.

"Colonel... Wong!" the general stated looking at Wong's nametag. "I haven't seen you around here before. Do I know you?"

"Yes, General Lee, I am in command of troop and airport

cleanliness, overnight guard duties, and I normally work at night and sleep by day. I often come through here to inspect while you are asleep, then I go out of the airport and inspect the missile launchers to make sure the guards are awake. We don't have the same daily schedules."

"Very interesting," the general thought. Wong could smell the man's body odor and knew this man was old school; he only bathed once a week. "I never knew that. Have we met in China?"

"Yes, I was a good friend of Colonel Rhu's at the airport in Harbin. I often noticed you coming and going."

"Oh, Rhu! He was a lousy airport commander, but good at chess."

"General Lee!" shouted a voice from the door the general had entered, and Wong nearly went into shock upon hearing an American voice.

"Mr. Westbrook, I will be one minute," replied the general in bad English and returned to Wong in Chinese. "Keep up the good work, Wong. Keep our airport clean."

"I have one question to ask, General," Wong continued, knowing that he was about to be dismissed.

"Hurry up, Wong."

"I am only in charge of the above-ground cleanliness, but my orders state the whole airfield. Should I get permission to check out the areas underground?"

For once the general looked surprised. "I suppose that would be in order. You are a colonel and only colonels and above are allowed down there. Get a special operations ID tag from Major Bong Fung at the operations office behind Hangar Two. Tell him that I sent you and I think a checkup should be done at least once a week. It stank of animal urine, or something that smelled horrible in corner areas when I was down there last week." With that and with Westbrook shouting at the man again General Lee did a half impromptu salute and headed back.

Wong went back to inspecting the corners of the hangar for cleanliness, in case anybody was watching.

If anybody had been watching, they would have seen the conversation and he decided that it was safe for him to poke his nose in a few more corners than just the large hangar. He walked into the living quarters and received quite a shock. They were much like the ones he had seen in Preston Strong's hangar in North Carolina. He had slept overnight there for one night. These were far bigger, had a large lounge where a colonel of equal rank to him was sitting on a couch reading a book. They nodded to each other and he continued through the rooms, only looking into open rooms.

There were several bedrooms along each side of a long corridor with the end room divided into a bedroom, a dining room and a private lounge. Lee was the name on the door and there was an orderly inside cleaning up.

"Twenty-one senior officers," he thought to himself. *"I bet the Americans sleep in the same rooms in the middle terminal."*

He found he was correct after walking out of one hangar and twenty yards later into the next. This time several heads turned to see who had entered, saw the rank and uniform and went back to their jobs. The lounge was in exactly the same place, one floor higher with the same open staircase leading up. This lounge had large glass walls and he could see a long table and a meeting going on. The guy Westbrook was there, three other Americans, several young and pretty American-looking girls serving drinks and food, and General Lee.

The two aircraft looked spotless. He had always wanted to get his hands on a Gulfstream V. A 747 was like an 18-wheeler truck compared to flying one of these babies. He decided to step inside and was confronted by a pilot exiting. He was American and had flight logbooks and maps in his hand.

"Can I help you?" he asked with a Texas drawl.

"I want to see if your aircraft is well cleaned enough for you,

Mr. Captain," Wong responded in his absolutely worst English and accent to boot.

"Sure, check it out. It smells a bit in there, and if the people around here ever washed a little more maybe the smell would go away." He arrogantly left the aircraft and headed for the meeting.

Wong quickly looked around. *"One modern anti-radar jamming device, front left passenger seat, just as Mo Wang had described. No transponder, no flight logs, no black box. One pretty clean aircraft!"* he thought looking around. He did notice a small and powerful-looking satellite phone/transmitter on the wall next to the main seating section of six comfortable leather lounge chairs. A few inches above the modern communications system was a padlocked Perspex box with two red buttons in it. He immediately left the first aircraft to check the second one. He ran his fingers down surfaces outside in case anybody was looking and then headed over to the second Gulfstream.

It was exactly the same, even the radar-jamming device was there and the radio transmitter and little Perspex box and its two red buttons, each the size of a dollar coin.

Wong was starting to worry. He had been visual for too long, but he needed to inspect the most important area, so he headed to find this Major Bong Fung.

"Looking for Major Bong Fung," Wong informed the corporal saluting in front of him.

"Who wants me?" shouted a voice from a rear office.

"Colonel Wong, on orders from General Lee," shouted Wong back pretty loudly and with authority. The man was out of his office quickly. "General Lee wants me to inspect the underground areas for cleanliness once a week and told me to tell you to authorize me an ID tag immediately."

"You don't want to go down there, Colonel, I've been told it stinks down there," replied the major looking directly at Wong.

"Precisely why he has ordered me to clean it up, Major! I

don't even know where the underground area is. Can your corporal show me?"

"You are a colonel. You are entitled to go down there at any time," was the reply.

"I don't like underground places and I don't like stinking smells, Major, but when the general gives orders, I must obey!"

"Of course, Colonel! Corporal Bo, issue Colonel Wong an ID badge and show him the door to get down there. Good luck, Colonel. Better you than me!" The major saluted and headed back into his office.

A color photo was taken and glued onto a badge that stated Hangar Three. The corporal headed out of the door, expecting the colonel to follow.

Colonel Wong quickly looked over the desk in front of him and looked inside the still-open drawer where the corporal had taken out the badge; he saw several others in there with photos on and left the room.

"You must return this badge when you leave Hangar Three," stated the corporal as he caught up. They walked through the heavy guard consisting of a jeep, two heavy machine guns behind sandbags and a dozen soldiers, all saluting upon seeing Wong's rank.

They didn't go into the hangar, but to a set of steps that went down outside the side of the hangar. It was at least a thirty-foot flight of stairs and heavily concreted around the entire staircase entrance.

"Code is 'Zedong007'," Corporal Bo stated to Wong smiling. "It never changes. I'm not allowed to go in there, only colonels and above and several of the white coats, we call them, engineers who come down here and check on things at night. Just show your ID to the guards the next time, and they will let you in. Daytime only, Colonel." He saluted and climbed the stairs.

On a Chinese box with ten numbers and letters, he spelt out Z-E-D-O-N-G-0-0-7 and the door automatically swung open. He went in, found a light switch, and the smell of a mix of cold nitrogen mixed with cold liquid rocket propellant hit his nostrils.

He walked down a concrete corridor and came face to face with two lighted corridors with a door at each end. The first one he tried was unlocked and he walked in, switched on a second light and came face to face with three rocket motors, exactly the same height as his head and several feet in front of his eyes. The smell was coming from small, external solid/liquid-propellant side-thrust motors steaming small amounts of coldness into the air a dozen or so feet above him.

"This was certainly a bad stinking animal," he thought to himself. He looked up and saw that he couldn't get any higher. He then realized he had walked down the exhaust escape corridors for the rocket and he went to the second door to find exactly the same set up. On the outer side of the second door, there was a flight of stairs and hitting the switch at the bottom of the stairs climbed the stairs to see what was on ground level in Hangar Three.

CHAPTER 11

The Time For Civilians Is Over

WITH VERY LITTLE TO DO BUT WAIT, the civilian pilots sat around waiting for their turn to get to the enemy.

Preston and Carlos were still upset and angry about the loss of Buck and Barbara. Buck had been a longtime friend to both of them and was an outstanding engineer. The sense of loss was beginning to get to them and for the first time since New Year's Eve Preston sensed that he and Martie were no longer really needed. Martie had suggested the night before that the U.S. Air Force was now better equipped, and their old-fashioned aircraft weren't really needed any more.

This time the enemy had modern weapons, modern Chinese missiles that could take them out of the sky before they even got into range of Cold Bay. Buck was the first real casualty of the war among their group of friends. They knew that they had won the lottery on New Year's Eve, being in the right place at the right time. If they hadn't had the fly-in, they would be among the hungry and destitute population out there.

Although they had continued to live the high life—flying and enjoying the luxuries the farm provided to them—they also had helped deliver food and supplies to the needy. They had witnessed nationwide loss and devastation and observed heart-wrenching despair and hopelessness on hundreds of faces of depressed people in line for food. They had also seen the resilience of many who, although they had nothing, would still be the backbone of this country, the country they all called their own.

Martie had spoken words of humility, how she was tired of this short and false life and being given everything they needed. They rode the roller coaster of good fortune for long enough, and it was time to get off and lead as normal a life as the U.S. offered for the future. She wanted to go and help her father, look after their new family, take back the farm, and go back to what "normal" had to offer.

Preston agreed to most of the ideas Martie proposed. He always underestimated the female sex on logical thinking.

To men, the thrill of action and adventure took priority over much of life. As long as a man had action, a cold beer, and a beautiful woman by his side, life was good.

Preston and most of his friends, other than Will and Maggie Smart, were in the top one percent in wealth in the country, before all this happened. Now all the wealth and security was gone, and money meant nothing. There was no communication with others around the country, or the rest of the world, and they hadn't seen the real death and destruction this world-changing event had affected.

They hadn't seen small innocent children dying of starvation, or mothers and daughters dying of exposure to the elements, or the millions of stories of horrible suffering in the northern and southern cities, around the country and the rest of planet Earth. They had seen only the excitement of the action and adventure most people only dream about, and slowly a sense of guilt crept into his thoughts. He began to see the big picture for the first time since New Year's Eve.

It was time they returned to reality. Let the soldiers do their job and the civilians go home to start a new life in this new country. The battles would end. They had already won the major ones, and now it was the time for family unity: help thy neighbor and go forward.

"OK," he said after spending most of the night lying awake and thinking. "Martie, let's go home," Preston stated to his wife. "We have new kids to look after, crops to grow, and a new life to start. You are right, let's go home."

Preston told Carlos over breakfast an hour later. "Carlos, you do what you want, but Martie and I are going to ask permission from the general to go home, back to North Carolina."

"Funny," replied Carlos, "Sally and I spoke along the same lines late yesterday. I'm sure it is a female ploy, but Sally has lost interest in military flying, and we all have a life to rebuild. I have work to do in the U.S. with the satellites, and with my father as president in Colombia, Sally doesn't want to be on the wrong end of a Chinese missile and I agree. We each flew a 747 for an hour and reached heaven. I don't want to fly one again. Will and Maggie are already back in California doing their thing, and I think the girls are right. Let the soldiers finish this fight. I'm getting interested in seeing if we could fly over to Europe. Preston, do you want to hear about my latest idea?" Preston nodded. "Once the work is done getting the satellites aligned, I was thinking of asking the president if we could start a sort of international information-gathering mission, to see what is happening in Europe and other parts of the world, and see if we, the United States, can aid other nations in engineering and electronics rebuilding. That sounds like a lot more interesting than getting a missile up my undercarriage. What do you think?"

Preston thought this over for a minute. Normally he was the idea man, but this one sounded like a lot of flying and since no information at all had reached American shores from Europe, apart from bits here and there from returning soldiers, maybe this idea could be a future path. He had heard that Europe was far worse off in electronics than the U.S., but more people had survived. The police forces had managed to control the violence more effectively than in the U.S. where there were guns and shooting everywhere. Further, with Michael Roebels, his new father-in-law, heading the U.S. reconstruction program, maybe there was merit to Carlos' idea. Plus it was time, the first time, for Preston and Martie Strong to actually travel and see the rest of the world. They had lived this false life for eight months now, and it was time for a new life.

With the general's permission, they flew out several hours later with Sally catching a ride in a C-130 heading to Edwards to pick up her Pilatus, left there weeks ago. First, she wanted fly down to Flagstaff and visit her parents. Carlos wanted to head to Bogotá, but would wait for Sally in California at *The Cube*.

CHAPTER 12

Major Wong And The Seals

THE LARGE ROOF HANGAR LIGHTS came on, first with a low dim light which made the interior of the hangar eerie.

It took a minute for the lights to brighten up and slowly the small lines of incoming light from outside disappeared as the hangar inside turned into daylight.

Wong stayed in one place and quickly looked around. The two heads of the 55-foot long Shaheen II rockets stood thirty feet or so out of their respective concrete tubes in the ground. He moved to a thick concrete wall built near the corner of the aircraft hangar, nearly wide enough and high enough to get a 747 inside. There was a protective curved, concrete wall in the corner of the hangar, and behind that sat several more jeeps, artillery pieces and a fourth small amphibious-looking Chinese tank, about twenty tons in weight .

As with the others, the tank was light enough to be carried in the Chinese transporter.

Behind the wall and through an armored glass door he saw a modern missile control center with the latest computers, screens, switches and flight control knobs. It appeared to be state of the art, and was inactive. He tried the door; it was unlocked. Inside he quickly studied the instruments, mostly radar and GPS guidance electronics. He noticed one screen that looked different. It looked like a manual, or radio-operated guidance system and he slowly put two and two together. Both of the Gulfstream Vs had similar equipment in place of parts that had been removed to make room, and this control center could be operated from the cockpit of the jet.

"Of course! They have satellite phone communications, they could also use the satellite phone digital keypads," Wong thought to himself. A person in the Gulfstream could control the direction of this missile by using the keypad of a satellite phone. It wasn't his area of expertise, but he would bet that both aircraft would have, maybe two of these systems; one for each missile. These missiles might not need GPS. They could be manually controlled and aimed from anywhere in the world, by typing in coordinates or compass directions for radio frequency guidance.

He needed to get back to report, so he quickly counted sixty vehicles stationed inside the hangar, around the two phallic symbols of destruction, and headed down the stairs.

"I think it is a small animal getting in there, like a large rat, or something which has really smelly urine, maybe a muskrat or even a skunk. I'm going to get it cleaned up tonight, tomorrow, or the next day," Colonel Wong stated to Corporal Bo handing in his ID. "Can you call a jeep for me? I need some fresh air to clear the stink from my nostrils?"

"Yes, Sir," replied Bo, picking up the phone. "The smell must be real bad for the general to complain. He hardly ever goes in there anymore." A jeep was called and the same lieutenant who had driven him across the airfield a couple of hours earlier drove up to the door.

"I want to clear my head. The smell is so bad in Hangar Three that I want some real fresh air. Lieutenant, drive me down to the old dirt runway south of the missile jeep out there. I need to walk and smell sea air, not the filth of that place."

"Remind me not to get promoted to colonel, so I never need

to go in there," laughed the man as he drove off to the closest gate, the same gate Wong had walked in through.

"Going out again, Colonel?" inquired the same two guards at the gate. "It is not often that we let anybody in and out. Do you have any orders from the camp commander?"

"No, not today, Sergeant. The aircraft could be flying out later today or early tomorrow, my head hurts from the stink in Hangar Three, and I thought to check on the outside jeeps and men after getting some fresh sea air," he replied trying to look as sick as possible. "If you don't let me out I could be sick all over your shiny boots, so open the damn gate!"

The poor sergeant wasn't going to go further on this topic and made a signal for the second soldier to open one gate. Who was he to cause more trouble than necessary?

"You sure you don't want me to stay and drive you back?" asked the lieutenant once they had driven through the old runway and further along to the beach.

"No, a good walk will clear my head and I can surprise the men in the jeeps by walking up from the south. It is a good opportunity to see how vigilant they are. Lieutenant, go back and if anybody asks where I am, tell them I went for a walk and will be back in an hour or two. General Lee might want a report on Hangar Three."

Major Wong let the sea air fill his lungs as the jeep drove off. He was surprised how many Seals had disappeared into the small, old buildings at the dirt runway, and returned to the buildings once the jeep had disappeared to see if anybody was still there.

* * *

Three hours after the Mustangs left, General Patterson held a meeting. He was sad to see his friends head out, but in a way he was thankful. Now he could be a soldier and run a soldier's war.

He still needed Carlos' brain though. With his phone and in front of the meeting, he called Carlos, now cruising over Vancouver. He described to Carlos the information that had come through an hour earlier on Charlie Meyers' phone from Major Wong.

"It's hard to understand what they have without seeing the equipment, General, but I think the major has assumed correctly. I believe the system or systems are back-ups for loss of GPS guidance, which means that those rockets might still be able fly where they want them to, within their 1,500-mile range. First, somebody must destroy, or at least deactivate any similar parts in or on the main control center in case there are more controllers out there. Second, those Gulfstreams should get into American hands, and I think Andrews is your best bet. Just a thought, but if the president were to offer Westbrook and his sidekicks a deal, I'm sure they would be more than happy to fly back to Washington to discuss the deal. They know that they can control the missile's flight from Washington, and sort of hold that as a ransom against the president if the deal isn't exactly what they want. Plus, I was wondering, how did these guys get our satellite phones?"

"I was just thinking the same thing," replied General Patterson. You gave out the lists of who got phones, and I think you said there were still a hundred locked up in the armory at Andrews, correct?"

"Correct, General. I would check to see who has authorized phones out of there. There is no place Westbrook could have got these phones, unless they got them before all this crap happened from Zedong Electronics, or from the Chairman himself."

"Yes, I think that is the answer. Thank you, Carlos. Fly safe."

The call ended and General Patterson left the meeting to make a couple of private calls. Twenty minutes later he returned to the men and women waiting patiently for him to work on a long list of items Charlie Meyers had asked for.

* * *

"The general thinks that the Gulfstreams might fly out of here tonight or tomorrow night," Charlie Meyers stated, having his own meeting a few hours later. "We have the second group coming in tonight and I have asked some of the men to bring in small slices of C-4 connected to a timer, so that we can distribute them around the airport's armored vehicles once we get in there. My only concern is those civilians. We need to get them out, and I just can't figure out how to simply walk 100 civilians out of one of the gates."

"Fly them out!" suggested Major Wong, still in his Chinese uniform and looking pretty out of place among the Seals. He didn't even sit like a Seal would.

"Major, I think that skunk smell did go to your head," replied Joe Paul. "But we are still in a free country so elaborate."

"I'm known by several, including the general in there. The aircraft I saw in there is a little bigger than a C-130 and must have flown in those small armored vehicles, those old Chinese amphibious tanks. You think they are Type 62s, correct?" Joe Paul nodded. "OK, you want to go in and paste the place with C-4. Then before they all go boom, I fly that aircraft out of there. Answer a question, Seal Team: How many men would fire on General Patterson's aircraft if he officially/unofficially flew out of Elmendorf?"

"Nobody without explicit orders," Joe and Charlie replied.

"Correct. Lieutenants, you give me some small guys, we dress them in Chinese uniforms. We grab the general in the hangar, get him aboard, then open the hangar doors and taxi out. I think it would be best to do this at night, the same time you guys go in. Then, I taxi the aircraft close to the civilian building, open the rear ramp, your guys take out the two guards, hurry the civilians aboard and then we all just fly away!" Charlie Meyers smiled. "I tell the tower over the radio, if your guys haven't already taken it out, that the general has a sudden and urgent appointment in China or something and, from the civilian building, I will have enough direct blacktop to fly straight out, as long as there's not a strong a tailwind. I stay low, 100 feet over the water, and hopefully nobody of rank at the airport will have the guts to fire on the general. If we do this after the Gulfstreams have left, which we have been told should happen, then there will be fewer people to make a decision about putting a missile up my rear end."

"OK," responded Charlie Myers. "We could use your aircraft noise as cover to take out the missile jeeps outside and the gun emplacements inside the perimeter, so that nobody can send you a gift, then fight our way into Hangar Three."

"No need if you can take out the missile emplacements first. Nobody seems to check them; they were all asleep when I inspected them last night. If you get your men to take them out, we take out the gate guards, several of us head to Corporal Bo's current place of employment, take white coats and a few backpacks of gifts with us, and I'll get you in Hangar Three before I head over to Hangar One. Just have three or four guys in Chinese uniforms waiting for me at Hangar One. If I'm found out and captured, at least you are in a position to take out the central control, add a few gifts to the rockets and then the guys in Andrews can take care of the Gulfstreams."

"So it all begins when the Gulfstreams leave here. What about possible phone, or radio messages to the Gulfstreams before they get to Washington?" Joe Paul asked.

"I think a second group of men silencing the colonels and brass in the VIP quarters, plus the American females and anybody else hanging around Hangar Two would be a good thing. If we can control those areas, and the airport's control tower before we start engines on that Chinese four-propeller job, then I think that any problems would be preempted. Or maybe we wait until the Gulfstreams land at Andrews, hopefully when it is still dark here, and Air Force personnel take the aircraft into custody and then phone us. I just wish I had Major Chong here. He could control the tower, or help me fly that thing out of here."

General Patterson was called and three more Chinese American soldiers, including Major Chong, who was a couple of minutes out flying a 747, were to be sent over with a third group with more explosives in thirty hours. The general reported that the president would contact Westbrook or Bowers in the morning, seven hours from the current time, and set up a meeting within twenty-four hours after that. "I will inform the president that he must ask for the meeting the same day, not knowing that these guys need ten to twelve hours to get in. Also, the meeting time will be early, so that it is still dark in Alaska. We are hoping that they will ask for the next day to give them time to fly their long route into Washington and he will then not accept any other time as he and his family will be leaving Washington for an undisclosed location for two weeks. He will also leak that to the government members in Washington to make sure the word gets back."

The fairly simple plan was put into motion. Since Colonel Wong was expected back by the guards at the gate, he decided to head back and make sure search parties were not sent out.

He was expected, and the same guards were awaiting his return. He entered making sure that they knew, and he knew that "Mao" was the password for the following day. They were put at ease when he actually told them the password and asked if they knew the next day's password. They said that they didn't, but the main guard house would know; one ran off and returned a few minutes later saying that 'Zedong' was the next day's secret word and Wong thought it a good word to have on the day they would begin destroying this enemy base.

He looked over Hangar One as it grew dark. He now was ignored, apart from the general seeing him walking around the brightly lit hangar and headed over to him. Wong saluted.

"You are still inspecting, Wong?" General Lee asked.

"Yes, Sir. I checked out Hangar Three's smell. It's a mix of animal urine and rocket fuel I believe. I'm trying to figure out how to get rid of the smell. Since the engineers are going in sometime tonight, I thought I would ask them for advice. It is better to be in there when I ask the question. What do you think, General?"

"I would assume so," a semi-dressed General Lee responded.

"The reason I am working late, Sir, is to sort out a new problem I was made aware of by Corporal Bo in the security office. There was a report that somebody, he didn't tell me who, was extremely sick today and the person thought it might be a contagious disease from either using a radio or a satellite phone. Was that your complaint, Sir?"

"If it is somebody getting sick, an officer, or a soldier, it must be a radio bug. Wong, you had better sanitize all the radio receivers here on base. There is one in each hangar and the main one in the airfield control tower. Only the American civilians have satellite phones, I believe. Even I wasn't issued one from the Chairman on his last visit. Can you imagine that?" the general stated, adding to his self-importance.

"The Chairman actually visited this airfield?" replied Wong in awe.

"Yes, several times once Hangar Three was complete. His last visit was around early November last year, just before he was to invade the world."

"Pity, I missed that," exclaimed Colonel Wong. "I met him once last year in Harbin. He shook both Colonel Rhu's and my hand when he left in November. Maybe he was coming here."

"Maybe," replied General Lee, walking off. "Check the radios, Wong. Make sure they are clean. Wong, make sure everything is clean!" he joked, walking off and thinking what a lousy job this silly little colonel had.

The silly little colonel found what he was looking for, several empty Chinese military backpacks in a stores section underneath the living quarters and he stuffed them in one bag and headed out of the hangar.

* * *

Twelve hours later the president was in contact with Peter Westbrook.

"It has been suggested by several civilians, and a couple of members of both Houses of Congress, Mr. Westbrook, that you and I should hash out an agreement of some sort. My generals are dead against it, but being a politician, I must play both sides, so I was thinking of discussing how to please both camps, and get this country up and running again. Many have been worried about the loss of money. Several congressmen and I need to discuss with you and Mr. Bowers what should happen for the rest of this year. Are you willing to fly back into Washington and discuss your ideas with me and the members of both Houses?"

"Yes, Mr. President, but this will be the last time. Mr. Bowers and I have the whole world to pick and choose from right now. China, I've been told, is needing leaders and outside help and actually needs more assistance than you and the United States need right now. Maybe we should move our headquarters and interests into China. There are far more people there than the current population of the United States."

"Mr. Westbrook, how are you obtaining this information?" asked the president slyly. "The entire world's global communications are down, there are no phones or communications even from here to London, yet you can obtain information from China? How is that?"

"Classified information, Mr. President," Westbrook replied confidently. "We have our ways and means. The whole system isn't down, just all the modern U.S. and European systems. Bowers and I aren't anywhere near the USA, and you and I are speaking on a satellite phone, aren't we, Mr. President? I assume you were handed one after beating off the Chinese bandits trying to invade your country. I'm sure you have several dozen phones around the country. Mr. President, it also sounds like you don't have very much in the way of communications, and you haven't heard that communications are normal in China and most of Asia. I just spoke to the head of their government yesterday in Beijing, and he stated that we would have carte blanche over there in our dealings with them. The yuan is still working fine in Beijing, Mr. President. This time we will meet at Dulles. I'm not happy landing at a military air base."

When General Patterson was told that a meeting was to be had in Washington in 24 hours' time, and the president relayed the information about Westbrook's bragging about China, he laughed.

"I'm wondering who is in the dark, Mr. President? He is doing well to hoodwink you. I'm sure he hasn't even headed over to China since the New Year, because he would have headed into Harbin, Nanjing or radiation in Beijing. Our powerful radar systems based in Misawa or Harbin would have seen them come in. He's playing you, and I think trying to find out how much you know. I'm glad you have finalized a meeting, and we will be ready both sides of the country once they touch down at Dulles. Mr. President, the nuclear threat is real and their aircraft will be boarded and taken over this time. I know they think landing at Dulles will be safer than an Air Force base, but their aircraft will be commandeered. All you have to do, Mr. President, is to have the enemy in position in the room. General Austin will have hundreds of men around and at all doors to the meeting room at Dulles. You must find out who is on our side and who isn't."

* * *

Thirty hours after General Patterson talked to the president, while he was having breakfast in the White House, there were silent, dark bodies swimming to shore just south of Cold Bay.

Due to the cold water Major Chong's teeth were rattling in his mouth, and he knew that if he opened his mouth, they would wake up the whole world. The dry suit was doing its job, but was a little big for him and several pints of icy water had leaked in during his ascent, and didn't seem to want to warm up.

His feet finally touched the bottom of the stony beach. Two Seals were propelling him together with a large floating water-proof bag of several packs of C-4 and detonators. The major was sure that this cargo added to his teeth losing control and making this weird noise.

It took both men to lift his cold body out of the water. He had the pressed Chinese uniform of a major in a waterproof air-tight bag in one arm. The outfitters had run out of colonel insignia after his colleague Wong headed out.

"Chong, are you there?" he heard his friend calling to him silently from out of the darkness.

"Yes, Comrade Wong. I need to get this freezing, crappy suit off me. There is water inside and it is freezing parts of my body. I don't think I'll ever be able to use them again."

They helped the major out of his suit and wrapped him in his dry sleeping bag.

For the next couple of hours of darkness, the third Seal team arrived after Major Chong. Only forty men swam to shore, floating in the rest of the baggage the major had floated in on; namely high explosive packs, timers, and detonators. The arrival twenty-four hours earlier had been delayed to get Chong aboard the submarine.

Lieutenant Murphy was the last man to reach dry land as the submarines quietly reversed and then slipped down the channel one at a time and away to the other shipping now a hundred miles south of their island base. General Patterson had asked

Admiral Rogers for the ships to retreat further out to sea, in case they were spotted by the two Gulfstreams after takeoff.

The three lieutenants got about setting up their plan of attack. They had 95 men against an army of 3,000. Fair odds they thought. No other weapons or equipment had been landed anywhere in the area, and they were told that it was impossible, other than by helicopter. So they were on their own, apart from thousands of Marines and two other Seal Teams currently at Dillingham an hour's flying time away, but ready to jump into the fight. The fighter jets and attack helicopters were over 15 to 45 minutes flying time away, and with a bit of accuracy the naval ships could rip the airfield to shreds, once the civilians were out of there. The frigates had the exact coordinates of the airfield on maps, and they would know their own from old-fashioned sea navigation, accurate enough at ten miles, to put several dozen nice holes in each aircraft hangar every minute.

The Seal leaders were impressed that the single 72-MM guns on each of the frigates could fire up to a hundred rounds a minute into a building the size of an aircraft hangar with 90 percent accuracy, when necessary. Once the Gulfstreams were flown out they just needed four hours to get back into range.

Three hours later and a couple of hours after dawn, the Seals heard the roar of jet engines and, minutes later they all made sure everything was under camouflage as the first Gulfstream swept by at a few hundred feet above the ground, and about a hundred yards to their west. They watched it as it turned right to head north. It stayed low, didn't climb as a normal aircraft would on take-off, and it disappeared quickly leaving two steams of dark exhaust fumes in its wake just above the horizon.

The second jet did exactly the same fifteen minutes later and followed the path of the first one and within seconds was also out of sight.

"Birds have flown the coop," stated Charlie Meyers into his

satellite phone and Alaska and the entire United States commenced preparations for battle.

Wong and Chong, dressed in their uniforms, carefully headed towards the closest enemy jeep. The men, checked for sleeping more times in the last twenty-four hours than in the recent six months, were alert this time.

"Halt, who goes there?" ordered a voice as they neared. "Show yourselves, or we shoot!" stated the voice in Chinese.

"Well done, soldiers," replied Colonel Wong standing up. He had tried to bend down as close to the jeep as possible, knowing the Chinese backpacks would give them away. "It seems my checking on you has paid off."

"Password," ordered the sergeant, brandishing his AK-47 at the two men.

"Mao," replied Wong. "Colonel Wong and Major Chong inspecting your admirable attention to duty, Sergeant Do!" The man and the rest of the five-man missile squad stood to attention and saluted. "Major Chong will be in charge of checks from tomorrow, and I think you should tell the men he is far stricter than me. He was part of the Chairman's personal guard unit until the Chairman left for America."

"Yes, Sir!" shouted the men in unison.

"May I ask one question, Sir?" the sergeant asked.

"Yes, replied the colonel.

"How did you get to the south of us? We had eyes and binoculars checking for you since we arrived at dawn this morning."

Major Chong felt a lump in his throat, and his face felt like it was going white, but his trusty colleague always seemed to have an answer for everything.

"Easy, we used the noise of the jets to walk through the open areas while you were all looking up at the flying aircraft. Were any of you not looking skywards when the jets went overhead?" Nobody replied, but nodded to each other. "Question answered, Sergeant. Keep up the good work."

The two men headed up the road towards the airport as if they owned the airfield.

"Pretty close one there, Chong. Our free time walking around here is getting suspect with a few of the men. As Charlie stated, he needs to know every internal fortification inside the airfield by tonight, so we are going to find you a clipboard, find my friend the lieutenant driving the jeep, and he will take you around, and you can make a map on the paper as he drives you to every post," stated Wong as they headed up the road. Colonel Wong often pointed his swagger stick in unimportant directions, In case anybody was watching them. Over several dozen soldiers were.

The password was given and they entered the gate. The colonel asked for a jeep, and this time a sergeant arrived driving the same jeep as yesterday.

"Where is the lieutenant?" asked Wong carefully handing his backpack to the major to place in the rear of the jeep.

"He took off this morning in one of the jets, his usual guard detail, Sir," the sergeant responded.

"Oh well, I hope he enjoys his trip. How many men does he command in the aircraft?" asked Wong.

"A full detail of twelve men in each aircraft, sir. Your friend, the lieutenant, is in the first one and my Lieutenant Fung and his men are in the second."

"Sergeant, this is Major Chong, my second-in-command for ground inspections today. I want a full report from the major by midday, so no tea breaks, understand?"

"But, Colonel, the checks are already in progress with Captain Chung Wo. He does it every day," the sergeant responded, puzzled.

"I know, but sometimes even officers need to be checked. We are checking more for cleanliness, cigarette butts and dirt, not the guard details, understand?" The man nodded.

First the sergeant was directed to Corporal Bo's office where a clipboard and paper were found, Colonel Wong's name tag retrieved and then Wong asked the driver where the main runway maintenance was located. The sergeant didn't know but he asked somebody sweeping a pathway outside Hangar Two and he pointed to the rear of the building next to the American prisoners' building on the other side of the runway.

The two guards were in place as usual and since he had arrived after inspection this day, the prisoners were doing odd jobs around the area, guarded by several smoking guards.

He found what he was looking for in the maintenance area; a sprayer used for spraying bugs. He used to have one at home and it had a line from the sprayer-handle to a backpack tank. It was an American model, he noticed as he had seen the sprayer before. He carried it out and asked the driver to head over to Hangar Three.

Here he issued orders for two guards to take the heavy packs out of the back of the jeep; he lifted the spray unit onto his back and ordered the men carrying the packs to follow him to the hangar steps. The lieutenant in charge of the large guard detail checked his badge and he reached the steps as the jeep headed out of view.

"Just leave them here," he ordered the two men as they reached the bottom of the long staircase. "They are full of cans of toxic spay for the smell in there. Tell your lieutenant that the general might be coming to inspect later today, so be prepared for a visit." The two men saluted and left the colonel and his twenty explosive devices as they returned up the stairs.

It took Colonel Wong two hours to find the best locations for the fist-sized blocks of C-4, including a timer and detonator Major Chong might have helped swim in with. The timers were set for a predetermined time, which gave them and the travelers in the jets, time to arrive and finalize plans. They didn't have the luxury of radio or phone detonators, and the timing had been carefully planned with all interested parties here, at Dulles and at Andrews to proceed with their agendas.

Charlie Meyers was hoping to carry in a few more packs later that night, but this mission was setup in case he and his men weren't able to get in.

There were no real openings, apart from underneath, in and around the rocket motors. Wong managed to squeeze a pack high up, inside, in-between and a foot away from the three rocket motor exhausts pointing downwards. He hoped that it would be cool enough to allow the rocket to get out of its hole before it exploded, but it didn't really matter; he hoped he wouldn't be anywhere near here when the explosives detonated. The magnetic attaching device would not let go once bonded to a metal and Wong had to be careful and analyze the location before clamping the charge to the rocket.

He placed a second charge right on the tip of the 55-foot high rocket. He found a high 12-foot section ladder, placed it up against the 25,000 pound missile, climbed up the remaining 30 feet and did his best to shape the charge to blend in with each of the rocket tips as best he could. He was quite surprised how sharp the tip was, and slowly molded the C-4 to cap the point. Only the timer stood out, but it was nearly invisible once he got down again. For the next hour he placed the remaining charges in and around the dozens of vehicles inside the hangar. He also found the mechanism which opened the hangar roof and placed his third and last one around it.

"Who are you and what are you doing here?" asked a stern voice from behind him.

"Colonel Wong on General Lee's orders looking for any animals making that foul smell in the underground area," replied Wong, slowly standing up, turning, and looking into the eyes of a well-muscled Chinese soldier, also a colonel. Holding the nearly empty pack in his left hand tightly he felt in his right pocket for the Glock and silencer Charlie Meyers had given him, and looked the man of equal rank straight in his eyes.

"How many of you stupid soldiers realize that the smell is not from an animal, but from rocket fuel. Are all you army soldiers so stupid?" the man responded looking at Wong as if he was a really dumb soldier.

"I'm sorry, Colonel Wo," Wong replied checking the man's name tag on his uniform "but I'm only in charge of cleanliness here on base, and yesterday the general asked me to check out this foul animal smell before he comes down here later today.

"How many times do I have to tell General Lee it is not from an animal? He is so typical for an army officer. He knows nothing about technology, only how to shoot people. Now, Colonel Wong, I will escort you out of here, and you are not to return to Hangar Three again, understand?" Wong nodded. "I will make explicit instructions at the security office that only General Lee, me and my men, and the engineers only, are allowed down here. People like you are not, and never were. Cleanliness! What a stupid department for a colonel. Now follow me."

Wong retrieved his second, now empty pack and the sprayer in the underground section and the larger man was about to lock him out and close the door behind him when he realized the colonel might find the explosives.

"Colonel Wo, I have just sprayed toxic animal poison in there. If you go back in there for longer than a few minutes, it could eat your lungs away. I was only following orders and was about to hurry out when you found me. I suggest nobody goes in there for at least twelve hours, or they might never come out again."

"Stupid idea you spraying poison in there! Don't you know how volatile rocket fuel is? And I'm certainly not getting my lungs damaged. I'll lock it and tell the guards not to allow anybody in until the engineers go in after dark," replied Colonel Wo, smartly stepping out of the door to save his lungs.

"I would also recommend giving the engineers the night off as well, or they should enter with gas masks. It states on the cans twelve hours, but maybe the manufactures are wrong. I would give it at least another six hours to make sure."

"That's fine, nobody needs to be in there until the aircraft return and everything is fully automated anyway. Colonel Wong, if I ever see you close to this hangar, my private domain, ever again, I will personally string you up and shoot you. Understand? Now go and tell Bo to destroy your name tag. You won't need it anymore."

After Bo cut up the tag, he headed over to Hangar One. His legs were still slightly weak from the surprise meeting with the Commander of Hangar Three and it took a while for his pulse to return to less damaging levels.

He looked around and saw two jeeps on the large airfield, both at opposite ends and it looked like Chong was doing his job.

His only concern now was the prisoners and he watched as Colonel Wo headed into Hangar Two before he headed into Hangar One. Wong needed the larger man to forget about him a little. He headed upstairs to the living accommodations and saw the lounge was empty. Most of the doors were closed to the bedrooms and he checked for the radio, which was supposed to be in the Hangar somewhere. It hadn't been downstairs, and he knocked on the closest door to the communal area, nobody shouted anything and he walked into an office with a radio sitting on the center desk. The room was empty.

Colonel Wong placed his second to last charge under the steel desk the radio was on and closed the door behind him.

Hangar Two was also pretty much empty. He realized that Colonel Wo must live in this hangar as he was pouring himself a cup of tea when Wong climbed the staircase and looked around the communal area.

"Following me around, Wong? Tell me, how come I have never seen you on base before?"

"I usually work while most of the men are asleep. Many areas of the airfield are cleaned at night by my staff when you soldiers are asleep. Because of my orders to spray Hangar Three this morning, I am late on my checks on my staff, which cleaned in here last night, Wo. Some stupid soldiers work while the real soldiers sleep," Wong replied not letting the bigger man dominate him.

"Well, tell your cleaning detail that my room, Room Three, needs the paper shredder emptied. It hasn't been for weeks," stated Wo, heading with his cup of tea to his room.

This time Wong, pretty angry, marched into the hangar's radio room and saw a man, a sergeant, behind the desk. "Sergeant, I'm not in a good mood and need to check this room. Go! Make yourself a cup of tea!"

The sergeant saw the look on Wong's face and headed out fast. He must have heard the confrontation between the two senior officers outside his closed door.

Within seconds the device was under the steel desk holding the radio and suddenly Wong realized that he was one charge short. He needed one for the control tower and wanted to hit himself on the forehead. He released his self-directed anger by reminding himself that his favorite colonel would go up in smoke if he was in his room, once the radio went into lift-off mode! He smiled, still felt pissed-off, and left Hangar Two.

He wanted to find the American girls, but they were nowhere to be seen, so he returned to Hangar One to "inspect" the cleanliness inside the aircraft he was hoping to fly out later that day.

Again the hangar was deserted and for an hour he sat in the left seat in the cockpit and went through the pre-flight checks of the aircraft. They were written in Russian on one side and Chinese on the other and were little different than checks he would have done flying a slightly smaller C-130.

A couple of hours later, he and Major Chong asked the driver to take them to the gate where he explained to the new guard commander that he and the major needed a walk and asked when the password changed from 'Mao' to 'Zedong'. The lieutenant stated at 2:00 a.m., after the midnight changeover of fresh guards.

The two men, now pretty well known, left the airfield.

"Wow!" exclaimed the three lieutenants when the two officers sneaked back into the dirt runway buildings south of the camp.

"You guys can join our Seal Team anytime you want," added Charlie Myers. "We couldn't have done any better than you. Both of you, not only have you fulfilled your mission planting explosives on the actual missiles, you got all the inner-defense positions. You have primed most of the place to go kaboom in eleven hours. Hey, Joe, we might as well go home, have a round of golf, and let these two air force dudes do our work for us." Lieutenant Paul, studying the map drawn by Major Chong smiled back.

Wong got on the satellite phone to General Patterson at Dillingham and brought him up-to-date on the improvements to the airfield and the general was grateful. He replied that the two Gulfstreams were expected in nine hours; he was transferring men and machinery into Dulles, the airport where the visitors wanted the meeting with the president for safety purposes; and, the meeting was due to start in ten hours.

For the last two hours of daylight, the three leaders of the 90 Seals and the two air force pilots planned the upcoming night raid on Cold Bay Airport.

Eight hours later, the first missile jeep was quietly taken out by the Seals, all now dressed in U.S. camouflage. The four semi-sleeping guards, double the number Wong had met on his first visit to the jeep, never stood a chance. Charlie Meyers told Wong and the others that he believed the higher guard activity was due to the Gulfstreams' departures. There could be a heightened awareness around Cold Bay Airport, China!

Within the hour, all seven jeeps were under the ownership of the Seals. Each jeep had two Seals disarming the missile system to make sure no missiles, manually or remote controlled would ever leave the jeeps again. The Chinese men, their throats cut lay underneath the jeeps, out of the way.

Wong and Chong led three Chinese-uniformed Seals to the southern gate, Sergeant Rodriquez and two other Seals who could actually fit into the small Chinese uniforms. The last two men looked disheveled, as if they had been asleep, their caps pulled down low over their faces.

"Guards, open up!" stated Colonel Wong as they approached the gate. It was just before 2:00 am, and it was the same time that the two Gulfstreams were about to head into Dulles in Washington.

"Password!" was the reply.

"Mao, or Zedong if it changed," replied Colonel Wong.

"Who are you and who are these other men?" ordered a guard who he had never seen before.

"Colonel Wong, my second-in-command Major Chong and two guards we found sleeping on duty. Open up, I need to report them and get them replaced immediately."

"We never saw you leave, Colonel. How did you leave the airfield?" stated a third soldier, a lieutenant, standing on a lit cigarette and walking up to the gate from the guard house several feet away after hearing the commands at the gate. The security had certainly been stepped up a notch since his last entry, and that worried Wong, but it was too late to retreat now.

"We headed out to check on the jeeps a couple of hours ago and left by the other gate, Lieutenant. Now open the gate I have my job to do. Who are you expecting, the American president... or the American Marines to sneak up on you? There is nobody else on this sad piece of property. Do I look like an American soldier, Sergeant?" stated Wong to the man waiting for orders from the lieutenant. "Sergeant, I will go with your lieutenant personally to the guardhouse, and he can phone the main gate to verify that Major Chong and I left. He needs to speak to Sergeant Cho, the man who opened the other gate for us. Now open the gate!"

The sergeant, not getting an order from his lieutenant who had already turned and was walking to the guardhouse, unlocked the gate and allowed the four men into the compound.

There were two lights above the gate, the second north gate was about 200 yards away, and their shapes could be seen by anybody interested. The guardhouse was purposely not in the well-lit area, Wong thought, for security purposes. As they entered, the two disheveled Seals walked up to the two gate guards, put an arm around them and shot them in the side, next to their hearts, three times with their silenced Glocks. Rodriquez was fast and hit the lieutenant, who had stopped in the darker area twenty feet away to turn around to see what the scuffles were about, with three out of three shots. They all watched as his body crumpled to the ground without a sound.

Immediately Charlie Meyers began opening a hole through the outside perimeter fence adjacent to the guardhouse with heavy box cutters. Both Seals passed the bodies of the still upright dead guards to Wong and Chong, and they headed out of the light and towards the guardhouse carrying the slumped-over men as best they could without getting blood on their uniforms They hoped that it looked to the other guards watching from 200 yards away like they were helping a colleague. It was too great a distance to actually see what was going on, and they were sure to get a detachment of men to come and inspect.

As soon as Sergeant Rodriquez reached the dead lieutenant, he silently rushed the guardhouse. He immediately saw the bright tell-tale tips of two cigarette butts by the back wall, where two, very quickly dead men were having a smoke break. The door to the guard house was closed, so he slid a fresh magazine into his Glock and, removing his night goggles, opened the door. Light streamed out of the brightly-lit room and the four men playing cards around a table each got a third eye as they looked up at him, and another four trying to sleep never knew what hit them as he sprayed the rest of his magazine into the heads of their sleeping bodies.

Within seconds, Wong entered.

"I hear men coming over from the other gate," said Charlie Meyers as he came in and looked around. A last man came out of the bathroom at the rear of the guardhouse and his forehead suddenly looked like he had a bad case of acne. The man slumped to the floor as Charlie Meyers hit him three times and then hit the cabin's light switch turning the whole place =dark.

"Get any bodies behind the building," Charlie Meyers ordered more men who were silently waiting by the open door. Wong knew all of the Seals had night goggles on, and while it took seconds for his eyes to get accustomed to the darkness, he heard bodies slithering about around him. "Here, put these on," said Charlie. His cap was removed and a pair of night goggles was fitted over his blind eyes. Suddenly he could see again. Although the view was all a dark green color, it was bright to the darkness he had just been in.

"Guard detail, six men fifty yards away and ten seconds until reaching the light by the gate," stated somebody.

"Rodriquez, Shaw, Mendez, take them out. Go!" ordered Meyers. "Marks, Santana, Perks, help drag the bodies back here!"

Men silently headed out and within minutes bodies could be heard being dragged into the growing pile.

Charlie Meyers asked Sergeant Rodriquez, still dressed in his Chinese uniform, to give a message to the men standing on guard at the gate and he headed over. "Message from Charlie, keep your Chinese uniforms and caps on, stay at your guard positions at the gate. When the next group arrives to see what is going on, mumble something. I assume they have less than a dozen guards left at the northern gate. Perks, Marks and Sammy Smith will protect you from the dark side; you know what to do and guys try and get some uniforms without blood all over them."

"Majors, we are heading to Hangar One. Men, bring all three packs of Christmas presents. Joe Paul, Pete Murphy, get your plans into operation and start taking out the machine gun and mortar posts. The Marines will be overhead in 59 minutes, explosions go up in 49 minutes. Let's go!"

The groups led by the three Seal lieutenants completed their mission of getting through the three new fence holes and headed in different directions.

Hangar One was minimally lit and quiet once the two guards at the small rear door had been taken out, Wong entered first, alone. He motioned to the rest that it was clear and six Seals silently sneaked in, going around the darker shadows of the outer walls and they dispersed into the large open space. Major Chong's job was to start the pre-checks on the aircraft while the small packs of C-4 were distributed around the vehicles inside, especially the three tanks and the more mobile jeeps with machine guns on them.

Colonel Wong, with four other Seals and one of the back-packs, headed over to Hangar Two. Again two guards felt the sting of a silenced Glock and were dragged into the hangar once Wong gave them the all clear. It was also minimally lit. The two missing aircraft made the lifeless hangar look larger, and the Seals began handing out gifts to the dozens of armored vehicles in this hangar. Two small, mobile fuel tankers were the most important vehicles in Hangar Two and received gifts while Wong crept up the stairs.

The lounge had three bloody Caucasian girls, half-naked and semi-asleep on the couches and a Chinese major and a lieutenant colonel, also half-dressed and snoring, on the other two couches. One girl spied him as he entered, and he put his finger to his mouth for silence.

He could see that the girls had been beaten, there was blood on all three of their gagged faces, and he crept down the staircase to tell two of the men standing guard.

Both men silently ran up the stairs and the girl's eyes widened as she saw American camouflage. She tried to make a noise, but luckily her gag kept her mouth silent. Six silent shots into the two snoring Chinese officers and a quick thud to the head from the butt of a Glock silenced the girl, and with a set of hand wire cutters the Seals quickly separated the other two girls, put two of them in fireman's lifts and headed down the stairs for Hangar One.

Wong looked around, placed a second charge under the desk in the radio room after checking to see that his first charge was still in place. Then he crept down the corridor to the end to open the last door to the largest room. It was locked and he waited for the two Seals to return.

This time Charlie Meyers arrived with three men, saw Wong at the end, and silently moved over to him. Wong motioned that the door was locked, and Charlie pulled what looked like a girl's hairpin from his upper jacket pocket and within seconds had the door open.

"Who are you?" questioned a scared female American voice in the dark room. Charlie pulled his night goggles down again and headed into the dark interior. There were two thuds, then what sounded to Wong like wire cutters in action, and he was handed a light female form in a fireman's lift on his shoulder."

"Tell two men to get in here. Wong, you take her back to Hangar One. One of the men will carry the unconscious American civilian male in here to the aircraft," whispered Charlie.

The others were guarding the entrance as he and the Seal headed down the corridor, down the stairs and over to Hangar

One. He passed several guarding the outside area and headed into the first hangar and gave both unconscious forms to men waiting in the door of the aircraft.

Colonel Wong rearranged his uniform as Sergeant Rodriquez and his two guys, still wearing their Chinese uniforms, entered the rear door carrying half a dozen fresh uniforms.

"No more guards, all deceased," Rodriquez stated smiling at him. We are heading over to the control tower, Sir. Remember to pick us up. I don't think Charlie needs these uniforms anymore and they stink. I don't want to have to fight the rest of these guys on the southern side on my own, Sir, so remember you are our ticket out of here."

Major Wong nodded. "Sergeant, your ride home will be taxiing past the tower in twenty-one minutes. That gives us fifteen minutes before fireworks, so I will not be hanging around. The rear ramp will be open and just treat us like you would a bus. Hop on."

With that he and two Seals headed up the stairs to the general's room. The door was closed but unlocked. This time he remembered to close his eyes, slide his goggles down from his forehead, and went in.

There were two sleeping forms on the large king-sized bed. The general and a fifth female form, again one hand was handcuffed to the bed. The Seals with him, in a blink of an eye hit both heads of the sleeping pair, cut the girl's handcuffs, lifted both bodies onto their shoulders and headed out of the room. Wong spied a desk with an open laptop computer and took it.

* * *

As Wong was entering the general's room, the last of thirty C-130s full of Marine parachutists was leaving the ground at Dillingham for the 55-minute flight to Cold Bay. The three F-4s and two F-5s were warming up and the dozen Z-10 attack helicopters were already a third of the way.

General Patterson was still issuing orders in *Easy Girl* on his satellite phone as she was next to take off. He wasn't flying this time as *Pave Pronto* took off in front of his aircraft.

* * *

Washington was a busy place; the two aircraft had just landed at Dulles, and General Austin was making sure everybody understood their orders.

General Austin was in charge of the military operations at Dulles. All military were low-profile with the odd guard standing around to make it appear to the two incoming aircraft that there was military presence, but not more than usual. Westbrook had warned them.

The two aircraft taxied into a large empty Delta maintenance hangar and the doors closed. Next to the hangar was a small jet terminal where the meeting was to take place. The president's helicopter could be heard heading in from the White House. Several senators and congressmen had already arrived in a couple of other helicopters from Capitol Hill, and there was no other air traffic.

Within minutes, the two CEOs, with six heavily armed American men in civilian suits, headed out of the side door and into the small jet terminal. As soon as they did so, two large air-conditioner vents supplied cold sleeping gas into the hangar. It would take at least an hour to fill the large area with enough gas to put everybody to sleep, and the noise was totally normal to those inside the hangar.

General Austin viewed the goings-on inside to make sure the aircraft's passenger doors were open and that the eighteen Chinese-looking guards, four pilots, and two American-looking male cabin attendants were not wearing gas masks.

The president arrived and with his usual secret service detail headed towards the jetport. He would be in the last group to enter.

"Good morning all," he stated not smiling at anybody, and headed towards the coffee machine and nice array of doughnuts and Danish on a table set up on one of the side walls of the large meeting room. The conference table was long enough to seat the dozen people expected and the president was shown to a chair at the middle of the table.

"Since we are all here," stated Peter Westbrook, taking the seat opposite the president, "we can get most of your goons out of here. We want complete privacy."

"Unfortunately, sir, two of our guard detail must stay on each side of the president at all times. That is normal protocol, sir," stated the president's head Secret Service agent in his usual dark suit and a man sat down on each side of the president.

"We will do the same, and we can then get started," replied Westbrook. "And you can turn off that camera up there," he added pointing to the blue dome on the ceiling on the corner of the room.

"The meeting is being recorded, and I cannot authorize that, Mr. Westbrook, sir," replied the head guard.

"Don't you have any say in the running of this country, Mr. President? Are you really the puppet we have so often heard about?" added Bowers.

"Taking the office of President of the United States of America, gentlemen, warrants this form of protection. I don't like it, but Congress and the Senate enacted all these laws decades ago, after the Reagan assassination attempt, and I have little say in the matter. Shall we get on? I see we have the Alaskan member, Washington State member and an Illinois member of House of Representatives and both Senators from Alaska, all of whom voted for you at the last meeting, correct, Mr. Westbrook?"

"Yes, a little one-sided, but since this is our last meeting, Mr. President, we have all our men right here."

Everyone at the table was finally seated twenty minutes later as they all stood up to help themselves to coffee and snacks. It had been a long flight and fresh coffee and cake were certainly a delicacy in this day and age. Everybody, apart from the president, who had already helped himself, and the four bodyguards from both sides, got up to fill plates and coffee cups.

The president was on the closest side to the closed door. Two mean-looking Secret Service men sat on either side of him. Opposite them were two tough American guards on each side of Westbrook, then Bowers, and finally the last five seats were filled with the congressmen and senators.

"Congressman Williams, I have considered you as a friend for over three decades, ever since we were in law school together. Why have you sided with these men?" the president asked the only African-American Congressman in the room.

"Sorry, Mr. President. A year or two ago these guys offered me the world and the whole of Illinois if I relayed Congressional information to them. A deal I couldn't say no to."

"So, Charles, you sold out the American government, its people and me to these guys for money?"

"Everybody in Congress was selling something to someone for money. I just got the best prize, a hundred million-dollar prize. It's just politics, Mr. President, and you should know that."

"A friend with the same law degree selling information for cash. Sometimes I think this catastrophic attack on our country was the best thing, to get rid of vermin like you, earning millions and selling out the American people," replied the president.

Suddenly both Secret Service agents felt a sting of a needle from the men sitting next to them and slowly slumped forward in their seats. The other two men stood up and headed towards the door, bearing large .44 Magnums in both hands.

"Your work, I assume, Charles?" asked the president, realizing that there were not meant to be any weapons in the room. Everybody except the president had been searched before entering the room.

"We learned a lot from the Colombian attack in their chambers, Mr. President, when we were briefed about it during the last meeting. I sent the information on, and I suppose these guys just copied it. And now may I add, as opposition to your party, Mr. President, how I have found your administration to be stupid, with a total lack of intelligence, and you should be the one tried for treason. You have done an abysmal job since you took office. There, I've said it!" stated the congressman proudly. "You just don't know how many years I've wanted to say that straight to your face, you stupid jerk!" Congressman Williams took a large bite of his doughnut and smiled at his ex-friend.

The president said nothing, but waited for the drug in the food to take effect.

"Crap! We've been poisoned!" stated Westbrook, feeling a little groggy, and he stood up, held the table with one hand, pulled something very small out of his suit pocket and drove a needle into the president's closest shoulder as he toppled forward.

Suddenly there was pandemonium outside as automatic weapons made hearing impossible. The president felt something enter his blood stream, and he felt a wave of laziness envelop him as he tried to get up and stop Bowers speaking to someone on his satellite phone.

Suddenly the world went blurry, he felt like he wanted to puke, and his head hit the desk hard.

Several Secret Service men flew through the breaking door seconds later. The first men inside got two before they themselves were hit and General Austin, with several medics behind him, headed straight for the president, got him on a stretcher and ran out with the inert body.

Bowers toppled over from the drugs in the Danish he had just eaten, and the phone flew from his hand.

Seconds before General Austin entered the conference room, he had ordered the attack on the hangar, exactly seven minutes before the charges were due to explode in Cold Bay, a third of a world away.

The men, wearing gas masks, entered through all the hangar doors, the people inside drowsy from the gas, and the soldiers with Glocks began shooting anything moving inside the hangar. One pilot jumped into one of the Gulfstreams and managed to push both red buttons inside the aircraft before several shots ended his life. It was all over in minutes, but unfortunately the red buttons did their job and a signal to several parts of the machinery inside Hangar Three started machines working.

* * *

Lieutenants Paul and Murphy were halfway through taking out the inner defense posts when the darkness disappeared and the whole roof of the third hangar began to open and began to light up the area with an eerie false light. Immediately they went to ground and took off their goggles.

They couldn't carry on. There was at least 200 feet between the defense posts and there was no way they could get across the open areas without causing suspicion. Joe Paul checked the map Chong had given him and saw that he was six machine-gun posts short on the eastern side. He assumed that Lieutenant Murphy was in the same predicament on the western area of the large airfield. It looked like the missiles were about to depart and seconds later both missiles slowly lifted out of the hangar areas and within seconds were high and disappearing. Paul looked at his watch. The explosions were still ten minutes away and it seemed that the charge Wong had placed on the roof mechanism wasn't programmed to explode early either. *"Damn!"* he thought to himself.

At the same time, General Lee, now awake, was being held hostage in the cockpit of the aircraft as the doors were opened and Chong started the first engine as the Hangar Three's roof doors opened. It took three minutes to start all four turbo-prop engines, and Major Wong already had the first two engines screaming to taxi the large aircraft out of the hangar by the time Chong had the fourth engine blowing smoke out of its exhausts.

Major Wong had the aircraft halfway across the tarmac and heading towards the control tower as the two missiles lifted off. He let the ramp begin to open. They still hadn't seen any men, and they had only seconds to get across to the tower and the prisoners' building before the place would be swarming with enemy troops.

"Seals, our job is done, there's not much more we can do. This place is going to go up like a July 4th fireworks display and anybody caught in here will be toast. We have six minutes to get as far away as possible. Head back to the holes in the fence and tell the men outside. Leave now!" ordered Charlie Meyers to the men in the hangar, its doors automatically closing, the aircraft a black silhouette fifty yards away.

A couple of officers hearing the noise of the missiles leaving ran down the stairs and made a pile at the bottom as Charlie's silenced Glock gave them a third eye. He replaced his magazine and was the last out of the hangar as all the lights around the airfield began to blink on.

Joe Paul and Lieutenant Murphy hoped this wouldn't happen and headed as far out of the light towards either end of the runway as possible. Lucky for them it took several blinks for the large lights to finally omit a powerful light, and they used this to get as far away as possible. They reached the furthest machine gun post towards the eastern end of the runway, blew away the several Chinese soldiers trying to figure out what was happening.

They hadn't expected enemy soldiers to be in the airport and looked at the approaching men puzzled.

"Take over the machine gun post, then shoot at anything that fires towards the aircraft. I'm sure they have tracer loaded, so just put rounds into the general area. Where is that aircraft?" Joe Paul stated, jumping into a foxhole and turning around to look down the runway as the runway lights slowly came on, and headed towards them at a fast pace. "Heads down, men!" he shouted as the area around him lit up.

Lieutenant Murphy, with less ground to run to the fence had men cutting holes, and they were already getting through and heading towards the old dirt runway as the lights came on. He didn't want to be close to the buildings when they went up.

Charlie Meyers and two men manning a machine gun post were the only Seals left in the area as he watched the blacked-out aircraft head in the vicinity of the prison building. As the lights came on he now could see that his three Seals were running next to it. The two men he had sent forward to get the prisoners ready had the men, women, and children outside the building, all lying down on the ground. He watched as the aircraft stopped, and the whole group jumped up and headed the twenty yards towards the rear of the aircraft.

He looked at his watch. They had forty-five seconds to go, as he noticed several Chinese soldiers leave a building further down the row to see what all the commotion was about. His gunner saw them as well and his heavy machine gun began its deathly rattle, spewing bullets towards the gathering men, half-dressed and still figuring out what to do.

He heard the four large engines scream, the rear ramp began to close and the aircraft lurched forward towards the runway, several yards ahead of it.

"Spray the area where you see enemy, Mendez! Use up what you have. We have thirty seconds to get out of here!"

Seconds later, the machine gun hot, its first metal case

empty, the three men ran for any available shadows and towards the guardhouse near where they had entered. It was going to be close, but at least they might survive, as the two Shaheen II missiles were already miles away, and it all depended on Wong's placement of the charges, whether they could take out vast parts of the American countryside.

Major Wong was concentrating hard in the left seat, while Chong was trying hard to keep with the takeoff checks. There were over 100 checks to do before takeoff, and they had cleared most of them when Wong was patted on the shoulder. He engaged the ramp closing switch and pushed all four engine controls forward.

"We have flaps and fuel flow?" he asked Chong as a burst of bullets hit the windows where Chong was sitting and his friend slumped forward. The side doors to the aircraft were still open and a Seal had General Lee's standing body filling the door. It didn't seem to worry the Chinese guards, or they didn't understand that the man looking at them was in fact their superior, they fired anyway and several rounds hit the general. The Seal let the body fall, lay down on the floor of the aircraft and began shooting back. The other two Seals blew a couple of windows out and also began firing into the area around the aircraft. They noticed tracer fire going in both directions as the speed of the screaming aircraft increased and the area began to darken as they left the main airport lights.

Suddenly the starboard outer engine exploded, and fire began to stream out of the rear of the wing. Automatic fire extinguishers erupted to quell the fire and Major Wong fed more power to the remaining three engines. He could hear screams behind him as a second engine began to flame to his left, this time his inner-port engine, and he pushed the two remaining controls forward realizing that they were already as far as they would go.

He didn't have time to check his watch as he pulled back on

the stick, the aircraft was heavily loaded with well over a hundred people on board and his speed was still 10 knots below takeoff speed. He had a hundred yards of runway to go as he felt bullets hitting the aircraft somewhere.

Then he was airborne, but barely, the outer fence was coming up fast to meet him as he pulled his bloodied hands back hard. He felt the undercarriage hit the fence and then he was away in the darkness.

Alarms were going off everywhere in the cockpit as he grappled with the stricken airplane. There was no way he was going to get far and he immediately turned to port. The whole area behind him lit up as hundreds of explosions erupted at once, literally blowing up tons of weapons and ammo, thousands of gallons of fuel and he felt a massive shock wave hit the aircraft seconds later. He was still turning but a split second before the expected explosions he was looking towards the direction the two Shaheen missiles were expected to go and thought he saw a minute explosion in the blackness, but his eyes had to leave the area and concentrate on getting all these screaming people down.

Thinking of what Mike Mallory had done in New York, he decided that the dirt runway was his only bet. The aircraft was at 500 feet, fire was spreading and there wasn't enough power to climb any higher.

Meanwhile Charlie Meyers had just exited the fence and was sprinting away when the world went bright a couple of hundred yards behind him. He turned and hit the ground hard as pieces of metal came at them, one large piece of hangar metal sliced right through Sergeant Mendez next to him as he fell to the ground. Charlie's eardrums blew out, and he covered his head with his hands and screamed as deadly pieces of metal flew less than a foot above his body.

The massive explosions subsided at this distance as fast as they had erupted and Charlie felt hands grab him and pull him away. He thought he heard aircraft engines and then a fire in the sky as he blacked out.

Major Wong, still semi-calm, was extremely grateful that this aircraft had been built so well. There were flames on both wings, He could see them by the light coming into the cockpit from above and behind and was being told by several screaming passengers as he nursed the aircraft towards the south. He was losing altitude. The engines were about to overheat and he looked for the old runway. The light from the continuous blasts now behind him displayed the darker dirt line of the runway and he judged that he needed at least 400 yards to turn 180 degrees and put her down facing the fires. He had about 300 feet of altitude left and it was going to be close.

Lieutenant Paul was running towards the end of the runway, as soon as the massive explosions died down several hundred yards behind him, where the aircraft's wheels had ripped open part of the outer fence. They just made the fence when the first parachutes opened up a few hundred yards in front of him and several new-sounding explosions began to pound the buildings behind him and his men. He thought them to be the 72-MM projectiles coming in from the three frigates ten miles away. He was supposed to be the eyes for the frigates and he found a slight rise, dropped behind it and with his satellite phone dialed up Admiral Rodriquez in charge of the ships' guns. They were firing a hundred yards short and south of the main buildings, in the town itself and within several seconds, he had them taking out the buildings where thousands of enemy were running around in all directions.

The aircraft was in its death throes as Wong brought her down fifty feet from the beginning of the runway. It didn't really matter where he brought her down. The ground was flat and he felt the broken undercarriage hit first. He had already managed to turn and fly level, but the joystick was dead in his hands as he worked on getting her down. He had engaged the ramp opening switch as he had turned in and a green light had come on, showing that it still worked.

With the undercarriage loose, the aircraft kissed the ground several yards in front of the runway, and proceeded to open a long furrow all the way down. Wong had closed down the fuel lines and engines seconds earlier and the aircraft took the whole of the 900-foot runway before coming to a grinding halt, taking out the building in which he had caught three hours of sleep a couple of hours earlier.

The force of the aircraft hitting the pile of rubble ended its forward motion and, unprepared, he hit his head on the side wall of the cockpit. He didn't remember anything else.

CHAPTER 13

The Final Cleanup

THE CHINESE SOLDIERS, many already dead or wounded from the powerful initial explosions, fought bravely. The 72-MM projectiles coming in at 300 rounds a minute for three minutes put an end to any organized defense of the airfield.

As soon as the barrage ceased, the F-4s came in with 500-pounders and leveled any remaining buildings. The Chinese soldiers had no choice but to retreat to the town buildings of Cold Bay, where the Z-10 helicopters, their own Chinese-made helicopters, began pounding the town with hundreds of missiles.

The Marines, landing several hundred yards out from the eastern end and northern side of the main runway, advanced and easily took what they could on the airfield. Many areas, especially around where the three hangars had once stood were burning so hot that nobody could get close.

Instead they worked around the areas even though several small explosions were heard from the raging fires, spewing hot metal everywhere. They concentrated on pushing west and south and came upon several entrenched troops which were swiftly dealt with by air support.

There wasn't one building standing at the airport by the time the Marines reached what was left of the southern perimeter fence. The remains of the 3,000 enemy were being bombarded by the helicopters and jets as they went in on alternate runs to demolish the town of Cold Bay.

Thirty minutes after the first massive explosions, white flags began to appear out of broken buildings and the Marines began a building-to-building search, bringing out unarmed Chinese troops, their hands high.

General Patterson, controlling the battle from the air in *Easy Girl,* gave the order to take prisoners. He had seen the fiery crash of the Chinese transport aircraft as it went down earlier, but up to now he had not had the time to inspect the scene. Now dawn was breaking and he commanded his pilot to fly over the old runway. He had turned on his satellite phone, turned off for the battle and it immediately rang.

"Patterson," he stated into the phone. He listened for several seconds as General Austin spoke to him and he responded with only two words, "Oh Crap!" before he hung up and looked down at the crash scene. The first of the three U.S. Navy Seahawk helicopters, flown in with medics from the Colombian frigates, was landing and there were civilians everywhere. It looked like Major Wong had done his job. The second and third Seahawks were heading in east of the runway and since both the old and new runways were destroyed, his gunship couldn't land; he could only watch from the air.

"Joe Paul to Easy Girl, *Paul to* Easy Girl, *do you read? Over."* General Patterson heard a familiar voice over the aircraft's radio.

"Patterson here, Joe Paul."

"We have two Seals dead, three injured. Can we get them lifted aboard one of the ships? Two of the injured are pretty bad. Over!"

"Affirmative, there is a Seahawk coming in to you from the east."

"Seahawk Two, copied that, going in."

"What is happening down on the other airfield, Paul?" the general asked.

"Sorry, but my men have headed the other way to help the Seals on the eastern side. I can't help you there."

"Roger that. Out! Seahawk One at aircraft crash site, can you give me a report? Over."

"Roger, we have one dead U.S. Air Force pilot, one injured pilot, one badly injured Seal, two dead male civilians, three wounded civilians and we are lifting off and ferrying the airman and injured to the vessels. ETA ten minutes and I've radioed ahead."

The Seahawk below him lifted off and headed out to sea.

The sun was now blinding as *Easy Girl*, at a thousand feet, headed back towards the western edge of the runway. The runway was badly pitted from the 72-MM projectiles and there were only 500 or 600 hundred yards at the end which had evaded bombardment. Not enough to get the gunship down.

For the next twenty minutes, reports came in continuously. The fighter jets were long gone and so were the Z-10 helicopters, apart from three which he had ordered to land on the undamaged western runway edge to conserve fuel and he was now alone in the sky.

Massive fires still raged where the hangars once stood. On the ground below him was a mass of bodies and live soldiers milling about and getting all the enemy soldiers into organized groups. There certainly weren't more than a few hundred, he could see from his vantage point.

"There is an open grass expanse of clear ground on the southern side of the runway, General," stated his pilot. "It is too short for us, but I believe a C-130 could get in and out if the outer fence was pulled down."

Orders were given and Marines ran to the fence and began man-handling it.

Ten minutes later General Patterson watched as the first

empty C-130 went in and stopped, feet to spare from the closest group of a dozen three-foot wide and deep holes made by the projectiles. The airfield certainly looked like it had a bad case of acne.

"Colonel Smith, Lieutenant Paul," stated the general over his radio as he circled the runway, "I have to leave the rest of the evacuation up to you. Get the civilians up to our new airfield; fly them into Elmendorf, then the prisoners, then yourselves. I will send in a bulldozer to bury the enemy dead. I don't want one person left here by the time the last C-130s leave. I have to go to Washington. We have won the war, but we have lost the president."

CHAPTER 14

New Government – New Laws

A WEEK AFTER GENERAL PATTERSON left Cold Bay, there were many heads bowed at a special sectioned-off part of Arlington cemetery. The funeral of the President of the United States of America was by invitation only.

Since the end of the last battle, nobody had been in command of the most powerful nation on earth.

The president and his two Secret Service agents had not been the only deaths in the meeting room. Watching live feed from cameras in the room, dozens of special agents had rushed the room when they saw the two Secret Service agents inside keel over in their seats.

Four of Westbrook's bodyguards standing guard outside the doors were immediately gunned down and three large Secret Service agents literally turned the double doors into splinters as they crashed through it. The two Westbrook guards inside shot two of the incoming men before a barrage of bullets took them out and General Austin rushed into the room with medics.

It was too late. A potent and deadly poison, Rican, had been used by Westbrook and his two guards on the three dead Americans. The drug the Air Force had used in the food was only a temporary knockout drug. Everybody who ate and drank the coffee and food was lying face down on the floor or slumped in their chairs; they came around in prison cells an hour or so later.

The president was first to help himself to the food and drink, taking specially marked doughnuts free of the drug, to demonstrate to the others that the food was safe. He did not drink any beverages as they were also laced with the knockout drug.

General Patterson arrived in Dulles aboard the 747 direct from Elmendorf twelve hours after the death of the president. En route he had ordered General Austin to lock down Dulles, Capitol Hill and the White House so tight that even the rats felt locked in.

The whole of Washington was like a battlefield when he arrived, thousands of soldiers making sure theirs was the only movement in the city.

When General Patterson landed in Dulles he was met by General Austin. Then, with six of the top military brass, they went to Andrews Air Force Base, where the president's body had been transported.

Totally at a loss, General Patterson asked General Austin, "What do we do now?"

"Well, you are Chief of Staff, Patterson. I can only assume that with no vice-president, no Speaker of the House, actually no vetted politicians to take over the Oval Office temporarily, you are the one in command... unless you want the First Lady to take over, and she is not in a position to do so at the moment. We broke the news to her several hours ago."

"Nobody ever thought that this country would ever be in such a position. Absolutely no leadership and only a couple of House Representatives we can't trust to take over," the general responded.

He had liked the president, getting to know him over the last several months. The poor man was just a normal guy. He even went solo in a Cessna, something that people in power would have been shocked at and never allowed; a total impossibility.

"Reminds me of that Clancy novel," replied General Austin, "when the Japanese Airlines 747 goes into Capitol Hill and only Jack Ryan is left to become president."

"Maybe we can learn from that," responded Patterson. "It is not possible, or logical, or probable, for a military officer to take over the leadership position. I'm totally against it. It has to be a civilian, and I think I know just the right man to be interim president until we can get this country going again. When are Admiral Martin Rogers and General Watson arriving?" General Patterson asked General Austin.

"Both are due in two hours. We have a 747 flying both men in. General Watson has just been picked up at Dyess and Admiral Rogers is on an aircraft from San Diego. Did we hear anything about the Shaheen missiles they launched from Cold Bay?" asked General Austin.

"Yes, we had satellite reports on the missiles," replied General Patterson. "Both missiles headed into the upper atmosphere as they were supposed to, and Carlos told me that it was impossible that the missiles were being directed by the satellites up there. He had set up a satellite communications blocker for any equipment that wasn't a satellite phone. It is how the system is going to be used until we need to unblock the communications, which we will do when the Russian rocket goes up from Harbin with the three satellites atop of it, shortly. We can only assume that the onboard computers could have been pre-programmed to follow radio signals, airport-system output or even signals from the Gulfstreams themselves to give them location coordinates. We are checking out the two aircraft here at Andrews as we speak. Both missiles were less than 10 miles apart and 120 miles high when they disappeared from our screens at the same time. We never heard any reports from anywhere after that. They could still have armed themselves and gone down, but I don't think that was at all possible with a pound of C-4 up both asses, as Major Wong reported to me. The experts believe both missiles were always programmed to arm their nuclear warheads once they had reentered earth's lower atmosphere but they didn't get that far. Major Wong said that he thought he saw a flash above him when he was trying to get his aircraft back onto the ground."

"How is our hero doing, anyway?" asked General Austin.

"Fine, he had two fingers amputated from his right hand and a couple of toes off his right foot, all done by a fine Colombian Navy doctor aboard one of their frigates. A second bullet messed his foot up pretty badly, but the doctor saved it, apart from the toes. There was a third bullet that went up through his flight chair and made a hole in his upper leg, which didn't hit anything vital, and he has a bump on his head the size of a goose egg. Apart from looking like a colander he's fine and I spoke to him a couple of hours ago. The doctor thinks that he might walk with a little limp, but his flying career isn't over. Unfortunately Major Chong was riddled by several bullets and he died at the aircraft's controls instantly."

"What other casualty reports have come in?" asked General Austin.

"Three Seals dead. One, Lieutenant Charlie Meyers, seriously wounded. Two of the male civilians aboard the aircraft were killed by gunfire, one an old man who was mayor of the town, and their leader. The other was one of the other CEOs, Weinstein, I believe. Wong got him aboard to bring him back for information, but didn't bring the other guy, Proker, I think his name was. Two other Cold Bay civilians are in intensive care aboard one of the other frigates steaming towards the West Coast, and I was told both won't make it. A young girl and her mother, I believe. Unfortunate! Major Wong did a good job getting that aircraft down. He saved everybody who wasn't hit by gunfire. The Marines fared pretty well; twelve men dead and several more wounded. The Marine wounded are also aboard ship, our own destroyer, and there is a good medical team of three surgeons aboard. The rest of the civilians are back at Elmendorf and the rest of the Seals and Marines are cleaning up. We have a dozer at the airfield and it will take a day or two to collect the dead enemy soldiers, but so far we have 467 male prisoners; several of the wounded are with medics, and still waiting for flights into Elmendorf. Most of the wounded enemy have burns so severe that they can't be moved and most of them will have died by now."

"I assume those initial explosions were powerful?" Austin asked.

"I was ten miles away and at 5,000 feet when the hangars went up. It was certainly better than the 4th of July. Major Wong believes that he actually saw Proker asleep when he went through Hangar Two, but he couldn't tell with night goggles. The young American girls filled us in a little more once they got to Elmendorf a few hours ago. I was told only Westbrook, his daughter, and Bowers left in the Gulfstreams; the two other CEOs were in command of the missiles with a Colonel Wo who actually knew what to do. Westbrook's daughter told us just an hour ago that if the team back at Cold Bay received a message that the automated systems to launch the missiles didn't work, they were to go into Hangar Three with this colonel and manually get them into the air."

"Who were all these girls? Where were they from?" asked Austin.

"University friends of Westbrook's daughter," General Patterson replied, looking through pages of notes he had collected over the last several hours. "She had just finished her final year at Yale, August last year, and her father had promised her a Christmas celebration with her sorority friends, eight of them, on a trip around the world in one of the Gulfstreams. They were expected to be at Cold Bay and visiting daddy over New Year's Eve. From then on things got bad for the daughter's friends, all very good-looking and intelligent girls. The Westbrook family suddenly had them carted away; they were used as entertainment, waitresses and sex slaves by the other CEOs and a few of the most senior Chinese officers. Westbrook's daughter and two others weren't among the girls rescued. We believe one girl had been raped, beaten and murdered by this General Lee fellow. Some of her remains were found in trash cans several weeks before we got there. The other, no sign. Westbrook flew in with his daughter and she was shot and wounded in the hangar with the rest of them. Lucky for us, she will make it to trial; the other girls reported directly to me from Alaska that she was in on the whole deal, and actually watched as her friends were abused by her father and the others."

Several hours later, there were arguments galore as a dozen members of the House of Representatives, the four senior military officers and two dozen citizens, including several from the usual group from North Carolina, were trying to figure out who would be the interim President of the United States.

"I can also break protocol and make one of us, a soldier, interim president immediately if I think that person will help get us to a fair election," fumed General Patterson. He had just been ordered by the interim Speaker of the House, somebody he certainly didn't know or trust, to swear him in as interim president. The Speaker of the House is constitutionally the next in line for the office, should the vice-president also be deceased or incapacitated. However, since this was a temporary appointment, this rule of succession may not apply. The row had been going on for ten minutes. With the arrival of Admiral Rogers, General Watson, and several other top brass, there were over two dozen high-ranking military soldiers in attendance, outvoting even the civilians present if need be.

General Patterson, Preston, Martie, Sally, an injured Captain Mike Mallory and several others could see the desperation in this man wanting to be president. The power attached to the position was certainly a big magnet. Knowing that it was against the system for a military man to become the head of state, the same desperation wasn't on the faces of the soldiers around him. Much like the situation in Egypt a year or so earlier, General Patterson understood that the military were purely there to make sure a peaceful change of power was enacted.

"You do that, General, and there will be hell to pay once we get Congress up and running again!" stated a senator.

"Only politicians can do a politician's job!" added the interim Speaker of the House.

"And where were you guys when the president and your country actually needed you, earlier this year?" added Admiral Rogers, unhappy and distrusting when he faced men like this.

"Defending our homes!" retorted one.

"Looking after our wives and children!" stated another.

"What? Did you expect us to leave our homes, our valuables and our families and come to Washington? Not on your life, Admiral. That is what you soldiers are employed to do. You take orders from civilians who are elected to office."

"Where were your men when we needed protection?" added another.

"In Europe, the Middle East and every other place you— Congress—sent us, even behind the president's back!" replied General Austin angrily.

"We were just doing our job," added another congressman.

"So were we!" responded Watson.

"And we were thousands of miles away from our own families, of which thousands of military families, women and children, perished, or have never been seen again! Thanks to you guys doing your jobs!" shouted General Austin, his face red with anger.

They were not going to get far, and the day was called to an end by the general to allow everyone present to cool down.

The next morning, and with a slightly quieter House Chamber, the meeting continued with General Patterson giving a short speech. It didn't take long for the fighting to start again.

"We have lost millions and millions of citizens, including thousands of military personnel and their families. The military has beaten three attempts to take over the government of this country," he began to a quiet audience of just over fifty people. "And all you politicians are worried about is which party, or which one of you is going to lead this country next!

"You know, I do not like politicians, most soldiers don't. The political agenda does not always reflect the needs of the people you represent, nor what is best for the welfare of this country and its citizens. Thank God I'm new and fresh to Washington. I got to know the president pretty well. He was a good, down to earth man, and I'm sure each of you is the same, once your political coat of self-preservation is removed. I've also seen the greed of Westbrook and Bowers, and I'm sure there are many others who used to be powerful, behind the scenes players who controlled Washington before all this happened.

"I don't know any of you personally, and I'm sure you can, or will all run for office again, once a proper and legal system is in place. But as Chief of Staff, and chief of all these soldiers around me, who have offered their lives for their country, I am not going to submit to anybody who comes out of the woodwork once the fighting is over and demands to my face that he should run this country. As Chief of Staff, this is my decision to make."

Several minor threats, mumblings and foul words were expressed at this statement by General Patterson, and he looked towards the Military Police Captain at the door and several armed soldiers marched in.

"You are taking over the government, General Patterson?" asked one senator, an older man who hadn't said a word since the meeting had begun.

"No, Senator, just trying to get this new country of ours on the right track."

"Then who do you propose?" the senator asked.

"A civilian, who has no political experience, with advisors from all walks of life, a good mix of good people; several of you politicians, several civilians and several high ranking soldiers from all our different forces, until we can have free and fair elections."

"We don't need amateur politicians in Washington. I'm totally against what you are planning, General!" interrupted the interim Speaker of the House, standing and pointing his finger at the general.

"Captain of the Guard, please escort this man to the outskirts of Washington, or the District of Colombia, wherever you feel it necessary to dump him. He is no longer needed in this Chamber and banned from Washington until he is fairly elected by his constituents, whoever they may be, to return to office!" ordered General Patterson angrily. And, under the Captain's orders, two soldiers physically escorted the angry and threatening man out of the room.

"Well, who do you propose should be the next president of the new United States of America, General?" asked the older senator calmly.

"I ask everybody in this room to take a piece of paper and write down a name of a person, one person, for consideration, whom you believe could be a good, fair and just interim president. No military personnel please."

Thirty minutes later, over four dozen pieces of paper sat in a pile in front of General Patterson, and had been sorted. A dozen of them, mostly from the soldiers and civilians had the same name written down, Mike Mallory. Most of the others had all different names, three had Preston's name on them and three had the oldest senator, Senator Shaw's name. Only three people in the room had more than one vote.

"Captain Mike Mallory, the Southwest Airlines Captain who has done more for our civilian population in the last eight months, than anybody else I know, was my choice and the choice of 11 other men here in this room. Senator Shaw from Montana and Mr. Preston Strong from North Carolina have three votes each and all others have one vote. Since we are a free and democratic society, I believe all three of these men should be given an equal chance to be interim president, a second person will become interim vice president, both positions for a minimum of one year, maximum of four years, or until a free and fair election can take place. Does anybody disagree? There was silence in the room.

Three days after the interim Speaker was thrown out and forty-eight hours before the funeral, everybody was present and seated in the House Chamber. First, two soldiers were helped in, both men bandaged and needing assistance. Those who knew the men stood and applauded Major Wong and Lieutenant Meyers as they were assisted to their seats.

It took time, but slowly Mike Mallory agreed to be interim president. Immediately upon being asked, Preston declined the positions of president and vice president. He believed he was not the right person.

With a vote of forty-three for and two against, Mike Mallory, dressed in his best suit and still wearing bandages around his head, was sworn in the next day as interim President of the United States of America.

Since there was no Chief Justice to swear in the interim president, the second most senior senator, after Senator Shaw, and who had been present for the last four presidential inaugurations, was authorized by the people in attendance to administer the oath of office; he replied that he would be happy to oblige.

Slowly a new group of leaders were formed. Jennifer Watkins, Maggie and ex-Detective Will Smart accepted the offers of joining the government and so did Joe, and Pam Wallace. Martie and Sally Powers refused the offer. Martie had work to do with her father and Sally, now married to Carlos, the son of Colombia's president and who had returned to Colombia for a few weeks, decided that it wasn't a correct thing to do.

After several more hours of discussion, Preston also refused his third offered position, Speaker of the House, but made a suggestion that he would accept a new position discussed a few hours earlier, U.S Overseas Ambassador. Martie was sure his suggestion for the post was due to her wanting to see Germany and there could be flying involved. Both of them had shown interest in seeing how the rest of the world was shaping up.

Standing next to General Patterson at the president's funeral was interim President of the United States Michael Mallory and interim Vice President Joe Shaw. Both had been sworn in on Capitol Hill a day earlier to head the Executive branch of government; the Legislative branch consisted of the forty previously elected members of the House of Representatives and the Senate.

General Patterson and all the people present at the meeting wanted a new president elected before the last one was buried.

The funeral was a solemn affair without the pomp and ceremony a funeral of this importance would usually have. The president's family was dressed in black; both General Patterson and Admiral Rogers gave eulogies for the man, a politician they had respected, and after a short and low-key military parade to the cemetery, a twenty-one gun salute was given with rifles over the grave, as well as by 21 artillery pieces positioned along the Mall.

At the same time, the U.S. military soldiers stationed across the country were working hard to address complaints from farming areas where farmers and their families were being harassed and threatened by former prisoners and the couple of hundred men who called themselves soldiers from several anti-U.S. organizations who had been hired by the CEOs for the pharmaceutical corporations.

Slowly the troubles decreased as those who were threatening farmers were caught. Very few of these small groups could stand up to the firepower of a Chinese attack helicopter and most did not survive to tell their tale. A couple did.

EPILOGUE

THREE WEEKS LATER, FALL ARRIVED and with fall came the first time the Law Courts were used in Washington for many months. Seventeen men and three women were on trial for treason, and six men and one woman for first degree murder.

The final story was told.

MonteDiablo had tried for years to get a foothold in the Chinese and Asian markets. Finally, three years before the event on New Year's Eve, they had their first meetings with Zedong Electronics. A deal was struck between the Zedong Electronics Chairman Wang Chunqiao, Peter Westbrook and Bill Bowers. Zedong Electronics would allow Westbrook and his cronies' complete control of the world's food and medical supply markets in return for information fed directly to him from the U.S. Congress.

Much of the information had to do with the state of the country and the economy. Equally important was information concerning the numbers and whereabouts of soldiers in the country; as these numbers were determined, they were actually decreased by the many paid, political friends of Westbrook and Bowers. Eleven members of the House of Representatives and three U.S. Senators were named as conspirators who used their political power to send more and more American troops overseas. These men, paid millions of dollars, had organized legislation to approve sending over 300,000 extra men out of the country just a few months before the invasion; they were sent in relatively small increments of 30,000 to 50,000. A couple of now-deceased high-ranking military officers, greedy for power and control, had worked the Pentagon to get these men shipped out, many without any other officer's knowledge.

Yes, numbers of troops being sent by the Pentagon overseas were presented to the president weekly, but the reports documented far lower numbers than were actually climbing aboard aircraft or ships.

Several of the surviving members of Washington were shocked at the size of the political atrocities that had happened right under their noses, and even the ex-interim Speaker of the House, who had been found beaten up and half-naked trying to get home, twelve miles from where he had been dropped off, was one of the names of the men sending troop numbers to Westbrook.

So were three of the surviving House members who had very little to say when the new government was installed; they also went on trial.

Vice President Shaw finally agreed with General Patterson that a thorough airing of the workings of Washington would be necessary for the country to clean itself of the old, entrenched systems.

From the prison inmates, three of them still alive and on trial, and two of the anti-government mercenaries also on trial, stories of what happened before New Year's Eve came to light.

Most of the prisoners had been released from prison a few hours before New Year's Eve. Three small prisons had been attacked in the northwest, the guards murdered and before dawn on January 1st, the first group had already been flown into Cold Bay.

Months before that, the anti-government men had been flown to the same location and worked side-by-side with Chinese soldiers building up the airfield as Westbrook and Bower's base of operations, following the New Year's Eve catastrophe.

The judge asked what had happened to the people who lived in the area. He had reports that there were still a number of American citizens missing from False Pass, a town of approximately eighty people.

One of the anti-government prisoners replied that he had flown into the town a few days before New Year's Eve. It had been bitterly cold and the people were told to lock their doors as a bad storm was brewing. They were captured without a fight, and flown into Cold Bay in the Chinese transport aircraft.

Once they arrived in Cold Bay, a troop of the Chinese soldiers took them away from the airfield, and they were never seen again. He believed that every man, woman and child was shot by firing squad.

Westbrook, his daughter and Bowers were asked what had happened to the civilians and none of them uttered a word. They just kept quiet and stared ahead.

A Chinese soldier was then presented to the court, and he affirmed the first man's assumptions. He had been ordered to drive a small bulldozer that had tried to make a hole to bury the Americans, but the ground was too frozen and all he could do was to move loose rubble like stones and rocks, it took two days, but a new hill was formed over the bodies.

After a week of witnesses and exhausting testimony, the news came that attacks on farmers had died down to zero. Final reports came in: 587 dead terrorists who were responsible for the deaths of 81 farmers, 35 farmers' wives and 16 children. All the remaining terrorists were killed; there was no mercy.

For two more weeks many of the government officials, civilians and military officers were in the court rooms. Preston and Martie wanted to hear the whole story and were shocked and sickened by the size of atrocities against the country and its people. Since New Year's Eve, they had been isolated from the realities that had happened around them. They had lived well and were fed and housed in the splendor they were used to. But these stories, one after the other, took away that curtain of safety. Back in their apartment at the Colombian Embassy, they discussed and speculated on what had actually gone on while they were playing war.

Carlos returned from Bogotá towards the end of the trials and Preston, Martie, Sally and he, often with the Smarts present, learned what their country and its people had actually gone through.

Reality smacked them hard in the face and feelings of anger built up in them again, as it did in most who attended the trials.

After a month of hearings, the first convictions were handed out. There was not one prison open anywhere in the United States, and the judge stated that one should be opened.

General Austin, now in charge of hospitals, prisons, and military bases suggested that the military could have one open in a few weeks. Northern Texas was the most likely area as there were over 300 other prisoners in military confinement in and around the Texas military bases, mostly remnants of the South American army, and who needed to be put away.

"Your Honor," General Austin stated. "It seems that many of the people currently in custody here, in Texas, and at army barracks around the country have one conviction for which they need to be sentenced: murder. Up to last year, the prisons were full and overflowing with these people and the country struggled to pay for the upkeep of inmates. Surely, a simple sentence of execution for murder is a fair price to pay for those who don't think twice about taking somebody else's life. It's time this country's laws became real and just again. I believe jail-time, or even the old African trick I heard while in Somalia, cutting off a hand for theft, should be reserved for lesser crimes. Why go back to the old-fashioned "civilized methods" which never worked. Our full jails proved it."

As usual there were people for and against the death penalty, and even after the deaths of millions of their countrymen and women; many did not want to see more death. Unfortunately they were not in a majority and "an eye for an eye" was accepted at the end of the day's discussions.

President Mallory signed his first law soon after that. "Death by Public Hanging" for people who planned, or committed murder, a maximum of 25-years, or life prison sentences for Treason and lesser time for smaller offenses. The word "Parole" was not part of the new law.

During the first day of sentencing, four former members of Congress and two former Senators were given life sentences, and two others received lesser sentences. The main sentences would be announced the following day.

There was no jury needed. The law was simple and sentences were determined by the judge.

The last day of legal proceedings was short. It took just two hours to hand out the death sentences. Carlos mentioned to Preston that the *Colombian Necktie* should be handed out to some of the people on trial for a punishment; even in Colombia he hadn't heard such gruesome stories.

Westbrook and Bowers were shocked at the change in law and objected, shouting out that they wanted proper justice and to be able to appeal their convictions. The last six men and one woman were extremely unhappy and condemned the new law in no uncertain terms.

When the judge added that these hangings would be carried out within twenty-four hours, in public, and in front of the courthouse, the condemned prisoners fell silent.

There was a new law in town, and the judge was not afraid to administer it.

Preston and Carlos stayed for the hangings. There were many people who did, but Martie and Sally were like many others, they headed down to North Carolina the night before in Sally's Pilatus from Andrews.

A week later, Preston, Martie, Carlos, Sally, Little Beth and Clint headed back up to Andrews in the Pilatus for their helicopter flight into arrived aboard Marine One for the day.

Mo's new friend, Tim O'Shaw, the Marine who had looked after his homes while he was away, was shocked at seeing so many VIPs in the small town of Ocracoke. He had cleaned up well over the months, looked good and was still waiting for the admiral who was yet to return.

He was given the bad news by Admiral Rogers that the remains of Admiral Peterson, the man who owned these units had been found on a floating Attack Cruiser off the west coast of Africa a month earlier.

Admiral Rogers now had dozens of vessels of all types and sizes, scouring the seas looking for still-floating military ships and, so far, only 119 out of 382 missing military vessels had been located. One, the USS Enterprise had been found, aground in the Middle East with several men and women, still alive on board. The only ship so far which still had live seamen on board... but that's another story.

The same church minister from Seymour Johnson was invited to conduct the ceremony as he had done at Prestonville, and the honeymoon was to be with best friends squashed aboard the cutter for a week's fishing. There wasn't much else anybody could plan for a honeymoon in this new age.

Tim O'Shaw moved into the admiral's old apartment and would now be Mo's neighbor and caretaker.

Welcoming eighteen people to the White House, President Mallory addressed the group, "Thanks all for coming and, we will enjoy the tuna you brought with you for dinner tonight."

General Patterson was missing, but Admiral Rogers and Generals Austin and Watson and three aides were at the meeting. Mo and Lee Wang were also there, as well as the three lieutenants from Seal Team Six, and six more Seal Team Lieutenants Preston had seen but never met. Mo's new wife, Lee's wife and daughter, and his sister Lu and her children were also in attendance.

Not often were children included in an official meeting in the Blue Room of the White House.

"This meeting is to initiate our new external governmental departments, including our external eyes around the world. We have no more FBI or CIA, or any external eyes, apart from a couple of people around the world who have our satellite phones and can communicate with us at Andrews. These new departments are now called U.S. Official External Operations and are on a need-to-know basis only, and under military command, not political command. As you know Andrews Air Force Base is being modified into the new Pentagon for the future and a hangar is being prepared for the leaders of our military to work together.

"As Carlos explained to all of you at our last meeting, our current four-satellite system will only last a decade or two at the most. Let me give you our latest good news. The Russian satellite was successfully launched from Harbin yesterday and, under the guidance of Michael Roebels and three former NASA professionals, they will be setting up its three-satellite payload in orbit during the next few weeks. These new satellites will give us extended viewing coverage over Western Europe and parts of Asia, including eastern areas of China.

"I will also give you the details of my speech to the new House of Representatives tomorrow, since many of you won't be there. In the last week we have had virtually zero crime or reports of violence across our country for the first time in the eight months since New Year's Eve. Thanks to the efforts of millions of farmers and helpers, we now have enough food stored for the coming winter. The lower temperatures are helping eradicate many onsets of plague and other lesser diseases in the northern areas of the country and, diseases and other problems in the southern area are now down to minimums. Thanks to the U.S. military and foreign aid from the Mexican Government, our southern areas are now safe, and will be under military control with 500,000 servicemen and women, who will be joining a group of 100,000 farmers and planting crops over the winter and into early next year. Another million acres of disease-free and good farming areas have been opened up in the southern states where only these farmers and helpers are allowed in.

"We currently have three dozen canning and bottling operations now running 24/7 across the country. Yesterday, Michael Roebels' team got a small coal-fired electric plant operational in Virginia. There is enough coal at the plant for the first half of winter, and we will have three trains a day taking coal to the plant beginning in February next year. This plant has enough capacity to light 100,000 homes in the area. Unfortunately, it will take us two more years to manufacture the grid parts needed to light the homes, but we have a fantastic new program in the planning stage and I will launch it during my Next Year's Eve Address. Until then power from this plant is being fed to seven large canning and bottling plants in the area, and Virginia is now producing half of our canned and bottled goods. Good news is that half of the canned goods are meat products like corned beef."

Martie looked at Preston and smiled sweetly.

"As many of you heard, our good friend, the last president, told us that some of our aircraft had been delivered, and more will be offered to other countries. Four months ago, we were asked for one aircraft from Australia and one of our five A380 Airbuses was delivered to the new Australian government shortly afterward. We had a satellite phone report from the Canberra government a few weeks ago that the aircraft is working 24/7, and is being used between Australia, New Zealand and Tasmania, delivering food and necessities around the area. They would like a second one, but currently we have decided to wait until next spring before we look at their proposal of swapping any needed supplies in return for a second aircraft.

"One Airbus A380 aircraft was sent into Russia at the same time; it lasted three flights and crashed; the same happened in China. That aircraft only made two flights, its last into Beijing for some stupid reason, and into the high radiation area. Nobody wants to go in and get it back, so Mo and Lee Wang have agreed to become our eyes in China and they are going to return there and base themselves at the Harbin Airport. The Harbin area is now empty of the supplies; we have transported everything we could into the San Francisco area and we still have the Harbin Airfield locked down with a battalion of Marines, and a second battalion guarding the base where the Russian missile is still being dismantled. The missile will be brought back to the U.S. and rebuilt, the rocket section at least. Carlos stated the missile could be useful for a yet unknown cargo into space.

"Mr. Mo Wang, one of our newest U.S. Citizens as of yesterday, and his wife Beatrice, also a new U.S. Citizen, will head a delegation to find out why the aircraft we really needed over here lasted less than a week.

"Preston and Martie Strong, I would like you two to head into Ramstein, Germany in about a week. We also sent an Airbus into Germany and the fifth one into Cape Town, South Africa just two weeks ago, and both have disappeared. General Patterson and I have decided that we need to reestablish Ramstein Air Force Base as a European/American base and will be sending over soldiers and the container ship still loaded with equipment. The navy has her at anchor off Norfolk Naval Base. This equipment was originally from our British bases.

"We have heard that there has been trouble in England, and it will be safer for us to set up a new sea base in Gibraltar, using our Chinese container ships and its airfield, and then fly equipment into Ramstein as our first European land base. At Ramstein there are a couple of Europeans, friends of our last load of troops, who only left there a couple of weeks ago, and are pleading for military help. We have a friend over there, a Mr. O'Meara who has one of our satellite phones and he and several others have defended the base and want help. Unfortunately, they only have a couple of hundred men; their army, we presume, is fighting back others daily, and trying to keep our base intact. I'm sending men in tomorrow. Preston, Martie, you have a week to clear up your airfield and get over to Germany.

"Also Preston and Martie, Sally and Carlos have permission from the Headquarters of U.S. External Operations, shortly to be placed under Admiral Martin Rogers' leadership at Andrews, to join you if they wish. We will have our Asian and our European sections and, the U.S. External Operations Department will branch outwards from there into the rest of the world. At Ramstein, Preston, there is a small air force of older English aircraft. I have been told three are now based at our old base and they need fuel and ammo.

"Apart from the new official U.S. Diplomatic transportation our diplomats will travel in, Preston, Martie, you will be taking your two Mustangs, three if Carlos wants to join you, and his wife's Super Tweet, her Colombian wedding present; all of these aircraft will be lifted aboard the flat surface of the container ship by a Jolly Green Giant, with tons of fuel and ammunition, and will be sailed over to Gibraltar.

"General Patterson is already there, and a Seal Team will be heading out later tonight with three 747s full of equipment. Seal

Teams Four and Five will be relocated with you, Mo and Lee Wang. Preston, Martie, Seal Team Six will be your official bodyguards while you are in Europe. We have heard that the above ground fuel reserves at Ramstein have been destroyed, but General Patterson thinks that the top-secret underground fuel tanks holding hundreds of thousands of gallons of jet and aviation fuels are still intact. If not we will supply you from here.

"Your job, Mr. and Mrs. Strong, since you have already decided to accept it, is to help the good people of Europe to become our allies and second, to see what we can do to bring peace and growth to Western Europe. Mo and Lee Wang, you will have the same job in China. My aim, ladies and gentlemen, is to have friends and allies around the world, ready to offer us aid and get aid from us in return.

"To get back to other matters here at home and to fill you in before you leave: The American currency will not be brought back until it is needed, and hopefully not on my watch. I have over a hundred of my most trusted assistants working the food and supply distribution points around the country. We have nearly a thousand old computers up and running, checking the food delivery systems daily. The new government's plan is to make sure everybody has their fair share of supplies handed out weekly; a mammoth task using a million people. Strict laws have been put into place for theft and misuse of our valuable supplies. Any misuse of supplies by anybody is a lousy new job—promotion to the Inspections Teams," stated President Mallory smiling. "A small, but I will assume, growing group of people who will lead others into the diseased areas looking for new problems! Not a position everybody wants right now.

"We are slowly bringing this country around, trying to make it a peaceful and enjoyable place to live. Many laws will be tough, but I'm trying to be as fair as possible.

"Last, due to the lack of electricity, the banking system is history, Wall Street and the whole monetary system is history, world communication systems are history and the entire GPS system, as Carlos told me, is total history. Virtually everything we, as a nation used last year is now nothing more than to be written into our future history books. Michael Roebels stated that he needs a decade to get parts of the country up and running, and three decades for the whole country. I will make sure he keeps his word; I certainly won't be president then, and many of us may not actually be alive then.

"It will be up to our next generation to see this country to its new future. Little Beth, Clint and you other children, that is why you are here today. It will be up to you and the other children out there to lead our future country to become the great nation it once was."

Upon leaving the long meeting, many said their goodbyes to the White House. Many at the meeting wouldn't see it for a while, some a long while, and they were transported back to Andrews.

The president would not be visiting "Prestonville" as often, but the wife and children of the late president had decided to move into the recently built log home on the airfield and become new citizens of Prestonville. Their gift to the town, organized from Washington and with help from the Air Force, would be a new school house.

Washington did have several new residents. The Smart family moved into a new government house, the old Chilean Embassy, to be part of the new government. The Smart kids promised the kids in Prestonville that they would visit often.

Joe was also moving north to Washington to be a proud member of the Confederate part of the new Government, leaving his farm to be run by his sons, and David, who was about to leave and try to return to Israel.

Most of the old and empty Embassies in Washington were housing the new members of the House of Representatives.

Washington was now full of a new kind of politics, and many hoped that would be the way it continued.

When the group flew back into Andrews, they saw that two freshly painted Gulfstream V's were waiting for them outside one of the hangars. Both jets looked like much smaller versions of the old Air Force One 747. Both had the official markings of diplomatic aircraft and both had "The United States of America–External Diplomatic Communications" in bold letters across both sides.

Preston's jaw dropped. "It would be fun to learn to fly these as well," he stated to Martie. "Carlos and Sally will certainly join us now."

General Patterson had given him the bad news days earlier, that they would not be getting any 747s; however, newly promoted Colonel Wong, in charge of the newly formed Military-Civilian Aircraft Wing, might give them lessons on the weekly flights down to Colombia. That had put an end to Preston Airlines, but after a few Yuenglings with the departing general, who was heading off to Europe, he remembered his beloved P-51 Mustang.

Two days later, Mo and Lee and their families said their goodbyes as they left Prestonville, the newest little town in North Carolina, Population: 40, for their flight to China. The Gulf-stream left the once again recently extended runway, bound for Hawaii after Beatrice and Marie, and the kids promised to keep in touch. Mo and Lee and their families were excited to be returning to Harbin, and several friends, including Colonel Rhu, and the ex-owner of the electronic production company were waiting for them... but that's in another story.

Tim O'Shaw was the new Mayor of Ocracoke, Population: 21, and in charge of Mo's two homes. He had a detachment of a couple of ex-Air Force members who had joined him; former Sergeant Perry and his family and several of his tech sergeant mates with their families, were setting up a new engine repair business at the town's airport hangars. Word got back to Preston that they were working on the dead engines of a fleet of modern fishing vessels of all sizes and, electric car engines were the rage of the day, hybrid to lawn mowers of all things, Preston told Carlos.

Carlos and Sally had arrived the night before from Bogotá in Carlos' DC-3, suntanned and happy, to say goodbye. Carlos was dying to check out the new rides and over a couple of Yuenglings, had decided to head over to Europe, as the general had asked, to help Preston and Martie.

Carlos and Sally, tired from traveling headed in for an early night, which left Preston and Martie, Little Beth and Clint, Oliver and Puppy on the softly lighted porch. For the end of September, the weather was cooling, and sweaters were needed to sit outside.

"Are we coming to Europe with you?" Little Beth asked, sitting close to her brother for warmth. Martie explained to them that they would be, but the first trip was dangerous and they would stay with the rest of the large airfield family until the second trip.

It was getting late, and it was time for bed. Preston had just twisted the tops of the last two Yuengling bottles on the whole airfield. There were other types of beers, but the Yuenglings had been hit hardest from all the visitors.

"Martie, do you realize that only nine months has passed since New Year's Eve?" Preston commented.

"I know. It feels like a lifetime ago, and so much has changed in so little time."

"The quickest I've ever heard of a couple getting married and having two kids!" smirked Little Beth.

"It's time for bed, guys!" stated Preston sternly swatting his daughter. "I promise that as soon as it is safe for you to come over to Europe, your mother and I will come and get you ourselves. Until then you will listen and take orders from Auntie Marie and the older kids, understand?"

"Once I have my last operation, can I become a President of The United States, like Uncle Mike? President Clinton Jefferson Busch... Now that's got a real nice American ring to it," stated Clint, always serious.

They all laughed at the tenacity of Clint. He was always thinking ahead of them, and on a totally different wavelength... but that is also another story!

"Go to bed, kids, give the dogs a bone, check on Smokey and we will be in to say goodnight."

The kids headed into the house and the screams and shouts died down.

"Our last two Yuenglings, hey?" stated Martie looking at the frosted bottle. "Maybe it's the right time to go to Europe. Hopefully they are still producing good German beer somewhere over there."

And they sat on the porch, sipping their beers, looking out at the cooling North Carolina darkness, and the beginning of a whole new world.

To Be Continued in...

INVASION EUROPE
The Battle for Western Europe

INVASION ASIA
The Battle for China

INVASION USA V
The New America

Please visit our website,
http://www.TIWADE.com
to become a friend of the INVASION USA Series,
get updates on new releases, read interesting blogs
and connect with the author.

BOOKS BY THE AUTHOR

The Book of Tolan Series (Adult Reading):

Banking, Beer & Robert the Bruce
   Hardcover and eNovel.

Easy Come Easy Go
   Hardcover and eNovel.

It Could Happen
   eNovel.

INVASION Series (General Reading):

INVASION USA I: The End of Modern Civilization
   eNovel – July 2011,
   Trade Paperback Edition – August 2012.

INVASION USA II: The Battle for New York
   eNovel – March 2012,
   Trade Paperback Edition – August 2012.

INVASION USA III: The Battle for Survival
   eNovel – June 2012,
   Trade Paperback Edition – August 2012.

**INVASION USA IV: The Battle for Houston ...
The Aftermath**
   eNovel – August 2012,
   Trade Paperback Edition – August 2012.

INVASION EUROPE: The Battle for Western Europe
   eNovel – April 2013.

INVASION ASIA: The Battle for China
   eNovel – June 2013.

INVASION USA V: The New America
   eNovel – August 2013.
   (Final Novel in this seven novel series)

About the Author

T I WADE was born in Bromley, Kent, England in 1954.

His father, a banker was promoted with his International Bank to Africa and the young family moved to Africa in 1956.

The author grew up in Southern Rhodesia (now Zimbabwe) and his life there is humorously described in his novel, EASY COME EASY GO, Volume II of the Book of Tolan Series. Once he had completed his mandatory military commitments, at 21 he left Africa to mature in Europe.

He enjoyed Europe and lived in three countries; England, Germany and Portugal for 15 years before returning to Africa; Cape Town in 1989.

Here the author owned and ran a restaurant, a coffee manufacturing and retail business, flew a Cessna 210 around desolate southern Africa and finally got married in 1992.

Due to the upheavals of the political turmoil in South Africa, the Wade family of three moved to the United States in 1996. Park City, Utah was where his writing career began.

To date T I Wade has written seven novels.

The author, his wife and two teenage children currently live 20 miles south of Raleigh, North Carolina.

Made in the USA
Middletown, DE
29 December 2020

30357108R00252